SUMMON UP
THE BLOOD

Jay Verney

Zen Kettle Books
BRISBANE

Zen Kettle Books
Contact (all enquiries): steaming@zenkettle.com
www.zenkettle.com

Publisher's Note: This is a work of fiction. Names, characters, places, and incidents are a product of the author's imagination. Locales and public names are sometimes used for atmospheric purposes. Any resemblance to actual people, living or dead, or to businesses, companies, events, institutions, or locales is completely coincidental.

Book Cover Design ©2014 Zen Kettle Design at zenkettle.com
Book Layout ©2013 BookDesignTemplates.com

Also available as an ebook

National Library of Australia Cataloguing-in-Publication Data

Verney, Jay.
    Summon Up The Blood.
Detective and Mystery Stories.
A823.3

ISBN 978-0-9873779-5-1

Also by Jay Verney

A Mortality Tale

Shortlisted for the **Australian/Vogel and Miles Franklin awards**

A wild summer storm has blacked out the streets. By the time she sees the young man in her headlights, it's too late. Stunned, Carmen drives home in the downpour. No one has seen her, but does this mean she'll get away with it. Teasing out the ambiguities of responsibility and retribution, Jay Verney explores Carmen's dilemma with a crisp, dry wit that will send you in search of her next novel.

'Superbly written, *A Mortality Tale* is a winner from start to finish.'

Stuart Coupe, *Sydney Morning Herald*

'An impressive literary debut.'

Herb Hild, *Courier-Mail*

'A deft blend of despair and optimism ... Jay Verney has taken an unfortunate accident and sharpened it like a scalpel.'

Michael McGirr, *Australian Book Review*

'An exceptionally witty, perceptive and challenging literary debut.'

Weekend Living

'Entertaining and thought-provoking ... funny and sardonic ... it's a ripper read.'

Susan Geason, *Sun Herald*

Percussion

When Anna Maher accompanies her mother, Maggie, and grand-mother, Veronica, to the United States for a war veterans' reunion, she is struck by the American way of denying death. The three women have a terrifying brush with their own mortality when a destructive earthquake hits Los Angeles.

On the other side of the Pacific, the remaining members of the Maher family face disturbances of a different kind. Brian's liver is failing to cope with his publican's lifestyle, his second daughter's marriage has split dramatically, and his grandson has high-octane plans of his own.

'Jay Verney ... combines a humorous insight into character and a deftly handled plot in this, her second book. [She] unleashes her talent for parody and offers dryly witty portraits. This a novel that, while serious about its characters and their dilemmas, teases with its satirical style.'

Dorothy Johnston, *Sydney Morning Herald*

'*Percussion* is a wryly humorous, absorbing novel.'

Sally Murphy, *Aussie Reviews*

'Worth the wait.'

Matthew Lamb, *Eureka Street*

'Perceptive and thoughtful.'

Gillian Dooley, *Radio Adelaide*

Spawned Secrets

The Global Financial Crisis is in full swing. Banks and businesses are closing. Homes are foreclosed. Bernie Madoff has been arrested. Jobs and savings are lost forever. People are angry, very, very angry.

A group of disgraced (and disgraceful) stockbrokers are enjoying a raniforest getaway weekend as a severe stormfront approaches.

A deadly secret blows in from their past, carried by a mystery stalker, 'Guy Friendly,' determined to execute each and every one of them with surgical precision and the wrath of an avenging demon.

Their only protection comes in the form of Garfield Fletcher, former ship's cook, jilted lover, and now, fake private eye, courtesy of his ever-so-slightly-shady cousin, Henry Pinkert.

The ink on Garfield's newly printed Certificate of Accreditation is barely dry when he finds himself up against the mystery killer who will inspire the most difficult choices Garfield has ever had to make.

In *Spawned Secrets,* award winning author, Jay Verney's third novel, all of these ingredients, and more, come together for a surprising climax and aftermath, as old friends reunite in the strangest of circumstances, and new friends face tragedy and betrayal.

For Lorrie, the one who counts

Imitate the action of the tiger;
Stiffen the sinews, summon up the blood

—HENRY V, SHAKESPEARE

CHAPTER ONE

Bogota, Colombia
[4.38N 74.05W]
Friday 7 July 2000

1

Already, several waves of hotel guests and visitors had passed through the lobby, and some evidence of their presence, temporary and hurried, had gathered on the large, marble coffee table in front of Dan and Livia. Empty and half-empty tea and coffee cups surrounded two ashtrays full of cigar and cigarette butts: the breakfasts of champions – gulped, inhaled, forgotten.

At Livia's end of the coffee table, a discarded morning newspaper's front page featured a colour photograph of several terrified-looking people surrounded by uniformed, armed soldiers. She turned the paper over; Dan didn't need that image in his head. How much easier things would have been had she stuck to her own plan and come alone, met her connections, and sealed the deal. In and out in a day or two, and home fast across the wide Pacific. She owed it all to Paul, she thought, but then tried to push aside her creeping sourness over his abduction of her neat, uncomplicated plan. There was no point in recriminations now.

She sat up straighter, glancing sideways at Dan, sitting next to her on the sofa. He'd been remarkably patient so far, for a six-year old in search of adventure. She watched his body moving slightly to the rhythm of the salsa-style muzak that seemed to greet them in every public area of the Casa Angelinos. He turned to face her, still squeezing the black squash ball in his left hand, and she knew, from the way he widened his eyes and raised his eyebrows, what his next question was going to be.

'Mum. Do you know where we are, Mum?' he asked.

'Hmm. I believe we are – here.' The required response in their mother-and-son tourist double-act. Livia smiled at Dan, dressed for any adventure in jeans, T-shirt and jacket, and hiking boots, accompanied by his ever-present backpack, every zippered pocket and available space filled with useful items: pencils, coins, lengths of string, rubber bands, a magnifying glass, the latest computer game, chewing gum, a foldup map of the world, old boarding passes, a squashed baseball cap with the embroidered slogan, 'Vote One Paul Clifford.'

'Mum,' Dan said, stretching the vowel and rolling his eyes, but he was smiling too. 'We are in the city of Bogota, which is in the country of Colombia on the continent of South America.'

'That we are,' said Livia, finishing her coffee. She set the cup down next to the other empties. The cars would be here soon, surely. They were half an hour behind schedule, although Livia had to wonder what kind of holiday demanded such precision timing as this one, and she answered herself: the political kind, the kind Paul specialised in as an ambitious parliamentarian in a government with the slenderest of margins.

'This country is surrounded by a sea, an ocean, and five other countries,' Dan declared.

'Really?' Livia scanned the lobby for Paul and their journalist friend – possibly Livia's future brother-in-law – Eamon Pearse.

'Guess which sea.'

'Pardon, sweetheart?'

'The sea, Mum. The ocean's easy. It's the Pacific, the same as ours, only on the other side.'

'Let me think.' She folded her hands on her lap and pretended to consider several options, briefly trying Dan's forbearance. 'I would have to say – the sunny Caribbean.' She looked expectantly at him.

'Correct,' he said, with some gravity. 'Now, for 20 pesos, and a trip to Guatavita La Nueva, can you tell me the names of the five countries?'

'Nice pronunciation, Danny boy,' Livia replied, genuinely impressed that he could name her day's destination with such fluency. He'd already fought and lost the argument to go with her to Guatavita La Nueva. It was business, she'd explained, and he would enjoy himself far more on the trip to the village and farms with Paul and Eamon. There would be animals to pat and other kids to practise his Spanish with while his father glad-handed the recipients of his Government's overseas aid.

Meanwhile, Eamon would be mooching around as usual, looking for corruption and fraud under every other farmhouse roof and local official's desk drawers.

'I owe it all to Eamon,' he said, bowing from the waist. 'Now, Dr Galvin, the countries? And be quick about it.'

'Um, um, Peru, and, ah, Brazil. And,' she paused, and Dan rose from his seat. Two men strode towards them. They were taller, larger versions of Dan in their jeans and boots, their T-shirts and bomber jackets.

'Dad, Eamon.' Dan sidled from behind the coffee table to greet them.

'Hello, boyo.' Eamon's Irish accent was the first thing that differentiated him from the rest of the group. He grabbed Dan and lifted him up as though he weighed less than nothing, bringing him to rest on his hip. 'Ready to go, I see.' He glanced at the bulging backpack.

'Yep. Ready.'

He was a natural with kids. Livia wondered if her sister, Greer, would ever get around to accepting his marriage proposal. She turned her attention to her husband as Eamon waltzed Dan away from them.

'Don't take your eyes off him, Paul.'

'Why don't you come too, and all three of us can spend the day not taking our eyes off him.' Paul followed Livia's gaze and they watched Dan laughing at Eamon playing the fool.

'They'd pass for father and son,' she said.

'What?'

'The colouring – that Irish look, you know?'

'No.' But he had to admit that Dan, with his fair skin and light brown hair, the green eyes, looked more like the Paddy than himself with his sprinkle of southern Italian genes courtesy of his maternal nonna. On the other hand, 'Luckily enough, he inherited his father's brains.'

'Right,' Livia said. 'Look, today's the only day the dealer could fit me in. Besides which, I arranged all this six months ago, and if the necklace is what I think it is, I want to get it today before someone makes a higher bid.'

'And yes, I know, I threw this junket together in five minutes flat.' He turned to face her. 'Look on the bright side, it's two more weeks with Dan you wouldn't have had otherwise. You've already been away for weeks with the bloody shooting competition in Florida and then that Hemingway thing. Six-toed cats. Who cares?'

'If you're near Key West, you visit the Hemingway house. And it was a day trip, Paul. And Dan was with me, he loves cats.'

'Whatever.'

'He would have been better off at home with Mum or Minnie, and in school.'

'Travel broadens the mind, Livia. Look at him. He's in the moment. Which reminds me.' He walked over to Eamon and Dan and left Livia to gather her things.

'Change of plans, Pearse.' He lowered his voice; there was no need for another earbashing from Livia. 'You and Dan will be up front. I'm taking a quick meeting with Señor Arroyo in the other car. It'll save time when we catch up with Livia later on.'

'Sure. No problem,' Eamon said, and turned to Dan. 'We can discuss Mayan blood sacrifices anywhere, can't we, Dan?'

Dan nodded happily as his mother arrived and swept him into her arms for a last hug and kiss. She buried her face in his hair and blew a raspberry into his neck, instantly raising goosebumps and giggles.

'Mum, I'm six,' Dan protested, but it was unconvincing. He was still young enough and sweet enough to enjoy his mother's full attention occasionally, and she was certain there remained a hint of baby scent in his tender scalp. She squeezed him tightly again, set him down and he made for the four-wheel drives idling in the pick-up area at the hotel's entrance.

'Keep your jacket on, darling,' Livia called after him as they all left the warm lobby and found themselves under cloudy skies. It was still cold, although the higher morning humidity made it more bearable, for her anyway, and the fog from earlier on had cleared. Fog always seemed to make a day seem that much colder, that much more miserable, Livia thought, even when it wasn't so bad in reality.

They gathered together in front of the first of the three black SUVs and Paul kissed Livia's cheek as Eamon assured her that their day would be a 'grand adventure,' and Dan would have hair-raising stories for her when they met up again after lunch.

Her car was at the head of the line and the first to leave the hotel. She ruffled Dan's hair, climbed in, and took a last glance at the three waving to her as her driver took off. Then Eamon and Dan took the rear seat of the second SUV, and Dan waved at his father through the rear window as Paul greeted Señor Arroyo. The two men stood chatting at the kerb as Eamon and Dan departed.

2

'We will catch them soon, Señor Clifford, I assure you.' Arroyo sat forward in his seat, apparently excited by the chase.

Paul nodded and continued to grip the seat as the driver – demented, Paul was sure – wove around and along the highway south of Bogota. They'd lost sight of Dan and Eamon's SUV earlier in the heavy city traffic. That would be Paul's story for Livia should Dan decide to offer a blow-by-blow of their morning together and illustrate his father's absence from much of it. Could he help it if this Arroyo was so laid-back about schedules and had kept him talking and greeting his friends – all of whom were mooching for international grants from Paul's ministry – as they stood outside the hotel? And furthermore, he didn't seem to understand that Dan was his, Paul's son, not bloody Eamon's. He only had himself to blame for that, he knew, spending so much time on business while Eamon took Dan here and there when Livia was off shooting at things.

'There is something –' Arroyo began, and strained against his seatbelt. He said something in Spanish to the driver, who began to turn his head from side to side. What was he looking for?

Paul leaned forward and looked out through the windscreen. Up ahead a couple of vehicles were parked on the side of the road. One, a white sedan, had its nose half-way down the steep verge. The other, a navy or black 4WD, was neatly parked parallel to the road, but its two offside doors were open. As they approached, Paul saw a body lying in the grass nearby.

The driver continued past and showed no signs of stopping.

'Wait,' Paul yelled at him. 'Turn around, go back.' Suddenly, his mouth felt dry.

'But Señor, it is too dangerous.' Arroyo stared at Paul. 'There are guerillas here – in the hills. Everywhere.'

'What? Don't be stupid. I told you – tell him to turn around. We're going back. That poor bastard on the ground might be alive.'

'Señor Clifford, we will call the police at the next town.'

Paul leaned over and grabbed Arroyo by his coat lapel, jerking him forward. 'They've had an accident. People could be seriously injured. We'll go back now. Now. Do it.'

Arroyo stretched away from Paul and spoke to the driver again. He took his time slowing down, performed an overly careful three-point turn and took them back to the cars. Paul jumped out first and ran to the man on the ground. Arroyo and the driver stayed in the vehicle.

'Get out here, Arroyo.' Paul gently rolled the injured man over and saw a large pool of blood seeping into the ground beneath him. His shirt was soaked in blood and he appeared to be unconscious. His face was streaked with dirt. 'Get the first aid kit, and help me get him into the car.'

'He's been shot, Señor,' Arroyo said, but he got out of the car and brought a blanket with him. He stood above Paul and the man, looking around him, then down at the man. 'He has lost too much blood. He will die.'

'He will if we don't get him to a hospital. Come on. We need to keep him warm. Are there any pressure bandages? Where's the first aid kit?'

'There is no kit, Señor.' Arroyo opened the blanket and draped it over the man's body.

At that moment, the injured man's eyes opened and he stared up at Paul and Arroyo, his face full of fear.

'It's all right,' Paul said. 'Tell him it's all right, Arroyo. Tell him we're taking him to a doctor.' Paul removed his coat, folded it a couple of times, and pressed it against the man's chest wound.

Arroyo leaned down and spoke to the man, who whispered back to him. He raised his arm and pointed towards the other vehicle.

'What's he saying?'

'There was a gang – they took people from their cars, let others go.'

'Is this his car?'

Arroyo asked him. 'Yes.' He spoke again, and the man responded, then turned his head to one side. 'He says they shot two other people, from the other car.' Arroyo stared towards the other car, a white sedan, whose front doors were open. 'They took the man and the boy.'

'Dan? Eamon? Is that who you mean?' Paul stared down at the man. He knew this SUV must be theirs, but even with confirmation he couldn't really believe what was happening. 'Are you sure?' He stood up and looked around. 'Dan?' he called. 'Eamon? Come out – we're here.' His voice rose to a shout and he began walking towards the other car. He looked inside, slid down the verge and pushed his way into the metre-high grass. 'Dan? Danny Clifford. Eamon Pearse, where are you?'

Arroyo watched Paul walking and shouting until he saw him stop suddenly a few metres in front of the sedan. He stood up and ran to join him. The bodies of a man and a woman lay side by side in the grass. They stared up at the sky, sightless.

'Jesus Christ.' Paul dropped to his knees.

'Señor, we must go – we must go now.' Arroyo looked back towards the road where their driver sat crouched behind the wheel of the car, gunning the engine.

'Please Señor, I beg you – our lives are in danger. We will be killed. They could be hiding anywhere.'

'But Dan,' Paul said, 'the car.' He ran back through the grass, sprinted up the verge and over to the SUV, climbing inside. He leaned over the back seat and pulled the blanket back from where it lay spread out over the tool box and several fuel containers.

'Dan?' He slumped back into the seat and looked around. The car was empty – no bags, no clothes, no toys. He looked down at his feet, and on the floor mat was a dark, wet stain. As he reached towards it, he saw that his hand was shaking. He touched the mat and turned his fingers over; the stain was blood. Blood everywhere he went. Something moved beneath the driver's seat and he jerked back in fright. His heart racing, he reached down and picked up the squash ball that had rolled out. It was wet, too. It could have been blood from the driver's wound. Maybe he'd been shot in his seat and then dragged himself out, looking for help from passersby. He wiped the ball on his trousers, gave it a squeeze, and put it in his pocket.

'Señor Clifford.' Arroyo stood near the door. 'The driver is dead. We must go –'

As he spoke, machine-gun fire shattered the car's windscreen and the driver's-side window. Paul threw himself onto the floor and Arroyo dropped to the ground. Their driver put his hand on the horn and left it there. Arroyo leaned up and found Paul's arms, using all his strength to pull him from the car. Together, they crawled through the dirt and past the dead man, using his body as a shield to bridge the gap between Dan and Eamon's SUV and theirs. The second they pulled themselves into the car, two things happened: the driver floored the accelerator, fishtailing onto the bitumen, and the windscreen of their SUV exploded into thousands of pieces.

CHAPTER TWO

Beijing, China
[39.55N 116.26E]
Friday 29 August 2008

1

'In conclusion, I would like to thank our respected guest, Dr Livia Galvin, for her generous donation to the Beijing People's Museum of Olympic Memorabilia. Not only is she an esteemed sporting ambassador for her country, and an Olympic gold medallist, she is a distinguished art scholar and gallery owner. We are, therefore, doubly blessed to welcome her today and to honour her with our gratitude and recognition. Dr Galvin.'

The speaker turned to his guest as flashing cameras lit up the museum's foyer. The two people on the temporary stage smiled at each other and shook hands. Together they lifted an open case from the table in front of them and held it up for the gathering to appreciate and photograph the contents.

'It's a shame we do not get to keep this beautiful case, Dr Galvin.' The smiling man, tall and handsome in his immaculate Italian suit, patted the side of the case.

'Yes, I'm sorry too, Professor Wu. It's far more impressive than the pistols.' The case featured graphic designs on its lid and base, together with a personal inscription to Livia.

'Ah, but the pistols, they won you an Olympic gold medal, and they will be most valued here at the museum. Are you sure you won't reconsider our offer to display your case as well? Even temporarily?'

'You're very kind. If it was up to me, you'd have it, permanently. I have no further use for it. But it was a gift from my family. They wanted it to be special.'

'It most certainly is.'

'Let me get the lie of the land when I go home. We'll see.'

'Very well. We had better give them a few more smiles.'

They stood together for another half minute until it was time for the next presentation in a different part of the museum. The media contingent moved off, leaving the foyer to the invited guests. Professor Wu Xiaoping, as chairman of the Museum's acquisitions committee, and its overall chairman, took precedence in the spacious foyer with its high ceilings and marble floor. The floor featured inlaid representations of the gold, silver and bronze medals presented to competing athletes, and, at the entrance, Chinese and English characters spelled out the Olympic motto: 'One World One Dream.'

As Professor Wu mingled with the crowd – it was a mark of special status to be seen with such an influential figure – Livia sought out Yani Lee, and confirmed his intention to drive her to the airport on Sunday.

'You and the professor made a handsome couple up there, Livia.' Yani looked uneasy, or was he still simply overwound after his Olympic security gig? He gestured towards the stage where a uniformed guard stood beside the table where Livia's donation to the museum rested. 'Wonderful propaganda.'

'The flashbulbs have blinded me to propaganda and everything else, Yani. Anyway, I thought you loved the Olympics. China's crowning glory now that she's overtaken the rest of the world in every other sphere.'

'Some may think so.'

'You were a loyalist to the end, my dear, but you begin to sound like a sceptic.' This wasn't the Yani Livia knew of old, her friend and occasional confidante. Admittedly, she hadn't seen him very often in recent years. Or perhaps the influx of foreigners during the Olympics had opened his eyes to other views.

'There's more to life than the People's Republic, Livia. And if you tell anyone I said that, I'll have to kill you.'

She laughed, and so did he, to be sociable, she suspected.

'Sorry if I'm out of sorts. My father is – well, he has a few financial issues at the moment, and his involvement in the Olympics hasn't helped. So much to spend on entertaining, blandishments, bribes, saving face at any cost.'

'Saving face? Isn't that old news?' And wasn't Yani's father, a high-level party member, also a wildly wealthy industrialist as a result of China's booming economy, just like Professor Wu with his pharmaceuticals. Of course, there was the school of thought that insisted that too much wealth could never be enough.

'Saving face as old news. It's an interesting idea. And speaking of face, I'll have to leave you for my parents. They're expecting an escort home and the number one son is it, today.'

Livia followed Yani's gaze and saw Bing and Antigone Lee taking their leave of Professor Wu. Livia and Yani walked together to the group and, once the Lees had gone, the Professor invited Livia to his museum office.

2

'This is a remarkable collection.' Livia replaced the last piece and stepped back to take in the entire wall. There must have been forty or more pieces carefully arranged beside, above and below each other on glass shelves – a small but select group of artefacts from the Professor's larger collection brought to his office to remind him of his good taste: bronze animals, vases, human figures in clay, pottery models of houses and other buildings, a stunning jade leopard inlaid with silver and garnets.

'The Han dynasty is my husband's downfall, Dr Galvin.' Professor Wu's wife, Zhang Lin, had joined them after her own presentation ceremony elsewhere in the museum. She was a small, neat woman who, despite her severe suit and self-contained manner, Livia had found to be warm and full of concentrated energy. 'I, on the other hand – well, you know where my heart lies.'

Madame Zhang stared at Livia's necklace, just as she had stared when they'd met at previous international conferences and dealers' conventions over the last several years. There was something in the woman's gaze that Livia knew she herself had lost long ago: that avid, unquenchable desire for certain objects of beauty, the proviso being, of course, that beauty, as the cliché went, was always in the eye of the beholder. Certainly, Livia was a dealer and a collector – usually on behalf of others – but her interest now was based in curiosity, in the psychology of the collector. And Madame Zhang was a collector, all right, perhaps a more passionate one than her husband.

'I know, Dr Galvin, talk is cheap, so I won't insult you yet again with an offer when I know you will not sell at any price.'

Livia forced a smile to her lips, but she felt the weight of the gold necklace. She had worn it every day that she'd been in China, to remind herself – as though she needed reminding – of the reason for her participation, the reason for her ambition to win. It was the golden equivalent of a hair shirt, the alternating barrel and tubular beads carefully cast, the small human figure in the middle, no more than three centimetres high, dangling helplessly, his little arms raised, the hands balled into fists. She took a deep breath as Professor Wu handed her a cup of jasmine tea.

'Thank you,' she said. 'It's always been my favourite.' It was time, she thought. She sipped the tea and concluded that he'd approve if he were here. 'You're right, Madame Zhang, I wouldn't sell this at any price.'

'Pre-Colombian gold. I don't wonder – it is rare to find very many artefacts outside museums. Private collectors, like me, we keep what we acquire, Dr Galvin. El Dorado is the legend of legends. Were you lucky enough to be present at Lake Guatavita for the total eclipse in 1977?'

'1977? I was 13, I had no idea about anything.' She set the cup down and unhooked the necklace, handing it to Madame

Zhang. 'Here you are, I'm forgetting my manners.' Removing the piece from her physical self would help with the transition, she knew. She'd realised years ago, before the necklace, before Dan, before Paul, that life was all about transitions when you came right down to it. One simple word full of everything imaginable.

Madam Zhang's face became more animated; her eyes lit up as she gently felt the beads and stroked the golden man. 'So beautiful. You will appreciate my sentiments, Dr Galvin, when I tell you that to want something and to be unable to have it, it is a physical longing, a pain that is felt – here,' she placed her hand over her heart, 'and here.' She moved her hand slowly to touch her forehead, all the while gazing at the necklace draped over her other hand.

'Yes, I understand,' Livia said, but her understanding had nothing to do with objects like this. She'd won a gold medal for Dan, and now, she realised, she could say goodbye to this reminder. 'That's why I'm giving it to you. I have the gold I came to Beijing for, and it's time to hand this on. It's yours, Madame Zhang, with my sincerest best wishes.'

Madame Zhang made no attempt to hide her shock. She looked at her husband, equally stunned, and then at the necklace. Her fingers closed involuntarily, possessively around the beads and barrels. The little man dangled in front of her.

'This is the last thing I expected, Dr Galvin,' she said slowly. 'It is too much. As much as I would like to, I cannot accept it. The protocols of dealing and selling are well established, you know that.' But her heart wasn't in it, Livia could tell.

'I have sound reasons for my decision, and I know you'll give this necklace a wonderful home. Your generosity in lending your art to galleries and museums is well-recognised and appreciated.' She paused. It had to work. 'Please indulge me in this.'

Professor Wu stepped forward. 'Perhaps we can reward each other appropriately, Dr Galvin.' He moved to his Han wall and selected a small bronze horse in full gallop. Its mouth was open, revealing bared teeth; its nostrils flared, straining for oxygen, and its eyes bulged. It suggested to Livia a state of exquisite pain, endured for two millennia already. Some of her clients would find it irresistible.

'Will you accept this as a token of our deep gratitude?' He handed it to her. 'It is one of the more beautifully-wrought animal pieces.'

Livia took it and held it by its hooves with both hands. 'Yes, I can see that.' She was no expert on Han dynasty art, but that didn't matter. The expertise required here related to diplomacy and, yes, Yani was right, it was a question of face. The horse saved face for the Professor and Madame Zhang. She had to accept it without demur. 'Thank you. Thank you both.'

'The act of collecting is like a purification of the soul,' Professor Wu said, watching Livia turn the horse this way and that. 'It is an art in itself.'

'I think my godmother would certainly agree with you, Professor.' Even if, these days, Minnie's collecting had more to do with gathering strays and lonely hearts, not to mention consciences whenever the opportunity arose to alert the populace to yet another development outrage at home.

'Madame Babitsky. Yes, I think she would. How is she?'

'She's very well, but she isn't actively collecting art anymore. She's involved in community activism. Preserving heritage buildings, that sort of thing.' Livia remembered that Minnie used to attend the international conferences and conventions that Livia inherited when she took over the Mesmer Babitsky Gallery. She would have had at least a nodding acquaintance with most of the dealers and collectors.

At that moment, there was a knock and they turned to see the guard, who had been standing on the podium earlier, at the door. He was carrying several items, including Livia's gun case, the slightly larger duffel bag she usually carried it in to protect it against scratches, and Professor Wu's briefcase.

'Oh, I'm so sorry,' Livia said. 'I forgot.' She moved towards the guard as Professor Wu said something in Chinese to him. Whatever it was, the guard seemed to tighten his grip on the items he held.

'Dr Galvin, this is one of my assistants. I should have explained to you earlier. As coincidence would have it, I am flying out to Australia this afternoon – government and diplomatic business. I would be happy to lighten your burden and take the bronze with me. And anything else that you would like to divest yourself of. I will have a courier deliver any items to your home if you like. Or elsewhere.'

'Oh – well, I was going to put a couple of things in the gun case for Mrs Babitsky. A flag, signed by some of the Olympians. I have it with me. But it's no trouble to carry the bronze. It will fit in the case – in fact, it could have been made for it.'

'Unfortunately, it may be a problem for our Customs officials. The spontaneity of your giving this beautiful item to my wife,' he gazed at Madame Zhang, still admiring the necklace, 'means that our reciprocal gift – humble as it is – requires official approval to leave the country. And Comrade Lee, who could have arranged such approval, has already left with his wife and son.'

Livia followed his gaze to Madame Zhang, apparently counting the gold tubular and barrel beads on the necklace. Already, it had become a kind of golden rosary in her hands. Livia wondered how soon it would be after she left the room that this collector of El Dorado's artefacts would ask her husband to hang the rosary around her slender neck and fasten the clasp. The thought encouraged a smile.

'However, if I carry it with me, the approval is automatic – it will save time, and unnecessary effort. Do you agree?'

'Do I agree? Yes, thank you.' A little bronze horse two millennia old, wrapped in the flag of another country, spirited out under diplomatic passage, and cossetted in the best foam moulding Livia's mother could find. What could she say?

'Excellent. Now, if you would be so good as to write the address for me, I will arrange delivery as soon as we arrive in your country.' Professor Wu's tone took on the brisk efficiency that must have helped to make his fortune, but he was still smiling politely, as was Madame Zhang.

Livia took a notebook and a gold Mont Blanc fountain pen from the Professor – apparently, they collected gold in all its forms – and wrote down the address: Minnie's office, situated immediately next door to Livia's gallery. She'd know what to do with it.

When she took leave of her hosts, Livia travelled through the busy streets in the official car they had called for her, comfortable in the silent, air-conditioned environment. She went back to the hotel to sit on her bed and contemplate the empty duffel bag and the remaining piece of gold in her possession. After a while, she went to the wardrobe and brought out her backpack. From it she removed a creased, home-made greeting card and read it once again: 'Shoot For Olympic Gold, Mum. Love From Dan, XOXOX.' Above this directive, there was a hand-drawn picture of Livia, blonde hair in unruly, crayoned squiggles, wearing what would, at a glance, pass for a green and gold track suit, her arm raised at a right-angle to her body, her hand holding a black six-shooter aimed at the black and white target drawn on the opposite page of the card. Red flames erupted from the gun and tiny, black bullets made their way across the pages to arrive in red blotches at the target's centre. Livia closed the card and placed it on the bedside table next to her gold medal. From a smaller, zippered compartment of the backpack, she removed a black squash ball, then fitted the backpack into the duffel bag, zipped it up and stowed it in the wardrobe with the rest of her luggage. She lay down on the bed and stared at the ceiling, counting each breath, squeezing the ball rhythmically in her right hand, hopeful of sleep.

CHAPTER THREE

Beijing
Sunday 31 August 2008

1

'Okay, Livia? Can you pass me the Laramies?' Yani turned to smile at her, raising his eyebrows in the direction of the glovebox. By way of compensation for his lack of focus on the road ahead, he accelerated.

'Truck, Yani.' Livia nodded at the oversized lorry cutting into their lane centimetres off the car's right headlight. Her legs and feet stretched out to imaginary brakes as the truck's bending shadow drew ahead of them. Its blinker signalled a left turn and it was gone as quickly as it had appeared. Livia leaned forward and flipped open the glovebox, pushing aside two pistols to reach the cigarettes, half-squashed beneath a box of ammunition.

'One weapon for each hand? Or each passenger? Is there a stash under my seat as well?' Livia pulled the Laramies out and squeezed the pack hard, hopeful of carnage within. She made no effort to remove a cigarette.

'It's always peak hour.' Yani ignored her comment and tapped out a martial beat on the steering wheel with his fingers.

'I thought you'd given these away. What's the tar content here?' She turned the pack around and around, feigning a search. 'It's so high, they're not game to list it.' She threw the cigarettes back into the glovebox. 'Cancer sticks *and* shooting sticks, all in one compact location. You can at least wait until I'm gone.'

Yani smiled again and said, 'Fair enough,' unflappable in the face of refusal.

That particular smile displayed his Chinese and Greek parentage to best effect, in Livia's opinion anyway. Mediterranean macho taunts Far Eastern delicacy, Greer said. Well, she would, wouldn't she? Livia knew it was a persuasive combination of charm and looks that ensured Yani got his way most of the time, with most people. She'd seen something deeper, too, something slightly off-balance and difficult to read with any accuracy. Whatever it was, it added positively to his particular brand of charisma. Except where cigarettes were concerned.

'You can drive if you want, Livia. It's quite safe.'

She knew it was a genuine offer, and not a comment on her truck reaction. She also knew driving here was sometimes safe for native Beijingers, but always traumatising for foreigners used to milder, less wayward conditions. There were so many traffic jams that when things finally moved freely, everyone seemed to turn into Formula One impersonators.

'No thanks. You're the designated driver on this family outing.'

Their first 'family' outing had been in Beijing over two decades ago when Livia and her sister, Greer, took their first trip to Asia. Yani had been their tour guide.

It was a very different city in the early 1980s – bicycles ruled the boulevards and hutongs; skyscrapers had only begun their invasion and takeover. They might have enjoyed a future together here, Livia and Yani, riding the challenge of unprecedented economic growth and the Communist Party's shameless lust for the juicy fruits of capitalism. But she'd realised – when had that revelation smacked her in the nose? – that in those far off days he would never have left his homeland by choice, not even for the love of a woman, not even for her. And in those days, she'd never seen herself as any kind of permanent ex-patriot. Nonetheless, Livia, whose biggest mistake had been to marry the ambitious, ethically mystified politician, Paul Clifford, had occasionally wondered over the years how hard it could have been for her to adapt to the People's Republic. Why hadn't love managed to find a way? Probably because, she had to admit, it had been a grand, intense infatuation between them, followed, fortuitously, by an intermittent, long-distance friendship.

'It's a wonderful day, isn't it?' He swerved into a faster lane.

'Wonderful. Yes, it is.' She replanted her feet on the imaginary brakes.

'Look at that sky, Livia.'

'It's a sky, all right.'

'But it's clean.' He paused. 'Cleaner, then. Yes?'

Air pollution in the city had been reduced by a government ban on industrial and other toxic, gene-scrambling, lung-shrinking activities before and during the Olympics. There were varying opinions about the ban's efficacy. It had to be better than nothing, didn't it?

'Keep the memory, Livia. It'll never be this fresh again.' He began to hum the Chinese national anthem, *The March of the Volunteers,* and his tapping fingers matched the rhythm. 'It's not far now.'

He relaxed his grip on the steering wheel and removed one hand as heavier traffic forced him to slow down. Now he began a tattoo on the driver's side window, the ring on his middle finger rapping sharply. Livia tried to ignore it and gazed out of her window in search of distraction. The streets were full of colour and people: locals, visitors, Olympians. Like Livia, many of the athletes and their families had stayed on after the Games ended. It was easier to be a tourist once the big event had drawn to its conclusion and the flame was out. The dust storms were still in Mongolia, the weather was bearable, if you came from a hot country. Everyone was safe; the ghosts of Munich remained in the shadows for another four years.

2

They stopped at a crossing, and Livia watched clusters of slow-walking, sweating pedestrians. Up ahead, a burst pipe sprayed arcs of cooling, rainbowed water into the air for anyone seeking temporary relief. It was hot enough in Beijing, all right, as hot as a pushy Australian summer.

They pulled away from the crossing at Yani's usual speed: fast, and sped through the unexpected shower. The traffic had thinned a little again, and Livia was surprised when she felt a bump from behind. It pushed them forward and to the left. Yani overcorrected the steering and they veered towards the bus in the lane beside them. He pulled away from the bus, and whoever was behind them, then slowed to the speed limit.

'I think we've been hit, Livia,' he said. 'Are you all right?'

'I'm fine. What was that?'

'I'm not sure. Let's turn off here and check the car.'

The precious car, an old, Beijing taxi, a collector's item from the 1950s that looked more like a party cadre's official transport, except that now it was air-conditioned, reconditioned, re-cushioned, re-engined, CD'd and carpeted, seatbelted, the black duco polished to within an inch of its ignition.

Yani turned off Fuxingmenwai Avenue, and drove and turned and turned until he found a quieter area. As he slowed down, a silver sedan overtook them and continued along the narrow street, coming to a halt in the middle of the road some thirty metres ahead, idling there as smoke issued from the exhaust pipe. The car's occupants remained in their seats.

'This is the car that hit us,' Yani said. 'They've probably stopped to apologise.' He spoke calmly, reached in front of Livia and opened the glovebox. He withdrew one of the pistols, released its safety and cocked it. 'They've been following us for some time.'

Livia watched the pistol intently. It was a Walther P5, smooth, compact, classy, one of her favourites.

'Do you think that's necessary, since they're going to apologise?' Her own weapons were behind glass at the People's museum, and for a moment she was more annoyed than afraid.

'I was never a boy scout, Livia, but I'm a policeman, so I'm always prepared, you know.'

'I'll take the other one, then. We can be doubly prepared.' For what, she couldn't say, and she didn't really want to know, but reached into the glovebox anyway.

'No, Livia. It's out of commission – the firing pin. Stay here, please.'

Yani opened the door, holding the pistol close to his thigh, and stepped onto the roadway. The driver and passenger in the silver car opened their doors, stepped out and turned to face him. Two dark suits, sunglasses, eyeless, blank faces, black gloves, focus. They began walking slowly towards Yani and Livia, simultaneously reaching into their jackets. For their business cards and insurance details? Livia wondered for only a moment as the pistols were revealed and pointed in their direction.

'Stop,' Yani yelled at them. 'Stop now or I'll shoot.' He crouched behind the car door and raised his gun, repeating the words in Mandarin.

But even as he spoke, the silver car's driver stopped, yelled something, and fired. The first and second shots shattered the door's window and appeared to hit Yani in the upper body, sending him backwards so that he stumbled and fell with the shower of glass. The third and fourth shots thumped into the reinforced-steel door. Would any other metal stop high-powered projectiles? Livia didn't know, but she was grateful for the protective shield the car offered.

She slid across the bench seat, thanking every god and goddess for Yani's obsession with old cars and column shifts. As she looked around for his gun – could they be so unlucky that it was too far away? – she saw his ankle holster, reached down, ripped the Velcro tab open and grabbed the familiar-looking PPK stainless, released the safety, cocked it and hoped the magazine was full. She had no time to reassure Yani, or herself, but risked a glance at his face, filled with pain and fear, and apology.

She crawled out of the car. Another two bullets passed close by as she peered around the door at the men approaching, still with that slow, confident stride. Who did they think they were – *Terminator* robots? But this was no film set they'd stumbled into, and the suits were far too close for her comfort. She was used to distant, inanimate targets, and rhythm, where was her rhythm?

The next three bullets hit the car door and the impact knocked Livia off balance and into the open roadway. There was no time for rhythm. She rolled onto her stomach and aimed at the closest man, firing off a double tap. He fell in mid-step, a surprised look on his face, still clutching his gun. She had already sized up the second assassin and caught him with another double as he fired and threw himself sideways. She was certain she felt the wind warp as his bullet passed her by. One of her shots entered the man's heart and the other cut through the arm of his coat before chipping the concrete gutter behind him.

There was no time for thought. She stood and ran towards the shooters, kicking their pistols as far along the street as her next adrenalin burst could manage. She stood between them as they lay on the ground, their confidence shed along with their lives. The second man down had lost his sunglasses and stared up at her, unblinking, calm. She backed away towards Yani's car, hesitant to take her eyes off the men, the PPK pointed at them, her finger still on the trigger.

Yani was leaning against the car, his left hand pressed against his right shoulder. Livia joined him behind the bullet-riddled door. She took one more look at the bodies on the road, removed her finger from the trigger, engaged the safety, and turned her attention to her friend. He'd begun to shake. His eyes were unfocused and she noticed a trickle of blood emerging from his hairline above his right ear. She crouched in front of him, wondering how to get help quickly when she smelt something familiar – a burning smell – petrol, oil, something else. Yani was whispering.

'What?' She leaned towards him. 'What is it? Where are you hit?'

'Move, now, move,' he said, his breath lost.

She didn't hesitate. She pulled Yani forward and around so that she could get behind him and drag him away from the car. As she grabbed him under his arms, she felt something harder than fabric beneath his jacket. Could he be wearing a Kevlar vest? It wasn't something to contemplate at the moment as she heard him groan in pain; she knew she couldn't stop once she had at least some momentum on her side.

As they struggled towards the footpath, she saw flames beneath Yani's car, and from the corner of her eye, she saw the first shooter moving sideways, awkwardly pulling a gun from his coat pocket. She pushed her knee into Yani's back to hold him up, pulled out the PPK, flicked the safety, raised her arm like the Livia in Dan's drawing, aimed and fired. The man slumped face down onto the road, his pistol skittering away from his hand.

She dropped her pistol, grabbed Yani and dragged him towards a recessed doorway, rolling him the last metre and a half and falling on top of him as the car exploded behind them, sending out heat and shock waves. With the greatest of efforts, she lifted herself off Yani's slumped body, pushing against the hot wind blowing at them from the flaming car, and it was then she felt a push against the back of her head. She knew without turning that it was the business end of a gun, but it wasn't the gun that caused her to swoon then, it was something from years ago, the memory of that smell: petrol, oil, and rubber, burning.

CHAPTER FOUR

Bogota
Monday 10 July 2000

They'd driven for only an hour, but the last half of the journey seemed to stretch and stretch. She knew time was elastic, but these minutes had become hours. She sat in the rear seat behind the driver. Paul sat up front. Noone in the car spoke, but they could hear voices on the two-way radio. The voices went back and forth, sounding, by turns, excited, angry, desultory, urgent; there was laughter every so often. She couldn't be bothered trying to translate the Spanish, even if the exercise might be a kind of calming meditation, and instead stared out of the window. The day had lightened, although there were scattered clouds above them and the remnants of yet another morning's fog lingered in the paddocks. They hadn't had time for breakfast. When the call came, at 5.30, she'd been ready to go, had been sleeping in her clothes since it happened; she was ready, always ready. Splashed water on her face, cleaned her teeth, as if it mattered; remembered telling Dan as she taught him how, 'Once you have clean teeth, you're ready for anything, my boy.' Saw his reflection in the bathroom mirror next to hers, nodding seriously, white foam on his lips.

And now, here they were, driving, slowing, passing a couple of farm buildings, nudging their way around several police cars, an ambulance. She supposed she should have taken a bite of something, simply to be sensible, but sense had left the world three days before, and who was she to challenge its absence now?

When the vehicle stopped, she flexed her muscles and felt the weakness in her legs, wondering if they would carry her through these moments. Paul, full of nervous energy as usual, bounded right out of the car and walked straight up to meet the official she'd seen leave a group of similarly uniformed men as they'd arrived. He'd begun to trudge towards them, his head down, avoiding eye contact even at a distance. She climbed out of her seat and walked unsteadily around the back of the SUV, and she could hear Paul already questioning the soldier, or policeman, whatever kind of officer he was. He looked to be in his fifties, with greying sideburns, although his moustache, entirely black, looked several years younger than its owner. He spoke English, and as she drew nearer, she heard the word she'd seen in the newspaper headline so long ago. Was it really only last Friday?

'These groups like FARC, and ELN, Mr Clifford, the AUC, they usually kidnap for ransom. Tourists, government officials, wealthy people. They finance their guerilla activities against the state. The ELN call this kind of operation *pesca milagrosa;* it means 'good fishing,' a bountiful catch.'

Her son was a bountiful catch. She took a few more steps
as the man continued, pushing her hands into her jacket pock-
ets. In the right pocket, she found the squash ball Paul had
handed her and gripped it tightly. Friday seemed closer again.

'As you know, in this case, these people set up a roadblock
and stopped the vehicles until they had plenty to choose from.
They take the rich people they think will be lucrative captives.
Children are particularly prized. As you can appreciate, they
fetch large ransoms, as do foreigners. I am surprised you were
not chosen, Mr Clifford. You are lucky in that respect.' The
officer made eye contact then, and another question waited,
unspoken: 'Why didn't you volunteer to replace your son?'

'I was several cars behind Dan and Eamon when we were
all stopped, there was nothing we could –' Paul began, as Livia
joined them. 'My wife, Livia Galvin.' He turned to Livia.
'This is Captain Rodriguez from the *Policia Nacional*.'

'My husband wasn't with our son,' Livia said, correcting
Paul. 'Not even close. Neither was I.' She heard her own
voice at a distance from herself. 'Eamon was with Dan.'
There. She'd said their names, their names were here, floating
on the air in front of her.

The captain nodded politely. 'Señora. My profound and
sincerest sympathy to you and your family. And to the family
of Señor Pearse. Words are no comfort for you, I think.'

But words had been comforting during the long wait.
Words strung into phrases: ransomed and released, kidnapping as fund-raising, victims found unharmed. Those words,
hopeful words, helped Livia to imagine her family belonging
to the 90 percent whose stories ended in reunion. Well, this
was a reunion, of sorts.

'Where are they?' She looked beyond Rodriguez and saw that the group of men he had been with had dispersed. What were they doing? They'd had plenty of time to secure the scene and sort things out. 'How did you find them?' Questions had their own rhythm, she felt, short, sharp questions. Direct. There would be answers, there had to be.

'A tip-off. By phone to the police headquarters in Bogota. Anonymous, of course. Perhaps you would like to sit down, Señora Galvin. You do not look well.'

'I'm fine, thank you. Where are they?'

'Captain, I thought,' Paul paused, seemed to reconsider, but then continued. 'I thought these people were interested in money. Why do this?'

Did he think discovering why would help them to understand anything but the most basic economics, the greed, the need for chaos to survive? Or perhaps the talking would wear them out, flatten them, make them invisible to even themselves. The worn, the flattened, the invisible, surely they would feel less?

'It is possible that something went wrong, Señor. Some of these guerilla groups, they – what is the term? – they subcontract their kidnapping activities to common criminal gangs. Or, sometimes, smalltime kidnappers, amateurs, abduct people, and then try to sell them to the bigger groups like FARC. They make mistakes, they get frightened.'

'There must be something –' Paul stopped and raised his hand, as though to point something of interest out to Livia, who saw them at the same time. She moved forward.

'No, Livia. No.' Paul went after her, and grabbed her arm, walking with her. 'You shouldn't do this. Not here. Wait until we get him back to the city.' Paul's face grew whiter.

Livia said nothing. She stopped walking and swayed forward and back beside him, then steadied herself. She placed her hand over his, still wrapped around her forearm. She gripped it tightly and squeezed until he suddenly groaned aloud in pain.

'Livia.' His voice was almost a shout. She let him go and he shook his hand and flexed his fingers.

She strode away from him and Rodriguez and towards the two gurneys being wheeled across the rough, damp ground of the farmyard. She could smell something burning: petrol, oil, rubber, all of them together, as she reached out and pulled back the first sheet. It was Eamon, grey-faced, blood smeared across his left cheek, his forehead and the left side of his jaw discoloured by bruises, matted blood in his hair. He stared past her at the sky, light blue like his eyes. She walked around the gurney and lifted the second sheet before another thought could stop her. There he was – pale, still, sleeping. She smoothed his hair, and placed a hand on his cheek. She pushed the sheet back and took his hand in hers and held it gently. His skin felt cold. There was a dark, bloody patch just below and behind his left ear. She knew it was the entry point of a bullet; she'd seen similar things when she was a much younger woman, but then she'd been stronger, harder.

'Danny,' she whispered. 'Where are you, little boy?' She leaned down and kissed his forehead. Her tears fell onto his eyelids and wet his lashes, and for a moment, just one moment, Dan seemed to weep with her.

Paul came to stand at the foot of the gurney. 'This isn't – this can't be –' He began to cry as Rodriguez and another man joined them. The stranger moved closer to Paul and put a hand on his shoulder. Paul acknowledged his presence with the merest of shrugs, but didn't move away.

After a few minutes, Rodriguez said, 'This is Señor Cordoba. He says he knew Señor Pearse.' Around them, the officers and the medics stopped what they were doing and waited, for something – a signal, a movement, another lead to follow, for the grief to stretch itself out a little more.

'I'll help you,' the man said, watching Livia intently as she continued to gaze at her son. 'I am a colleague and friend of Eamon's. It would be an honour if you would consider my offer to help.'

Livia glanced up at the man who'd spoken. He had thick, greying hair and a full beard, sunglasses, and he wore a dark suit. In his left hand, he held the strap of a camera bag. His voice sounded familiar, with the trace of an accent that sounded Middle Eastern, but with a name like Cordoba, that was unlikely. What did it matter? She couldn't believe she was thinking of such things. She could hear her heart thudding in her ears, and she felt as though she might simply drop down on this hard ground with the scratching chickens and the whimpering dogs, and will herself to die. Instead, she asked another question.

'Did you catch them?' Who should she ask? Rodriguez, or the man who'd arrived to offer help? She looked at them both in turn, and returned to contemplating Dan's face. She would carry this image, along with all the other images of Dan, smiling, laughing, frowning, questioning, inside herself for as long as she lived. That was what mothers did, she thought, what they must do. They carried the lifeblood; even when it had been stilled, even when it had become unbearably heavy, they carried it. She didn't need Señor Cordoba's camera to help her with reminders.

'I am sorry to inform you that they have escaped,' Rodriguez said.

'Escaped?' Paul stood with one hand on the gurney. He looked to Livia as though he might just drift away entirely if he let it go. 'What are you doing to find them?' Every word was an effort.

'Everything we can, Señor. Everything, but I must warn you that these people are like the mist. They come and go, they live in the forests, they are protected by villagers, they rule through fear. They have many resources, and people will not bear witness against them.'

'I'd like to take my son and Eamon away from here,' Livia said. 'Now.' This time she knew who to instruct, and she could see the relief in Rodriguez's eyes as she spoke. He must have sent some kind of silent signal out to his troops, because almost instantly there was movement. People appeared from the farmhouse and the barn, the ambulance officers covered the bodies and, slowly, moving around and away from Paul and Livia, continued their procession with the gurneys to their vehicles.

As she was walking towards their car with Paul, Rodriguez caught up with her and handed her Dan's backpack. She took it from him in silence and without warning, she was over-whelmed by a great nausea. She held the backpack to one side and leaned forward to vomit. There was only bile, and little of it. She wiped her mouth with the back of her hand as Paul tried to hand her his handkerchief and Rodriguez tried to look genuinely concerned. Who knew, perhaps he was, even after years of such scenes must have hardened his heart. What she did know was that there was no point in encouraging him to do his job. He would do whatever it was they always did in these cases, which was irrelevant now as far as she was concerned.

She transferred the backpack to her other hand, and Paul stared at it as though it might contain a ticking bomb, but he said nothing, instead wiping his face with the handkerchief he'd offered her. In the car, they sat in the same seats as before, Paul in front, Livia behind the driver, though this time she balanced Dan's backpack on her knees and held it with both hands. Cordoba arrived at her window and she wound it down once she realised he wasn't going anywhere until he spoke to her.

'I will find them for you, Dr Galvin,' he said. 'I promise.' His voice was soft and steady, and still she couldn't shake the notion that she'd heard it before. There was something in the way he pronounced certain vowels, the flatness of them, that made him sound like the kids she'd grown up with who'd come from other countries and learned English as a second language.

'Do your worst,' Livia replied. 'It makes no difference now.' She felt so tired.

'I am so sorry for your troubles,' he said, his voice breaking, and he moved off quickly as their car took off simultaneously, before she could respond.

It was the phrase her mother used with the greatest of respect whenever there was a death and she'd go and visit the family of the friend or relative who'd died, dragging Livia or Greer, or both of them with her. Greer, her mother, Uncle Con, Minnie, the family. What could she say to them? How would she explain? Questions with answers and no answers. She withdrew the squash ball from her pocket and began squeezing it in her right hand, clinging more tightly to Dan's backpack with her left. She watched the ambulance up ahead leading them home.

CHAPTER FIVE

Strait of Magellan Chile
[53.10S 70.56W]
Sunday 31 August 2008

1

'It's very adventurous of you to brave the deck with me in such weather, Mademoiselle Skelloe. And after midnight.'

The man who spoke was in his early sixties. He had greying hair, but his moustache was a luxuriant black. He wore a calf-length, woollen overcoat buttoned from top to bottom. He tugged at his black gloves and stamped his feet. The boots were heavy and thick and reduced his agility, but they were warm and protective in this godforsaken tail-end of what he regarded as the greatest of the Americas.

'The pleasure is entirely mine, Miguel.'

The attractive, dark-haired woman standing beside him was 20 years his junior. He had charmed her at dinner when they discussed everything but what was on his mind: getting her into his stateroom and his bed, gazing into her blue-grey eyes as he seduced her. He'd suggested this late-night meeting on the freezing deck after she'd told him how much she loved to experience nature's extremes. This was the part of the cruise she had most looked forward to, negotiating the Strait and rounding Cape Horn, sailing to Tierra del Fuego and Patagonia. Poor old Patagonia. Tourists thought of her as being so mysterious, when she was merely another outpost of stony ground and uncompromising weather.

'It isn't easy, travelling alone, Greer, whatever they may say about greater independence.'

'I like the opportunity to meet people, interesting people. Like you, Miguel.'

She turned to him, smiling and happy, her face flushed, he was certain, with the pleasure of his company, as much as with the midnight freeze. He could still bring out the best in women.

'Who'd have thought a property developer could be so fascinating. Of course, I only have my cousin, Karl, the mogul, as a comparison.'

'Your cousin?' His intonation suggested he was far more interested in her stories than in speaking about himself. An unselfish man for this lovely woman, a man who would listen forever and a day if it guaranteed access to her body. And it wasn't even a sacrifice, lending an ear – he was an excellent listener, even to the hopeless and helpless, even to those who had nothing, really, to tell him, after all.

'Let's not bother with Karl.' She turned back to the sea. 'When do you think we'll cross the border, Miguel?'

'Oh, it'll be a while yet. Not tonight.'

They stood together leaning against the rail as the breeze picked up. Did she move closer, or was it his imagination? He had never been able to decide if he preferred to make love to strangers in the country of his birth, or elsewhere. There was no choice with his wife – a stranger in a different way – who refused to leave Bogota and their walled fortress of a mansion for love or money. And he – well, he refused to become a victim of circumstance, a prisoner for no reason that he could fathom. He'd done his job all those years, and he'd been rewarded, and rewarded himself at times. Now it was over, and he enjoyed a new, lucrative career, courtesy of his former employer. People should move on, in his opinion, take up their lives and prosper, as he had done, even if, at times, he missed the thrill of the breakthrough, the breaking of a spirit, especially the contracted ones.

'I was wondering – I suppose it's the trip that put the thought in my head – I was wondering where I'd choose to die, Miguel, if I had a choice, that is? At home, or somewhere else entirely? Somewhere exotic.'

'But what is exotic these days, Greer, when one has the chance to travel almost anywhere at a moment's notice? Look at us.'

'Yes, look at us,' Greer replied. 'So where, Miguel? Colombia or Chile? Patagonia?' She paused. 'If you had a choice.'

'What a strange question, my dear. I have no intention of dying for a very long time. And not even then, if I can help it.'

He laughed at the notion that occurred to him. 'If I could make a pact with the devil, I'd happily sell my soul for immortality on this earth. Yes, I would. No doubt about it.' So many had regarded him as the devil made flesh at different times, when he was merely an instrument guided by greater forces, well, a government minister, and the lure of profit.

'Really? You would do that, Miguel? Surely life would become boring after a while?'

'Not with money, and the right connections.'

'Both of which you possess in abundance, of course.'

'Of course.' Miguel was the director of this conversation. He wanted nothing more than to get out of the cold, this frosty, moonless night, and warm himself over this woman. The occasional seduction was one consolation of these clandestine business trips. 'You know, Greer, the cold, such cold as this, which is abnormal, can make a person morose, and gloomy. What is the word? Joyless. Perhaps you would like to sip a brandy or champagne with me in my stateroom. A pick-me-up, a little joy, before bed.' And even greater joy.

'Miguel.' Greer turned to him. 'There's nothing I'd like more than a stiff drink at the moment. Unfortunately, I gave it up years ago. I found it interfered with my work, which requires great precision, and devotion. Not unlike your work. Or rather, the work you used to do.'

He couldn't see her face as well as before. Some of the deck lights had been turned off. Cheap bastards. 'I don't know what you mean, my dear.' He felt unbalanced by her comment, unsure of his next move. What did she mean? Wasn't she a psychologist? How much precision could such a menial job require? He realised that he'd concentrated on his own pleasure at the expense of his usual level of vigilance. How could this woman – ?

'Let me explain. It's important.'

Her voice became soft, and almost, yes, almost loving. He was being paranoid; he'd probably caught his wife's disease.

As she spoke, Greer moved closer, gently turning him around to face the ship. She leaned into him, as though to kiss him, pushing him against the railing, smiling once more.

'Eight years ago, outside Bogota,' she said, 'a little boy and a man were murdered at a farmhouse. Dan Clifford, 6 years old, and Eamon Pearse, a journalist. Apparently, it was a tourist kidnapping gone horribly wrong. Do you remember? You were the investigating Captain.'

'That's quite a time ago, but yes, my dear, it was a terrible incident. We searched and searched but never found the murderers. To this day, I regret our failure. That little boy. His parents, they were broken people.' What did she want to hear from him about this? Was she another of those journalists in disguise, dredging up old horrors for some feature story in a U.S. paper? Something else to bring his beautiful country into disrepute, as if the drugs weren't enough? 'Let's leave the deck – we can discuss this inside, somewhere warm, with brandy.' He took a step, but she raised her hand, gently placed it on his chest, and pushed him back.

'You see, Miguel, I found out a few things about the killers, and I thought you might like to know. For closure, as they say.'

'Why would you want to find out? And how did you do it?' He heard his voice – it held a note of fear, despite his effort to lighten the tone. He had to get a grip. He stood up straighter.

'I research PTSD – Post Traumatic Stress Disorder – and this is a project I've been working on for – well, the last eight years, on and off.'

'You want to interview me about it, is that it? You've discovered that I was a policeman in the anti-kidnapping squad, and you are interested in my – what did you call it? PTSD?'

'Not exactly *your* PTSD, but you're close. You're right, you know, it is bloody cold out here. The thing is, Eamon Pearse was found to have been tortured – severely beaten, broken ribs, a broken leg, missing fingernails – he was investigating the whereabouts of art treasures stolen by the Nazis from the Jews in World War Two. As you may be aware, many of these treasures were brought to various South American countries when psychopaths like Mengele fled Europe. Most of them, with the collusion of governments down here, simply fell off the face of the earth, along with their art. But Eamon Pearse, he was always a determined type. That's what got him into so much trouble.'

'I can imagine.' Although he didn't have to imagine on this particular occasion. All he had to do was remember. He would see where she was going with this – he may have to contact his old employer if the worst came to it.

'But I think the people who took him thought he was investigating the drug lords.' She raised her eyebrows, as if to ask for his confirmation.

She had nothing, then. He allowed himself the hint of a smile, the shape of his lips his wife insisted on calling a smirk.

'We think that if the operation had been planned, the child and his father, two foreign nationals, would have been the targets.' The smirk deepened. 'But the boy was separated from his father and went ahead with the other fellow. If only he had been with his mother.'

'Really?'

'A child should be with his mother. It was neglectful of her to go off so selfishly. We think it turned into an opportunistic crime, in any case. They saw the child, they saw that he was foreign – blonde hair, fair complexion, and so on – and they saw much more money to be made in ransom. And the man he was with – he, too, looked Nordic.' The perfect crime, in fact, if he said so himself. 'Now I think we should leave the deck. It is far too cold for a fragile young woman like you.'

'Not Nordic, Irish. Whatever the story, the outcome was what it was. And here's the best part. My research shows that you were in charge of that particular cell of kidnappers, Miguel.' She smiled the sweetest smile at him as she delivered the verbal blow.

'What?' He smiled sweetly in return. 'You surely mean, my dear, that I was in charge of a particular cell of the anti-kidnap squad. Your informant is sadly mistaken.' Why had he begun to sweat in this temperature? It must be nearly at freezing point, and yet, when he looked at her he felt strangely feverish. It was almost as though he knew her from another time.

'I caught up with one of the gentlemen involved in the kidnapping. He was very helpful. He said you were also extremely helpful over many years – the policeman who never got his man, as long as there was a profit in it. Furthermore, you enjoyed personally inflicting the torture on Eamon Pearse. And you, Miguel, ordered the murder of the little boy because he saw you briefly by mistake when they brought him out to take a pee. You thought he could have identified you.'

'These things aren't true, Greer. You must believe me.' He would have to kill her, and the freezing ocean would be his friend tonight. Surprise was the thing. Some of the women he'd known had been quite strong, and feisty, for their inferior size. She was speaking again.

'And here's something to chew on for these last exciting moments, Colonel Miguel Alonzo Rodriguez. Dan Clifford was my nephew, and Eamon Pearse was my fiancee.'

Before he could act, he felt a surge of pain so severe that he was momentarily blinded. His eyes filled with tears, and his arms and legs felt weak. The bitch had cut his throat. No, wait, there was no blade, no blood. She'd punched him so hard in the larynx he was speechless. He gasped for breath and words, but merely opened and closed his mouth in silence, like one of the fish in his wife's aquarium.

'It's a little something I learned in the Middle East, from friends. All the power is in one's focus.' Greer held him up and stayed close. 'You can't hurt anyone, anymore, Miguel, but you'll have a more comfortable death than the innocents you tortured and murdered. I've heard that drowning is like going to sleep. I, for one, wish you nightmares on the way down.'

Her voice was angry but controlled. As he tried to focus on her words, he felt a tremendous, terrible pain in his groin, but still he couldn't cry out, or even move himself more than an inch, and he was twice her size. What had she done, the whore? Kneed him, cut him? He knew people who could deal with her. Would deal, once he'd managed to tell them.

'You murdering bastard.'

Did he see a tear in her eye? She was regretful, she was, but then she disappeared from his misty vision and he felt himself being lifted, pushed up against and over the railing. He could do nothing about it. How could she be so strong? By the time he hit the water, he'd managed to wave his arms uselessly in farewell.

Greer heard the faraway sound of a splash. It could have been a flying fish having some nocturnal fun, if flying fish swam in these waters. She leaned forward, searching the ocean for the man's dark shape. There was nothing. Midnight had swallowed him at last.

2.

'It's like that movie about the aliens, one of my favourites.'

A man emerged from the darkness where the deck lights had been turned off and joined Greer at the railing. 'Someone says that in space, no-one can hear you scream.'

'Thank god for the gym and training with those ballet dancers in London. He was a heavy one,' Greer said, moving closer to the man.

'The burden of all those deaths?'

'I think he wore that burden lightly, Uncle Ari,' Greer replied.

'Please, darling, Purser Cordoba.' The man put his arm around her shoulders and kissed her cheek. 'This cold is a killer for we temperate zone people. You're shaking, bubeleh. Are you all right?'

'I hate being around that kind of evil,' she said, leaning into him, his warmth. 'He was definitely a psychopath. They all were.' She wasn't sure if it was the cold or the thought of the intimate contact they'd had over the years with other members of the Rodriguez gang.

'Perhaps not all of them, but they went close. They were greedy, stupid people, desperate some of them. But there are no excuses. That monster, Rodriguez, he killed for sport, to terrorise the weak, the vulnerable.' He paused. 'How do you feel about this action, tonight? Are you all right, now that it's happened?'

She turned to him, studying his kind face. 'You mean do I need counselling now that I've finally despatched someone all by myself instead of relying on you to do the heavy lifting?' She looked out again to scan the waves for a bobbing, living body about to scream for help despite his fractured voicebox.

'Something like that, yes. Come, let's move and keep warm.'

They stepped away from the railing and walked slowly along the deck arm in arm. Greer knew that she was still in operative mode, her heart and soul yet to engage with the notions of guilt and remorse that accompanied the actuality of killing someone. She'd had enough experience as an accomplice, after all.

'I don't think I'll know for a while how I feel. I'm glad he's the last of them, I know that much.'

'You may be glad, but we don't know for sure that he's the last, liebshen. I have always thought there was another tier, above Rodriguez. I'm looking into it. I have a few useful connections with the government administration in Colombia. The old guard who've been in the paddock for a long time, since before the reforms.'

'Don't say that, Uncle – Purser Cordoba. This vendetta, if that's what it's been, is over now. The next task is finding a way to tell Livia that won't bugger up everything.'

'You understand my feelings about this – Livia should never know. It could cause a lot of problems for your relationship, the family. Have you spoken to them lately?'

'Not since Livia won her medal the other week. I'll call at the next port. We wouldn't want to encounter a phone trace, would we?'

And she didn't want to discuss what she might and might not tell Livia. She hadn't begun to consider the simple mechanics of it, either. How, for instance, would such a conversation begin: 'Dearest sister, I have hunted down and killed the man who murdered your darling son and my lover. Revenge is ours. Amen.' Would Livia even be grateful? Had Greer turned herself into an avenging angel for the sake of gratitude? She knew she hadn't. She knew how powerful she'd felt on this deck only minutes ago – triumphant in the face of evil undone and destroyed at last. It frightened her. Ari must surely have felt the same as he despatched the other killers to oblivion. But she couldn't talk to him, not yet.

'Come, I'll see you to your alibi and a nice hot chocolate.'

But Greer steered them back to the railing.

'He'd last only minutes,' Ari said, 'if he wasn't already dead from the sudden stop. It's a long way down and the water's like concrete at such speed. You know that. Otherwise, hypothermia will do the trick. And then, there's the most obvious of all – drowning. It's almost impossible to swim in layers of leather and wool. And those warm, thick boots. A waste.'

'Purser Cordoba, physicist and footwear expert,' Greer said. She felt her heart beginning to slow at last, the adrenalin settling. 'Now that I'm on a cruise, maybe it's time to retire and go home for good.' She was determined not to consider the possibility of a boss above Rodriguez, directing traffic, ordering deaths. 'Even Colonel Rodriguez died in his own South American waters at least. He's not too far from home, and who knows what the current is capable of?'

'Not that he had a choice. Anyway, what would you do in retirement?'

'What I do now in my other life, counsel victims of trauma, run Avalon full-time instead of being a blow-in when it suits me. Eat fish and chips at the bay, and soak up the light. You could come, too.'

'Another sunny place for shady people,' said Cordoba. 'Come along now, or you'll be answering questions in the morning instead of sleeping in.'

'Do you think he felt anything, really?'

Their voices became indistinct as they strolled away from the railing and into the darkness. The deck lights came on and dimly lit the spot where Colonel Miguel Alonzo Batista Rodriguez had stood imagining the seduction of his killer. The air blew in fresh cold gusts across the ship, cleansing its timbers and steel, its railings and portholes of any trace of his presence. As for the colonel, the last things he heard before the ocean claimed him were the liner's mighty engines, thrumming, purring, roaring in his ears, their rhythms a peculiar comfort as he sank and sank, and then slept.

CHAPTER SIX

Beijing
Sunday 31 August 2008

1

When she awoke in the ambulance, Livia tried to convince the two medics that she was okay. But she realised, after a few minutes of haggling – during which she reached a world record for the most repetitions in a conversation of 'Okay,' accompanied by pointing stupidly at herself – that it would be easier to let them take care of her.

She lay quietly as the vehicle rushed through the streets, wondering where they were headed, and hoping that Yani had preceded her, hoping that his Kevlar vest had protected him. At the hospital, she was taken into the Emergency centre and examined. Her heart rate and blood pressure were checked – two more 'Okays;' and then a doctor arrived who spoke English far better than Livia had ever spoken the few words of Chinese Yani had taught her. He told her that Yani was in another part of the hospital being assessed. He performed neurological tests as Livia explained, following his finger up and down and from side to side, that she'd simply fainted, probably from the shock of, well, everything, and specifically, from the physical impact of Yani's exploding car. No good purpose could be served by describing the dreams she'd had of Bogota.

In the end, she was bruised and muscle sore from throwing herself around on the hard road and the effort of dragging Yani to safety, but her only real injury was a simple gravel rash. The doctor applied a soothing salve to the palm and wrist of her right hand and bandaged it. He gave her a tetanus shot – 'to be safe' – and she asked him if she could see Yani.

2

'There will be a complete recovery,' Yani's doctor explained to Livia as he left the room, leaving her to wish she had such confidence in her prognostic abilities.

Yani had a slight concussion, and a shard of glass had lacerated his forehead, just above the hairline; the amount of blood he'd apparently lost from that injury made it look much worse than it actually was. A bullet had grazed his right arm, and he'd taken a hit to the chest, but the Kevlar had saved him. He hadn't even cracked a rib. She supposed it hadn't occurred to her own Olympic committee to include such accessories in the official uniform kits.

She drew the visitors' chair up to the bed and sat down, watching Yani's face for signs of movement, and consciousness. As she sat, she held his hand, and tried to remember details of what had happened. It was more than likely that someone would ask her at least a few questions about the incident, wasn't it? Or would they rather get a pesky foreigner out of the country as soon as possible? The two men who'd shot at them didn't look Chinese, but did that mean anything? The driver had yelled something at Yani before firing his first shot. It had sounded, on reflection, like 'Lee.' She held Yani's hand more tightly.

'They knew you, Yani,' she said. 'I think they did.'

She began to wonder how security conscious the General Hospital of the Chinese People's Armed Police Forces might be. Very, was the word that sprang instantly to mind, if the name of the place was any guide. But it was also a vast enterprise, consisting of a number of large, multi-storey buildings and bustling crowds inside and out. She squeezed his hand again, and this time, after a few seconds, he squeezed back.

'Yani, it's me, Livia.' She half stood and leaned over him, kissing his forehead.

'Say nothing,' he whispered. 'Tell noone.'

She leaned back and stared at his face. 'What? Say nothing? Say nothing about what? Don't tell them what?'

Behind her, the door opened. She turned to see a lean, middle-aged man in a dark suit. His face was a mask of blandness. He had to be police or military intelligence with that bearing and demeanour. Every experience she'd ever had with such authorities told her so. She turned quickly back to Yani to confirm that he'd drifted off again.

'Dr Livia Galvin? I am Inspector Bao Jinmin from the Xicheng police district. It is a pleasure to make your acquaintance.'

He came to stand at the foot of Yani's bed and bowed slightly. Livia found herself bowing back as she responded.

'Hello. Inspector, do you know what happened? Who those men were?' She spoke quietly, willing the policeman to do the same.

'We are working on several investigative leads, Dr Galvin. I have come to see my comrade, Inspector Lee. We are all worried about him.'

'Of course. Yani's resting. They say he has a mild concussion, but he should recover completely. Luckily, he was wearing a protective vest. Do you all have those Kevlar things?' She could at least find out if it was Yani alone who thought he needed protection. Or if he should have been offering her his spare, if he had one.

'Kevlar vest? We wear them on training exercises, and of course, if there is a true emergency.' He seemed to be quite uninterested in Yani's self-protective paranoia. 'Were you injured as well? Have the hospital staff assisted you?'

'The hospital has been very thorough, and no I wasn't injured, not really.' Livia held up her bandaged hand. 'I'm fine, thank you.' There didn't seem to be much point in discussing with this stranger the finer psychological ramifications of having killed two people, even if they'd been intent on killing herself and Yani.

'That is good news. And please accept my heartfelt commiserations on the loss of your precious Olympic pistols in the car explosion.'

'I appreciate those kind thoughts, but you needn't worry. The Beijing Olympic Museum has my weapons, and an acquaintance took the gun case back to Australia with him last

Friday after the presentation. A bit of luck.' Could they so matter-of-factly discuss such things when two people were dead? Apparently, they could.

'That is very fortunate. And your passport, identification papers? Perhaps we can help you with your documents? Replacing your gold medal?'

'Luck, again. Thank you, but I always take the most important documents out of my luggage when I travel, and I keep them close.' She patted her stomach. 'It's a kind of money belt. It has big enough compartments for my passport and a few other pieces of paper – traveller's cheques, personally valuable things.' Dan's 'Shoot For Gold' card. 'I'm wearing the medal, too.' She tapped a spot above her diaphragm. 'But the medal box is gone.' And the squash ball and Dan's backpack had gone up with it in black, acrid smoke, along with everything else in the car. And two men were dead, for heaven's sake.

'I will need you to make a statement, Dr Galvin. And the sooner the better, before your memories become hazy. Would you accompany me to the police station?'

'I'm unlikely to forget this, Inspector, but let's get it out of the way.' There wasn't anything to be gained from sitting with Yani. Even awake, he was making no sense – tell noone. Who would she pick to tell in a country of over a billion citizens? What would she tell them? The sooner she gave Bao what he needed, the sooner she could resume her life, and continue visiting Yani until he fully recovered. She felt jittery, anxious to be on the move. She should have been on the plane home by now. She'd have to ring them all; she'd have to check back in to her hotel. She'd have to re-establish her equilibrium, but she couldn't see that happening any time soon.

She went to the side of the bed, and kissed Yani goodbye. Bao moved no closer to his colleague than the end of the bed, neither touching nor farewelling him. They left his room and entered the elevator, where they stood on a large Taiji pattern. It was one of the hospital's symbolic touches, Bao explained, small-talking on the way down. It featured on elevator floors all over the hospital, and was designed to promote integration and harmony among people everywhere, and with the universe. Or at least to remind everyone of the value of good intentions. Livia knew the Taiji as the symbol for yin and yang, two black and white commas snuggled together, head to tail, forming a circle, dots of their opposite colours in the centre of each larger comma dot. She stared down at the floor and took a deep breath. Let the commas do their work and help her to pause.

STAFF-IN-CONFIDENCE

ENGLISH TRANSLATION

Transcript of Interview with Dr Livia Galvin held at (Xicheng) West City District Police Headquarters, Beijing – August 31, 2008

Witness Description – Dr Galvin:

DOB: 22nd April 1964. Ht: 170cm. Eyes: Blue. Hair: Blonde. Race: Caucasian.

Subject:

Fatal Accident and injuries – one foreign national, one Chinese citizen, two unidentified persons.

Inspector Bao Jinmin:

Interview commences 16:32 with Bao Jinmin,Inspector, Xicheng Police and Dr Livia Galvin, witness to events occurring near Yuetan Park at approximately 14:30 today August 31, 2008. We apologise for this inconvenience, Dr Galvin, but we ask you to bear with us.

Dr Livia Galvin:

That's fine.

IBJ:

May I first of all congratulate you on your Olympic success. I think that I did not do so when we met earlier.

DLG:

Oh. Thank you.

IBJ:

And I would like, also, to apologise on behalf of our officers at the scene. They are very sorry they had to draw their weapons. But you will understand that they could take no risks.

DLG:

I understand, Inspector. I'd do the same in their shoes.

IBJ:

Thank you. This should not take long, I am sure, Dr Galvin. Before I continue, may I confirm that you lost clothing and items of luggage in the fire?

DLG:

That's correct.

IBJ:

You may be eligible for compensation through the Olympic authorities. But you did not lose your Olympic equipment?

DLG:

No. The museum has the pistols, as I explained earlier.

IBJ:

Forgive me, this interview will formalise the information, so that you may use the transcription as an official document, should you wish to proceed with a compensation claim.

DLG:

I understand. And you also know, then, that the case the pistols were in was also saved. Along with an Australian flag. But the medal box went up with the car.

IBJ:

You did not mention the flag when we spoke before. You sent it to Australia, or do you have it with you?

DLG:

No, I sent it to Australia, in the gun case. It went home to my godmother, Mrs Babitsky. The flag is a gift, along with another memento. She works next door to the gallery, so it's convenient. The gallery's only opening a couple of days a week at present.

IBJ:

Thank you. Just one other detail, for our records. You are a medical doctor?

DLG:

No. My qualifications are in art history, but my thesis focussed on the psychology of collecting. Not much use when people are shot and bleeding.

IBJ:

Fascinating, Dr Galvin. Now, if you will – you were on the scene when the accident occurred?

DLG:

Accident? It wasn't an accident, Inspector.

IBJ:

Excuse me, I should be more specific. The traffic accident in which our Inspector Lee's vehicle was involved.

DLG:

He works for you? I thought he worked in security?

IBJ:

He is an Inspector in security, Dr Galvin – an Olympic transfer. He is still a policeman. Could you tell me what you were doing with Inspector Lee today? You were a long way from your hotel, the Huadu. In fact, you had travelled in the opposite direction from the airport.

DLG:

Inspector Lee, Yani, suggested a final look at the city before I flew home. It was a last minute decision, we were actually on our way to the airport, but he said we had a little time to spare, so we changed direction.

IBJ:

And where were you going when the accident occurred?

DLG:

The Beijing Zoo. We were going to stop there. Yani knew I wanted to see the pandas again. They were asleep last time.

IBJ:

Pandas sleep a great deal, it is true. Westerners take an inordinate interest in them, awake and asleep. After the zoo, what had you planned?

DLG:

I'm not sure. It was Yani's tour. Perhaps Beihei Park.

IBJ:

You were going to meet someone in Beihei Park.

DLG:

As I said, I'm not sure if we were even going there. And who would we meet?

IBJ:

You must have speculated about where you were going. You've known Inspector Lee for some time, I believe.

DLG:

Yes. Almost 25 years, on and off. I met him in Beihei Park when my sister and I were here in 1984. We walked across the frozen lake with him. He was our guide.

IBJ:

Could you hear the cracking?

DLG:

Pardon?

IBJ:

The ice cracking, Dr Galvin. You heard it?

DLG:

As a matter of fact we did, yes. And the water must have frozen in mid-ripple. That's how it looked.

IBJ:

What did it sound like?

DLG:

Sound like? [Pause of several seconds]. It sounded like a live
thing. It sounded sad.

IBJ:

A high-pitched, mournful sound.

DLG:

You walk on water?

IBJ:

On occasion. I like to listen to the world, Dr Galvin. You
must have had a great deal of trust in Inspector Lee, to walk

the lake with him. In any case, it is you who walks on water after today's events.

DLG:

Yani's a local, and my sister wanted to do it from the moment he mentioned it.

IBJ:

So you still trust Inspector Lee.

DLG:

Trust him? He's my friend. Of course I trust him. He's my sister's friend. And he's a friend of our family.

IBJ:

You were going to Beihei Park. Possibly. You don't know if you may have met with anyone there. Your sister perhaps? She is in the city with you this time? To witness your success?

DLG:

My sister? No, she couldn't make the Games. My mother flew home the other day with my cousin, Karl. They have businesses to run.

IBJ:

After Beihei Park, where, I wonder? Did you loop the city before the accident?

DLG:

We travelled approximately south from the Huadu hotel, turned into Jianguomenwai and drove past the Museum, Tian An Men, the Great Hall, the Forbidden City. We were on our way to the Zoo when the car hit us from behind. I realise now that it was deliberate.

IBJ:

How did you find yourself in that area? You said you were on Fuxingmenwai when your car was hit.

DLG:

Inspector Lee was looking for a place to stop so he could check the car. The main streets were busy, as usual, so he took a few turns, and we ended up in that narrow street. I had no idea where we were until later.

IBJ:

And this vehicle. You'd seen it previously?

DLG:

I didn't see it. Yani noticed it eventually, but then it was too late.

IBJ:

You trust Inspector Lee and he wouldn't put you in danger for any reason, would he, Dr Galvin. Not deliberately.

DLG:

I don't know what you mean. I think it was a case of mistaken identity. I didn't know those men and neither did Yani. They thought they knew us, obviously.

IBJ:

Mistaken identity. And yet Inspector Lee's vehicle is somewhat distinctive.

DLG:

There were plenty of those cabs around when we were here 24 years ago. A lot of people must have bought them as collectors' items. Yani thought I'd enjoy driving in one of them again. And who would know I was with Yani?

IBJ:

I do not know, Dr Galvin. The men you shot carried no identification. Their vehicle was reported stolen three months ago. Their weapons are untraceable. I wonder why they didn't simply run you off the road and kill you before you could react? With Inspector Lee unconscious, as you saw at the hospital, there could be memory loss, so therefore we rely on you to tell us what has happened, what you know.

DLG:

What I know? I don't know anything. I don't know what they were after – something of Yani's, or my souvenirs, my medal? That's ridiculous. And they had their own guns, they didn't need mine, or Yani's. They were intent on shooting us, killing us.

IBJ:

And you were intent on killing them.

DLG:

What? I've never killed anyone before. I shoot targets, not people.

IBJ:

People can be targets, Dr Galvin. I understand that other members of your family are rather more familiar with death. And you are an expert with weapons, of a sort. It was a great advantage today, your accurate response. Was it a response, or was it a pre-emptive strike? There don't seem to be any witnesses, or none who will come forward.

[Sound of chair scraping floor]

DLG:

You've seen Yani's car, what's left of it. It's full of bullet holes. And just so you know, my family runs legitimate businesses, Inspector. Check the corporations and companies registers, check the international antiquities registers, check the repatriation registers for the return of stolen artworks and antiquities to the victims of theft, Holocaust survivors, Iraqi museums – my sister is in human services, she's a psychologist, for Heaven's sake.

IBJ:

Please Dr Galvin, calm down. Please sit down.

DLG:

I am calm. This is as calm as I get, with two dead men rolling around in my mind like gigantic boulders. You'll find my uncle's name in those registers, and my mother's – they're the sort of people who re-unite the rightful owners with their possessions. My mother went home via Thailand to participate in a handover ceremony for some priceless bloody Siamese *tchotchke* that was stolen a century ago. My uncle brokered the deal to have it returned.

IBJ:

Dr Galvin, please sit down.

DLG:

I had to defend myself and Yani, Inspector Bao.

IBJ:

Which may be how you managed in this terrible situation today. A split second to react, it appears. And precision shooting. This is what I would expect of an athlete like yourself. Only –

DLG:

Only what, Inspector?

IBJ:

Someone like you, Dr Galvin, with such perfect aim – you needed to shoot each man several times to be sure?

DLG:

I shot one man twice and the other three times. He tried again to kill us. I know how many times I fired. I saw them go down. I'll see it for the rest of my life.

IBJ:

Of course. The ballistics reports will help when they are completed. Please don't worry about it.

DLG:

Of course I'm worried about it. I'm not an assassin, I'm a target shooter. Look, I don't know anything about these fellows. All I'd like to do is visit Inspector Lee again before it's too late. My visitor's visa is about to expire, as you'd be aware. And I need to phone my family before the media gets involved in all of this.

IBJ:

You are an important guest of the People's Republic of China, Dr Galvin. You are safe from the media here.

[Knock at door].

IBJ:

Excuse me, Dr Galvin. Interview suspended at 16:55.

IBJ:

Interview recommences 17:05. Dr Galvin, you are free to go. Your lawyer is waiting for you outside. Your flight can be re-arranged and your visa extended so that you may visit Inspector Lee once more. Your attorney, Comrade Sun, will have more details for you.

DLG:

Attorney? What attorney?

IBJ:

An attorney, a lawyer, Dr Galvin, who represents you. He also has the permission of my superiors to remove you from our jurisdiction.

DLG:

But what about the gunmen? Aren't you going to find out who they are, what they wanted? What about Yani? His life could still be at risk. Is he being protected? Who else could be involved, Inspector?

IBJ:

The incident will be determined as self-defence. Inspector Lee will confirm this when he awakes. The gunmen are dead, and you are almost breathing your fresh Australian air again. My best wishes to you.

DLG:

Wait a minute.

IBJ:

Interview terminated at 17:08.

CHAPTER SEVEN

Beijing
Monday 1 September 2008

The Yin-Yang commas weren't helping her this morning.
She stood on the black one as the elevator took her to
Yani's floor. She hoped he'd be awake so she could ask him
what Bao was really after when he'd interviewed her. Were
his colleagues also as thoroughly interested as the Inspector
had seemed to be in people's qualifications and whether or not
they'd want to claim compensation for lost track suits? Maybe
he was obsessive-compulsive, or maybe he thought she'd shot
the carjackers with her competition pistols as well as the Walther, and then thrown them into the flaming car to melt, assuming there could be no evidence linking her directly with
their deaths. Did he think she hadn't watched forensic proce-
dural dramas on TV?

On the other hand, could he be searching for ways to distance her from the entire horrible incident to avoid international embarrassment? But how much more linked could she
be? Forensics were irrelevant. She'd readily explained what

had happened, and in more detail than she'd given her mother on the phone the night before. Even with Bao's assurance that the media in China was highly regulated, she hadn't wanted to risk Rosanna reading a River City morning paper's hysterical beat-up and wondering if her little girl was alive or dead, or rotting in some prison beyond the Great Wall. Ever since Bogota, Rosanna's anxieties were readily and robustly aroused – tertiary PTSD, Greer called it, trauma by association – whenever anything didn't go quite as planned, so it was just as well she wasn't with Livia as she entered Yani's room and found his bed empty and Inspector Bao sitting in the visitors' chair.

'Inspector,' she said. 'This is a surprise.'

Bao stood and nodded a greeting. 'Dr Galvin. You slept well?'

'Not really. Is Yani coming back soon? I might go and get a coffee while I wait. Would you like one?' Something wasn't right; the room felt empty despite their presence.

'I do not think we will see Inspector Lee today.'

'Is he all right?'

'He decided to leave us during the night. I hoped you could tell me where he is.' Bao's voice was neutral, but the muscles around his lower jaw were working away at remaining slightly less than outraged.

'Me?' She hadn't a clue about the motivations or identities of the two men whose lives she'd taken, let alone Yani sleep-walking out of the hospital. Say nothing, he'd said. Right now, then, he'd surely be proud of her saying nothing about the nothing that she knew. Rosanna must have sent a larger dose of psychic anxiety over the phone lines than Livia had reckoned on, because she felt a sense of panic rising, and she didn't know what to do. She didn't have her pistols to take apart, clean and reassemble – one of her few calming techniques. The squash ball was gone. She couldn't even rub the little golden Colombian man any more.

'I wish you well on your journey home, Dr Galvin.' Bao moved towards the door.

'Wait? I can't leave when Yani's missing, if that's what you're saying. He could be disoriented, lost somewhere. He has concussion.'

'I have spoken with your embassy – their officials have arranged a seat for you on this evening's flight.'

'I'm telling you I can't go until I know Yani's all right.' What if Yani hadn't left under his own steam? What if he was languishing in a prison right here in Beijing? But what had he done except to be shot at by people who seemed to know him? And what about the bulletproof vest? He'd been expecting trouble.

'Your visa has expired, Dr Galvin.'

'No, it hasn't. It runs out at the end of the week.'

'You are in danger of being deported if you refuse to leave voluntarily. If you are deported, you will be banned from the country in future. I wish you a pleasant journey. My assistant will drive you to your hotel and on to the airport.'

Bao nodded once more, left the room and was replaced by another man, who waited for Livia to accompany him back to the elevators. She couldn't look down at the commas for fear of throwing up, and on every floor, as she and her minder shuffled like conjoined twins to let people on and off, she wondered if Yani was in a room somewhere, waiting for her to come and find him.

CHAPTER EIGHT

River City, Australia

[27.28S 153.01E]
Monday 1 September 2008
Arthur Street, New Farm

'That should do it, Tibor,' Minnie said. 'That's the last of them.'

They tidied the table and finished filling a garbage bag with stray napkins, paper plates, polystyrene cups, and sandwich wrappers. The wind had picked up a little, and they were glad to be going in for the night. It might be officially Spring according to the calendar, but the weather made its own decisions.

'Can I drive you home, my dear?' Tibor asked, as they wheeled the foldup table into the shop and manoeuvred it into the corner against the rear wall. 'You've surely done enough today.'

'I want to get this press release faxed and emailed.' She went to the desk and picked up a hard copy of the group's latest fund- and consciousness-raising project. 'It's early yet.' She smiled at her friend, trying to somehow alleviate the anxiety she saw in his face. 'And I might even have time to do my 10 chin-ups before bedtime.'

'I don't like you being here alone, Minerva, not after the phone calls. Not even with your chin-up power.'

He was one of the old guard who still addressed her by her full name. Their friendship had lasted through the decades from the circus years when they'd performed together in the trapeze troupe. They'd stayed in touch even when separated by oceans and continents and by marriage to their respective partners, until Tibor, widowed, had returned to River City to enjoy his retirement.

'Pranksters, Tibor, that's all. I could hear them laughing. Probably children. Anyway, who could object to a bunch of senior citizens trying to save the city we all love.'

Tibor shook his head. He knew he'd get nowhere with her; she was determined and focused, and that was that. They were attributes that had kept them safe under the big top.

'Promise me you'll lock the door behind me, and wait for the security guard to walk you to your car. Or you could go next door to your gallery and stay the night in the loft.'

'I don't think that will be necessary, Tibor, and I don't have a key to the gallery these days. It's been Livia's place for years, you remember.' But more often these days, he didn't. 'Did you manage those deliveries?'

'Of course. You know me, one hundred percent reliable.'

'To the right people in the right order?'

'Minerva, please.'

'All right, Tibor.' She could check the deliveries herself, tomorrow.

'I can skip tonight's game and stay with you. It's no trouble.'

'No, Tibor. It's card night, and you can't leave them short of a fourth. Besides, who else is going to fleece them?' And the other three would make sure he exercised his grey cells to the maximum; that could only be a good thing for Tibor's memory.

He forced a smile to his lips as she walked him to the door and they embraced, to any casual observer a handsome, older couple, some grey in their hair, a few lines around their eyes, but both straight-backed and fit-looking, the beneficiaries of having lived athletic lives.

'Farewell, my friend,' she said. 'Don't stay up too late. Remember, it's a big day tomorrow. We need to check the inventory for the auction catalogue.'

'Goodnight, and lock up, Minerva.' He held her hands a moment longer, then stepped outside and waited, watching as she pushed the dead-bolt across the doorframe and turned the key. He raised his hand in a half-wave and disappeared as the darkness beyond the shop's lighting welcomed him.

Minnie returned to her desk and set to work with the press release announcing a charity auction with guest auctioneers and speakers to raise funds for, and awareness of inner-city heritage and housing issues. She faxed and emailed it to her list of media outlets, and then decided to skip the chin-ups in favour of applying another coat of paint to the north wall of the office. It might even become a feature wall if she could decide on a colour other than creamy sailcloth; a consultation with Livia was in order when she arrived home. Their last phone call had been so rushed she'd had no time to discuss anything other than Livia's request and agree to it. It was a sweet thought, such a gift for someone they both loved so dearly.

She'd opened the paint tin's lid and begun stirring when she heard a knock. Turning to face the clear glass front door, she smiled when she saw the man outside. There were sandwiches and cake in the fridge, and she'd rustle up a pot of tea for him. He could keep her company while she rollered the wall, although she knew he would insist on helping, too. She went to the door and unlocked it, noticing as she did, that the night had turned much cooler.

CHAPTER NINE

River City

Tuesday 2 September 2008
International Airport

1

During her marriage to Paul Clifford, Member for Claythorne, and currently Minister for Local Government, Public Works and Housing, Livia Galvin had gradually developed what she called an allergic reaction to the variety of minders and hangers-on who populated the political and bureaucratic circles in which her husband dwelt, and in which she, too, found herself as supportive spouse from time to time. The allergy had spilled into her Olympic activities as well, minders in any area of endeavour being alike in so many respects, from their possession of superlative spin-doctoring skills to their ability to convince you that night was day and lies were truth.

This morning, then, as she disembarked, after a sleepless night, from her Beijing flight, and felt her skin prickle and her eyes moisten, she knew that allergens were present. Soon enough, two groups of suits approached her, raptor-like, from each side, as she made her way to Customs. With practised flanking movements, they cut her out, like some poor zebra or antelope, from the rest of the passenger herd.

'Dr Galvin.' A tall, grey man in a beautiful charcoal suit moved in closer and walked beside her. 'Gerald Bannerman from the Minister's office. May I take your bag?' With practised ease, he reached out and slid the bag from Livia's grasp, handing it on to a slightly shorter man in a beautiful navy suit, who rejoined the other four in the defensive line they'd formed behind Livia and their superior.

Livia, who had had no choice, after the explosion, but to buy new clothes and toiletries and something to stash them in, had let the bag go without a second thought. None of what it contained mattered. What mattered was still close to her in her money belt. She must remember to remove it and show the contents to the Customs people, lest they suspect her of smuggling ivory or other forbidden goods. She couldn't bear to lose Dan's card. Suddenly, she felt even more grateful to Professor Wu for taking the bronze horse and the gun case off her hands.

'We'd like to speak with you before your press conference this morning,' the first suit said.

Livia couldn't remember his name, and she didn't care about that either.

'Would you come this way please?'

He nodded in the direction of a series of closed doors off to their left.

Livia stopped walking and, with great precision, so did the rest of her new entourage. Some allergies, she realised, are incurable, and must be endured until the irritation passes. 'Which Minister?' It couldn't be Paul's office, surely? 'What press conference?'

The first suit blinked. 'The Minister for Foreign Affairs and Immigration, Dr Galvin. And it's your press conference. We convened it to clear things up, to minimise the speculation, the half-baked ideas about what happened in Beijing that will inevitably appear in the media. We think it's best that you speak to the press in person, without any filtering by third parties, like us.' He glanced back at his pack of suits. 'We've already cleared you through Customs.'

Livia felt like laughing. 'How does anybody know anything about what happened in Beijing?' I was there, she wanted to say to him, and I don't know what happened.

'There was a leak – about the car-jacking, and the shooting. Please, this way.'

She was too tired to argue, and too wary to mention Yani's disappearance, but in the small meeting room into which they all managed to cram themselves, she raised one objection.

'I'm under no obligation to speak to the media,' she said, sipping from the glass of water one of the suits had kindly placed in front of her.

She hoped it was true, hoped that her Olympic contract was void now that she'd retired, but no, a suit insisted after a small silence, she was still obligated, if not technically, then morally. And as a loyal citizen, another added helpfully.

'You're not joking, are you?' she said, fearing that the hysteria of sleep deprivation and the aftershock of Beijing were about to claim her. She rubbed her eyes and the room became pleasantly blurry for a moment or two.

'And besides,' the first suit continued, 'the way things went with some of our other sports, we need to be co-operative with the press. More importantly, Dr Galvin, we need to reinforce that we have nothing to hide. It's imperative that we avoid any continuing awkwardness with Beijing. We have nothing to hide, that's correct, isn't it?'

'We?'

'You, Dr Galvin. I was using the royal 'we.' I meant you. You don't, do you?'

'If I knew, I'd tell you, just so I could go home to bed.'

'As a matter of urgency, you need to put this to bed now, Dr Galvin,' said another suit, seizing his chance for relevance, emphasising 'this,' whatever it might be.

'Paul didn't put you up to it, did he?' She wondered, but only fleetingly, if her ex-husband could have anything to do with this particular episode of spin, if somehow he thought his ex-wife's activities in Beijing could be bad for his career, despite the gold medal and the distance of several years of divorce.

'Paul who?' The first suit was genuine in his query.

'Never mind. All right, but there's a time limit.' Livia had done her share of press conferences, for sport, for the art gallery. There were even a few after Bogota, at Paul's urging, and she knew that they were all about control, who retained it, and for how long. She was glad she'd asked her mother not to come to the airport to pick her up.

2

'We've teed up the first few questions to move in the right direction,' the first suit told her as they approached a much larger room where a contingent of journalists and photographers waited. The camera flashes began before they sat down at a long table in front of the gathering.

'Ms Galvin, where to from here with your career?' The question, following a nod from the suit who'd mentioned putting 'this' to bed, came from a man whose sharp grey suit suggested he might work in the Minister's office.

'I announced my retirement in Beijing,' Livia replied, stealing a glance at the clock on the wall. Ten minutes, no more, and less if it could be managed.

'But you've retired previously, Ms Galvin, before the 2000 Sydney Olympics. Can we be sure it'll take this time?'

This questioner was a journalist. Livia recognised him from the local rag, the only daily in town. There was a tinge of sarcasm in his tone, but you couldn't blame him for trying. Would any of them dare to mention Dan this time around?

'There was a reason then, and there's a reason this time. I'll never shoot again.'

'And these reasons, are they connected, in your own mind? Is your retirement now, associated as it is with these two deaths in Beijing, linked somehow with your son's violent death in Bogota? Are all these tragic events telling you something, Ms Galvin?'

There it was, plain as day, potential for a screaming beat-up, using Dan as part of another headline.

'You're talking rubbish,' Livia replied. 'I announced my retirement before the shootings. And not that it's any of your business, but my son only ever wanted the best for me.' How had Dan suddenly begun to sound like some kind of mentor, a parental figure? She tried to picture his card to her, snug in her money belt.

'And clearly, as you've just admitted, you have shot again, Ms Galvin, if these reports are accurate. Not just once, but at least twice.' That same sarcastic tone.

The first suit twitched beside Livia as she remained silent. Perhaps he didn't have the experience she'd had in this milieu. Not that she'd ever had quite this experience. The other media scrums she'd been part of had been gentle by comparison.

'Dr Galvin has made no such admission, and you know it,' he said, his indignation and anger obvious. The event was getting away from him.

'So what about your bodyguard, the driver who was seriously injured if these reports are to be believed? What's his story?'

'He's not my bodyguard.'

'Who is he then, your Chinese lover?'

'He's an old friend, for God's sake, and he was injured trying to save me. He had no chance. He needed help.' That did it. 'Whatever you say, say nothing.' Why hadn't she had that phrase from the bogs tattooed on her retinas? Rosanna had warned her often enough over the years, along with all of her other Irish relatives whenever anything contentious arose in relation to the family's business. Say nothing, tell noone. Yani knew the drill; he could join the family without delay.

'So you shot the car-jackers, he didn't?'

'They gave me no choice.' Of course, had her mother been present at this very moment, the entire press conference, if it had ever begun in the first place, would be over right now. Rosanna never stood on ceremony, she took no notice of officials – government, political, or otherwise – and anyone who attacked her family deserved to have their eyes removed with hot pokers, and their tongues cut out and stuffed down their throats for dessert. But Rosanna the Terrible wasn't present. And so it continued.

'No choice but to kill them, Livia? You're a crack shot, aren't you? They would have had no chance, never mind your mate.'

'Exactly what are you accusing me of?'

'Just like your grandfather, old Wolfie Galvin, the Squizzy Taylor and Al Capone combined of his time.'

'My grandfather? Al Capone?' Weren't they stretching the bow a couple of generations too far now? 'That's it. Show's over.'

As the first suit rose from his seat in an attempt to regain the front foot, the atmosphere changed as another journalist entered the room and strode down the side aisle to the front. He asked a question before the bureaucrat could object.

'Do you have any comment, Dr Galvin,' the reporter asked, 'about the discovery earlier this morning of an elderly woman's body at the CLEAR office next door to your gallery? She was found by the security guard who checks your premises.'

'What elderly woman?' Livia sat very still.

'There's an unconfirmed report that the dead woman is Minnie Babitsky, the woman who owned your gallery before you took over. Now Chair of CLEAR.'

'Can you comment, or confirm, Ms Galvin? Are you involved with her lobby group, and do you think this is related to her opposition to lucrative CBD development proposals?'

'I've been on planes for the last 14 hours.' Livia answered automatically and stood up, unable to think of anything – as she looked along the table at all the beautiful suits – but a comment Minnie frequently made about such people: 'As useful as an ashtray on a motorbike.' She felt like laughing, but caught herself and pushed her chair back. It tipped to beyond the point of no return and fell with a crash to the floor. The first suit scrambled to right it as Livia walked out of the room pursued by calls from the pack.

In the hall, gazing around her and then down at the carpet, which appeared to be swirling at her, Livia realised the air was suddenly much cooler. She breathed deeply and looked over to where a journalist was waiting in front of a TV camera for her cue. She moved a little closer so she could hear.

'The pistol shooters' poster girl,' the reporter began, 'Olympic gold medallist, Livia Galvin, returned to Australia early this morning following an alleged shootout, still shrouded in mystery, on the streets of Beijing that resulted in the deaths of two men, only to be confronted with the suspicious death and possible murder of her godmother, Minerva Babitsky. Mrs Babitsky, 66, was a campaigner for the preservation of River City's heritage, particularly in inner-city areas. She recently set up a lobby group known as CLEAR, Citizens Leading Education Against Redevelopment. Police are refusing to speculate at this stage as to whether or not her death may be linked in some way to her CLEAR activities. It's been rumoured that Mrs Babitsky had received threatening phone calls in recent weeks and –'

Livia stepped back. The press conference journalists, along with the suits, were emerging from the room. They jostled and argued with each other, and Livia could see the first suit behind a pack of reporters, waving at her. She wanted to go to the TV woman and ask her how she could be sure it was Minnie, but forced herself to walk away from them all. Somewhere deep inside, she knew it was Minnie. She walked faster, and broke into a trot, which she maintained until she made it out of the building and into the sun. She hailed a cab and directed the driver to the one place where she knew she'd find, if not answers, then plenty more challenging questions.

CHAPTER TEN

River City

Tuesday 2 September 2008
West Bend Heritage Hotel

L ivia heard the music as she walked down the steps from the private car park and across the verandah to the kitchen. It was Benny Goodman, Minnie's favourite jazz musician. Minnie had converted most of the family to Benny and his contemporaries, and successors. Not a day went by in Minnie's house without a few good hours of musical massage from Benny or Woody Herman, Glenn Miller or Billie Holliday, Ella Fitzgerald, Louis Armstrong, the Duke and the Count. Rosanna would be playing Benny for comfort, Livia knew.

At the kitchen's screen door, she paused and located her mother at the big table next to the sink. She wore a cream pantsuit, pearls, newly coloured (auburn highlights) and styled hair, and a butcher's navy and white-striped apron. She had her hands in a large mixing bowl, probably crumbing flour and butter. Livia guessed that it would be one of Great-granny Skelloe's pie recipes, the ones Rosanna used to teach her children, and for a while at least, her only grandson, how to cook. She pushed the screen door open.

'Mum,' she called across the spacious room.

Rosanna turned and Livia could see that she'd been crying. Her face suggested Maureen O'Hara: feisty, the flawless, pale skin, the vivid blue eyes usually waiting for a challenge, ready for a fight. It had been several years since Livia had seen her mother this distressed.

'Livia.' She removed her hands from the mixing bowl and rinsed them under the tap, wiping them on a tea towel as she crossed the floor. 'Livia.'

The two women met in the middle of the kitchen and embraced. They held each other for a long time, and Livia could feel her mother trying to contain her sobs as they stood together.

'Mum? What's happened to Minnie? I called her the other day.'

Rosanna stepped back and held Livia by both arms. 'How did she sound? Was she all right? Did she seem worried?'

'I – she seemed fine. She was herself – happy, busy, rushed off her feet.'

'You'd better tell the police about the call. In case it means anything.'

'What could it possibly mean, Mum?' And what, she wondered, remembering the journalist's provocation at the airport, would grandad Wolfie think of them being on good terms with the law?

'What did Minnie say to you?'

'She said she was looking forward to seeing what I sent her from Beijing.'

Rosanna raised her eyebrows in puzzlement.

'A flag for the birthday girl, and a bronze horse for Minnie – last minute – a gift from a chap who runs the Olympic museum.' She paused. 'I gave his wife the necklace.' She might as well get that fact out and away. With any luck, it would float out to the car park on Benny's music.

'You gave it to her?'

'I didn't exactly give it away.' Yes, in fact, she had, never expecting the return offering from the Han dynasty. Minnie would have loved it. 'We both know it was time. Anyway, let's not worry about that now.' She went to the kettle and topped it up before turning it on. 'Tea?'

Rosanna nodded, dabbing at the tears on her cheeks.

'It's a good thing you're home, Livia, after the car jacking. You'll be safe now.' She moved towards her daughter and they embraced again.

Safe, Livia thought. There's a relative term. 'Let's finish the pie.'

'Con's in hospital.' Rosanna floured a board and rolled out the pastry; Livia poured the tea. 'An infection related to the bypass. He's been overdoing it. You'll call in to see him.'

'Yes, Mum. But how bad is it?'

'He's worse since he found out about Minnie, very distressed, but not as bad as Karl would like, I think.' Rosanna's tone always changed to something near icy when she mentioned her nephew.

'Mum. Karl's ambitious, but he wouldn't want his father signing out prematurely.' They both knew Livia's cousin Karl,

Con's only child, was driven by one overriding ambition: his succession to top dog in the family businesses, access to everything profitable, and the sooner the better.

'That's enough about Karl.' Rosanna straightened her shoulders and took a deep breath. 'You know, the police asked me where I was around the time they believe Minnie died. Do you think they're asking everyone?'

'I don't know. They think she was murdered?'

'I don't know, Livia.' She unrolled the pie top from the rolling pin onto the shell filled with spiced mince. 'I wish I'd been there. I might have been able to help her, save her, the poor little thing.' Rosanna began to cry again as she pricked the pastry with a fork and basted it with egg. 'And how are we going to tell Sibyl about her sister?'

'Mum,' Livia put her arm around Rosanna's shoulders. 'Mum, Minnie wouldn't want you to be so upset. Neither would Sibyl, for that matter, if it wasn't for the stroke.' What else could she say? She took the pie from her mother and slid it into the oven.

'You're right,' she said, 'you're barely through the door, exhausted, and here I am upsetting everyone. You need to get some sleep, Livia. Your bed's made up. I'll phone Gordon and see if he's tried to tell Sibyl, if he thinks it's the right thing to do.'

Rosanna could fake unflappability when she had to, but as the years passed, it seemed to Livia that the trick became harder. She was anxious to get to the gallery, but she'd stick around for a little while. Could being near to where Minnie had been when she died somehow help her to understand what had happened? Or cause even more confusion?

Livia poured herself another cup of tea as Rosanna started on the apple pie, kissed her mother's cheek and left her to Benny's musical comfort. She'd be able to think more clearly, about Minnie, about Beijing and Yani, if she could sleep for a while. On the flight home, she'd kept jerking awake, feeling as though she was falling from great heights, unable to remember her dreams.

She walked across the covered verandah – the kitchen, along with the laundry, formed a separate building – and into the main hallway on the ground floor, past the dining-room on one side and the Private Ladies Lounge on the other. As she reached the billiards room, she heard a familiar voice behind its closed door.

'So he went out for a drink, and never came home,' Karl said, his voice sounding kindly and interested, a combination that didn't manifest very often in her cousin.

'We thought he'd met up with old friends, since he's been away overseas for so long. But then the hospital phoned us early the next morning.'

The stranger's voice seemed to break and there was silence for a few moments.

'How is Michael now?' Karl asked.

'He has rehabilitation therapy every day, for his spine and his hands. They broke his hands, Mr Galvin. They stomped on them. Why would they do that? His jaw is still wired. And the judge said there wasn't enough independent evidence against these fellows. Michael knew them. He went to school with them. He's an eyewitness, for Christ's sake.'

'If they were his friends, why would they beat him up, Ron?'

'I thought I'd already spelled it out, Mr Galvin. Michael's gay. At their trial, they claimed he propositioned them that night, provoked them, and they responded like good, red-blooded males – they roughed him up, they said, and left him in the park to sober up, but they had nothing to do with the serious injuries. You know Michael doesn't drink, Mr Galvin. Or at least your father knows. They left him there to die. He's been your father's best designer for years. Now he could be finished. His mother – she's distraught.'

His father sounded distraught, too. He began to cry in earnest, and Livia wondered how Karl, who wasn't the most sensitive person she knew, would cope with such obvious distress and grief.

'You know he's getting the best care, Ron, through our health plan.'

Karl knew about the corporate health plan? He'd been doing his homework, all right. He really was intent on ascending the throne.

'It isn't enough, Mr Galvin,' Ron said, still sounding tearful, but now there was a note of anger in his tone. 'I was hoping to discuss this with your father.'

'You can discuss it with me, Ron. My father is ill, very ill.' Karl's business tone kicked in. Ron should have read the cues – it didn't pay to imply that Karl was second fiddle when he saw himself as first violin.

'I'm sorry to hear that, Mr Galvin. All right, then. Michael could have residual brain damage, but even if he overcomes all these obstacles, he won't ever completely recover, and neither will his mother and I. Not while those three live their happy lives free and clear. Suspended sentences for this assault and no convictions recorded. I saw them laughing outside the court. There's nothing I can do, but your father – you – you can do something.'

'What might that be, Ron?' Karl would make him spell it out. He was nothing if not thorough.

'You can do what the court couldn't, what they wouldn't do – teach them a lesson in respect, show them there's no excuse for such terrible, such murderous behaviour.'

Ron sounded as though he was winded.

'You'd like some help from your friends. From Michael's true friends.'

Livia could visualise Ron drawing himself up, biting the bullet of future indebtedness.

'Yes,' he said. 'Yes, I would. Definitely.'

'You don't think you'll change your mind, Ron? Have an attack of conscience? You're a law-abiding citizen, just like all of us.'

'I'm all out of conscience, Mr Galvin. Why do you think I came here?'

'As long as we understand each other, Ron. You call me with the names and current addresses of these fellows, and we'll see what we can do for you. All right? You never know what might happen.'

Livia realised that the voices were moving closer to her. Karl was ushering Ron out of the room. She darted down and across the hall into the Private Ladies Lounge just as the bil-liards room door opened. The lounge was deserted for the moment, so she swung around behind the bar and busied her-self fixing a Coke and ice. Karl and Ron walked into the lounge, and Ron nodded at Livia as he continued on his way, offering another thank you to Karl before he disappeared through the exit.

'Livia. Livia Galvin, as I live and breathe. How are you, cousin? Big adventure over there in Cathay. Talk about your *Fifty-Five Days At Peking*.'

'It was no Boxer Rebellion, Karl.' Livia had always found somewhat unappealing the fact that she and Karl had similar tastes in film. For some reason, their favourites matched, and one of them was the Charlton Heston, Ava Gardner classic about the Boxers and foreign legations in Beijing, and the Chinese Empress, all of it mixed up into a confused Hollywood blockbuster of the first order, or more accurately, the second, just like Karl's attempt to become Don Corleone in the billiards room. She could barely believe her ears.

'Whatever. Do you know Ron Morris? The bloke who was just here.' Karl slid onto one of the bar stools. Did he expect her to serve him a drink? He'd be waiting a while.

'No.'

'His son designed your gun case for the Olympics, among other things. The one the family gave you.'

'Yes, I know the one you mean.' But she'd been so overwhelmed by the family's thoughtfulness, she hadn't thought to ask about its provenance.

'Well, since then, he's been in a brawl and now he's a basket case. His father wants the gun case as a memento of his son's former glory. Dad thinks it's a good idea, too.'

'When did he tell you that?' Livia must have missed the earlier part of the conversation. She'd have to improve her eavesdropping.

'When did who tell me what?'

'Ron Morris – when did he tell you that he wants the gun case?'

'When we were talking in the billiards room, cousin.'

'Karl, I don't involve myself in your affairs, but since when did you turn into the Godfather?' She couldn't ignore it, and if Con was out of commission, she'd have to be the one to reign Karl in. Who else was there?

'What are you talking about?'

'Don't play coy. Who do you think you are, coming into my mother's hotel and doing grubby deals with poor, vulnerable people like Ron Morris? If the police ever found out that you were meeting here to organise thugs and assaults, Mum could lose her license.'

'Don't be stupid, Livia. Since when did you turn into little miss nosy parker? And who's going to tell the thin blue line? You?' Karl leaned towards her across the bar and she stepped back a pace. She must be losing her grip.

'I'll tell you once, Karl. If you want to do that sort of business, don't do it here. I won't have my mother put at risk in any way or upset any more than she has been.' She stepped forward. 'Uncle Con won't stand for it. And neither will I.'

She picked up her Coke and retraced her steps around the bar, leaving Karl to welcome a group of laughing, loud, very happy women who looked as though they'd already engaged in some serious drinking. As she passed them, a thought worthy of Minnie occurred to her, and she whispered to one, 'See that guy over there at the bar? He's the stripper – don't take no for an answer – that's part of his act, playing hard to get.'

It wasn't much, but it was something. She allowed herself a tiny smile as she walked up the stairs to her bedroom, serenaded by the laughter from the Ladies Lounge.

CHAPTER ELEVEN

River City

Tuesday 2 September 2008
Fortescue Street, Spring Hill

1

Minnie Babitsky's house is a sliver perched between a tall block of units on one side and her park on the other. The house was her father, Max's business and their home when he set himself up as an art restorer and valuer on their arrival in Australia from Europe in 1955. On rare days, when the humidity was at a particular level, you could smell hints, mere whiffs of turpentine and oils from decades past, the odours still present in the timbers and floorboards where Max, and later, Minnie's husband, Ari, had worked. It was comforting in a way, ineradicable evidence of their lives and labour.

The park next door was a donation to the environment by Minnie of two house blocks of greenery and shady trees and space in which passers-by could stroll or sit, or stop at the fountain and have a refreshing drink of water. The park benches wore brass plaques with inscriptions dedicated to loved ones (two and four-legged) since gone to glory, or else commemorating significant events such as the release of Nelson Mandela from prison on February 11, 1990, or the granting of the vote in federal elections to Australian women on June 12, 1902. It was an eclectic mix, reflecting Minnie's tastes and those of the people who cherished her park.

Whenever Livia visited or stayed with Minnie as a child, she would sit on the bench with the most mysterious plaque of all, the one that simply stated: 'Ariel Moishe Babitsky, disappeared October 10, 1972. God help you. Shalom.' That was Uncle Ari, Minnie's lost love. What did Livia know about him? He'd been Max's protégé and later, his business partner. Ari had disappeared into the night never to be heard from again, a victim of the world's strange vibrations and manipulations. But he'd also been Livia and Greer's godfather. In childhood, Livia used to hope that by sitting near his plaque, carefully tracing its words with her fingers, she'd somehow learn his fate, and once she had, well, there'd be nothing for it but for him to return to Minnie and to all of them, resuming his life as an artist and art restorer.

Livia stood across the road from Minnie's collective at 221, 221B and 223 Fortescue, thinking these thoughts and picking out the dark shapes in the park: benches, fountain, shade sails, rotunda, barbecue, flora, a possum scuttling along the TV cable suspended above the footpath. She'd tried to sleep, and failed, borrowed Rosanna's car, and found herself driving, not to the gallery, after all, but here, to what had been her second childhood home.

The house was dark and there was only the suspicion of a moon to illuminate its roof above the three slender stories. She locked the car and made her way across the road. Halfway down the side of the house, she located the fuse box and, directly below it, a small maiden-hair fern garden landscaped with stones and rocks Minnie had collected during her travels or been presented with by friends returning from abroad.

The rock she was after didn't stand out unless you had a real interest in geology, or you were a burglar who knew about such ruses. When you picked it up, it felt much lighter than a rock of its size should be; it had a hollow centre for the key. In the darkness, with everything the same grey colour, it was more difficult than usual to find. Livia felt underneath several rocks of a certain size for the fake rock's flat bottom and sliding plastic opening. The ground was damp and soft, and she could feel it pushing in underneath her nails.

She paused to listen to the rustling and shuffling in the garden behind her. Toads. She kept searching, more gingerly, and found the rock, and its key, in the garden's rear corner, conveniently placed near the downpipe. She removed the key, replaced the rock, and walked slowly down the side path and around to the back verandah, aware now of the possibility of more toads barring her way, listening to their rustling behind her. She blamed Rosanna for ingraining her fear of them, and of spiders, cockroaches, flying insects of every kind, and anything with feathers, anything spiky or wriggly, 'girly' fears that Greer had somehow managed to avoid acquiring. How did she do that, Livia wondered, inserting the key and turning the lock.

Usually, at this point in a visit to Minnie's, you could hear Benny Goodman or another jazz great playing up a storm. Minnie and her sister, Sibyl, inherited Max's LP collection and Minnie updated it with CDs when the technology changed. Tonight there was silence.

Livia pushed the door open and reached around for the light switch. She flipped it, and nothing happened. She tried again, with the same result, then pushed the door wide open to let in what light there was from outside. It made little difference, but she knew her way around, and not every light bulb could have blown. They couldn't have disconnected the power already.

As she stepped into the kitchen, she smelt stale air mixed with a hint of souring apple and another smell, old and familiar: floor polish and the residual bite of methylated spirits, Minnie's favourite cleaning product. She moved forward into the gloom, trying to decide which light switch to aim for, and simultaneously felt the air cooling and something, something big and strong, thump her in the back. She had time enough to prevent her face from messing up Minnie's lino by putting one arm out as she fell. When she landed, her right elbow took most of the initial impact, and she saw a body flash past on her left. It was breathing heavily. She rolled over with the intention of scrambling under the kitchen table, when another big something leapt on top of her and planted its feet on her chest. There was a bark, and an answering bark, panting and more panting, and bad breath in her face.

'Caddie,' she said as loudly as she could, but it came out as a whisper from her airless lungs. 'Caddie, girl.'

Was it Caddie? It was the first name that sprang to mind. Livia stared at the black nose centimetres away from hers, and tried to smile her friendly, dog-loving smile. Another bark, a deep, scary, business-like bark. She felt hot air on the top of her head and rolled her eyes back to see a large mouth and a long, pink tongue moving closer.

'Tilly? Tilly.'

If it was them, she hoped they'd pick up her scent and recognise her, even though she hadn't seen them for a while. She wouldn't move until they made a decision, one way or the other.

'Caddie. Tilly.' A voice called out from near the back door. 'Caddie. Tilly. Good girls.' She heard footsteps on the verandah and coming closer.

'Who's there?' Livia tried not to speak too harshly and risk spooking the dogs, who seemed to be waiting for their next scene to begin. 'Caddie, it's me girl, Livia. Tilly, it's Livia.' If she could get the dogs on side, together they could deal with whoever had come in. 'Liebschen,' she said, suddenly remembering one of Minnie's words of endearment. 'Liebschen,' she said again.

'Liebschen,' the male voice repeated. 'Liebschen, liebschen.'

It seemed it was a word he liked, too.

'Hello,' she said to the voice and the dogs. She slowly raised her aching right arm – as much to confirm it was unbroken as to make contact with Caddie – and placed her hand on the dog's shoulder. Caddie turned her head quickly and began to sniff at Livia's hand.

'Caddie, it's me.' There was a moment of recognition for Caddie at the same moment Livia heard a growl above her and felt Tilly's tongue and wet nose on her forehead. Caddie followed suit and licked her hand, took a couple of steps back and turned to face the man in the doorway. At that moment, Livia was blinded by light. The dogs flinched and she sat up, shielding her eyes until they adjusted from the darkness.

'Who the hell are you?' She pulled herself to her feet and stood between the dogs, who showed no signs of returning to the man they'd arrived with. He may have been about 30. He had dark hair and green eyes, and he wore blue jeans and a white T-shirt with an embroidered badge of some kind on the left-side pocket. Was he the local security, a neighbourhood watch representative?

'The hell are you?' he said. 'I'm the man next door. Caddie, Tilly.'

The dogs looked up at Livia briefly and then walked over to the man next door. Turncoats. He bent down and put an arm around each of them, pulling them close and ruffling their fur.

'May I ask your name?' There was something about this man that wasn't quite right, Livia decided.

'Name? Call me Ishmael. You're Livia.'

'How did you know that?'

'Know that?' He paused. 'I've seen you in Minnie's photos.' He glanced off towards the lounge-room where Minnie kept her book collection and assorted treasures. 'Why are you here?'

'That's a good question, Ishmael. I don't really know. I suppose I just wanted to be near Minnie, somehow.'

Ishmael looked up and Livia could see that his eyes were wet with unshed tears. 'She's gone,' he said. 'I can't believe she's gone.'

'I'm sorry. I can't believe it either.' Before they could bring out the tears in each other, Livia adopted Minnie's and Rosanna's preferred option in crises. 'Would you like a cup of tea?'

2

Ishmael disappeared to his apartment next door while the kettle boiled, and returned with an envelope, holding it out for Livia as she placed the teapot on the kitchen table.

'What's this?'

'It's Minnie's Will – her last Will and Testament. There's a key. I don't know what it's for. Minnie said you'd know when the time was right.'

Livia felt the outline of a key as she took the envelope from him. She ripped it open and removed the contents. She scanned the three-page document, which named Livia as Executor and an heir, along with Greer, of Minnie's estate. There was no mention of a key. A spare for the house, or the CLEAR shop next to the gallery? When the time was right? She added it to the others on her key-ring, refolded the Will and returned it to its envelope.

'Do you know what's in here?' she asked Ishmael.

'You're the Executor, and an heir, with your sister. Sibyl, Minnie's sister, gets half, and you and Greer share the other half. I was a witness.'

'You're 'I. Darrow'?'

He nodded, and over tea and shortbread biscuits, Livia discovered that the man next door had witnessed other things as well. He'd been watching from his place when she'd arrived. He was about to take the dogs for a walk and had brought them into his apartment, hoping they'd find the novelty of a different place a motivation to eat. He believed they'd sensed that something was wrong this morning. They'd been wound up and skittish, even before the police had arrived with the terrible news and searched through Minnie's house, disturbing the dogs, and Ishmael, even more. The detective in charge had told him they were simply confirming that her house hadn't been burgled, and that all was otherwise in order. They'd asked him where he'd been the night before, as though he could have had anything to do with harming Minnie. He had noone to confirm that he'd been home alone in his apartment, but he wasn't concerned about his lack of an alibi; his only concern now was for the dogs' welfare. Already, he was worried about them fretting and becoming malnourished. He'd been Minnie's official alternative canine-carer and walker since he arrived a year ago and, reading between the lines, Livia suspected that Minnie and the dogs unofficially adopted him from about day one. Livia hadn't met him before, he told her, because she hadn't visited at the right times and she'd been too busy, what with all her Olympic training and travelling to shooting competitions around the world. But Minnie had kept him well-informed about her goddaughter, of whom, he said, she was very proud.

Ishmael seemed different because he had a syndrome he called Asperger's, a type of autism, 'not extreme,' he emphasised, but it had been part of his life for as long as he could remember. He worked as an accountant in his father's company, three blocks away. Livia gathered that the autism meant his communication skills weren't exactly what most people would find entirely normal, but give him a complex tax case – give him 20 of them, preferably – and he'd fly like Superman. Repeating what people said to him was a means of calming his anxiety; it helped him to focus and follow the conversation. It was lucky, he said, that he worked for his father. His mother had died four years before and now Minnie and the girls, Caddie and Tilly, were the ones he cared about most in the world, the ones he truly felt for. He'd followed her into Minnie's, he told Livia, because he was worried about what would happen now that there was no-one to look after things: the house, the park, but most importantly, the dogs. As Livia had opened the back door, worrying about the toads in the bushes, Ishmael had been at the fuse-box turning off the power as a precautionary measure. He knew that the dogs – two oversized Heinz Hounds, as Minnie called them – could handle themselves and protect him from whatever lay within: Livia, as it happened.

'Will you live here now, Livia?'

They were at the sink washing up the cups and saucers.

'I don't know, Ishmael.'

'Stay tonight, with the dogs. Maybe they'll eat something with someone in the house. Someone they know.'

Livia glanced down at the two of them, lying under the kitchen table, looking as depressed and abject as she felt. Did they need to go to the vet for a check-up? How could a vet cure fretting, grief? Could she stand the thought of them starving for another night for lack of company, despite Ishmael's entreaties and enticements? But why couldn't Ishmael move in, even temporarily? They knew him better than anyone alive now.

'I have my routines, Livia,' he said, his voice getting quieter as he went on. 'I can't change my routines. Where I live is right for me. It sounds stupid, but that's the way it is.' He trailed off.

'No, Ishmael. It isn't stupid. It works for you,' Livia said, forcing some optimism into her voice. 'That's the beginning and the end of it.'

Ishmael looked at her in surprise, and a little of the overwhelming sadness Livia had seen in his eyes seemed to lift.

She knew all about routines, and how to use them as comforters in crisis. Breaking down a pistol and putting it back together blindfolded used to work, after the 10th or 15th or 20th repetition. And there had been the squash ball. She'd have to find something else.

'Please, Livia. Will you stay?'

'I haven't brought anything with me.' As though that mattered. She returned to the table and sat down, fidgeting with the envelope containing Minnie's Will. Almost immediately, she felt the weight of something heavy and warm on her foot, and looked down to see Caddie resting her head. The dog raised her eyes to meet Livia's and Livia remembered when Minnie had brought the two puppies home from the pound.

They'd grown bigger, so much bigger, but the eyes were the same: 'soulful,' was Minnie's description. She'd called them her 'little dears.'

'Let me think about it,' she said, as Tilly placed a paw on her other foot.

CHAPTER TWELVE

River City

Wednesday 3 September 2008
Fortescue Street, Spring Hill

1

It was hard to breathe and there was nothing Livia could do to take in a clean, deep lungful of fresh air. She was covered from head to toe in heavy, wet canvas and the heat was overwhelming. No matter how hard she tried she couldn't seem to move her legs or pull the smothering cover from her face. She knew that Minnie was somewhere out in front of her, but she couldn't see her clearly, only the form of her body disappearing around the corner of an unfamiliar building. She tried calling out, but the words wouldn't come.

Somewhere, an alarm rang. She should follow Minnie and see that she was safe, but for some reason she was paralysed, and couldn't take a step. The alarm rang on, her heart pounded faster, and she woke in darkness. Panting to get her breath back, she found that she'd managed to tangle her right arm in the sheet and fling both arms over her head as she slept. The crooked angle encouraged a dull ache in her right shoulder and pins and needles from her elbow down to her fingers.

She pulled the sheet away from her face and sucked in the cool night air, realising simultaneously that the phone was ringing and one of the dogs was dozing contentedly across her legs. So much for paralysis. She must have chosen Caddie's half of the futon Minnie kept made up in the guest bedroom for visitors and wayward godchildren. Livia sat up and patted Caddie's flank, then flattened her feet and eased them out from under the dog's belly. She staggered across the hall into Minnie's bedroom and sat on the edge of her bed, wondering why there was no answering machine to record pesky 3am callers. She picked up the handset with her left hand, opening and closing her right hand, shaking out the numbness, and feeling the sting from the Beijing gravel rash on her palm.

'Hello.' Livia's voice was croaky, her throat dry and scratchy. 'Just a minute.' She coughed a couple of times. 'Hello?'

'Madame Babitsky?'

'Hello? Who's speaking please?' Obviously, it was someone who didn't know that Minnie was dead.

'Madame Babitsky, s'il vous plaît.' The voice was male, and hesitant. The accent could have been French, although speaking French was no guarantee of that.

'I'm sorry, Madame Babitsky isn't here,' Livia began. 'Madame Babitsky n'est pas ici.' She had minimalist French in the form of rudimentary phrases and a small vocabulary, both useful and useless when she travelled for shooting competitions. 'Je suis vraiment désolé, mais Minnie est –'

The caller hung up before she could say the word. Morte. She's dead. Caddie wandered into the room, followed by Tilly, who'd been downstairs somewhere. Livia lay back on Minnie's pillow as tears formed in her eyes. How many others who didn't know would eventually feel the loss as they innocently phoned with news and greetings? As far as Livia knew, Minnie had friends and acquaintances around the world from her years with the circuses; and Ari had maintained alliances with Max Mesmer's and his own networks of colleagues in the art world. Who knew how many of them Minnie had kept up with after Ari's death?

Tilly pushed her muzzle under Livia's hand and waited for a rub. Had the voice sounded familiar? She wasn't sure she wanted him to phone back, if it meant breaking sad news.

'Come on,' she told the dogs, 'we'll have a drink and chase the demons.'

She flicked on every light switch she passed on the way down to the kitchen. Illumination would help her to rearrange her thoughts into a more satisfactory state.

'We're 27 degrees 28 minutes south of the Equator,' she informed Caddie, presenting her with a fresh bowl of water, 'and 153 degrees east of Greenwich. We're about as far south of the Equator as New Delhi is north of it.'

She placed Tilly's bowl in front of her, but Tilly showed no interest. The dogs weren't impressed with latitude and longitude, either, regurgitated from a 'Did You Know' radio segment.

When the phone rang again, Livia picked it up on the first ring.

'Bonjour, parlez-vous Anglais?' She would at least attempt to communicate with the man in his own language. With luck he'd speak better English than she spoke French.

'That isn't Minnie,' said the most familiar voice Livia knew.

'Greer?' Livia slid down the doorframe and sat on the floor. 'Greer?'

There was a brief silence.

'What are you doing there, Livia? What's happened to Minnie?'

She spoke quickly, but her tone wasn't urgent or panicked.

'Minnie. Minnie's dead, Greer.'

Greer waited.

'Some time late on Monday night, or early Tuesday morning, I'm not sure. She was at the CLEAR office next to the gallery. The police are investigating.'

'What's that mean? Was she attacked?'

'I just got home from Beijing. Nobody knows anything. I came over to feed the dogs. A man called before you – he spoke French, but he hung up before I could tell him. All I know is what's been on the news. Mum said the police asked her where she was on Monday night.'

'Mum? Why would they ask Mum?'

'How should I know?' Livia said. 'Everyone's a suspect until proven otherwise?'

'Have they done a post-mortem?'

'I don't know. They'll have to if it's a suspicious death.'

'You don't know much, do you?'

'Apparently not.' Livia hadn't thought about a post-mortem, but that was surely what they'd do, to determine the cause and time of death, even if nothing else came to light. 'Uncle Con's in hospital.' She knew that much. 'A post-bypass infection,' Mum said. Greer usually did the calling – she changed her mobile phones like other people changed their socks – so Livia took the opportunity to mention this other significant family news. Beijing could wait for another day, and besides, to all intents and purposes, it was over, and would remain a mystery. There was no point in telling her that Yani had disappeared in such circumstances.

'Has Karl taken over yet?' Greer asked.

'He'd like to.'

'We're – I'm coming home, I was on my way, but I'll make it faster. When's the funeral?'

She hated the phrase so much now, she responded in French. 'Je ne sais pas. I don't know, Greer, I don't bloody know. All right? Where are you?'

'Punta Arenas – in Chile. It might take us a while to arrange flights, but as soon as, Liv, as soon as. Stay safe.'

'Greer? Greer?'

She was gone.

2

Livia let the phone hang off its hook and stayed on the floor. Greer was right. She didn't know, and hadn't learned much at all. How could she find out more? It was coming up to the hour, and there was a local news broadcast linked with the national breakfast show. A suspected murder would surely be of continuing interest to the media, especially if it remained unsolved. The thought occurred to her that an arrest may have been made already. The police wouldn't bother to call her.

She went to the lounge-room and turned on the television. Soon enough, the newsreader began the update on Minnie's death and then the talking head cut to a shot of the CLEAR office and the Mesmer Babitsky Gallery in Arthur Street. A familiar- looking man dressed in a dark suit was walking up towards the camera past the gallery and the office. The voice-over introduced him as 'Tibor Restik, a close friend of the dead woman, and deputy chair of the CLEAR Management Committee.'

Tibor faced the reporter and told her that he was devastated by Minnie's death. 'I believe I know what happened,' he said, 'and I shall leave no stone unturned until I find the perpetrators.'

'You say you know what happened, Mr Restik.' The earnest reporter, all of twelve years old as far as Livia could tell, stood facing Tibor, a microphone under his chin. 'Can you reveal to us what you think occurred here on Monday night?'

'No, I can't.' Tibor was quite definitive. The reporter looked worried. When you reach a dead end, where do you go? But Tibor wasn't finished. 'I do not wish to spook the guilty party, or parties, by elaborating on my suspicions here, but I am offering a personal reward for information leading to an arrest.'

Tibor proceeded to give the reporter and viewers his mobile phone number. Livia grabbed a pen and notebook and took down the number. The reporter thanked Tibor for his

time and reiterated the importance of anyone with information calling the police, indicating that investigations were
continuing and a number of people of interest were being interviewed.

Tibor's anxious face was replaced by a detective called Greg
Petersen, the Senior-Sergeant in charge of the investigation.
Petersen stressed that members of the public shouldn't take
matters into their own hands.

'While we appreciate the support of citizens like Mr
Restik, I cannot stress enough the importance of calling the
police if you have any information relating to this case.' His
voice was flat and monotonous; he'd been well taught at the
academy to suppress his emotions while simultaneously appearing disinterested but committed.

'And what action have you taken so far, Detective? Is an
arrest imminent?'

'We're questioning a number of people about the events of
Monday night and early Tuesday morning. At this stage, forensic evidence is still being analysed. There are several possibilities and we're looking into them all as a matter of
urgency.'

'Detective Mirror,' Livia told Tilly as she came to sit beside
her. 'He's looking into everything for us.' She didn't feel a
surge of confidence in this sharp looking man in a suit. Was
Rosanna one of those possibilities, for heaven's sake? What if
they had nothing to go on? What then? Had Minnie been a
specific target, or was there a killer out there preying on the
elderly of River City? That would be the next screaming
headline.

She went to the kitchen phone and dialled Tibor's mobile number. A robotic female voice asked her to record a message that would be returned as soon as possible. She waited for the tone, told Tibor who she was, and asked him to call her on her mobile or Minnie's landline. She went to the fridge, found a block of cheese, cut off a wedge and ate it on her way upstairs. In Minnie's bathroom, she washed her face, found a new toothbrush and brushed her teeth, borrowed Minnie's hairbrush and brushed her hair.

'It'll have to do. Come on, girls,' she told the dogs, 'you're going for a walk with the man next door. That might help your appetites.'

By the time she'd put their leashes on and walked them around the side of the house and out to the front where Rosanna's car was parked, Ishmael had arrived at the gate. His surveillance methods were nothing if not attentive.

'I'll come with you next time,' she said, smiling and handing him the leashes.

He smiled back, a tentative smile, but it was something.

'There you go. A new day. We'll get through this, Ishmael. We will.'

He nodded. 'Yes. Robert Frost said, 'Life goes on.' Minnie told me that.'

'Minnie told me that, too, a few years ago. She was right, of course.'

Livia, waving Ishmael and the dogs off on their stroll, remembered the day. It would have been Dan's tenth birthday, January 31st, 2004. Another Olympic year. She was finally going through all the boxes she and Paul had packed up when they divorced and sold the house. She'd brought them to the gallery, determined to be ruthless and cull them to the bone. She opened the box containing Dan's Bogota backpack, still bulging with his things. Minnie was with her when she unpacked it and found Dan's card. In her memory, she heard Benny's sweet saxophone playing 'Happy Birthday to You,' just for Dan. 'Well, sweetheart,' Minnie had said, shedding a tear with her, 'as the great poet said, 'Life goes on.' Time for Dan's birthday present, don't you think?' And she was right. Life went on, she began again, and missed the cut in 2004 for Athens, but she made Beijing, and nothing could taint that golden birthday gift, not even the car-jackers, if that's what they'd been. She looked around her as she stopped at a red light in Boundary Street, and flicked the door locks.

CHAPTER THIRTEEN

River City

Wednesday 3 September 2008
Mesmer Babitsky Gallery and CLEAR
Office
Arthur Street, New Farm

'Do you think we can? Are we allowed?'

'I have a key. What could be more kosher than that, Trina? But we'll use the back door.'

Livia and her part-time gallery manager, Katerina Miller, ducked under the blue and white checked police tape and Livia let them into Minnie's shopfront office.

'What about fingerprints?' Trina asked in a whisper.

'I think they've finished with the fingerprinting,' Livia whispered back. She looked around at the dusting powder that covered as many surfaces as fingerprints might attach themselves to. 'Why are we whispering?'

Trina laughed nervously and ran a hand through her short, blonde hair, a sure sign of anxiety in Livia's experience of her friend and business associate.

'You don't have to stay if you feel uncomfortable, Trina.'

'No, no, it's all right. It's just – if I'd been at the gallery the other night, maybe – I don't know – things might have been different.'

'Trina – the gallery doesn't open on Mondays,' Livia said gently, 'and there wasn't anything you could have done. That's all there is to it.' She put an arm around Trina's shoulders and they stood together surveying the space.

The shop was divided into two rooms, a smaller private room at the back, which housed a kitchenette and storage space, and a larger office facing the street, where the Citizens Leading Education Against Redevelopment had only recently begun their crusade.

There were drop sheets spread across the floor in the front room, and on top of them were several paint tins, one still open, and one overturned beside a roller tray whose paint roller was half way across the room. Skins had formed on top of the paint in the open tin and what was left in the tray. Paint had soaked into the drop sheet and mingled with a darker liquid next to a ladder lying in a V-shape on the floor, leaving a congealed, almost-dry mess of cream and what might have been blood. Was that the spot where Minnie was attacked? Or was a crime committed at all? Had Minnie fallen from the ladder and hit her head on the corner of the desk? It could be that simple. The paint roller could have landed where it did if Minnie had lost her grip on it as she fell.

'Watch out for wet paint, Trina,' Livia said, stepping past the ladder.

'Does this look like a crime scene to you, Livia?' Trina was near the front door inspecting the locks. She turned and walked back to the kitchenette area and did the same at the back door.

Livia followed her and noticed a red lacquer box sitting on a bread board on the bench near the sink. She recognised it as the container for the bronze horse Professor Wu had given her. Like so much else, it featured a layer of dusting powder, too. She picked a tea towel from the back of a chair and used it to protect her hands as she opened the box and confirmed that the horse was still inside.

'If it was burglars or junkies, you'd think they'd have taken this,' Livia said. 'Surely it'd look valuable to even a doped-out addict.'

'So would the laptop.' Trina gestured towards the desk in the front office, half-draped in a drop sheet and revealing Minnie's laptop sitting next to an equally portable multi-function device.

'And anything else worth a dollar.' Livia went to the desk and removed the drop sheet. She looked around the room but there was no sign of the brass paperweight of Big Ben Livia had sent Minnie from London. Maybe it was back at Fortescue Street. Who would steal something like that and leave the rest?

'There's no sign of forced entry, Livia, not that I can see,' Trina said. 'You don't suppose she let someone in, someone she knew?' Trina looked even more anxious.

'Someone she knew,' Livia repeated, thinking of people – usually victims' partners or close friends – who'd appeared on television begging for witnesses to come forward, pleading for information, all the while knowing that they were it, the guilty parties. They were like arsonists who waited in the crowd to watch the fire they'd started. Tibor's earnest face from the morning news floated into her mind's eye. Tibor? Impossible. But could it be someone Minnie decided to allow in because of who they were, not necessarily someone she knew? Officials, or authority figures – council workers fixing roads or searching for water leaks, approaching Minnie – for help with what? Who would be out late at night being official? She could only think of the police. What about someone who pretended they were injured and needed help, who asked to use her phone to call an ambulance, or the police?

No, Minnie was generous and kind, but she was smart, too, and she wouldn't deliberately put herself in danger, however innocuous or harmless a stranger might appear to be. There had to be something more to it. The thought that had continued nagging at her pushed itself forward again. A friend, someone she trusted so much she would let them in, no questions asked. But who? And why? Her friends were her biggest supporters, helping her with CLEAR and any number of causes over many years. And her art world colleagues – who among them would visit unannounced, who among them would hurt a hair on her head? If they thought she retained links with art dealers or had a collection herself – Livia hadn't seen evidence of one – could someone want something, some collectible so badly they'd literally fight Minnie for it?

'There was a woman in Beijing who said that not being able to have an art work you wanted caused a physical longing, real physical pain.'

'What are you getting at, Livia? You don't think Minnie's death has something to do with the gallery, do you?'

'I'm not sure what I'm getting at, Trina. Let's go. There's nothing here – Minnie's not here.'

The two women returned to the gallery and Livia went up to the loft apartment on the third level, showered and packed a bag. She re-joined Trina in the gallery, which Trina had closed the day before after learning of Minnie's death.

'Did the police talk to you, Trina?'

Trina nodded. 'Yesterday, after they – after they took Minnie away.' She sniffed and reached for a tissue on the reception desk. 'They asked me where I was on Monday night and Tuesday morning. I told them I was at home with Jill, playing Scrabble.'

Jill was one of Livia's many Skelloe cousins – she and Trina had been together for the best part of twenty years. 'How's Jill?'

'Upset – she knew Minnie so well. And I told the police she couldn't possibly have any enemies, she was too lovely, and kind.'

So how, then, could anyone who knew Minnie, intentionally hurt her? She was no saint, but she had no enemies that Livia could think of. Strangers, then, people who were against her campaign to curb redevelopment and preserve the city's heritage. It wasn't entirely unknown for protesters who caused too much trouble and cost developers too much money to end up in the concrete foundations of CBD skyscrapers in cities around the world. Or to be left to die in their campaign office?

'If Jilly has any theories, I'd love to hear them. Did the police actually tell you anything, or was it one-way with the questions?'

'I asked them about any on-going danger in the area. They said to make sure I locked up, that noone's here alone after dark, and to be wary of strangers. An art gallery is full of strangers every day, Livia.' Trina was angry as well as fearful.

And if one or more of those strangers decided they wanted something they couldn't live without – God knew what it might be, the Mesmer Babitsky was hardly the Guggenheim, but then there really was no accounting for taste – they may have decided to try and access the gallery from the adjoining shop, and encountered Minnie, staying up late to paint.

'We'll close for the rest of the week. What do you say, Trina?'

'Yes, let's do that.'

Livia could hear the relief in Trina's voice as they locked up and made their way out to their cars. They could close the gallery for a week, or two, if necessary, but would the police track down the killer, if there was a killer, in that time? Wasn't there a theory that the first 24 hours were the most crucial to an investigation? Or was she remembering something else, something about kidnappings and single days in which to find the victim alive. Dan hadn't been saved, nor Eamon, and eight years of single days on, noone had been caught. For the first months and years, she and Paul had kept in touch with the authorities in Bogota. After the new President took over, and introduced harsher laws against the criminal and revolutionary gangs, things seemed brighter, more hopeful for a time. But it had come to nothing, as she'd always feared it would.

That couldn't happen to Minnie, could it, not here, not now? Someone in River City knew what had happened, it was simply a matter of finding them. One day at a time was the only way she knew how to cope with life after Dan, and she'd had to begin with single hours, and sometimes, when things were truly bad, single minutes. Single minutes, then, she thought, driving out onto the street and past the gallery. The police tape fluttered in the breeze like bunting. Anyone would think a party was on the way.

CHAPTER FOURTEEN

River City

Wednesday 3 September 2008
4th Floor, Police Headquarters, CBD

1

Detective Senior-Sergeant Greg Petersen sat down and placed cups of coffee on the table between them. He smiled at the man sitting opposite him in the interview room.

'Let's start again, shall we, Mr Courtney? Or would you prefer Warrant Officer? I understand you had a sparkling career in the military. A decorated soldier.'

'Courtney, Douglas Peter. Date of birth: 1st of the 8th 1950. No fixed address.' He was weary. He'd had enough of this fellow with his smart-Alec attitude. He felt foggy and tired and jangly, all at once. He wanted out, but he knew how to conduct himself.

'Very nice. Of course you weren't a Warrant Officer when the Viet Cong captured you, were you? You were a humble

Lance Corporal, doing your national service. I'm surprised you carried on with a career after being a prisoner of the enemy for two years. Says something about your resolve, doesn't it, Warrant Officer, your survival against the odds?'

'Courtney, Douglas Peter. Date of birth: 1st of the 8th 1950. No fixed address.'

'I'm sorry, yes, it's former Warrant Officer, isn't it? And these days resident of the streets of River City.'

Doug reached for the coffee and picked it up with both shaking hands. As he brought the cup to his lips, the door in front of him opened and another man strode in, a man who looked like the people who ran the restaurants in Chinatown. At first, he was startled; the shock of seeing that face threw him back in time for a moment or two. Then he realised the man wasn't Vietnamese, he was Chinese. Another detective? Or had he come in especially to take Doug's dinner order? A snort of a laugh escaped from him and some coffee sprayed onto the desk.

'Something amusing, Mr Courtney? Are you remembering killing Mrs Babitsky and it's still a happy memory for you?'

Doug raised his eyes to meet Petersen's and held the other man's stare until he looked away to the new man. 'This is Inspector Bao, from Asiapol. He's observing our interviewing techniques.'

Inspector Bao nodded at Petersen and then at Doug.

'You don't mind, do you, Mr Courtney?' Petersen said. 'Of course you don't.'

'May I speak with you outside, Detective?' Bao asked.

Doug kept his eyes on Petersen, who waited a beat and then rose from his chair. Was it a well-rehearsed double act, or had this visitor interrupted him at what he thought was just the wrong moment? If his mind had been sharper, he'd be tempted to stir Petersen up a little more than he'd managed so far. He tried another sip of the coffee as the two detectives left the room.

2

'What is it, Inspector?' Petersen had been told to be polite towards the visiting policeman. After all, Bao's visit was apparently part of SCIALEP, the Sister Cities Inter-Agency Law Enforcement Program. Even so, there had been no advance warning. Bao had appeared out of the blue with the explanation that there had been a cock-up at the Beijing end with the arrangements and offered a thousand and one apologies for any inconvenience. Blah, blah, blah, was how it went, and his boss had simply told him to wear it. No harm done, he supposed, and he might score a trip to Beijing in return, although he'd much prefer Hong Kong and the casinos.

'Do you think you are making progress with this witness?'

'Suspect, Inspector. He's a suspect. We're making progress, and we can hold him for a while longer – there are outstanding charges relating to vagrancy and public drinking if we run out of interrogation time.'

'He strikes me as an individual who is determined. I have been observing from the other room since I arrived.'

'He strikes me as the kind who'd accept an old lady's hospitality then kill her without a second thought. His determination ran out a long time ago. Any that he has left, he buys in a bottle these days.'

'Do you really think so, Detective? He was a prisoner of the Viet Cong for two years, was he not?'

'So?'

'He would have been tortured, Detective, of that you can be certain. Unless your country allows for certain protocols beyond the humane, you may learn very little, unless he chooses to offer it freely.'

'Well, we've got diddly otherwise, mate. Maybe we can export him to Beijing and you can take over with your proto-cols.'

'Diddly?'

The visitor appeared oblivious to the insult, unless, of course, he took it as a compliment. 'Never mind,' he said. 'Even the no-hopers get lawyers sooner or later. Time is of the essence, Inspector. Care to join me for the confession?'

CHAPTER FIFTEEN

River City

Wednesday 3 September 2008
Fortescue Street, Spring Hill

1

'What we need is music.' Livia stood on Minnie's verandah in front of Caddie and Tilly. They still looked forlorn despite Ishmael's earlier attentions, and the dry food in their bowls remained untouched. She let herself into the house and went to the CD player next to the fruit bowl. There was a Benny Goodman CD already waiting. It must have been the last disc Minnie had listened to before she went to the shop. Livia pressed 'Play' and a jaunty track that sounded like the 1920s filled the room. She opened the fridge door and moved bowls and containers. Soon, Caddie joined her, and then Tilly – moved by the music perhaps to think that Minnie was home at last and somewhere in the house?

'Where does Minnie keep your meat now?' she asked them. 'I should have asked Ishmael, shouldn't I?'

Caddie turned her head slightly, and Tilly kept staring into the fridge.

'I know,' Livia said, reaching down to rub their heads, 'you're impressed with my search and seizure skills.'

She returned to the verandah and noted that the freezer was padlocked. The key. She unhooked the keyring from her belt loop and tried the key that came with Minnie's Will in the lock, but it didn't move. Raising her eyes to curse the god of security, she saw a small key hanging from a wall hook above the freezer.

'The best hiding place can be no hiding place at all,' she told the dogs. 'Remind me to read you Poe's 'Purloined Letter' some time.'

Once the fog cleared after she'd opened the freezer lid, she could see plastic packs of dark red meat labelled 'Kangaroo' in black marker, stacked neatly in the upper baskets.

'You're going to be very impressed with me shortly.' Livia lifted a couple of the bags to show the dogs, who raised their noses to the frozen meat.

When she looked back into the freezer, she saw what was underneath the dog food: four small plastic zip-lock bags containing something that looked like exotic dried herbs. Livia hadn't seen it often, but she was almost certain that it wasn't parsley, sage, rosemary, or thyme. She looked around her and closed the freezer lid, returning the purloined key to its hook. There was no need to change Minnie's routine if it had worked so far. But had it, she suddenly wondered? Surely noone would kill for marijuana. Surely noone thought she'd carry supplies with her to the CLEAR office and try to rob her there, and how would they have known it even existed? Everything had a way of becoming public knowledge; even details of the car-jacking in media-suppressed Communist China had escaped to the world.

She returned to the kitchen and microwaved the meat to room temperature, then took it out to the dogs. She sat on the top step with a cup of tea, waiting as they sniffed at their bowls and tried a little, then a little more. They obviously liked company when they ate, as well as some mood music, and it gave Livia time to think about where else Minnie might have stored her leafy crop, and in what form; or if she had any more at all. It wouldn't be a good look if the police returned to conduct further searches in their quest for a motive, and somehow, drug theft seemed too easy an explanation to Livia. Finding Minnie's pot might stop their investigation in its tracks, especially if their resources were demanded elsewhere for bigger, nastier crimes, although what could be bigger and nastier than murder, she couldn't say.

She stepped off the verandah and went to the shed in the far corner of the yard. It was empty except for a couple of benches on which Minnie kept supplies of bird food and cuttlefish bones. There was a small collection of tools and handyperson materials in one corner. Back inside the house, she walked through the rooms, checking cupboards and drawers, but if the freezer was the storage area, shouldn't she be looking for a growing area? The thought was almost preposterous, but she went upstairs and up again to the top of the house, and pulled down the hinged access door and its sliding ladder that led into the roof space. Here at the very apex of

Minnie's home there were excellent views of the Terrace hospital, where Uncle Con was a patient, and the upper stories of CBD high-rises. The attic space, she was relieved to find, was empty but for dust, cobwebs, and a few dead cockroaches.

Her elbow had begun to ache again after pulling herself up the attic ladder, and she was occupied with rubbing it when she entered the kitchen, and looked up to see the silhouette of a figure standing silently at the open back door.

'Jesus,' she heard herself yell as her muscles tensed and her heart instantly sped up.

'Hi, Livia.' He raised his arm in a half-wave. 'I'm on a break.'

'Ishmael. Sorry. I wasn't expecting you.' She recognised her state of hyper-arousal as a consequence of the events in Beijing. Her internal fight or flight responses were still on high alert. 'I'm glad you're here. I need to ask you something.'

The dogs joined them in the kitchen as Livia decided on the best approach. What if Ishmael knew nothing about the drugs? But he must have seen them in the freezer, unless his Asperger's meant he didn't notice certain things, or simply couldn't identify the grass as a drug.

'Ishmael,' she began, 'you knew Minnie well enough. I've been away a lot over the last couple of years, and I was out of touch with a lot of the daily stuff, you know, my family's usual life.'

Ishmael nodded, but there was confusion in his eyes.

'Do you know if Minnie had visitors very often? Strangers, maybe? Or people who seemed –'

What would they seem, exactly? Mad with reefer fever? Wild-eyed and overwound? They'd seem like ordinary people, which would be just what they were. She cursed herself for spending so little time with Minnie in the year and a half before the Olympics.

'There's Minnie's club,' Ishmael said.

'Club?'

'The people who come to play cards, and talk about books. Sometimes they watch movies and drink coffee. They all like to smoke.'

'They like to smoke. How do you know?'

'Minnie closes the windows and curtains and turns on her air-conditioning.'

'Did you go to these club meetings, too?'

'Of course.'

'So you're a club member.'

'Me? No, I'm not.'

It was time to stop asking closed questions, as Greer would describe them. 'So if you weren't a club member, what did you do?'

'I helped Minnie get everything ready. Brought up the tobacco from the basement, if the freezer stock was low.'

The basement. A vague memory returned from Livia's childhood of a basement under Minnie's house. During her earlier walk around the house, she hadn't seen any evidence of an entry door to a basement, but she hadn't been looking for it either.

'Can you show me the basement, Ishmael?'

'Of course. You're Minnie's Executor.'

Ishmael led her into Minnie's study and closed the door. It could have been a music room or a box room in other generations. There was one small window covered by a holland blind. Three walls were lined with bookshelves; the shelves were weighty with the books and jazz LPs and CDs Minnie had collected over the years.

Livia turned to face the other wall, the one she enjoyed looking at the most. Ishmael paused, obviously a fan, too. On the wall were framed photographs of circus performers and circus advertisements. Minnie was in a few of the photos, caught in mid-flight, or posing with trapeze artists like herself, men and women who risked their lives every night high up under the big top. There they were in their sparkles and tights, athletes in their primes, their undoubted vigour and precision preserved for respectful gazes to appreciate. Some of the pictures and circus ads were autographed, flamboyant strokes and curves, completely incomprehensible. In one photo, Minnie stood between a younger Tibor Restik, and Uncle Con, the three of them smiling as though their youth would last forever and they'd remain inseparable pals, the Donald O'Connor, Debbie Reynolds and Gene Kelly of the circus set.

Above the desk was Livia's favourite item, a keepsake from the Skelloe Brothers Circus, one of Minnie's old trapeze swings. Its ropes hung from ceiling hooks and the bar was just as it had been the last time Minnie swung on it: red paint faded to bare wood, traces of chalk from her hands still visible. Livia sat down in the chair behind the desk and gazed up at the swing keeping watch over Minnie's important documents. There were several leather-bound scrapbooks on the desk, the latest one open at a page that featured a newspaper article about Livia's recent Olympic success.

'Minnie liked to keep bits and pieces about the family,' she said by way of explanation to Ishmael, who'd picked up an older volume and begun to turn the pages.

'Livia, look at this,' he said, clearly impressed.

Livia leaned over and read, for only the second time, the report of the most significant event of Greer's and her, childhoods.

From the Daily Sun-Telegraph, January 27, 1974

CIRCUS TERROR – MAN-EATER EATS MAN!!
Little Girls Tame Big Cat

A Daily Sun-Telegraph Special Feature by Bill Malone with Carol Elms and Jenny Steele

A man is fighting for his life after being mauled by a tiger at Manly's popular Skelloe Brothers Circus yesterday afternoon.

Circus visitor, Con Galvin, 37, was critically injured when he entered the caged performance arena under the Big Top to save his 9-year old nieces, twins Livia and Greer Galvin.

It is believed that the girls were left alone with the tiger, 8-year old Lakshmi, known as Laki, when Mr Galvin's son, Karl, 14, lost control of an impromptu tiger-taming demonstration. He fled the cage, presumably seeking help, but left the girls behind with Laki.

It seems the young Mr Galvin ignored earlier pleas from a nearby circus performer, Minerva Mesmer, to stay away from the tiger.

Miss Mesmer, a trapeze artist performing nightly as La Tournoyer (The Twirler), then saw Con Galvin arrive on the scene.

'When Mr Galvin ran into the big cage where the girls were it was like everything froze,' said an obviously distressed Miss Mesmer, whose lowering rope had tangled, preventing her from reaching the ground in time to help the girls.

'Even Laki didn't move, but then she must have felt threatened, or something, because she rushed at Mr Galvin and knocked him down. She rolled him around and slashed his leg. She could've killed him with another swipe you know – there was blood everywhere and Mr Galvin was screaming at the girls to get out and save themselves.'

Miss Mesmer said that what she saw next from her perch high above the scene left her breathless.

'And then, I couldn't believe it – Greer picked up the tamer's whip and started cracking it at Laki and yelling at her to get back. And she did, the little devil, she got right away from Mr Galvin.'

Meanwhile, Greer's twin sister, Livia, dragged her uncle out of the cage and sat on his leg to stem the flow of blood.

'The size of her,' Miss Mesmer remarked, 'she's a slip of a thing with the strength of ten, just like Sir Galahad.'

The sisters were hailed by police, ambulance officers and witnesses as heroes and life savers. When big cat handler, Gerhard Benzler, a star from Zirkus Bavaria, reached the Big Top, Laki was safely in a corner of the cage eating her favourite snack, chicken liver, tossed to her by the quick-thinking Greer.

'Without a doubt,' said Mr Benzler, 'the little girls saved the man's life. They were amazingly cool. Laki is a great cat, but you must always remember even the tamest tiger is still a hunter, a carnivore.'

Mr Benzler added that tigers 'are wild like Bavaria's bears, big and wild and easily frightened. But ferocious, too. They must be shown respect.'

'The boy, Karl, should stick to pussy cats, I think,' Mr Benzler suggested, 'and leave the big cats to his baby cousins.'

Although family members declined to comment on Mr Galvin's condition or the events leading up to the attack, it is believed police and animal welfare authorities are investigating how the incident occurred. Laki remains safely in her cage at Skelloe Brothers Circus, while Mr Galvin is officially listed as being in critical but stable condition.

The Big Top will be open for business tonight.

DAILY-SUN-TELE

FAST FACTS FROM *THE SOURCE:*

1. Karl Galvin is not a tiger tamer or professional animal handler. He works for his father as an administrative assistant.

2. Twins Livia and Greer Galvin are holidaying with their injured uncle, who is rumoured to have strong connections with Sydney's Underworld.

3. Con Galvin has never been convicted of any criminal offence.

4. Family members, including the twins' mother, Rosanna, are enroute from River City to the bedside of their stricken relative.

5. Rosanna Galvin is the younger sister of the three brothers who own and operate Skelloe Brothers Circus.

6. Con Galvin's father, and the little girls' grandfather, Wolfgang Charles Galvin, was a well-known racing identity and patron of the arts.

7. Wolfie Galvin's involvement in illicit gambling, alcohol and a host of other rackets in the 1930s, '40s and '50s, made him a Mr Big, if not *the* Mr Big of this country's organised crime outfits.

8. Connections of Con Galvin insist that he is a hard-working, legitimate businessman and patron of the arts.

2

'Were you afraid, Livia?'

'Terrified. We were terrified,' Livia said. Apart from the terror, or rather because of it, she and Greer had found out, very early in their lives, exactly what they were capable of in the face of fear. 'But look.' She pointed to the photo on the wall opposite the desk. 'We loved her, too. And she was the most frightened, the poor thing.'

It was a shot of Gerhard Benzler, the big cat handler, standing beside Lakshmi, his left arm draped casually around her neck. She looked as sweetly docile as a lamb on Valium. Perhaps not that docile, but close.

'If you could just step into a picture –'

'What's that, Livia?'

'Step in there and cuddle Laki. She was a great cat, you know. Mr Benzler was very protective of her after that.'

'How would you do that?'

'Do what?'

'Step into the picture.'

It was a literal world for Ishmael, and he brought Livia back to the room.

'It would be difficult, for sure. But the basement, that must be easier.'

'Yes, Livia. Easy.'

Ishmael picked up one of the chairs that sat in front of Minnie's desk, and Livia took her cue to pick up the other one and move it off the Oriental rug. Then he flicked the brakes on the desk's castors and slowly pushed it back and away from the rug. Minnie had had the desk fitted with castors so she could move it herself: she valued her independence, even in matters of furniture moving. Ishmael squatted down, reached under each corner of the rug and unhooked it from small brass rings screwed into the floor.

'Help me roll this up, Livia.'

When they began rolling the rug, Livia saw the brass hooks sewn into its underside. Beneath the rug, flush with the floor, was a trapdoor with a circle of metal inlaid into the timber near one edge. It could pass for an eccentric Victorian-era floor decoration, at a pinch. Ishmael took what Livia had thought was a paperweight from Minnie's desk: a small but heavy object shaped like a solid bucket and painted black. He placed it on top of the inlaid metal on the trapdoor, slid his hand through the bucket handle and pulled.

'It's a magnet?'

'Of course.' Ishmael spoke as though such items were in common use in every home for just this purpose.

'After you,' he offered, as we looked down at the narrow set of steps disappearing into darkness.

She shook her head and gestured for him to go first. 'You know where you're going.'

As Livia followed him down, her eyes adjusting to the dimness, she noticed that the air was fresher and cooler. It seemed to be a large room, though it was difficult to tell in the gloom. Then, Ishmael parted a curtain towards the back of the room and bright light beamed out at them.

'This is where the tobacco grows,' he said.

Four medium-sized plants were reaching up towards the lights and a miniature sprinkler system.

'Minnie says the water timers 'let you set and forget'.'

'Does anyone else know about this, Ishmael?'

'No-one, except me and Minnie.' He paused, stared at Livia as the realisation hit him, and said, 'Me and you, Livia.'

At that moment, a loud ringing noise startled both of them.

'What is it, Ishmael? A fire alarm? Let's get upstairs.'

Ishmael didn't reply, but nodded and led Livia from the plant room back into the gloom, up the stairs, out of the study and into the lounge-room, where the ringing continued, though at a much lower volume. Livia found the source at last.

She picked up the phone's handset. 'Hello.'

'Livia, it's me.'

'Hang on a minute.' She didn't wait for a response, but clamped her hand over the mouthpiece. 'Ishmael, why didn't you say something?'

'It's Minnie's phone, Livia.' He looked at her with what appeared to be genuine surprise. What was he thinking? That if he knew the deafening clang in the basement was the phone, then so should she?

'Okay,' she said. 'So there must be a speaker or something in the basement.'

He nodded. 'You can change the volume,' he said, 'up or down. On the speaker downstairs.'

'Would you like to do that – turn it down, I mean. And would you like to put everything back the way it was, please?'

'Yes,' he said, nodding as he disappeared through the study door.

'Mum, I'm sorry I haven't phoned.'

'Are you all right, Livia? I've had a call from Minnie's lawyers. Her funeral is tomorrow at the Holy Mother and St Jude. The post-mortem is done and Minnie's body has just been released.'

'Tomorrow? Isn't that a bit soon? What about people from out of town? And overseas?' What about the people in town, and hadn't anyone heard the term 'unseemly haste?'

'The lawyer said Minnie wanted people to have as short a time as possible to grieve and cry and be sad. They were her instructions – burial without delay, so the law firm has made all the arrangements. Her lawyer said Minnie left instructions for a memorial party to be held in three months, so everyone can put it in their diaries and look forward to the stories. I told him I'd call you – they're calling all the others on Minnie's list.'

Rosanna sounded as shocked as Livia felt, but she had to admit that the posthumous plan was Minnie all over. It was always on with the show with her, and if you couldn't keep up, well, there was a mouthful of dust waiting.

'Mum, Uncle Ari was Jewish, and they have speedy burials. So do the Arabs.' And it shouldn't have surprised any of them that Minnie would give her lawyers lists and detailed instructions. She wouldn't have wanted her loved ones to be burdened with such tasks.

'Ari's been dead for 30 years, and Minnie wasn't Jewish. I don't think she was anything in the end; the church service is for family and friends. But Livia, have you heard anything from the police? Do they have a suspect if it really is murder? The lawyers didn't know.'

'Try to stay calm, Mum. I haven't heard anything.' Rosanna's wired state and mention of the police reminded Livia of what was in the basement. Could Rosanna be a member of this marijuana club of Minnie's? If Livia asked her, that would be that, and she wasn't sure how Rosanna might react to knowing that Minnie was growing illicit drugs in her basement and what's more, handing them out to people at meetings. It could only be worse if she'd been selling the stuff. It seemed that Yani's advice was applicable in almost any circumstance: tell noone, say nothing, not even to her own mother.

'Well perhaps no news is good news, for a change. It might mean it was just a tragic accident, or natural causes, or –
'

'Mum – are you okay?' Her mother sounded less sure of herself than usual.

'People are dying, Livia.'

'Mum. Don't worry – we'll sort this out. Please don't worry.'

'Go and visit your uncle, all right?'

'Yes, of course.'

'Go and visit, Livia.'

Too often in the past, Rosanna hadn't had the opportunity to talk to and be with people before they left her life forever, or threatened to. Con had almost died after Lakshmi; Livia's father, Ed, had called Rosanna from Europe and announced he'd met someone else and wouldn't be back; and then there

was Eamon, her future son-in-law, and the last straw, her beloved Dan.

'It's only around the corner,' she said, and rang off.

CHAPTER SIXTEEN

River City
Wednesday 3 September 2008
Terrace Hospital, Spring Hill

1

A t the Terrace Hospital, a five-minute walk from Minnie's house, Livia took the stairs to the second floor, and followed framed prints of various saints along the corridors and past the nurses' station. Near door 21, she heard a familiar voice.

' – haven't had much to do with that side of things, Dad. You and Gordon have been the artefacts experts – but there has to be a replacement. Both of you are unwell. We need to discuss a transition. The gardener project, for example, is –'

'No such thing, Karl.' Con's voice was firm, but quiet, not his usual strong baritone.

'Dad, I don't know all the details, but –'

'No, you don't.' The voice was weakening a little. 'Because there are no details, my boy. Forget about the gardener.'

In Livia's experience, Karl, who hated being interrupted, had never been known for his patience. She could tell, listening at the door, that there was no more than a tiny measure of it left, and it was all being applied to Con's resistance to any kind of transition.

'But Dad, that's why it's time for some decisions. We've got the future to think of, and I need to know more about certain aspects of the business, including the specialty items. I have investment opportunities, but there are outstanding obligations that I have to meet first.'

Livia agreed with Karl about the importance of transitions, but there was one thing more important, one thing that transitions were entirely reliant on for their success: timing.

'Uncle Con.' Livia breezed through the door. 'And Karl, how lovely to see you again so soon.' She returned her attention to her uncle. 'Mum phoned me, Uncle C, I'm sorry it took me so long to get here.'

'Are you all right, Livia, since Beijing?'

'Yes, I'm fine. Perfectly fine,' she replied. There was no point in discussing her fear and anxiety with someone already burdened with his own affliction. The interruption had stopped Karl in his tracks; that was all she'd wanted. Sometimes, the best way to deal with her cousin's overbearing presence was to pretend he wasn't there at all. She went to the bed and leaned down to kiss Con on each cheek, their standard form of greeting to each other since Livia's childhood.

'We're in the middle of a meeting here, Livia. Why don't you run along like a good girl and come back tomorrow.'

'Meetings and hospital rooms – a contradiction in terms, wouldn't you say, Karl?' Livia pulled up a blue visitors' chair and sat down close to her uncle's bed. She leaned forward and took his hand in both of hers. 'But I'd be happy to take the minutes, if it's that important.' She smiled at Con, who managed a weak smile in return.

'Never mind.' Karl moved to the end of the bed and touched Con's blanketed foot. 'We'll talk later, Dad.'

Livia stood and walked to the door with her cousin. 'What's your problem, Karl? That sounded more like a threat than a date.' She spoke as quietly as she could, hoping Con wouldn't overhear them. 'He's your father, and he needs time to get better.'

'Forget about it. It's none of your business, Livia. You set those bloody women on me at the pub, didn't you?'

There was nothing like a not-so-subtle change of subject when things were heating up. For Con's sake, she went with the flow.

'I thought you'd enjoy the attention, Karl, since Sylvia's on vacation. Doesn't Armani have a velcro tear-away range of suits, for people in your line of work? There's nothing like a bit of self-revelation to clear those nasty cobwebs.'

Karl stared at Livia for a moment, clasped his hands together one over the other, and began turning his wedding ring round and round, a sure sign of suppressed anger. He seemed ready to continue the conversation, but then checked himself. 'Don't tire him out.' He left the room without a backward glance at his father.

When Livia returned to the bedside, Con had drifted into a shallow sleep. She sat and waited. Unlike Yani – the last per-

son she'd visited in a hospital – at least Con was still here, as
he had always been there for the family. When she and Greer
were children, Karl, five years their senior, would try to
frighten them by describing Con as The Enforcer, painting
pictures of a demonic figure severing the ears of his enemies
and slurping out the blood, stabbing barbecue forks through
the hearts of traitorous associates, kneecapping wayward em-
ployees with his large, bare hands, strangling naughty little
girls until their eyes popped and rolled down their cheeks.

The scary images worked for a while, during the years before their godfather, Uncle Ari disappeared, and before their
father, Ed, decided to remain in Europe. They'd had little to
do with Con – he lived in another city and they knew him as a
dark-suited figure with a deep voice and a stern look, who
smelled of spicy tobacco, who came and went apparently at
random, a constant traveller within and outside the country.
It was easy for Karl to create any kind of personality for Con
when he visited with the twins during school breaks.

But after Ari and Ed departed, Con took a greater interest
in the girls. Livia could remember one memorable occasion
when he strode into the dining-room at the hotel not long
after Rosanna received Ed's news of his new love and life in
Amsterdam. Con knew that Rosanna was feeling particularly
fragile. He took Livia and Greer by the hands and out to the
street, almost marching them down the block to Mr
Godolfus's café and ice-cream parlour. He placed large, Nea-
politan banana splits in front of them, and explained that he
felt it incumbent upon him, as their interim godfather, and his
brother, Ed's, keeper, to provide them with some of life's little
luxuries from time to time. He proceeded to make them offers

they couldn't refuse and still call themselves kids: rolls of Life-savers, Steam Rollers and Fruit Tingles, and white lolly pack-ets of Mr Godolfus's famous acid drops. Thereafter, Con Galvin, Karl's demonic, blood-sucking strangler, was Uncle C: sweet, soft, protective, caring, reliable Uncle C. And as the years went by, and Livia researched her family a little more, she discovered that Karl's fantasies were fuelled, not by his father's activities, but by his grandfather's, Wolfie Galvin, and by Gustav Galvanisch, the great-grandfather and German immigrant who changed his name to Gus Galvin, and inte-grated himself and eventually, his son, into any and every ille-gal scam going in those Squizzy Taylor-Al Capone times. Con, on the other hand, was the one who'd begun to take the family businesses towards legitimacy, and now Livia suspected that he feared a return to the old days, courtesy of Karl.

2

Con opened his eyes and turned his head towards Livia, smil-ing at last after his unconscious visit to who knew where?

'Livia,' he whispered.

'Uncle C,' she said, and took his hand. 'How are you today?'

'Not as bad as I look, my dear. The drip is working.' He shifted his gaze to the bag of clear fluid suspended from a hook.

'Mum said you had an infection, after the bypass.'

'No – a reaction to the drugs – they've changed them – I'll be fine.'

Livia wondered if Karl was aware of the positive progno-sis, or if Con's own body had been informed. 'Are you sure?'

'I'm not checking out, Livia – there's the future to consider.'

She wasn't sure if he was taking the mickey out of Karl's earlier comments.

'You're a big part of it, now that my beloved Minnie is gone.' He pressed a button on the remote control near his hand and the bed brought him to a half-sitting position.

'Minnie?'

'Livia, most of us, we're bred, fed, led, and dead. That's okay for some. Not you. That's never been you. It wasn't Minnie either. There's a lot to do – I have to sort Karl out first, let him know where he stands, that he can't run the art businesses. Then we'll talk, you and I. Minnie didn't get the chance.' He began to wheeze and then came long, slow, breath-taking coughs.

'I'll get the nurse,' Livia said, but Con shook his head and pointed at the water bottle on his bedside table. She grabbed it and held it close as he sipped from the straw in between coughs.

'Karl,' he said, as his breathing returned to normal, 'is up to something. Let me attend to that. All right?'

'Yes, yes, that's fine,' Livia said, not wanting him to say another word, even as she wanted him to explain. What about this future he seemed to have planned for her? And Minnie's death, was it accidental, what did he make of it? He'd been out of action for a couple of weeks already, and he was still very weak. 'Just relax. I'll be around – I'm not leaving town.' Her future, whatever it might be, belonged to her and noone else, not Minnie's ghost, nor Con's fevered plans. And just because she ran a gallery didn't mean she had any interest in the family's art and artefacts trading.

Con nodded, and pressed the button again, lowering himself back to resting level. He looked to Livia like the last person who could sort anything out, let alone a son like Karl, intent on securing his inheritance before his fiftieth birthday, less than a year off. She waited as Con drifted off to sleep again, and slipped out after dusk when a nurse arrived to check his progress and write more illegible words and numbers on his chart, as though such figures could predict an outcome for a man like her uncle.

CHAPTER SEVENTEEN

River City

Wednesday 3 September 2008
Fortescue Street, Spring Hill

1

Half a block from Minnie's house, Livia could see that the front door was open. A shaft of bright light cut across the verandah and down several steps. She was certain she hadn't left the place unlocked. As she quickened her pace and drew closer, she saw the dogs on the stairs, sitting just beyond the reach of the light: two dark, furry bundles, ready to scare any passerby into the next dimension if they dared to enter the yard; or else they'd be licked to death, depending on the canine mood. Caddie and Tilly weren't so far from puppyhood that they couldn't be bought for the price of a mutton shank and a furless tennis ball.

She called out their names as she walked up the path and stopped to give them each a rough-house hug as they met her

163

at the bottom of the steps. They returned her offering with licks and panting half-barks, and, for a moment or two, Livia enjoyed the fantasy that they'd been waiting for her, her own faithful, dependable pets. Then someone darkened the doorstep and she looked up.

'Ishmael. What's going on?'

'Going on. The CLEAR meeting, but not really a meeting. Not all members are here, Livia, not all.'

It was Minnie's heritage preservation committee, members of which Livia had met briefly in previous months when she was home on flying visits and they'd be here at Fortescue Street planning CLEAR's future. Minnie had managed to gather some of her old circus cronies together. That was before she leased the office next to the gallery.

When she walked into the house, Ishmael followed her and closed the front door behind them. She heard a switch click and something came to life with a hum; the air-conditioning system.

'We didn't think you'd mind, Livia,' said Verity Price, a woman in her early sixties, if Livia was any judge, and CLEAR's Secretary. 'Minnie used to say, no matter what, the show must go on.'

'Of course, that had a lot to do with her old trapeze artist days, you understand,' said Cosmo Dacey, a grey man, also in his sixties. Livia couldn't remember his committee role.

'You remember her trapeze artist days, don't you, Livia?' Ruth Gold asked. 'Minnie was La Tournayer – The Twirler.'

'Yes, I remember,' Livia said. She congratulated herself on remembering all of their names, and she also remembered the someone who was missing.

'You don't have a quorum, do you?'

'Not for a proper meeting, no,' Verity said. 'This is more in the way of a –

'A memorial meeting,' Ruth said, and the others nodded their agreement.

The minute Ishmael had turned on the air-conditioner, they'd begun their equivalent of a tea ceremony. Verity poured cups of tea for everyone, while Cosmo and Ruth set about rolling and lighting the joints.

'Medicinal purposes only,' Ishmael explained. 'In some countries, it's already legal.'

'I have no problem with that,' Livia said, and she realised as she said it, that she truly wasn't concerned about these quiet, serious people seeking a little pain relief from something that, if it had been marketed and promoted as cunningly as alcohol or nicotine, would be sold in supermarkets, and specialty shops, and attract about the same level of criticism.

'We'll save Tibor's for him,' Ishmael announced as the others settled in to finishing their smokes.

Livia wondered if perhaps Tibor was grieving in the old-fashioned way, by sitting at home and staring at the wallpaper, trying to will Minnie back to life.

'He's probably gone bush,' Cosmo said. 'He does that sometimes when things get on top of him.' He leaned over and picked up three small plastic packets of herbs, pocketing one for himself and handing the others to Ruth and Verity, who dropped them into their handbags. Cosmo noticed Livia watching him. 'Small enough for personal use only, so if by unlucky chance any of us were caught, we couldn't be convicted for dealing, only possession.' He smiled at Livia and stood up, which seemed to be the cue for the others to rouse themselves, too.

Ishmael and Livia saw them off to their cars, and Livia sent a few thoughts to the patron saint of pot smokers, whoever she might be, to protect the CLEAR committee from police patrols and sniffer dogs. Ishmael made himself scarce as soon as the cars drove off, patting the dogs and thanking Livia for her patience. Livia was left to sit on the steps with Caddie and Tilly.

'She wasn't just a woman of substance, as you and I always knew,' she said to her companions, 'she was a woman of controlled substances, too.' She put her arms around them and felt their soft warmth. 'Minnie, darling,' she said to the night, 'any other surprises?'

As if by way of reply, a car pulled up in the driveway behind Minnie's Renault, and Verity emerged from the driver's side. She'd left the engine running.

'Forgotten something?' Livia asked as she reached the bottom step.

'I'm very worried about Tibor, Livia,' she said. There was anxiety in her eyes and her face looked pinched. Before Livia could speak, she continued. 'I know it's a lot to ask, but would you come with me to Tibor's place, to make sure he's okay?'

'Of course. And I'd be happy to drive, if you like.'

2

Tibor lived on the river at Norman Park, no more than fifteen minutes from Minnie's across the main traffic bridge, in one of two small flats built-in under a house that hadn't been discovered and redeveloped. The river frontage alone would be worth millions. Whoever lived here wasn't interested in profit, yet. The yard was overgrown, there was no fence, and the paintwork had moved beyond powdery and flakey to disintegrating.

'His car's gone,' Verity said as they pulled up. 'There are no garages for the flat people. They park on the street.'

'Maybe Cosmo's right,' Livia offered. 'He's gone bush.'

'We'll check anyway, now that we're here.'

Verity led the way down the garden path beside the house. There were no helpful spotlights, or garden globes to illuminate the inky blackness. Livia heard rustling in the garden to her right and instinctively moved closer to the wall of the house, stepping on something soft that wriggled under her foot. As they neared the door to Tibor's flat, something made a plopping sound out on the river metres ahead of them.

'Fish,' Verity said. She reached down and lifted the welcome mat, felt around and came up with a key.

'Shouldn't we knock first?' It was late, and what if Tibor was enjoying himself with a lady or gentleman friend? Who were they to barge in, Livia thought? On the other hand, Verity knew where to find the key.

'He isn't here, I'm sure,' she said, a despondent tone in her voice.

She was right. His flat consisted of two rooms. They walked into the main room, which was a combination lounge-dining-room-kitchen. Everything was in its place and tidy. Verity rolled a sliding door back and entered the bedroom. It featured a double bed and built-in cupboards. Beyond this room, through another sliding door, was a narrow *en suite* consisting of a small shower at one end, a toilet at the other, and a miniature handbasin in the middle. The bed was made and the *en suite* was neat as a pin. The place reminded Livia of a motel unit from the 1960s. The two women stood in the bedroom and Livia surveyed Tibor's hospital corners. Verity went to a door in the wall and pulled it open.

'His camping gear is still here.' She sounded disappointed and tired.

'What do you want to do, Verity? We could call the police. That detective who was on TV is investigating Minnie's death.'

'No, no,' she said, 'not the police.'

Livia's suggestion seemed to give her a surge of energy.

'He could have had a call on his mobile, after he appeared on TV. Maybe the police can trace it, and then find out where he is.'

'Not the police.' She looked around the room and sighed. 'The police have already interviewed us about Minnie. And adults can choose when and where they want to travel,' she said, more to herself than to Livia. 'Or disappear, or whatever it is he does, whether or not their friends like it or loathe it. Come on. I've wasted enough of your time, Livia.'

Verity led them out of the flat and locked up, returning the key to its place beneath the mat. She was quiet during the drive back to Fortescue Street, and when they arrived she thanked Livia for her patience, kissed her cheek, and drove off without another word.

3

Inside the house, the air-conditioning hummed along, and seemed to have removed any trace of telltale marijuana scent from the immediate vicinity. Livia turned it off, found Tibor's mobile number and dialled it. This time there was no answering service, the phone simply rang and rang. She hung up and went to the back door, calling the dogs in for the night. They followed her as she turned off the lights on the ground floor and made her way upstairs.

At the top of the flight, both dogs stopped and became alert. Livia hesitated to turn on the hall light and listened for what they'd already heard coming from farther away. Then there were footsteps on the front verandah, followed by the doorknob rattling. The footsteps went back down the stairs and were lost, then sounded again on the side path. They stopped again – near the hiding place for the spare key? – then started up, travelling towards the back of the house.

Livia darted down the stairs, into the kitchen, and over to the back door, checking again that it was secure. She waited for the footsteps on the back stairs and the verandah, then flicked on the floodlight, and looked out the window.

'God help us,' she said to herself as the dogs lolloped into the kitchen, waiting for the game to start. She opened the door before he could attempt a break-in, and he half fell through it and into the kitchen; the dogs began to growl.

'It's all right,' Livia said, 'it's your cousin, Karl.' She patted Caddie's head. 'What brings you here, Karl? I was about to go to bed, at long last.' She had no intention of making him welcome, even though Minnie had always seemed to retain a soft spot for him.

'I was concerned.' He looked about the kitchen, settling finally on Tilly's hopeful, sweet face. 'About them. Whether anyone had remembered they were even here. Everything happened so suddenly. And then there's security – you know, there are people who read the papers to see who's died and then find out where they lived, and go and burgle the place.'

'No, I didn't know that, Karl.' Why did he seem overwound, she wondered? Had this become his normal state now that the corporate presidency was in sight?

'So,' he said, sitting himself down at the kitchen table, 'is anything amiss?'

'I don't think so, Karl. Minnie's funeral is tomorrow, by the way, at the Holy Mother.'

'Yes, I know, the lawyers phoned me. They've been phoning everyone. Sylvia won't be able to make it. What are you doing here, anyway, Livia?' He didn't seem the slightest bit interested in the arrangements for Minnie.

'Like you, Karl, I wanted to check out the house, make sure it was okay. Then I discovered I'm Minnie's Executor, so, here I am.'

'You? You're her Executor?'

'I was surprised too. It tends to concentrate the mind.'

There was more than surprise in Karl's eyes, but he quickly collected himself.

'Well, make sure you do a good job. Do you know –' He stopped in mid-sentence.

'Do I know what, Karl?'

He looked around the kitchen. 'Never mind. Does Minnie have a security system? You should make sure it's on. Who knows what she could have hidden in this place?'

Did he know the half of it, Livia wondered, remembering the basement's bright lights encouraging those four little plants to grow. Come to that, did she?

'She has a security system, Karl.' Livia glanced down at the dogs. They'd come to sit at her feet, and were keeping a wary eye on Karl.

'I mean it, Livia. Watch yourself. In fact, you should go back to the gallery, and let me organise this. Better yet, go and keep your mother company at the Bender.'

'Thank you for the heads up, Karl. I can't imagine why you care so much all of a sudden, but I'm a big girl now. I can look after myself.'

'Rosanna's very upset about Minnie. You're upset about Minnie. You should be together.'

'We're all upset, Karl, even you, apparently, and I'm in contact with Mum, so don't worry.'

She spoke more slowly for emphasis, staring him down until a vibration passed between them that ensured Karl knew his cousin was going nowhere despite his suggestions.

'Don't let that business in Beijing go to your head,' he said, leaning forward, as though she needed reminding.

But which business did he mean? The official business on the firing range, or the business in the hutong? Either way, it didn't really translate to River City and Fortescue Street.

'I won't, Karl. Goodnight.' She stood to emphasise the benefits of taking his leave.

He took the hint, glancing down at the dogs as he rose. Then he bent slightly and put one hand out, apparently intent on patting Caddie, but something he saw in her face caused him to draw back and flex his fingers. Caddie, for her part, half-sneezed in Karl's direction, and strolled to the back door to form a guard of honour for his departure, wagging her tail appreciatively in anticipation of his exit.

'Don't say you weren't warned, Livia. Goodnight.' He flicked the floodlight off before stepping outside and, in his dark clothes, disappeared from view after he'd taken only a few steps.

4

Outside, Karl stayed in the shadows as much as possible on the way back to the car. He was furious, but he had to concentrate. He stopped near the corner of Minnie's house and waited, listening for the sounds of the city, for footsteps too close, looking for shadowy figures like himself. Then he sprinted across the lawn and the footpath, stabbing the button on his keys to unlock the car. Once inside, he immediately locked the doors, and stared around him one more time before taking off. Two blocks away, he pulled over and dialled a number on his mobile.

'I need more time,' he told the party at the other end.

'The time is up, Mr Galvin,' came the reply.

Karl waited a beat.

'I don't need to remind you that you haven't exactly been successful yourself, despite your apparently privileged position. Don't make the mistake of attracting more attention to this than it deserves.' He believed, for the moment, that his voice was hard enough to disguise any residue of fear. He thought he'd achieved the right combination of respectfulness and firm direction.

'I repeat to you, the time is up. Where is it, Mr Galvin? The delivery is overdue and that is unacceptable.'

'So unacceptable you start killing little old ladies after your own man fucks up.'

'You are mistaken, Mr Galvin. The death had nothing to do with me or my people. I gather the police regard it as a crime of random street violence. As to the other, I shall take care of my man, as you call him. My reputation is at stake, too, Mr Galvin, and perhaps, in the short term at least, my life. This means that your position is the same as mine. Don't forget it was you who initiated this project.'

'I'm attending to the problem. Try not to kill anybody else.'

Karl closed his phone without waiting for another denial and another warning that his time was up, as though he was some game show contestant. He found that his hands were shaking and he was beginning to sweat. He reached over to turn on the air-conditioning, and leaned back in his seat. Why bother reminding the fellow when they both knew exactly who the project manager was, and what an irony? That had been his first mistake: not directing all the traffic himself. Karl should have known the old boy was fading, despite his past successes. He should have taken the reins years ago, but instead found himself frustrated at almost every turn. But there were some turns where no-one could thwart him, now or in the future. All he had to do was clean up this mess and make it right. He'd satisfy the shopper, and then be invited to join the bigger, better plans that would ensure his international success.

He flipped open his phone and tried another number. Sure enough, the old boy's service was turned off. He couldn't be bothered leaving a message; he'd see him tomorrow at the funeral, if he made it that far. It was sure to be an ordeal. Karl had loved Minnie Babitsky, too, in his own private way. For some reason, she hadn't turned away from him the way some of the others had done after the accident with the tiger. He didn't think it was pity, either; there was a kindness in Minnie that sometimes seemed to him transcendent and far beyond the ordinary. It couldn't be true, could it, couldn't be some terrible coincidence that she'd been killed by some homeless no-hoper who saw an opportunity, or whose brain finally melted after too many nights of whatever it was they drank or sniffed or stabbed into their veins? Surely it was better to die for a substantial reason, for something worthwhile?

He rubbed his face with his hands, checked the street again, quickly started the car and took off. It wouldn't do for Karl Galvin, entrepreneur and cultural connoisseur, to be suspected of trying to pick up one or both of the prostitutes making a beeline for him in his wife's black BMW sports job. He'd go home and rest, and soon, he'd find what he was looking for, with or without the old boy's network. Time wasn't up, not yet.

CHAPTER EIGHTEEN

River City

Thursday 4 September 2008
Grounds of the Holy Mother and St
Jude Retreat for the Aged and Infirm
Border Road

1

'Thank you all for coming – short notice, I know.'

Most of the congregation had walked the 50 metres from the chapel to an outdoor area distinguished by a large terracotta-coloured concrete slab with the outline of tiles stamped into it. The slab was protected by a green Colorbond roof, and the option of lowering thick, transparent plastic blinds around the four sides should the weather turn windy or rainy.

'I'm sure Minnie would have appreciated it, but she won't appreciate any tears, so keep smiling, whatever you do. And please remember there'll be a memorial party for Minnie in a few months' time to make up for the speediness this week. So let's consider the memories of Minnie some of you shared during the eulogies as the warm-up act for the party down the track.

'Right now, I'd like to publicly express my personal thanks to Minnie Babitsky, Minerva Helena Babitsky, nee Mesmer, for all the wonderful things she did for me and my sister, Greer. Greer couldn't be here for this farewell, and we ran out of time to tell Minnie personally how much we love her and how glad we were to have her in our lives.'

Livia turned to focus the congregation's attention on the poster-sized photograph of Minnie taken during her circus heyday. She sat on the same trapeze that now hung from the ceiling in her study at Fortescue Street. Her smile almost out-dazzled the bling on her costume. In her instructions to the lawyers, Livia discovered, Minnie had expressly forbidden an open casket or any viewing sessions, supplying instead the circus photo, so she'd be remembered at what she regarded as her brightest and best. Livia returned her gaze to the assembled crowd. There were people from circuses and councils, from holy orders, art galleries, environmental groups, and protest movements, from the media and the police, and from the streets of New Farm, the people she and CLEAR tried to help with hot meals and warm blankets.

'As you know, Minnie is my – was my godmother, and my family had a long association with her and, unfortunately, a shorter one with her husband, Ari, who was our first godfather. It was because of Minnie – and by association, Ari, through his family ties – that Greer and I were able to live and work on an Israeli kibbutz, and to travel through Europe staying with their art world friends and circus families. Minnie encouraged my interests in pistol shooting and art history, and if she ever thought it was a strange combination, she kept that thought to herself. She was a thoroughly decent human being, never judgemental, as you all know, and Greer and I could have had no better education. It was all due in large part to Minnie, our godmother, with the unconditional support of our mother, Rosanna.'

She glanced over at Rosanna, standing near one of the tables laden with food, and nodded. Rosanna smiled back at her, but Livia could tell her attention was elsewhere. Even a function as apparently informal as this one brought out the Sergeant-Major in her mother, which was one of her strategies for coping with the shock and grief.

'I know you'll all have similar stories of support and loving friendship to share, so please accept this as an invitation to present them at Minnie's big Wake in three months time. It'll be here at the Holy Mother and St Jude Retreat. This place is the lifetime work of Minnie's and her sister, Sibyl's ancestor, Mother Magda Mesmer, founder and benefactor of the Order. Please stay a while today to celebrate Minnie's life.'

There was a smattering of applause, a 'Bravo,' and the odd 'Hear, hear,' as Livia stepped down from the temporary podium and joined her mother at the table.

'Well done, darling,' Rosanna said as they embraced, 'but I don't feel like kicking up my heels, or smiling.'

'Minnie would have,' Livia said. What else could you do but grin and dance in the face of your own suspected murder?

'Verity Price – you know Verity?' Rosanna asked.

'Yes, I saw her earlier.' Livia had seen Verity in the crowd at the service at around the same time that Rosanna asked her to leave early and ensure that everything was ready for the reception. Rosanna had stayed with Con throughout the service and interment; he'd been granted a leave pass from his doctors for only a couple of hours.

'She told me Tibor Restik didn't come to the funeral. She seemed really upset about it.' Rosanna looked around her and moved closer to Livia. She lowered her voice. 'You don't think he had anything to do with Minnie's death, do you?'

'No, I don't. Definitely not.' How could she sound so certain that Tibor was an innocent party, even to herself? His disappearance, and his close relationship with Minnie could only look bad for him. 'Where's Uncle Con?'

'He's gone back to the hospital. Elias took him after the cemetery service.' Elias was Con's body man, bodyguard, and all-round personal assistant. He spoke very little, but he was worth his considerable weight in gold for his street smarts and the level of his devotion to Con. 'Livia, don't forget to talk to Sibyl and Gordon while you're here. Now that Minnie's gone, I don't know how Sibyl will be. Who knows what she understands anymore? When I phoned Gordon – well, he seems to be getting more and more nervy about everything, and frail. I've never seen him so stressed.'

'Don't worry, Mum, I plan to see them both – I just haven't had time since – ' There was no need to finish the sentence.

'I know. But Gordon's a very old friend and business associate of your uncle's – Con will appreciate your interest. See him and Sibyl today, and then make a date for next week – you can have lunch, just the three of you. You'll have to discuss

Minnie's estate with Gordon – he has Sibyl's power of attorney, but make sure he's with it when you talk to him. Lately, he seems to be having trouble keeping track of conversations.'

'Okay, Mum, don't worry about it now,' Livia said.

Rosanna had decided it was time to bustle in order to shake out her anxiety – Livia recognised the symptoms: ordering people around, organising lunches, hovering where the wait-staff were loading up their trays. She moved off to give herself a break and had taken a few steps when she heard her name called.

'Dr Galvin, hello.'

She turned to the familiar voice.

'Bao Jinmin, from Beijing.' He nodded at Livia and offered a slight smile. There was another man, of Caucasian appearance, hovering just behind Bao and to his right. An interpreter? The inspector was a fluent English speaker.

'Inspector.' Livia looked at Bao. He was out of context, here at Minnie's Wake. For a moment, she was back in Beijing, in the interview room, shaking in shock after the terrible shootings. She forced a hello, but she could tell he knew he'd upset her.

'Forgive me for surprising you. I am visiting as a representative of Asiapol, as part of the Sister Cities program. There are many of us coming and going, making our small contributions to closer ties.' He didn't introduce her to his offsider.

A waiter strolled up to them with a tray of drinks. Livia set her empty wine glass down and took a fresh one. Bao selected an orange juice. His offsider took a few steps back and moved off to stand a short distance away.

'May I offer you my condolences, Dr Galvin, on the sad loss of your godmother.' He half bowed towards her.

'Thank you. I can't understand how something like this could happen to someone like Minnie.'

'Oh?'

'Someone full of the joy of life, someone so generous, so open to helping others. She was altruistic, and she had a social conscience.'

'Perhaps just the sort of person, however, who could find herself in harm's way. An irony of modern life.'

'Whoever it was, Inspector Bao, if I find them before the police do, they should be glad I gave my guns away.' She swallowed half the liquid in her glass and felt its comforting warmth.

'Did your Australian flag make it home to the right person, Dr Galvin?'

'You have a good memory for detail, Inspector. I suppose it did. As you can appreciate, I haven't seen it or had an opportunity to discuss it with anyone. Have you heard from Inspector Lee at all?'

'I believe that Inspector Lee is in your fair country.'

'Here? What would bring Yani here?'

'I couldn't say, Dr Galvin, but I hope to catch up with him.'

Livia finished her wine and placed the empty glass on a passing tray. Some unspoken signal brought Bao's assistant back to them.

'Would you excuse me?' Bao said. 'I must return to the city to prepare for a presentation to your esteemed metropolitan police officers, and I would like to speak briefly with some of the Sister Cities officials here.'

'This way, Inspector.' They were the first words Bao's offsider had spoken, and for some reason Livia wanted to laugh. It must have been the wine – she hadn't had a drink in months – and the sun, and all of Minnie's friends gathered and mourning, trying to lift each other's spirits.

2

The two men moved off into a cluster of nursing home residents and elderly CLEAR activists, and Livia was left, momentarily, on her own, gazing at the slow-moving group of mostly grey- and white-haired mourners, punctuated here and there by the younger, faster catering staff in their black-and-white uniforms, moving smoothly through the sway of suits and dresses, of Zimmerframes and wheelchairs. She grabbed another glass of wine as a waiter walked by. It must have been her solitariness, she decided later, that attracted the detective, who'd brought his especially winning ways with him to the Wake.

'I've had some trouble catching up with you, Ms Galvin.'

The man stood beside her in a dark suit. He could have been the catering manager Rosanna had hired to oversee the function, but he was dressed far too well. There was a sheen of sweat across his brow. He offered his hand, and she shook it before she could check herself.

'I'm sorry. Have we met?' She withdrew her hand from his hot, crushing grip and stared down into his thin face. His eyes were so dark it was difficult to distinguish iris from pupil, and the effect was mole-like, even rodentine. Livia knew perfectly well who the man was – she'd seen him on the television news

– but the nicety of an introduction wouldn't go astray, especially if, as she suspected, he wanted to talk business in this inappropriate setting.

'Detective Senior-Sergeant Greg Petersen, Homicide. I'm the officer in charge of the investigation into Mrs Babitsky's death. I believe you were in the air when it happened.'

'Yes, returning from Beijing.' If he wasn't going to waste any time on small talk, then neither was she. 'You said suspected murder. Was the post-mortem inconclusive?'

Ignoring her question, he continued with another of his own. 'Did you have any contact with Mrs Babitsky in the days prior to her death?'

Yani's warning to say nothing to anyone suddenly entered her mind, and she wondered if she should apply his mysterious instruction here. 'I couldn't be certain. I often text and phone Minnie regarding art deals and other matters.'

'We're checking her phone records, Ms Galvin.' Somehow, he made the statement sound like an accusation.

'I would hope so, Detective. Once again, was the post-mortem inconclusive?' One thing she'd learned from years of shooting competitions and art auctions was persistence in the face of resistant targets and elusive works of art.

'The post-mortem told us what we already suspected.'

'Which is?'

'Ms Galvin, there are many ways to compromise a case, and disclosing potentially significant information is one of them. Once we've concluded our interviews with persons of interest to us, such as yourself, we'll reassess the situation.'

Persons of interest, such as herself? She took a long draught of her wine to stifle the urge to laugh in his face, but he seemed deadly serious.

'So, you've got nothing, Detective,' she said. Perhaps a counter-provocation would encourage a more definite response, and for a hopeful moment Livia thought she noticed a slight stiffening in his body, or at least in the immaculate suit. It was obvious that he was grinding his teeth; she could see his jaw working away and she didn't think it was chewing gum in there. But he was well-trained and she sensed it.

'I don't like to bring this up at such a sombre event, Ms Galvin.' He paused.

But you will, Livia thought.

'If you'd gunned down two people in River City the way you gunned down the two in Beijing, you'd be answering a lot more questions from people like me. River City isn't as stupefied by the golden glow of Olympic success as Beijing.'

She was surprised by the sudden change in direction, and wondered what he'd learned about the Beijing incident from international contacts. What had Inspector Bao told him? What could he tell him apart from what had actually happened: that she'd acted in self-defence to save herself and Yani, that she'd had no choice, that it was as big a mystery to her as it must be to them?

'What sort of questions would you be asking, Detective? And how do you know what I was asked?'

'You're a crack shot, as your gold medal obviously proves. Those fellows had no chance, a pair of common car-jackers. Surely someone with your talent could have shot to wound rather than kill?'

Petersen's provocations were better than her own, she decided, but she had to resist this one. She realised, all of a sudden, and very clearly, that the men in Beijing were neither carjackers, nor common. It was Petersen's re-telling of Bao's initial assessment that made it sound so false, concocted. She tried to stay calm as an image of one of the dead men's faces appeared in her mind's eye. Change the subject, that was a strategy.

'Mrs Babitsky had many, many friends who cared deeply for her, as you can tell by the people who've come here today, even at such short notice.'

'Unseemly haste, some might say, Ms Galvin.'

'I thought so myself at first, but it's the way Mrs Babitsky wanted it. Her lawyers followed her directions to the letter, and as her Executor, and a close friend, I fully approve. No drawn out delays, or elaborate services.' At least not until the big party, to which this man was definitely not invited. 'A brief, formal farewell in the chapel, the interment, and this gathering. I assume you attended all three, so you must know there are a lot of people counting on you to find the murderer.'

'You're a major beneficiary of Mrs Babitsky's, aren't you, Ms Galvin?'

'What's that got to do with it?'

'You and your sister, Ms Greer Skelloe? Where is she, by the way?'

'I couldn't be certain, Detective. Out of town. Why – do you suspect us of something illicit? You surely couldn't –'

'As major beneficiaries of Mrs Babitsky's considerable estate, from what I can gather so far it stands to reason that such largesse invites inspection from the likes of me. It suggests motive at the very least, the hiring of a third party while you were above ground, as it were, flying home to River City with your gold medal.'

'This is a joke, isn't it?'

'With your family's history? No joke, Ms Galvin. Murderers are more often found among the victims' loved ones than anywhere else. You must appreciate that the police investigate every avenue and your family offers a very wide avenue for investigation.'

Livia felt her blood pressure rise. Was he smiling at her? Was it a smirk? He meant her grandfather and great-grandfather, of course, and probably Con, too. She thought of Con sitting in the chapel earlier, his grey face registering the grief he felt and the effort it had taken him to leave his hospital bed to come and honour Minnie. Somewhere deep inside her, somewhere visceral and hot and unchallenged by reason, she felt a responsibility to defend them, Con and her forefathers, even though she'd barely known Wolfie, her grandfather, and had only read of Gus's exploits in old papers that Con had kept as an archive of the family's move from its illegal exploits to business legitimacy.

'If you're reduced to attacking dead men, Detective, not to mention my sick Uncle, there's no hope for you. If you want to take it up to me, go right ahead, but you'd better be sure of your ground, because I have enough contacts to bury you.'

'What did you say, Ms Galvin? Are you threatening a police officer in the performance of his duty?'

Petersen looked both indignant and pleased with her reaction.

'You may be performing, but you're not doing your duty, Detective. And I meant your career,' Livia said. But she felt her face flush with a combination of fury, embarrassment and confusion. Where had that come from, the wine? Or was she channelling the old boys now? How stupid could she be? Obviously, Minnie's death had overwhelmed her more than she could say. And the killings in Beijing, what kind of delayed effect were they beginning to impose? She put her wine glass, half-empty, on the table. Petersen followed her movements and then took a deep breath and exhaled slowly and deliberately, as though he was ending a meditation exercise.

'Please forgive my intrusion into your gathering, Ms Galvin. I may need to speak with you again. I assume you have no plans to travel in the near future?'

He was as cool as the cucumbers on the Wake's sandwiches. And she felt like a floundering person of interest. She took a deep breath and felt light-headed.

'No plans,' she said, as he handed her his business card and then held out his right hand for her to shake. A gesture of goodwill after what he'd said? She was in no mood for goodwill. She took his hand and gripped it, squeezing until she felt some give and he disengaged first.

'If you think of anything,' he said, his voice tight again with anger, 'I'm only a phone call away. Good morning.'

3

Was it a fishing expedition, Livia wondered, watching the detective walk off towards the car park, rubbing his hand. Is that what Petersen was conducting here, attending the funeral of someone he'd probably never heard of before Tuesday morning? Did he suspect that the murderer might be present? She'd seen movies where the police went to a victim's funeral for that very reason. But was life imitating art, or vice versa? And how could he possibly consider throwing her and Greer into the pool of suspects?

'What did he want?'

The voice was right behind her left ear, and when she turned to face him, it appeared that Karl was trying to shrink himself behind her.

'He's not a very nice person,' Livia said.

'Police aren't supposed to be nice, except to kids, sometimes.'

Karl still appeared rattled and worried. At the funeral service, he'd become visibly upset, barely stifling his sobs. His wife, Sylvia, was away with her friends at a makeover resort that Karl referred to dismissively as the Body and Sell scam. Consequently, he had noone to lean on, and noone to blame, temporarily at least, for his shortcomings. Was that why he'd come to Minnie's late last night, because he was at a loose end without his wife to badger?

'Have you found that gun case yet, Livia? Dad wants to give it to Ron Morris, remember? I'll need it as soon as possible.'

'Yes, you made mention of that already, Karl. Surely there's plenty of time. Noone's going anywhere anytime soon. And just out of interest, how do you know the case is here in River City?'

'You told me the other day at the Bender.'

'No, I didn't. You asked me about it, and I didn't realise at first that you couldn't know unless Minnie told you. For all you knew, it went up in flames in Yani's car.'

'It must have been Minnie, then.'

He was lying, Livia was certain. She was equally certain that he wouldn't explain, for the time being anyway, and she was just as certain that she could try his non-existent patience further. 'Oh, must it?'

'All you need to know is that Dad wants the case to give back to Ron Morris.'

'I've never thought of Uncle Con as the type to recall a gift so he could present it to someone else, especially an inscribed one, with my name on it.'

'Special circumstances, Livia. Don't try to be deliberately difficult. And if Minnie left you any instructions, or anything in her Will that you don't understand, I need to know about it.'

'I'll sort it out, Karl. There's a member of the fourth estate I have to catch up with right now, before he starts harassing anyone.'

Livia walked off in the direction Petersen had taken, sure that Karl would not pursue her after his earlier irritation at the detective's presence. Perhaps he thought Petersen suspected him of foul play as well.

4

'Livia, at last.'

Grady Crabtree, investigative journalist, friend and some-time colleague of the late Eamon Pearse, and, briefly, Livia's high school sweetheart, strode up to her and folded his arms around her. She returned the embrace and they stood that way for a few moments.

'I'm so sorry about your godmother,' he said, stepping back to assess what he saw. 'You've lost weight.'

'Over here,' she said, and they moved to the shade of a tree. The day was mild enough, but direct sunlight took its toll. 'What's happening with Minnie's investigation, Grady?'

'I thought you'd have all the details from Detective Petersen. From where I was standing, it was an animated conversation.'

'He's a prick. He seems to think I hired someone to bump Minnie off while I was flying home from Beijing so I could inherit a third of her estate, the idiot. But tell me, what's he really like?'

Among other investigative interests, Grady did some police reporting for the local rag, The River City News, jokingly referred to as The Guano Gazette. It was the only show in town as far as newspapers were concerned, and literally had no competition, which meant that quality sometimes took a back seat to complacence. Grady was an exception to this rule; his investigations had produced jail time for the rich and fatuous as well as the uniformed and political. He had a number of enemies to go with the journalism awards.

'You'd have to go back to the stud book to get an accurate picture of him, but prick will do for the moment.'

'Stud book? He's got form, then?'

'He may have form himself, that's to be determined. The police are a wilier bunch these days with their business and psychology degrees. But his grandad certainly does have form, or did. Remember Gerry O'Shannan?'

Livia shook her head.

'Sure you do. Gerard Xavier Francis O'Shannan. Former Assistant Commissioner of Police. Did three years in the metal motel for corruption after the Royal Commission. Should have done another 20 in my book.'

'That Gerry O'Shannan. It all becomes clear. Well, his grandson told me buggerall. So I'm relying on you.'

'I'd like an exclusive on the events in Beijing – and not just the story the Olympic suits told you to spread.'

He looked both hopeful and confident, standing there in his charcoal trousers and sky blue dress shirt. She felt touched that he'd made an effort to wear something other than his usual blue jeans and T-shirts and Blundstone boots. He'd had a haircut, too; the ponytail was gone, replaced by a conservative collar-length style. Was there a promotion in the offing?

'Done, but can it wait a few days? I'm in the middle of all this family stuff, and my Uncle Con isn't well. Mum hasn't seen me for ages, and if the gallery was my partner, it'd be suing for separate maintenance.'

'As it happens, I'm a patient man, and a happier one as a result of your response. And in anticipation of your request, I made some enquiries. Petersen's got very little at present. Mrs Babitsky died from heart failure – surprise, surprise, don't we all, in the end – but she had a fractured skull, too. Hit her head on the corner of the office desk when she fell. But did she fall, or was she pushed?' He stopped speaking. 'Would you like to sit down? You look pale.'

Livia took a few deep breaths. She hadn't anticipated the depth of feeling that would arise when she heard what actually happened to Minnie physically on the night she died.

'No, it's all right, Grady. Go on.'

'There are DNA tests, of course, still ongoing. Fingerprints that will cover almost the entire homeless population of New Farm and surrounding suburbs. They've been coming and going for dinner ever since Mrs Babitsky started the renovations and the soup kitchen. Blood at the scene that doesn't match hers, AB negative, rare apparently. And it doesn't match the combination eyewitness and potential suspect they've been interviewing. And her friend, Tibor Restik, appears to have gone missing. Another victim, or the perpetrator?'

'What eyewitness?'

'A homeless guy. He's a Vietnam Veteran, apparently. The usual story: broken marriage, substance abuse, PTSD, job losses, bankruptcy, out on the streets. He's the perfect candidate for a fit-up if they can't find anyone else, and there's extra pressure for a good monthly cleanup rate.'

'So you don't think he's the murderer?'

'Who knows? Sometimes there's no resolution. Lack of evidence, motive, reliable eyewitnesses. Or they could get lucky when the highway patrol pulls someone over for a broken taillight and they find stolen items they can link to Mrs Babitsky.'

'It can be that random?'

'Afraid so. That's why they have cold case files that go back a very long way. You should sit down, Livia.' Grady steered her over to a bench seat facing the grotto devoted to St Jude, one of the nursing home's patrons.

'I'm all right. Thanks, Grady. I appreciate it.'

'Call me and we'll talk about Beijing.' He leaned down and kissed Livia's cheek. 'I've got a deadline.'

5

After Grady left, Livia remained in the grotto, and tried to piece together what she'd learned. For one thing, Tibor was still missing. It was inconceivable to her that he could have hurt Minnie, but what could have prevented him from attending the funeral of a beloved friend? The surprising Inspector Bao from Asiapol was as cool and polite as he'd been in Beijing, but was there more to his visit than Sister Cities' activities? Was that an excuse to chase Yani down, and where was Yani? Why hadn't he contacted her? For all she knew, he was dead in a ditch somewhere in a Beijing hutong.

The detective investigating Minnie's murder had so little to go on, and Grady had confirmed it, that he was reduced to bullying Livia and virtually accusing her of the crime. Karl's only interest was in retrieving the wretched gun case. She was beginning to wish she'd never accepted it as a fancier replacement for the sturdy, plain old case that had seen her through every other shooting competition. And why was Karl lying about how he knew that she'd sent the case back to River City ahead of her return?

'Livia?'

She moved her gaze from St Jude to the man who'd come to sit beside her.

'Paul.' She felt very tired; it must be the sun and the wine and Minnie; the overwhelming Petersen. And then there was Karl.

'Just paying my respects, Livia, to the family. Minnie loved Dan and he loved her – she was like a third grandmother for him – and we'll always have him in common.'

He spoke quickly, and it was as though he was excusing his presence before he'd even begun. She couldn't be bothered playing along, so she sat quietly, waiting for him to continue. But he seemed to get a message from somewhere and was silent for a while. They both contemplated the grotto, St Jude's statue surrounded by climbing ivy. She wondered idly if it was devil's ivy; that seemed about right in this upside-down world where the innocent paid for the crimes of the evil.

'Did you keep any mementoes from the Olympics?'

'Pardon?'

'The Olympics. I heard about the car-jacking.'

'Most of my stuff went up with Yani Lee's car.'

'Because I heard you disposed of your Colombian necklace in Beijing. Before the incident.'

'How did you know about that?'

'Your mother mentioned it when she rang to give me the funeral details. And I'm in touch with the Wu's from time to time with this Sister Cities program. Dr Wu is still quite taken with your generosity. She told me it's the crowning glory of her Colombian collection.'

'It was time, Paul. That was me realising it was time. You disposed of the past by having your affairs and marrying your electorate secretary. I disposed of it by giving away the necklace.' It was her equivalent of the monk's hair-shirt, a constant reminder of her failure as a mother, a priceless penance whose beauty she could never enjoy.

'All right, Livia, I get the message. You know I'm chairing the committee organising this Olympics memorabilia display for the Museum. Another part of the Sister Cities program. Pity you gave your guns away, too.'

'As far away as possible, Paul. I'm retired, and the guns can stay retired in the Northern Hemisphere.'

'I was only half-expecting you to win gold, Livia. Otherwise, I'd have put you on the list earlier.'

'Flatterer.'

'I suppose you have no idea where the gun case is? At least it has that nice graphic design on the lid. That's noteworthy. Did you leave it up there, too, or is there a slight chance we could have it for the exhibition, it's emptiness a metaphorical reflection on absence, if you will.'

'Always on the make, Paul.' She smiled. 'And so philosophical for a pollie. The gun case is here somewhere in River City. Unless Minnie gave it away. It could be anywhere, I suppose. Karl wants it, too. Something to do with Uncle Con.'

'Well, if you see it, remember my request. I'm surprised you'd let it out of your sight. It's a work of art in itself.'

She was about to say that she'd sent it home safely with the flag inside, but thought better of it, knowing that her ex-husband would begin an urging campaign to have her offer it up as well for the Sister Cities spectacular.

'What about your gold medal? Can we borrow it for a few weeks?'

'Why not? There's nothing to be gained by locking it in a drawer.'

'It's all together, isn't it? Case and medal?'

'The case went up with Yani's car, but I was wearing the medal. It's not damaged. Nike meets the East.'

'Whatever. Good. That'll do,' he said, and she half expected him to rub his hands together like Uriah Heep and demand she hand it over there and then.

'Paul, you don't need to keep coming to these things. Today, it's a special occasion, as you say. But we've been apart for a long time now. You don't need to keep putting us on your agenda.'

'It's no trouble. Really.'

And then she saw, in action, exactly why it was no trouble, really. Karl reappeared from behind the grotto and joined them for long enough to hand out fresh drinks and then draw Paul away with him. The two men walked into the old olive grove where they began an earnest discussion. Business of some kind, with a few animated hand gestures, until Inspector Bao arrived, striding quickly across the open paddock before Karl, or Paul, realised he was there. It didn't seem to bother Paul. He grew even more animated to see a representative from River City's sister metropolis in his midst, and she could tell, from years of living with him, that he'd begun a spiel to win over Bao and impress him with his knowledge of Beijing and her many ancient and modern attributes. He would add Bao to his list of thoroughly exploitable foreigners. It wouldn't hurt, either, to enhance his post-politics prospects with any current or potentially future power-broker. Being a member of a minority government tended to encourage politicians in marginal seats to plan ahead with a fastidious attention to detailed smooging.

Karl, by contrast, appeared deflated. He was still and silent, with Paul doing most of the talking, but even from her vantage point of some distance, Livia could see that the eye contact was between Karl and Bao, not Paul and Bao. What was that all about? And why was Karl, self-described corporate mogul, behaving like a backroom boy suddenly thrust into the limelight without his script? Maybe Minnie's death had affected him more than he'd care to admit, especially with his father so unwell, and with Gordon Trembath, their old family advisor, growing frailer by the day, or so Rosanna had insisted. Which reminded Livia that she'd decided, after her conversation with Rosanna, to visit with Sibyl today rather than wait for next week. But it would be prudent to check with Gordon before she put that plan into action. He liked to know who visited and when, and why. He was a naturally suspicious kind of person, a character trait that her Uncle Con had said ensured their business success in many arenas over the decades of the family's association with him.

She turned her attention from the threesome in the grove to the dwindling crowd of mourners and saw the glint of Sibyl's wheelchair spokes before she saw Sibyl with Gordon slowly pushing her along the opposite grotto path.

6

'We're going in now,' Gordon said.

Livia wasn't sure if he was speaking to her or to Sibyl. It didn't matter, she supposed, in the circumstances.

'It's been a big day,' he continued. 'We're going in, yes.' He looked as though he was gradually deflating like a balloon. He had shrunken inside his suit, so that it looked like it belonged to his plumper, taller brother, and he appeared greyer somehow.

Livia tried to make conversation even though Gordon obviously wanted to depart the scene. She explained that she'd moved into Minnie's house, at least temporarily while they decided what to do about the dogs.

'And I've only scanned it quickly,' she added, 'but in her Will, Minnie says she wants me to stay there and preserve its heritage value, and the neighbourhood's access to the park. To uphold CLEAR's ideals, she said.'

'Minnie's death is a tragedy, Livia. It should never have happened.' His voice shook and he took a deep breath, all the while gripping Sibyl's wheelchair with white knuckles.

'What do you mean, Gordon?'

'Look after yourself. Support your family, Livia. They're who matter. The family. Blood is more important than anything, remember that.'

'Actually, I disagree, Gordon. But we can agree to disagree, can't we? You're not blood, but I value your friendship as though you were. The same way I love Sibyl and Minnie. It's loyalty that matters, surely? Whether it's blood or not.' She searched his face for the usual comfort she found there. But today, there was none. He was distracted and distressed, and as for Sibyl, she grew softer around the edges every time Livia saw her. Eventually, she'd simply meld with the environment around her and disappear.

'I'd be happy to take Sibyl back to her room, Gordon. You look a bit tired.'

'I'm so sorry about what happened, sweetheart.'

'We're all sorry, Uncle Gordon.'

'In Beijing as well, Livia. You couldn't have known.'

'We had no choice with those men.'

'I can't understand how they could get it so wrong. Amateurs.'

'Pardon?'

He seemed to be talking to himself and as he became more flushed from the effort, Sibyl seemed to grow paler out in the fresh air of a Spring day.

'I can take Sibyl now, Gordon, if you like. Why don't you have a cup of tea and a bit of a break.'

'Be careful, Livia. Be very careful.'

'Don't worry, Gordon. Sibyl's safe with me.'

But Livia couldn't shake the notion, as she wheeled Sibyl away, that she and Gordon had been talking about two entirely different things.

7

Livia decided to test the theory that nurses knew everything that went on in their institutions. She stopped the first nurse she saw in the foyer of the high-care building and asked her if she knew Sibyl and Gordon Trembath. Instantly proving Livia's theory, she confirmed that she knew them, of course she did, and furthermore, that she was the charge nurse for Sibyl's floor. In addition, she said, she'd been a little worried about Mr Trembath lately.

'He's been so quiet over the last few days, and a bit teary, too. But before that, he'd talk and talk to Mrs Trembath.'

'What about?' Livia asked, trying not to appear too eager.

'Wonderful stories, I don't where he got them from – it was like listening to Sherherazade some days. I'd stop and listen at the door for a bit on my rounds.'

'That must have been pleasant.'

'He reminds me so much of my grandfather, but the stories, they're altogether different. His latest was about sending precious things all over the world because they had a great designer. Sounds like God, but goodness knows what it could mean. I think I missed the first few chapters of that one.'

Livia was beginning to think she'd missed a few things, too, in her grief over Minnie today, and with the wine, but maybe it wasn't too late. 'Did he mention any specific precious things or a person?'

'He often talks about art works to Mrs Trembath. She loves her art, you know. He talks about a lot of people. They sound like Chinese names, and somebody named Karl gets mentioned quite a bit.'

'In relation to an art work?'

'Oh, probably. I suppose I was distracted by the other residents coming and going, dear. They all have their needs, you know. You're listening at the time, and it's very interesting, it truly is, but afterwards, it gets all so mixed up. Did I hear it there, or was it on the news, or was it that new BBC serial on the ABC? And sometimes he speaks in German – well, I think it's German.' The nurse glanced surreptitiously at her watch, pinned to her uniform above her left breast.

'Ah,' said Livia. 'Yes. Sorry to keep you.'

'No trouble at all. It's lovely to see the young ones visiting.' She looked down benignly at Sibyl. 'Isn't it, Mrs Trembath?'

Sibyl glanced up at the nurse and then down at her hands, one folded over the other in her lap, the skin seemingly whiter than chalk. Was that skin shade even possible?

8

Cosmo Dacey helped Livia settle Sibyl into bed. He'd been sitting there when the two women arrived, waiting. Apparently, he spent a lot of time at the Holy Mother and St Jude, helping out, and so did Ruth Gold and Verity Price, and before he disappeared, Tibor Restik was a regular, too.

Sibyl still looked frail and too white, even indoors where the light was more forgiving. But her eyes were bright, and there was clearly vibrant life in the old girl somewhere, even if it only shone for short periods.

'Sibyl doesn't talk much these days,' Cosmo said. 'It's the aphasia.'

'Aphasia?'

'Difficulty conveying what you want to say – you know what it is, but actually saying it, uttering it, is very hard, sometimes impossible. The neurones have to try and build new pathways for speech.'

As though on cue, Sibyl began to whisper. Livia leaned closer but she couldn't make out the words. One sounded like 'Mercedes.' Another could have been 'Makita.' Luxury cars and power tools: what did they have in common?

'Sibyl speaks in an old Bavarian dialect sometimes,' Cosmo said. 'She studied several languages in her earlier years. Maybe a different language can be a way around aphasia.'

'Can you understand what she's saying now?' Livia asked. If Cosmo knew her well enough, he might also be able to decode the aphasic messages. It seemed important to make sure Sibyl knew they were listening.

'Mercedes? Is that it, Sibyl?' Livia asked.

'Mercator?' Cosmo raised his eyebrows at Livia in puzzlement.

'Mercator? What's that?'

'It could be a substitute word for something she can't say – because of the aphasia.'

That made a kind of sense, but Sibyl looked worried that they hadn't really comprehended her. She took her hand away from Livia's.

'Maybe it is 'Mercedes',' Livia suggested, but Cosmo shook his head.

'I don't know,' he admitted. 'Does 'Mercedes' mean something else, in Bavarian? Or is it really 'Mercator,' whatever that is?'

Sibyl nodded again and resumed whispering, but still Livia couldn't get past 'Mercedes' or 'Makita' or 'Mercator,' or even something that sounded like 'Mycaterer.' Perhaps she was simply trying to compliment the caterers at Minnie's Wake.

Eventually, Livia said, 'I don't understand, Sibyl, I'm sorry,' and held her hand again. At that point Sibyl seemed to give up, too, or else she felt too tired to continue. She closed her eyes to both of them.

9

Livia decided to return another day, when Sibyl had recovered whatever strength remained to her after the exhaustion of attending Minnie's funeral. She was fumbling with her car keys, and cursing her aching right elbow, when she almost ran into a figure in a suit.

'I'm so sorry.' She stepped back and took in the familiar face, glad to see it wasn't a frail resident. 'Mr Morris?'

'You're Miss Galvin,' he said. 'Hello. Please accept my condolences on your loss.' He half-inclined his head in a gentlemanly greeting. His manners went well with his dark grey suit, light blue shirt and navy tie, and hardly suggested a desire to have certain people beaten up. He looked like an old-time draper.

'Thank you. How are you?'

'I'm visiting Michael.' His tone implied something close to the opposite of feeling good about life.

'Michael's here?' Livia was shocked. She'd thought the home catered exclusively to the aged, but that other word, 'infirm,' concealed a multitude of conditions apart from being old. 'I was so sorry to hear about his injuries.' She hoped he wouldn't ask how she knew.

'He has some brain damage, they think. There's nerve damage to his hands from where the thugs he used to call friends stomped on him.' But Ron Morris was too consumed with his son's ill-health to interrogate her, and the effort of his revelations seemed to wind him. Livia waited politely as he looked around the grounds. 'There aren't many places that care for younger invalids. Young Mr Galvin helped us with this place.'

Another surprise move by Karl, but even though the grounds were beautifully landscaped, and the old olive grove beckoned from a distance, Ron Morris might as well have been staring at the fires of damnation. His pain was so raw, Livia wanted to reach out and hold him, tell him that somehow, everything would be all right, the way Rosanna used to do when she and Greer were kids, and everything usually did turn out to be okay, with a few notable exceptions. But it wouldn't be okay now for Ron Morris's son, and it was quite possible that it never would be. She realised that Karl and Con were probably right. There was one small thing she could do.

'I've been looking for the gun case, Mr Morris,' she lied, promising herself that the search would begin immediately. 'I didn't know until recently that Michael designed it, but I understand you'd like it back. Don't worry, I'll keep searching until I find it.'

'You mean the case you had for the Olympics?'

'Yes.'

Ron Morris was momentarily confused. 'I appreciate the offer, Miss Galvin, don't get me wrong. But you're mistaken. The last thing his mother and I want to do at the moment is remind Michael of what he's lost. That case is a work of art itself, something Michael may never create again.'

So Karl was lying, but why did he want an empty, obsolete gun case? Was he trying to impress someone with the artwork on the outside, and if so, who?

'I'm afraid I'll have to keep moving, Miss Galvin. Thank you for your kind offer, I know you meant well.' Ron Morris half-nodded at Livia and turned away, obviously anxious to see his boy, perhaps hoping St. Jude had already interceded to effect a miracle cure.

'Of course. And thank you for your sympathies. Give my regards to Michael.'

Livia picked up Ishmael on her way to the car park. She'd noticed that he'd spent most of his time helping Rosanna with the catering and clean-up. He told Livia that Rosanna had said he reminded her of her grandson. Livia let the comment go, but began to wonder what it was about Ishmael that invited comparisons with Dan, and what it was about him that had caused Livia to feel comfortable with him, despite his difficulties with socialising. Maybe he was simply a kind and decent fellow, and that was something that Livia, and her mother, had wished for Dan, watching him as a baby and a toddler: that he would grow up to be a kind and decent fellow.

They drove home past the cemetery where Minnie's remains had been interred only hours earlier. It seemed strange to Livia to feel that she was leaving Minnie behind in the mausoleum way down at the rear of the grounds. She wanted to turn in and pay a visit, but it would have to wait, and Ishmael seemed anxious to get home to the dogs. They were due for a walk, he said, and he couldn't understand why they hadn't been brought to the funeral to say goodbye to Minnie. When she thought about it, neither could Livia.

CHAPTER NINETEEN

River City

Thursday 4 September 2008
Fortescue Street, Spring Hill

As she walked down the shady side of Minnie's house after seeing Ishmael off to his apartment, Livia thought of sleep. The idea of an afternoon nap seemed like a fantasy, but she could make it real today of all days. There'd be time enough later to search for the gun case and satisfy her curiosity. The jetlag that she'd pushed away after the flight from Beijing was catching up with her, which may have been why she didn't register, at first, that the back door was ajar. She walked through the open door into the kitchen and looked beyond to the lounge-room. She returned her gaze to the kitchen, in which every drawer and door, including the oven door, had been jerked open or pulled all the way out and dumped on the floor. She walked over to the fridge door, also open, and pushed it shut. There was a puddle of water on the floor in front of it. She grabbed the paper towel roll, tore off a wad of sheets and placed them on top of the puddle, then stood there for a minute, watching the paper absorb the water and the grey wetness stain through the layers.

She couldn't think what to do next, so she walked through the rest of the house, downstairs and up, confirming that the entire place had been trashed to a greater or lesser degree, even the attic room. Its access door was still open, the ladder hanging down. In Minnie's bedroom, Livia's brain sparked at last and she remembered the study. She took the stairs two at a time and ran over to the open study door, certain it had been closed since the night the CLEAR committee members visited.

She was reluctant to look inside, but forced herself to take a couple of steps through the doorway. The chairs had been knocked over and a lot of the books were on the floor, the drawers from the desk thrown into a toppling heap in the corner and surrounded by their contents which, it appeared, were mostly old bills, pens, pencils and envelopes. The carpet was still at perfect right-angles to the walls, unmoved, and the bucket paperweight remained on the desk top, brown and unobtrusive.

She went back to the lounge-room where she'd dumped her bag, and found the card Detective Petersen had given her at Minnie's Wake. She picked up the phone and began to dial the number, but stopped midway through. Ramifications. What would be the consequence of calling this man, given their conversation earlier? She gently replaced the handset on its cradle. Remembering the basement's contents, she imagined the worst: Petersen arriving with an entire investigative team, ready to tear the house apart to find his killer, or their motive. Would sniffer dogs be able to detect those plants

downstairs beneath the floor? The beagles she'd seen on television news reports at airport drug busts had appeared to be
extremely efficient. Cadaver dogs could sniff bodies metres
below the surface of rivers and lakes. The dogs.

The dogs. Whenever they were absent, Livia had assumed
Ishmael had taken them for a walk, but they'd already been for
their walk this morning, and Ishmael was in his apartment.
Caddie and Tilly should have been asleep on the verandah,
waiting sensibly for Livia's return, and their afternoon treats.

She called out to them from the back door, but there was a
silence about the yard that she knew was the silence of an an-
imal-free zone. Their vibration was nowhere to be felt.
There was no sign of a disturbance on the verandah, the only
place in the house that remained tidy. She unlocked the freezer and lifted the lid to confirm that everything was in place.
The dogs' water bowls were more or less full and there were
still a few biscuits left in their food bowls. Their leashes were
gone – Ishmael could have put them down somewhere else –
but the harnesses still hung from their hooks on the wall near
the freezer key. She called their names again as Ishmael appeared from the side of the house.

'Livia? What's wrong?' He looked around for the dogs and
returned his gaze to her.

'Do you have them?' She knew he didn't, but the question
was automatic.

'I walked them this morning and brought them back here,'
he said, obviously upset. 'I'm sure I closed the gate, and anyway, they don't stray. They're not like that. I'm responsible
for them, Livia. I'm their minder.'

He scanned the yard again, and so did Livia, hoping they'd magically appear from the shed, or from behind a shrubbery, satisfied that the game had been a roaring success.

'Sit here,' she said, sitting down herself on the top step.

Ishmael followed suit and began untying and retying his shoelaces.

'Listen,' she said, after his third re-tie, 'I want you to stay calm – someone's burglarised the house, and I think they must have frightened the dogs off.' Livia didn't want to imagine anything other than that they were scared and took flight, and she needed to relieve Ishmael's guilt. 'We'll grab some water and look for them now. They're probably nearby waiting for us to make an appearance.'

Ishmael leaned forward and rested his head in his hands. 'Who, Livia? Who could it be? Would they hurt the dogs? Why would they hurt them? Have you called the police?'

'Not yet, Ishmael. We'll have to do something about the basement before we call any police in. Come on,' she said, 'remember what Minnie always says: talk doesn't cook rice, and besides, the dogs must be hungry by now.'

She was determined to think positively as they organised themselves into a posse, grabbed bottles of water and one of the dogs' water bowls, and headed into the late afternoon. They walked the nearest blocks, calling out to the dogs, looking for telltale signs of car accidents involving furry animals, describing Caddie and Tilly to anyone they passed in case they'd seen or might see them, cursing themselves for not bringing paper and pen with them to ensure the people they met had their phone numbers. They gave them the name Babitsky, told them it was the only one in the phone book, and implored them to ring if they saw anything resembling two canines on the loose. Finally, Livia returned to Minnie's, grabbed a notebook and pen off the floor in the trashed study, and returned to the street, where she and Ishmael stayed until dark, reluctant to go home, but in the end having no other practical choice. When they returned, Livia called the pound and local veterinary surgeries, enquired, unsuccessfully, about lost dogs found, and left Caddie's and Tilly's descriptions with all of them.

She offered Ishmael a meal, but he said he couldn't eat while the dogs were who knew where in the night. She attempted to reassure him, and herself, by pointing out that they were robust, healthy and large dogs, and could fend for themselves for one night. In fact, they'd probably be out on the verandah in the morning, looking more sheepish than canine. But Ishmael, just holding himself together, didn't buy it, and trudged off to his apartment, leaving Livia to sit in the kitchen and stare at the back door, and wait.

CHAPTER TWENTY

River City

Friday 5 September 2008
Fortescue Street, Spring Hill

1

The red numbers on Minnie's digital bedside clock blinked out 3:11am. In Livia's dream, she and Dan and the dogs were at the beach. They frolicked along the sand and splashed into the shallows, flicking water at each other, happy together. It was a cloudless, cool-not-muggy summer's day on the bay, a tourism marketer's dream.

They found themselves under a shady Moreton Bay fig tree eating fish and chips as the dogs lapped at their water bowls and gnawed on mutton shanks. Livia smiled at Dan and he smiled back at her, coming to sit beside her. They threw handfuls of bread pieces out to the seagulls and Dan placed a banana on a branch of the fig for the possum to collect at her leisure. Mother and son embraced and toasted the day with glasses of Coke.

Livia turned onto her back as Dan and the dogs stood up and walked towards the ocean, now flat and quiet, not a wave in sight. Half-awake, and with the beach fading, she listened for the waves to begin anew. As she did, the dim red light from the clock disappeared from her peripheral vision. Somewhere, a motor hummed down to silence. The power had gone off.

She heard a rolling, rattling noise that sounded as though it was coming from the back yard. She sat up and stood up, instantly tripping over her shoes and stumbling towards the door. She staggered back to the bed and felt for the miniature torch Minnie had thoughtfully left on the bedside table for visitors. It was small but good enough to throw a beam a metre or two. A series of repetitive thumps combined with the rattles and sounded closer to the house. Could it be sleepless Ishmael searching for the dogs with a wheelbarrow in case one was injured, or worse? Ridiculous. A family of drunk scrub turkeys making their way home, via the verandah, to the stand of leopard gums in Minnie's park? What were they carrying with them, luggage?

If it wasn't Ishmael, and it wasn't the dogs, or itinerant turkeys, it wouldn't necessarily be sensible to leave the house. Livia's eyes had adjusted to the blackness, but it was still very dark, the moonlight – such as it was – obscured by cloud cover. She visualised herself earlier in the night locking the front and back doors and sliding their barrel bolts home. All of the windows were security grilled and as far as she knew there were no other points of entry, unless the basement sported an exit for when the police arrived or the plants began burning under overheated lamps, a thought that reminded her again that calling Detective Petersen to attend to whatever was outside, especially when the inside of the house was still in disarray, was out of the question.

She played Minnie's torchlight around the floor, and noticed that her hands, usually rock solid, were shaking slightly. She found her jeans and T-shirt, discarded when she finally left the kitchen, exhausted after hours of willing the dogs to come through the back door. After a moment or two, she realised that the noises downstairs had stopped. But had whoever was making them gone, or had they decided to waylay her when she ventured out? Or were they trying their luck, very quietly, with the back door?

The digital clock flashed on and blinked its automatic reset time: 12:00. She had no idea of the real time, but figured it must be near 3:20. Whoever it was – he, she, they – had efficiently completed their task. She'd bet that they were the ones who'd cut the power and then restored it. And if they were the ones, and it wasn't a coincidental load-shedding exercise by the power authority, it seemed unlikely that they were waiting around to be exposed by the movement-sensitive floodlight trained on the back verandah.

Livia crept downstairs as quietly as creaking steps would allow, kept the house unlit, and, when she reached the kitchen, crawled on her hands and knees to the window near the back door. There was a dark, boxy shape on the verandah that hadn't been there before, but she couldn't tell exactly what it was. She flipped the manual switch for the floodlight and turned on the overhead verandah light as well.

The verandah light was an insect repelling bulb and its colour diffused the floodlight sufficiently to create a sickly yellow effect. A gecko, surprised by the light, dropped onto the freezer lid and scuttled over the side. The boxy shape was a wheelie bin, a big, dark grey council rubbish bin on two wheels. That explained the rolling, rattling sounds, and the thuds as it was pulled up the stairs.

She continued staring at the bin, wishing that Minnie had invested in another floodlight angled towards the yard, which was all but pitch black. She was tempted to phone Ishmael and ask him to come over, but she couldn't be absolutely sure he wouldn't be brained by the vandals who'd dumped the bin. Wait, or go; wait, or go.

'Bugger it,' she whispered, drawing back the barrel bolt, and turning the deadlock.

No knife- or gun-wielding thug swooped to the door and pushed it open, but the fridge motor made her jump as it turned over with the subtlety of a Boeing engine. She gripped the doorknob and slowly turned it, opening the door a crack, and then half a metre and a metre.

Outside it was truly the dead of night; not a snake moved in the grass. She glanced around her and out to the yard, and then focussed on the bin. A rope, or something like it, was dangling down the side that was in shadow. When she moved closer, she realised it wasn't a rope, it was a dog lead. She swallowed a rising sensation of nausea.

In fact, there were two leads, clipped together to form one long lead. One end disappeared beneath the bin's lid and the other dangled down the side and onto the floor. Her fingertips, she suddenly noticed, were cold. What if a vindictive neighbour, some latent psychopath, had decided to take his revenge for Caddie and Tilly barking occasionally without notice and late at night? What if she stood here all night and poor Ishmael arrived and opened the bin instead? What if the dogs were in there, barely alive, and saveable? Time-wasting idiot.

She pulled on the leash and it came up and out easily from beneath the lid. So far so good. She gripped the lid's handle and pulled it up and over as quickly as she could. It banged against the side of the bin. Nothing stirred inside.

'Caddie?' she said to the open bin, her stomach in knots, heart banging along. 'Tilly? Are you there, liebschen?'

Not a sound. She leaned forward and over the opening. A cloth resembling potato sacking was draped over something. There was a wet stain on the sacking: blood? And there was a strange smell, a combination of old garbage and something else, something almost coppery. She closed her eyes, waited, opened them and pulled the sacking off and out like a bad magician.

It was a body, a human body. It was a dead body – no living being possessed quite that quality of stillness. The shirt was torn, the right arm positioned at a strange, sickening angle. Did 'they' break it, or dislocate the shoulder so the body would fit? She moved around to the other side to get a view of the face. His head rested against the side of the bin. She looked down at him and realised she knew him. A terrible feeling overcame her: fear and panic and anger and surging adrenaline. Dread. She felt clammy and hot and cold as she staggered to the stairs and vomited over the baluster into the yard. Her breath came in heaving gasps, as though she'd sprinted the block, and her eyes were watering so that every-thing was blurry. Her fingers and hands burned with heat now; her heart thumped and raced. She fell rather than sat down on the top step, the bin behind her, the black yard ahead. She began to shake as though it was mid-winter in Beijing and she was standing naked on frozen Beihei lake.

She tried to pull herself together, using a technique Greer had taught her: a kind of meditation for want of a better term, nothing like the visualisations she practised before shooting competitions, but it usually achieved the same desired result: calmness. She began to count her breaths, willing them, and her heart, to slow down, and she listened to the night, tuning in to every noise, allowing them to come and go. Her stomach continued to protest its desire for further emptying, and she was glad she hadn't eaten anything since lunch. She heard a car door slam, streets away; there was the hum of an air-conditioner to her right – on such a mild night?

After a while, she knew her legs would hold her up, and she knew she had to look at him again, to be certain.

She grasped the hand-rail and pulled herself up, forced her-self to turn her back on the black yard, and took the two steps to stand beside the bin and view the body again.

It was most certainly Tibor Restik, Deputy Chair of CLEAR, close friend of Minnie Babitsky. Verity had been right to worry, but how had this happened? Who had Tibor made contact with after his television appearance? He may have looked robust and strong, but he was an old man, an easy mark.

'Tibor, what happened?'

In the quiet night her voice was loud and, as she stared in at him, she thought about bringing the bin inside, out of respect, and out of sight. But then what? And how had he been killed? Clearly, it couldn't be an accidental death. In the yellow light, the black eye and the bruise on his lower right jaw looked much worse than they may have been, and suddenly that rationalisation was her hope against hope that he didn't suffer. Didn't suffer? He was murdered, stuffed in a rubbish bin with a dislocated shoulder, or broken arm, or both, bruised and battered – the bloodstain on the potato sacking had come from a long gash on his forehead – and she hoped he didn't suffer?

She wanted to touch Tibor, to somehow reassure him, and herself, that someone cared, someone had found him. She stretched her hand out and into the bin, and rubbed his cheek. His skin was still warm, so perhaps he hadn't been dead for long; they'd brought him right here. The noises she'd heard of the bin rolling through Minnie's yard meant that they'd come through the yard of the vacant house behind; nothing would have appeared amiss at the front of 221 Fortescue. There was noone to see anything at this hour, but there would be soon. She closed the bin lid and turned to go, stepping on the edge of the potato sacking. She picked it up, lifted the lid again and draped it back over Tibor.

'Goodbye,' she said, replacing the lid.

She scanned the area one more time and went back to the kitchen, simultaneously switching the verandah light off and the kitchen light on. She slid the barrel bolt across the door-frame.

She glanced around, taking in once more the handiwork of the people who'd probably killed Tibor, and felt herself sagging. They'd done her a small favour, though, in leaving all the cupboard doors open. It meant she could scan the shelves easily. There, for instance, was Minnie's Chateau Tanunda, her favourite brandy. She picked it off the pantry shelf and scanned the benches for an intact, upright glass.

'Playing ladies at this hour?' She unscrewed the cap and noticed that her hands were still shaking. She took a long swallow, shuddered, coughed, and felt the instant warm comfort of strong liquor. When Greer and Livia were younger, Minnie's remedy for everything from a gravel-rashed knee to period cramps was to dissolve a heaped teaspoon of sugar in a small glass of equal parts brandy and water. It was an acquired taste, but Livia couldn't remember a time when it didn't do the trick, possibly because of the associated loss of brain cells.

2

When the phone rang, it sounded more like an alarm clock. She picked the handset off the wall bracket and held it to her ear, but remained silent. Had they been watching her from a distance, waiting for her to come back inside so they could ring and make threats? But about what?

'Livia? Are you there? I can hear you breathing. Have you been out for a run?'

'Sorry, Greer. I thought you might be someone else.' She pulled out a chair and sat down.

'Who?'

'I don't know. How are you? You wouldn't happen to be anywhere near home, would you?'

'Not far now, but not close enough to bring you breakfast in bed. Is there something I can do for you at a distance?'

'I'm not sure, maybe just talk to me, okay?' Livia generally felt calmer listening to her sister's voice, so like her own. She could sit and think about what to do.

'As a matter of fact, I do need to talk to you, seriously, when I get home.'

'Talk now.'

'This has to be face to face.'

'You're not getting married, are you?' All of a sudden, Livia had a vision of her sister walking down an aisle strewn with the bodies of the people who'd died in the last week or so: the Beijing shooters, Minnie, Tibor, and maybe, just maybe, the dogs. She shook her head. The brandy must be stronger than she'd remembered.

'Married? That ship sailed quite a while ago, dear. Look, I'd rather not say right now. I really need to do this in person.'

'Then let me tell you something.' And she proceeded to explain Tibor's arrival on the verandah, the dogs' disappearance, Karl's odd behaviour, the appearance of Yani's boss from Beijing at Minnie's Wake, and Detective Petersen's accusations. The effort of articulating the strange events, of expressing her fear to her oldest and most trusted friend had the same effect as the breath counting exercise – she felt as though it was out there now with all the other stories in the universe, no longer ripping around inside her and shredding her thoughts. Let the universe help her.

'Is the house secure? What do you think you should do?' Greer asked. 'I mean, is it entirely out of the question to call the police? Some other police station, so Petersen doesn't get involved. Are you all right?'

'I'm all right, I think, and yes, the house is locked up tight. Petersen would get involved, somehow, and he already sees me as a prime suspect. Imagine what he'd make of finding Tibor on the back verandah. And Minnie's marijuana in the basement and the freezer.'

'Hang on. What was that last thing you said?'

'Never mind, Greer. I've got a dead man four metres away from me.' She could hear herself speaking more firmly, but she wasn't winding up again. She sounded calm enough to carry on, for a while.

'Con. He'll fix it. Or rather, he knows people who can. Call him now, Liv.'

'He's in hospital recovering from a severe reaction to the drugs they put him on after the bypass surgery. I can't call him at this time of the night, Greer. I can't call him, period.'

There was silence at the other end of the line, and then, 'Uncle Gordon. I understand he was a great cleaner in his day.'

'What day was that? And how would you know?' Cleaning, as it was called – removing all evidence of a criminal act, usually murder – wasn't something that was spoken of in public places, or by anybody at any time, really. You had to know the right people, and to know the right people in that line of work, you had to belong to the wrong kind of people as far as the law was concerned.

'Never mind what I know. Call him – he's always owed Con more favours than he's ever repaid. I'll get home as soon as I can. Be careful.'

'I can take care of myself, G. Just get here, okay?'

3

Livia knew she had no choice. She wanted to wait and weigh up the options, and she knew that there was no time left for waiting. Technically, she might be regarded as an accessory after the fact of murder, but it was the only decision she could make at four in the morning. She dialled Gordon Trembath's number.

'Karl?'

'No, it's Livia, Uncle Gordon.' There was no response. 'Livia Galvin, Rosanna's daughter. Con's niece. We spoke at Minnie's Wake yesterday.' Further silence.

'I – yes, Livia. Darling. Are you all right? What time is it? Is Karl with you?'

'No, he isn't, Uncle Gordon. I need your help.'

'What's happened? Are you safe? Have they come for it again?'

She glanced at the barrel bolt to be certain it hadn't rusted out in the last five minutes.

'I'm safe, Uncle Gordon. What do you mean? What are they coming for?'

This time there was a longer pause.

'Is there something here at Minnie's I should know about?' It couldn't be the marijuana.

'Never mind, sweetheart. I must have been dreaming.' His voice sounded strained. 'It's this business with poor Minnie. Such a terrible thing when you can't feel safe in your own office without drug addicts attacking you. I thought they might have worked out where Minnie lives, looking for valuables to steal. What's happened, Livia? Is that it? Burglars?'

She described what had happened in the last hour.

'Leave now, Livia. Go to your mother's straight away.'

'I'm not leaving, Uncle Gordon.' What if the dogs came back from their odyssey, only to find they'd been deserted again? And, the thought hit her like a cold blast, if she left Ishamel on his own, would he become a sitting duck? 'They' might be well aware of his friendship with Minnie.

'All right, I can't force you. Someone will be there soon. The darkness at least is our friend, Livia. But I want you to think about leaving – your Uncle Con would have you out of there in five minutes, no argument.'

4

Livia returned the brandy to the pantry, put the kettle on and made toast. She'd learned from experiences in other countries when she was much younger, that the more routine one could make one's extraordinary days, the greater were the odds of surviving such days. Routine was its own form of meditation, and besides, there was no advantage in being blind drunk when the cavalry arrived and already the power of the alcohol had made its presence felt. She hadn't been a serious drinker in years, with her exhausting travelling and training schedules, and the drug tests imposed by Olympic protocols meant that it was easier to ban the lot and adopt an ascetic diet. This morning's brandy, combined with the wine at Minnie's Wake had made her painfully aware that her resistance was low. But it hadn't stopped her from noting the lack of conviction in Gordon's suggestion of burglars and drug addicts. Livia supposed it was possible that Minnie could have retained some valuable art from her dealer's days, and that this knowledge had leaked to someone unscrupulous. But most addicts committed crimes of opportunity. Wouldn't it be too much trouble to track down Minnie's residence, break in and trash the place for something that may or may not exist, whether it was an art work, or a CD player? And they hadn't trashed the CLEAR office, or stolen anything, of value or otherwise, including Professor Wu's bronze horse.

She'd try to set aside time to talk with Gordon about his suspicions. Surely between them, they could work out whether or not there was anything that required special security in Minnie's house? But not now, not today. Today was Tibor Restik's day. What secrets did 'they' think he harboured, the poor old bugger, an ex-circus performer, retired for so many years? But what was he alluding to when he said on television that he knew what 'they' wanted?

A soft tapping at the kitchen door interrupted Livia's speculations. It had been no more than fifteen minutes since she'd spoken with Gordon. She recognised Jerry, the barman from the Bender, when she looked through the window before opening the door.

'Ms Galvin,' he said, cheerfully. 'Good morning.' Jerry was a big man who worked out eight days a week. Livia never worried about her mother's safety as long as he was on duty, which was most of the time.

'Jerry. I didn't know you were in this line of work.'

'Not many people do, Ms Galvin, only the ones who need me,' he said, as two other men Livia had seen at family gatherings, nodded hello. The four of them formed a circle around the wheelie bin and the three men pulled on surgical gloves. Jerry introduced the other two as Bernard and Pete. He lifted the lid and pulled the sacking off Tibor, and the three of them peered into the bin. The kitchen light illuminated the verandah just enough for them to see the work ahead of them.

'This isn't your bin, Ms Galvin?' Bernard asked.

'No, it came with – with Tibor.' But it had to come from somewhere, from someone else's yard, someone who'd report it missing.

'Good,' said Bernard, 'that's good. Thanks.'

He and Pete manoeuvred the bin to the edge of the verandah and carefully rolled it down each step to the ground.

Pete said, 'We'll take it through the back yard.'

Were they really criminals, these men? They had to be if they were interfering with a corpse. Great criminal minds, or some criminal minds, thought alike, then: obviously, there was no need for a front-of-house entry and exit when the service entry was available and unobtrusive. There was something positive in the buy-up of the houses Livia had noticed on Allenby Street when they were looking for the dogs: they were a good cover for removing a murdered man to a more convenient location.

Even as she marvelled at Gordon Trembath's apparent efficiency, and the professionalism of his cleaning crew, she felt the nausea rise again as the roll and rattle of the bin receded. Was she truly an accessory after the fact now?

'We'll be going, Ms Galvin.' Jerry checked the floor to ensure it didn't look like a crime scene.

'Just like that?' Livia asked. The situation had become surreal; a dead man had come and gone from her godmother's verandah in less than an hour.

'Just like that,' Jerry repeated. He picked up the dog leads from where she'd dropped them and placed them on top of the freezer.

'What will happen now, to Tibor. To his body, I mean?' She had to ask.

'It's best that you're in a position of ignorance, Ms Galvin, if you don't mind. What the politicians call plausible deniability.'

'Oh.'

'Is there anything else we can do for you?'

'Um, no. Thank you, Jerry.' If Jerry was now a cleaner, did that mean he'd been a murderer as some kind of pre-requisite apprenticeship? She pushed the thought away.

'No problem, Ms Galvin. I'll see that the boys take care of the package, and then I'll be outside.' He handed her a business card. All that was printed on it was the letter 'J' followed by a mobile phone number. 'Mr Trembath insisted. You won't know I'm there, but I'm in the vicinity. Good morning.' He nodded.

'Good morning, Jerry.'

Livia watched him trot down the stairs, where he turned his head towards the side of the house in some kind of acknowledgement, then continued across the yard. He disappeared into the darkness as another figure rounded the corner of Minnie's house and walked quickly up to the stairs.

'Karl. What are you doing here?'

He took the steps two at a time and joined Livia on the verandah.

'That's a fine greeting, cousin.'

'Are you still worried about security?' she asked. 'If so, there really might be something to worry about now.'

Karl looked at her and then walked into the kitchen. He looked around at the mess. 'If you're too stupid to leave, Jerry's standing watch, at least until daylight. Gordon phoned and asked me to make sure everything went smoothly.'

'Lucky you have such perfect timing, then,' Livia said, trying to quell her natural inclination to bait him.

Karl continued into the lounge-room and sat on the sofa. Livia followed him; there seemed to be little alternative. 'Are you moving into cleaning as a career now? I could really use some help tidying up the house.'

'God you make some ridiculous suggestions. I have more important things to worry about than your problems, Livia.'

'Then why are you here?'

'Have you found your gun case yet. Time's getting away from us, and Con really needs to do a few things like this before the worst happens.'

'Hand it back to Ron Morris, you mean?' She raised her eyebrows. 'As a dying gesture?'

'What else?'

'Karl, quite apart from dying gestures – and I wouldn't be phoning Skelloe Funerals yet – you're here because of my problems, as you quaintly describe them. Here's my problem:

there are people after something that Minnie had in her possession. Look around you. I'm not the best housekeeper in
River City, but I'm not this bad. They thought it was here,
and maybe it still is, but I doubt it. With everything that's
been going on, and the questions people have been asking me,
I'm starting to join the dots. Yani and I are attacked in Beijing,
Minnie's found dead, presumed murdered for no good reason
that anyone can think of, the inspector in charge of the case
turns up at Minnie's funeral; now, Tibor Restik, Minnie's
close friend, is dead. Has it got anything to do with drugs, or
some secret paintings that Minnie kept for herself, or frustrated developers? I'm thinking it goes back to Beijing, and,
somehow, my gun case.' If that wasn't a bait, Livia didn't
know what else to offer.

'Your gun case? I want it – Con wants it for Ron and his
son, that's all.'

'Forget the Ron Morris story – I talked to him yesterday after Minnie's funeral. As far as he's concerned the gun case is
radioactive – he doesn't want anything to do with it, and he
doesn't want it shoved in his son's face to remind him of what
he's probably lost. I don't think Uncle Con knows anything
about this, either. So what are you up to?' She might as well
lay it all out. What could he do but leave in a huff?

'Up to?' Karl clenched and unclenched his fists. When she
made eye contact again, Livia saw that his pupils were pin
pricks, even in the dull ambient lighting of Minnie's
loungeroom. What was he taking, and why? When he spoke
again, he'd turned the volume up and leaned towards her. She
could smell alcohol on his breath.

'You have to find it, Livia, before there's another death on your hands.'

Karl had always had a way with words. He could find just the right means, with his particularly selfish outlook, of placing a linguistic shiv between the fourth and fifth ribs of his targets. Livia suspected he enjoyed watching her obvious shock at his accusation, but she wouldn't wait passively for another twist of the knife.

'Do you remember when Greer and I lived in Israel and Europe? We learned a lot about the way people use others to achieve their ends. In fact, sometimes we helped them out. But we looked for the reasons behind their actions, too, because we were naturally curious people. Surprise, surprise, they usually came down to one or all of three things: profit, power, and passion. Ring any bells with you, Karl, the three P's?'

Karl remained silent but stood up and began walking around the room.

'Because it rings bells for me,' Livia continued. 'Having the house trashed and a dead man turning up on the doorstep focuses the mind, if it doesn't send you mad. And the dogs are missing. Caddie and Tilly – they were gone when I got home from Minnie's funeral yesterday afternoon.'

'Noone would hurt the dogs,' Karl said.

Because Karl had a soft spot for pets, especially dogs, he'd convinced himself that everyone else must feel the same. Noone had been more relieved than him when the decision was taken to spare Lakshmi the tiger's life.

'Karl, you sound so certain, but look around you. Tibor Restik, an old man who never harmed anyone, is dead in a wheelie bin.'

'He could have had a heart attack. What if he met with someone after that TV story and it was all too much for him?' He returned to the sofa and his legs seemed to collapse under him as he sat down.

'Maybe it was, but Minnie was killed in her own office,' Livia said, urgency in her voice. 'The dogs have disappeared – they left their leads hanging out of the bin. What the hell does that mean?'

'They?'

'What?'

'You said 'they'? How do you know there's more than one?'

'I don't. It's a manner of speaking. But I wouldn't be surprised.'

'You need to leave. Go to the gallery, or better still, the Bender. Jerry can't hang around forever. It isn't safe here.'

'You think?' Livia knew he was right, but she also knew that she'd made a promise to Minnie, one she intended to keep. If they'd muscled their way into Minnie's office and killed her, then trashed her house, stole her dogs, and murdered her best friend, what was next? If she left the house now, what would happen to it? Would they torch it, or bomb it to register their anger and frustration? Could it really be the gun case that was so valuable? What had she missed when she'd had it with her twenty-four-seven? The answer was easy: she hadn't been looking for anything in the first place. She got up from the sofa and went to the kitchen, took a bottle of mineral water from the fridge, and brought it back to Karl.

'Here. Have a drink. Relax. You look dehydrated.'

He took a foil strip of pills from his inside coat pocket and pushed two of them out onto the coffee table. He downed the pills with a swig of the mineral water. He looked up then, and saw her watching him.

'Want some?' he offered. 'Calmatives.'

'Prescription?'

'Sylvia's brother.' Karl's brother-in-law was a cosmetic surgeon. Livia had always thought his dispensing of drugs at the drop of a hat to family and friends was irresponsible, but his constant mantra was 'adults can make their own decisions, I simply offer them access.' Of course that depended on how you defined an adult, and at the moment, Livia wondered if she was talking to a grown-up, or to circus Karl, the frightened boy with no idea.

'No thanks.' Minnie's calmative of choice, brandy, was still doing its job, but if what Karl was swallowing was supposed to calm him, it was having entirely the opposite effect.

5

She left Karl and went back to the kitchen and the walk-in pantry. Spending so much time here as a child meant that the house, with and without Minnie's help, had offered up most of its secrets and quirks to Greer and herself, although the basement had eluded her attentions.

She opened the pantry door, took a step in, felt around under the waist-high shelf, pressed a release button, and gently pushed until a section of the pantry's rear wall about a metre wide moved back several centimetres. She slid it to the left to reveal a cavity a little over a metre deep and as high as the kitchen ceiling. She stepped in and fumbled for the light switch. A bare bulb lit up the space to reveal three pistols hanging on the wall in front of her. Beneath the pistols, on a shelf running the length of the cavity, were cleaning kits and ammunition for each weapon. It was the remainder of Ari Babitsky's strange collection of firearms memorabilia. There was a German Luger, a Czechoslovakian .38, and a Smith and Wesson revolver with an inlaid mother-of-pearl handle. The rifles he'd owned had disappeared years ago, but for some reason Minnie had kept these. They were compact and attractive in their own way, and Livia knew that Minnie came in here to clean them twice a year, on Ari's birthday, the 18th of January, and on her own, June 22nd. Comfort comes in many forms, and this had been one of them for Minnie. Livia selected the .38, checked that it was empty of shells and that the safety was on, closed the cavity's door, and the pantry, and took it out to the lounge-room. She placed it on the coffee table in front of the sofa where Karl sat, and sat down beside him.

'Where did you get that?' He drew back from the coffee table and stared at the gun. He looked frightened.

'It isn't a snake, Karl. It won't bite you, and it isn't loaded.' Livia leaned forward and picked the gun up, laying it flat on the palm of her hand. 'If you want one, for protection, I can give you this. You seem very worried. It makes me wonder exactly what the gun case is all about. Are you going to tell me the truth?' She had no intention of giving him any kind of weapon, but the challenge of it might scare something out of him.

'Minnie trades in guns?'

'No. It's mine, Karl.' It wasn't a lie, not really. Half of the estate belonged to her and Greer now. It wouldn't do for Karl to know more than he needed to about Minnie's hiding places. 'The gun case?'

'It must be found. That's all there is to it. You should know where the fuck you sent it. And why did you send it the way you did, anyway – you said you wouldn't let it out of your sight. You said it was a wonderful gesture by the family, for Christ's sake. And you send it off with a stranger as though you couldn't care less about it anymore.'

Karl appeared to be getting more strung out rather than calmer, but his sources were accurate.

'Professor Wu isn't a stranger,' she said, although she had to admit he was right, up to a point. It was a very personalised case, down to the heartfelt inscription from the family. But it was the special graphics that set it apart. They were a mon-tage of stylised miniatures in a high-tech version of *cloisonné*, designed to highlight her eclectic taste in art. There were Pi-casso's *The Sculptor*, Hopper's *Nighthawks*, Sydney Nolan's *Ned Kelly*, Van Gogh's *Bedroom in Arles*, Artemisia Gentileschi's *Judith Slays Holofernes*; and in the centre of the lid, an image of a Chinese dragon to symbolise Livia's year of birth, and the fact that she was a Beijing Olympian. The colour filter the designer used reflected Livia's preference for the dominant spectrum of colours found in Outback landforms: ochres rang-ing from yellows and browns through to reds.

Apart from the dragon, the pieces were taken from the diptych hanging in the foyer of the Mesmer Babitsky Gallery and which Minnie had commissioned for Livia in honour of her assuming its ownership. The inscription, etched on a titanium plate, was a quotation from Shakespeare's *Henry V*:

Imitate the action of the tiger;
Stiffen the sinews, summon up the blood.

The couplet had brought a smile to her face when she first read it, but she couldn't explain why to them, not after they'd gone to so much trouble. Shakespeare was Greer's favourite writer, not hers, but the sentiment was true, and over time, she'd come to love it. It complemented the copy of Rosa Bonheur's *Stalking Tiger* placed above the plate on the case's base. Rosanna had said the tiger reminded her of her family's circus years with the big cats, and especially of Livia's and Greer's bravery when Con had been attacked.

'You're right, Karl, it is mine,' she said, 'and therefore my responsibility. I'll find it, but I want to know why it's so dear to certain individuals. Did they follow it from China? And it's so bloody important that they're killing people, actually killing people, people who couldn't defend themselves.' Defenceless people, as Dan and Eamon had been. 'Nothing's that important, Karl. In fact, I'm having a lot of trouble believing it.'

'I'm not sure if that's the reason, Livia. I think mistakes have been made. They're a bunch of amateurs.'

'Unlike you.' If that wasn't an example of projecting his own inadequacies onto these faceless bastards, then nothing could be. 'Why, Karl? Why did you get involved in this? Don't you have enough money?'

Then she remembered Karl's half-joking but deadly serious catchcry, the one he yelled from the rooftops whenever a corporate deal went his way: 'When too much money just isn't enough.'

'I don't know any more than what I've told you,' he said.

'And the day I believe that, Karl, is the day I accept that Dan's and Eamon's murders were just another example of God's will.'

'The gun case – it's extremely valuable, art-wise.'

He stared at her but couldn't hold her gaze, turning away to face the lightening sky outside beyond the kitchen door. They sat in silence for a while, Karl sipping his mineral water, Livia encouraging thoughts of a smiling Dan Clifford on his first day at school rather than the lifeless little body outside the farmhouse in Colombia. That was the empty shell, the form he'd abandoned – she hoped he'd taken his soul off to a much better dimension, one where guns and thieves and greedy power-trippers like Karl didn't, and couldn't, exist.

Karl sat up and glanced around the room.

'Look, the truth of it is, I'm helping Gordon with one of his projects. All he's told me is that the gun case is valuable, it was supposed to be part of a deal that seems to have gone belly up.'

'Because I sent it back to Australia?'

'It's beginning to look that way. His opposite number, the project manager in China, may have changed direction, or had it changed for him. And Gordon – he hasn't been the best lately.'

The car-jackers, Livia thought, they must have been after the gun case, but she'd already sent it home days before the ambush on the way to the airport. She'd put Minnie in mortal danger by sending it home to her with the flag and the bronze horse. Professor Wu and his wife could have been in danger, too, at least for a short time. And Yani, did he suspect that they were targets – one of the men had called out his name, she was certain of that. But who was this project manager who may have hired the assassins?

'When you speak to Gordon,' she said, 'and I hope it's very soon, ask him to contact his opposite number. Or maybe Gordon can delegate that task to you. Maybe you'll know who to contact. Tell him to give me some time to find the case.'

'Livia, I don't know if Gordon can guarantee that, and anyway, if noone else has found it, where do you think you're going to look?' He blinked several times, as though waking up at last. 'Who do you think you are, anyway, ordering me around? Ordering Gordon to do things.'

'It's a process of elimination. And I'm sure it isn't here, if that's what you're wondering. I've got skin in the game, Karl. I shot two men to death, Minnie's been murdered, Tibor's been killed. The dogs are missing, probably dead, too.'

'I have to go,' he said, standing. He was unsteady on his feet. 'Do what you can, but whatever you do, don't go near the police. And remember, I'm a target, too, Livia. So is Gordon, and come to that, Sibyl. You can't trust anyone, so don't go babbling to anybody.'

He walked through the door to the kitchen and then turned back to her.

'You should keep searching the neighborhood for the dogs. I'm sure they'll turn up.'

'Wait. What do you –' But he was gone. She heard his footsteps on the path beside the house, and then nothing. He'd hit the grass running. He knew far more than he was telling her, but there was a chance he might be able to warn off whoever 'they' were, for a while.

Could it be possible that the designs on the lid and the base were more than simply copies of her gallery work? Maybe it was the materials they were made from – some kind of new precious stone, or did they disguise something more valuable underneath. Even small paintings and sketches, if they were by the right artist, could be worth the combined GDP of several third world countries. Unless, of course, it was entirely a cover, and she'd been inadvertently carrying drugs in some new sniffer dog resistant, X-ray repellent form, disguised as art, or suspended within it.

6

Who knew who was the next target? She couldn't be certain of anything at the moment and Karl was right about not trusting anyone. She phoned Elias to make sure that Con was always protected by either Elias himself or another of his trusted colleagues. She phoned Rosanna and asked her if Minnie had mentioned receiving the gun case and bronze horse.

'She was sending it over here,' Rosanna said, and paused. 'But I never saw it. She must have forgotten.'

'Why was she sending it to you, Mum?'

'She said that even though you'd told her to do what she liked with it, she knew that one day you'd decide you wanted to keep it as a memento, so she said she'd send it to me to put away for you.'

'And you're sure you didn't get it?'

'Livia, I may be in my seventh decade, but I'm not demented yet. And do you know what time it is?'

'It's really important, Mum.'

'And I'm really sure, Livia. It isn't here. But –'

'But?'

'Minnie said she'd ask Tibor to drop it over here on one of his rounds. He might still have it and he's just forgotten. You should ask him.'

'Thanks, Mum. Good advice.'

'What's this all about, Livia? Don't you have enough to worry about being Minnie's Executor?'

'Yes, I do. I'll talk to you later, Mum. I love you. Bye Bye.'

Had Tibor tried to give the case to someone – the right someone or the wrong someone? – and they'd killed him for his trouble? They'd contacted him after he'd appeared on TV and rashly given out his mobile number. Why not simply take the case from him, if he had it with him, and let him go, or go to where it was, and secure it? Because either way, then there would be a living grenade on the loose who could dob the lot of them in at any time. They were thieves, big time thieves. Drugs seemed unlikely – in such a small space, they'd have to be the most powerful chemicals ever created, and the most miniaturized, to be worth a fortune, worth this much effort. In the world Livia knew, if they were collectors, or representing collectors, they would be focussed and determined. She believed that Karl had very little idea of how ruthless certain sections of the art world could be, especially in the darker regions of indeterminate provenance and the competition for rarities. That was where the sun very rarely shone. But murder?

7

One of the wonderful things about living in River City was its position on the 27th parallel, where the weather was described in advertising by the state tourism authorities as 'beautiful one day, perfect the next.' They had tried to extend the description to the whole state, but River City and its immediate surroundings were where temperate demonstrated its true meaning. The winters were never too cold, the summers were never too hot, if you allowed for a little global warming and the odd heatwave. But even the heatwaves seemed to joke around: a day or two here, a day or two off, another day of discomfort, but not for long. Once the sea breeze blew in from the bay at dusk, it was all over bar the shouting. A little more sweat, a cooling julep on the verandah, a slow-twirling overhead fan in the bedroom, the wooden louvres creaking back into place, and the evening was all yours.

As Livia walked out to the car where Jerry sat, she looked up at the brightening sky and took in a few deep breaths of morning. The air was crisp and cool, and the hint of summer, even so early in spring, was apparent. The humidity was rising and the wintry bite had gone from the post-dawn chill. There were crows and magpies and peewees circling or sitting in trees and on powerlines. Livia knew they were waiting to be fed; it was one of Minnie's morning rituals, her own dawn offering to the sun god, every day.

'Jerry,' she said, as he wound down his window, 'I'm fine now, thanks. I have a friend arriving shortly and he'll be able to stay a while. Uncle Con won't mind if you leave.'

'Are you sure, Ms Galvin?'

Jerry was in two minds, Livia could tell. Gordon Trembath had employed him on this job, but Con Galvin was Livia's blood kin. Did invoking the latter trump the former?

'Yes. In fact, I'll be happy to know that you're at the Bender, looking out for my mother. Like you always do.' She smiled and he smiled: the trump card had been played.

As she turned to cross the street, she saw Ishmael walking out of his building's foyer, bottles of water in each hand, and intercepted him on the footpath. She looked over at Jerry, about to take off, and pointed at Ishmael with a nod. Jerry gave her the thumbs-up and took off.

'I have a good feeling, Ishmael,' she told her neighbour.

'Why, Livia?' Ishmael looked as anxious as he had the day before.

'That's a good question. I don't know exactly why, but I've decided that we have only one choice: to look on the bright side.' And she'd been heartened by Karl's secrecy, of all things. She hoped she wasn't reading too much into his last cryptic remark about being sure the dogs would turn up, and somewhere in the neighbourhood as well. She hoped it wasn't the drugs talking, or delusional optimism.

'The bright side. Yes, Livia, that's better than the dark side.'

They began to walk the block, and the ones beyond Fortescue, hoping to run into a jogger or walker who'd seen something. They walked until the sun had burnt their skin pink. They were in Allenby Street, behind Fortescue, and Livia was about to suggest a walk down to the café for morning tea, when a black and white cat sprinted out of the yard of one of the vacant houses.

'That was Arachne,' Ishmael said. 'You know, Minnie's stray.' He moved ahead of Livia.

A round of muffled barking came from somewhere up ahead.

'Did you hear that?'

Ishmael nodded and they quickened their pace.

'Funny name for a cat,' Livia said, listening for more barks.

'From myths and legends. Minnie loves myths and legends.' Ishmael was smiling for the first time in days.

'I think I'm going to love that cat.' As they entered the yard, they heard whimpering. Livia undid the latch on the gates to the car park under the house.

'Caddie, Tilly,' she yelled into the gloom.

'Over there.'

Ishmael ran to the rear corner where the laundry tubs were, and where Caddie and Tilly were wagging their tails and crying. Livia joined him and they dropped to their knees and embraced the dogs. It was cool and airy under the house, but apparently there was no water for them. Livia found a plastic ice-cream container in one of the tubs, rinsed it out, and filled it up. Both of them drank copiously, nosing each other around and away and back again, but despite their excitement at seeing Livia and Ishmael, and their desire to drink, they seemed sluggish.

'Tilly's hurt,' Ishmael said as he watched her wobble away from the water and towards the front of the house. He caught up with her and checked the paw she was favouring. 'I can't see anything in it, but it could be bruising, or muscular.'

'The vet, Ishmael,' Livia said, patting Caddie as she sat down again and put her head on her paws. 'We're going now.'

She wanted to get them away from their prison and out to the light. Whoever had locked them up here may have had no intention of freeing them; on the other hand, they hadn't done away with them either. Perhaps the dognapper knew they'd be found, sooner or later, but why hadn't the dogs been barking to be freed? Their silence until now was strange. With her limited veterinary knowledge, Livia supposed it could have been dehydration and fear combined, but it seemed more like they were too groggy to manage anything other than a bark at Arachne and a whimper at their arrival. Drugs? Could they have been sedated?

'I'm sure they'll be okay, Ishmael,' Livia said, registering his panicked look. 'Don't worry, they're not going to die.'

'I'll bring the car around,' he said, walking quickly towards the open gate, 'so Tilly doesn't have to walk.'

8

'Severe bruising, and from what you've told me about their behaviour, they'll be getting over some kind of sedation. It'll work its way out of their systems.' Tanya gazed at the X-ray of Tilly's paw, which appeared normal in every respect. She rubbed Tilly's head as she sat on the examination table, and ran her hand over her back in long, smooth motions, as though she was brushing her fur. Ishmael appeared mesmerised by the action. 'What happened, Livia? I heard you were taking care of Minnie's place.'

The Skelloe hotline was vast and efficient. Tanya Skelloe, the family's vet, ran the City and West Bend Veterinary Clinic. She was one of Rosanna's many nieces and nephews, and the first and only person Livia had thought of when Tilly needed help.

'It's a long story,' Livia said, which was true, but there were demons in the details. She decided that the sanitised version was appropriate for the time being, and probably forever. 'Someone burglarised the house and got rid of the dogs while they did it. Ishmael and I – ' Livia turned to smile at Ishmael, who, after initial greetings had remained silent throughout their visit, ' we searched and searched yesterday, and this morning, there they were under a house in the next street.'

'Are you all right? That must have been horrible.'

'Yes,' Livia replied, 'as a matter of fact it sucked.' She realised that a certain weariness, combined with a revitalising anger, had entered her being.

'I recommend a few days of rest and recreation,' Tanya said, 'and plenty of fluids.' She touched Livia's arm. 'For the dogs as well.'

Ishmael reattached their leads before they left the examination room. As they said their farewells to Tanya, Livia's mobile phone rang, and 10CC's Art for Art's Sake filled the reception room. It was Trina's joke; she knew very well that Livia had never had the slightest interest in making millions out of the gallery. All she wanted was a quiet and peaceful life in a dimly lit environment, where the 'furniture' graced the walls and the rooms were largely empty.

'Trina, how are you?'

'Livia, do you remember Doug Courtney?' Trina asked.

The group continued walking out to the car park, where Ishmael put the dogs into their harnesses in the rear of his station wagon.

'Doug from the lane?'

Livia tried to remember Doug Courtney, and a slightly blurred figure in a duffel coat and faded blue jeans emerged, a man with greying, curly hair, and, she heard Minnie's voice, 'kind eyes.' Minnie tended to make decisions about people by the level of kindness she perceived in their eyes. The fact that Doug had light brown eyes, like her late husband, Ari, didn't hurt his kindness rating either.

'Yes, Doug from the lane,' Trina confirmed.

'Doug, the Vietnam veteran. One of Minnie's dinner pals.' Minnie and CLEAR were among several groups who tried to keep the homeless of River City from being constantly hungry by providing hot, nourishing meals at least once a day.

'The very one. Are you busy?'

'We've just finished being busy with the dogs,' Livia said. 'What do you need? Is Doug all right?'

'I think you should come to the gallery, now. I don't trust the phone lines, Livia, okay.'

'Sure – Ishmael's taking me and the girls back to Minnie's place. I'll pick up my car there and see you soon. Are you safe, Trina?'

'Yes, perfectly. Don't be long.'

CHAPTER TWENTY-ONE

River City

Friday 5 September 2008
Holy Mother and St Jude Retreat
Sibyl Trembath's Room

' **A** nother death, liebschen. How many more?'
Gordon Trembath sat at his wife's bedside. He
leaned forward, then back in his chair, and forward again. He
stood, tried to smile at Sibyl, and walked to the window, with
its view of distant airport runways and the bay beyond. Another perfect day in a paradise of dark blue ocean and bright
blue sky.

'I should never have agreed to this project with Karl.' He
turned his back on the window and faced his partner and best
friend. 'So many times I've told Con to change his plans. Karl
shouldn't inherit – give him money, I said, give him something to do, but don't give him the reins. And I thought this
would get him out of our hair at last. He's a Jonah, that boy.'

Sibyl gazed up at Gordon, who'd begun to sweat despite the mild day. His body had been playing nasty games with him lately. Sweating in cool weather, shaking in warm sunshine, and the headaches – he had to do something about them, as soon as this mess was cleared up.

'You know, darling, I thought it was the ideal balance of profit and power, an illusion of control, anyway. Karl was to be the southern hemisphere connection, but it wouldn't impact on Con, not really. Now Karl says the gun case was delivered to Minerva from China. Livia sent it home early for some reason.'

Gordon returned to his seat near Sibyl. His hand trembled as he grasped her fingers and gently rubbed the fragile skin.

'I don't know if you understand, you're the only one I can talk to. It was too late, too late to stop it. Someone came after the case. Bing Lee says he doesn't have a clue what's going on, and now he's worried about Yani. I'm so sorry about Minnie, my sweetheart.'

He began to cry, silent spasms rocking his body as tears rolled over his cheeks. He tried to check himself, aware of the effect his reaction could have on Sibyl's delicate condition.

'I must talk to Livia,' he said, sniffling, 'before anyone else dies. The girl's in grave danger.'

He rummaged in his coat pocket for a handkerchief, which fell to the floor as he pulled it out. He leaned down to retrieve it, but gasped in pain before he could reach it, and clutched at the mattress to push himself back into the chair. The effort seemed to take all his strength and breath. His face was burning with heat, and something else.

'God, Sibyl,' he said, 'it hurts.' He held his hand to his head and opened his mouth to speak again, but slumped forward before he could utter a word, pinning Sibyl's arm underneath his shoulder.

Sibyl, reaching and reaching with her free arm, managed to curl two fingers around the emergency button on the opposite side of the bed. She pressed and kept pressing, knowing the racket at the nurses station would annoy the duty sister. Soon, she heard footsteps approaching down the corridor. The nurse bustled into the room, ready to chastise Sibyl for her insistence.

'Mr Trembath?' she said, quickly realising that Mr Trembath wasn't able to answer, or to move. His face was powdery grey, his mouth slack and open, the tissue around his lips a cyanotic blue. His eyes were wide open and filled with fear. The nurse felt for a carotid pulse in his neck as she grabbed the emergency button from Sibyl's hand. She held the button down until the others came running.

CHAPTER TWENTY-TWO

River City

Friday 5 September 2008
Mesmer Babitsky Gallery
Arthur Street, New Farm

1

He looked different in clean, new clothes. Minnie had always been able to bypass the street odour, the frequent intoxication, and see through the worn out gear, 'the totally buggered look,' as she called it. She always saw the man he'd been, before the horrors of Vietnam got to him so badly that he couldn't function properly anymore.

Minnie was the only one he'd talk to about his tours, and his capture and torture. Livia had only ever heard one of the many stories of his time as a combat soldier, and that one had been enough, even tidied up and retold by Minnie. He'd been with the rest of his patrol when they'd come under attack by Viet Cong guerillas. The fighting was intense, and close up, some of them in hand-to-hand battles. Then a series of mortars landed around them; deafening, shrapnel-throwing mortars, one of which must have hit a landmine, he realised later, because the even bigger, double-bunger explosion stopped them in their tracks. Everyone tried to scramble to safer parts; a Huey, one of the big Iroquois helicopters, flew into the melee to evacuate what was left of the patrol. They managed to drag three wounded into the chopper, but had to leave the dead for later. Once they'd dusted off, and he'd begun to breathe more deeply, he realised one of the medics was staring at him. He followed the man's gaze down the front of his fatigues – strafed with blood and what was most likely human tissue – and to his thigh, where, staring up at him, was a bloodshot and bloody eyeball trailing its optic nerve along his leg. The medic leaned over and scooped the whole thing into his hand, peeled his surgical glove off and over the top of it, tied the top of the glove into a knot, and flung it out of the open chopper door. 'That belongs to someone,' he remembered telling the medic, wondering if it was someone he'd killed. The medic replied, simply, 'Not anymore, mate,' and returned to working on his patient.

'Doug, how are you feeling?' Livia asked.

They sat in the gallery's private office, where Trina had made Doug a pot of tea and set out sandwiches and fruitcake for him. She'd found one of Livia's CDs of big band swing music and it was playing quietly through the gallery's speaker system. The music was one of Minnie's touches, a means of helping some of her street friends, like Doug Courtney, to calm down after bad experiences.

'Not bad,' he replied, picking up his cup in both shaking hands.

Livia wanted to reach out and help him, but restrained herself and instead concentrated on the cup as it moved from table to lips and back again. Not a drop spilled, so far.

'Trina told me you remembered the gallery's number.'

'From the sign – out the front. I see it every day.'

'Of course.' It pays to advertise, Livia thought.

'They couldn't keep me locked up forever, and without a lawyer. I'm not a terrorist.'

'And I posted the bail,' Trina said, sounding pleased with herself.

'But how did you end up being arrested, anyway?' Livia felt uneasy about the situation, and wondered where the three of them were headed now that he was here, and, she assumed, legally their responsibility as a result of posting bail.

Doug explained, between bites of sandwich and shaky sips of tea, that he'd been caught up in a police roundup on the morning of Minnie's death. They were after anyone in the area, and after the previous evening's activities, he'd been distraught and exhausted and he couldn't think of anywhere else to go except the lane, his lane, hoping that somehow, Minnie wasn't dead. They'd found him, eventually, beneath a pile of cardboard boxes that served as shelter in fine weather. He'd told the interrogators nothing, he said, not even the Chinese one. What did they expect, after what he'd been through in Vietnam?

'A Chinese detective? Do you mean a visitor from China, or a local.'

'No – a visitor, so he said.'

Inspector Bao was getting around very efficiently in River City, using his official status, no doubt, impressing Detective Petersen and company.

'So what can you tell us that you didn't tell the police? Do you know what happened to Minnie?'

Doug had been late for dinner, the dinner Minnie put on every night that she could manage, and he'd turned up after everyone else had gone back to their digs. Minnie was painting when he arrived, but she took him out the back to the kitchen and set him up with a meal. At some point, he heard a knock at the front door and Minnie talking with someone, then the door opening. At first, he ignored the conversation, but when he heard the words 'drug smuggling,' he listened more carefully.

'It sounded so – well, incongruous, someone saying 'drug smuggling' to Minnie.' Doug stopped and looked at Livia, then Trina, for confirmation that they, too, thought it was out of context. Trina nodded her assent.

'What kind of drug smuggling?' Livia asked, feeling a strange sensation making its way along her spine.

'Diplomatic – diplomatic cover, they said.'

'There were two people?'

Doug hadn't heard them identify themselves at the door through the steel mesh grille when they arrived. But he was certain they must be officials of some kind, or else she would never have opened the door to let them in.

'They said that Minnie could have received a package in the last few days from China, and that they were certain it contained illegal drugs. They wanted to search the place, then and there. And they wanted her to take them to Fortescue

Street to search there as well, if the package wasn't in the CLEAR office.' Doug had a little laugh then, and broke a piece of fruit cake into smaller pieces. Was he a delicate eater because he'd been starved by his captors in Vietnam, and every crumb counted? Or was it a simple nervous tic?

'Did they describe the package?' Trina asked. 'Was it there, in the office?'

'Minnie told them she wouldn't be able to help them. She said her lawyer should be present, and surely they needed a warrant. She asked them why they'd come visiting so late at night and she said they could wait until the next day.'

'What did they think of that?' Livia asked.

'They didn't get time to think. Minnie called out to me and I came into the room – as soon as they realised I'd been there all the time, they said they'd come back in the morning, and they left.'

Livia waited while Doug took a bite from a slice of cake.

'That's it? So they didn't hurt Minnie?'

'No,' Doug said. 'Not them.'

Doug had left at Minnie's urging, he explained, not long after the two men departed. She assured Doug that she'd go to her car with the security guard, but that Doug should get himself settled for the evening. She made her usual offer of a bed for the night at her place, and, as usual, Doug politely declined. For years, he'd lived outdoors; ironically, it was the only place where he felt safe – from what, he couldn't exactly say, but it had to do with feeling trapped, observed, vulnerable to attack. Open space, even in a lane in a big city, was preferable to a closed-in bedroom in a house, small or large. The last few days of being locked up had almost, almost, but not quite, broken him. He'd clung to his friendship with Minnie, he said, knowing she was with him, supporting him, from somewhere in the universe.

'Minnie gave me $20 – to buy something with a bit of quality. I went around to the bottleshop – it's a few blocks away. I'd had a few sips by the time I got back, and I went straight over to the lane to sort out my bed. People steal your bed if they get a chance.'

By bed, Livia assumed Doug meant cardboard boxes beneath him as a mattress, and over him as a blanket. It didn't seem like much of a life to her, and yet he went on. Did he hope for a new start one day? That his family would magically return to him? She wanted to tell him that it wouldn't happen, that he'd have to pick himself up and decide he wanted to live, as she had done years before. It was the only option, unless you planned to check out permanently.

'I nodded off, I suppose. I usually do. I don't know how long it was, but this sharp rapping noise woke me. I was pretty cranky – good booze to go to sleep with, and then this hoodlum wakes me up.'

'What hoodlum?' Trina asked. 'There are still hoodlums?'

'Not a hoodlum – no, he wasn't, not really. He was well-dressed, in a suit, like the two earlier ones. In fact, right then, I thought he could have been one of them. Minnie let him in, so I – I thought I'd better go over there and help out.' Doug lowered his eyes, and concentrated on lifting crumbs from his plate with his thumb and forefinger.

'And did you?' Livia watched him closely, searching for evidence of deception.

'I was a bit staggery by then, but I got up and by the time I got across the road, they sounded like they were arguing. I couldn't make out the words, but Minnie, she grabbed his arm all of a sudden – they were standing close to each other – and tried to steer him towards the door. But he pulled away from her and I don't know, maybe she hurt his arm – a little lady like that – but he pushed her back into the desk. It all happened in two blinks, Livia. Minnie picked up her Big Ben paperweight and – you know, it's bronze, it's heavy.'

'Yes, I bought it for her,' Livia said. Would this man have been so angry if she hadn't had such an effective weapon to hand? The answer didn't matter now.

'Well, Minnie, she almost seemed to lose control of it, like it was too heavy for her.' He paused for a moment. 'Unless it was me, I'd had a few, and I suppose I could have thought I saw something that wasn't there.'

'Just describe what you saw, Doug, that's all right,' Livia said. 'You're our only witness, mate, you're it.'

'It was like a roundhouse punch, the Big Ben in her hand, swinging at him from way back. And it got him on the side of his head. He backhanded her and she stumbled, her foot went in the paint tray, and she fell. I'm sure she hit her head on the side of the desk – she kind of bounced away from it.'

He stopped. The effort of recreating such a horrible scene was taking its toll.

'Take your time, Doug,' Livia said, 'there's plenty of time. Have another cuppa.' She was glad of a moment to regather.

Doug sniffed and nodded. Livia poured him another cup of tea, leaving room at the top for shaking without spilling to occur.

'Livia,' Trina said, her voice low, 'with all of this, I'm sorry, I meant to tell you that Rosanna phoned. She said your Uncle Con has turned the corner, he's much better. He can have visitors – oh, and she arrived just as I was leaving to pick Doug up from the watch-house. You have a visitor, upstairs.' Trina smiled. 'Some good news in all this bad stuff – Greer's here.'

'Greer? At last. That is good news, and Uncle Con, too,' Livia said, still watching Doug. She wondered if a man so damaged would be able to concoct a story like the one he was telling. Was he capable of killing Minnie, if he'd been drunk and aggressive, and thought she was annoying him, or if he couldn't get money out of her, as usual? He'd been trained to kill in the Army, but that was different, wasn't it? It didn't exactly translate. And he'd never seemed the violent or aggressive type to her, nor, obviously, did Trina think anything but the best of him. She hadn't hesitated when he rang, putting up her own money.

'She's asleep – jetlag.'

'I'll go up later. Doug?' Livia spoke softly, not wanting to spook him.

'This fellow rushed over to her, as though he couldn't believe it. I saw him with his fingers on her neck.'

'Trying to find a pulse?' Livia offered.

'Yeah, that'll be it, like he was shocked he'd done it. I started yelling then, and I came through the door. He took one look at me, knocked me aside, and ran out. He wasn't that big, but solid. I went to Minnie, but she wouldn't wake up – I didn't know what else to do, so I called triple 0. I got some paint on me – my shirt, and shoes – left footprints for the cops to follow, I suppose.'

Livia hesitated with her next question. She knew it was a long shot.

'Have you seen any of these men before, Doug? In the gallery, maybe? Or around the streets?' And were the three of them connected with each other? Was the third man the boss, coming in after the other two had messed things up?

'They're not locals, Livia,' Doug said, the disappointment apparent in his tone. 'I almost wish they were.'

'Do you recall what they looked like?'

'Average – dark hair, short back and sides, one had lighter skin than the other, about my height, six feet. They were Ken dolls, Livia.'

'There was nothing remarkable about them, then. No outstanding features. What about the third fellow, the last one?'

'He wasn't exactly the same, not exactly. There was a hint of something else there. Maybe he was shorter and stockier, too. But not by much. His skin, it was hard to tell – all of them were covered up in suits. They were like catalogue models.'

Livia realised that Doug was frustrated at his own lack of ability to force some distinguishing characteristic out of what amounted essentially to three crash test dummies: nameless mysteries, like the Beijing assassins.

'Maybe you'll remember something else, down the track,' Livia suggested.

'Maybe, but if I ever saw any of them again, I'd know them, for sure.' Doug looked up and found Livia's eyes. 'They might be Ken dolls, but if you find them, I'll be your witness. I'll know them.'

'Thanks, Doug.' It dawned on Livia that Doug himself could be in danger. He'd seen the three men, and they must all have registered his appearance, and smell. They'd know he was likely to be a street person, and knowing that, would they have the hide to return and take care of the one eyewitness to their visits and crimes? They couldn't know that he hadn't said a word to the police.

'Doug, are you doing anything at the moment? Do you need to be anywhere?' Livia asked.

'Be anywhere?' He smiled a genuine smile for the first time that day. 'Only at my springtime residence, across the road.'

'Can you stand being here for a while? I won't be too long. Maybe Trina can give you a tour of the latest acquisitions.' Livia moved to the office door and looked out to the gallery.

'Sure. Come on, Doug, bring your tea with you.'

Trina, Livia knew, was anxious to make Doug's bail time worthwhile for him, as though she was responsible for his entertainment as well preventing him from going to ground where the police couldn't find him. But avoiding the police might be the most important move he could make for the next few days, or at least while Inspector Bao was in town. Who knew what his connections were, or why he was really in River City?

2

Greer thought her sister's face had aged, but only a little, and it was probably the lack of sleep, the jetlag, the grief. Why couldn't all women age backwards, why was it only nuns who possessed such a gift? It must have something to do with the simplicity of their lives, those wardrobes full of the same dresses, the absence of disbelief. Did they still wear habits?

'What are you thinking?' Livia asked, coming to sit on the side of the bed.

'How are you?' Greer pushed herself up onto her elbows and smiled at the one person she knew would never let her down, not deliberately anyway. Would Livia be disappointed to learn of her activities in South America? Would she feel let down by her sister's take on what she termed ethical revenge?

'As they say in the comedies, love, fine, under the circumstances.'

She pronounced love and under as 'loov' and 'oonder,' two British variations. Was this the only time the two of them truly relaxed, when they were together, and alone? Greer gestured for her twin to come closer, and, when she did, she grabbed her in a bear hug. They held each other for a while, feeling the samenesses, and the differences, thinking of themselves 'kicking each other stupid,' as Rosanna had described it, before they were born. They spent most of their time apart – in different hemispheres – as adults: trying to make up for that earlier lack of space, was how Livia explained it.

'How are you, pet?' Livia asked.

'I'm here, and that's good, but I'm sorry I missed the funeral. And I wish I'd been around to help you with that other matter.'

'I don't even know where Tibor is now,' Livia said. 'I don't know if I want to know, either, the poor bastard.'

Livia explained Karl's visit after Tibor's body had been taken away, his insistence that the gun case had to be found, his lies about why he wanted it, and the conversation Doug Courtney overheard between Minnie and two of the men who visited her the night she died. Greer tried to make sense of it, but pieces were missing. The trail led back to Beijing, that seemed plain enough, whether it was drugs or art.

'I had a phone call – from Yani,' Greer said, testing the waters.

'Yani? Isn't he calling the wrong twin? I've been worried about him since he disappeared in Beijing. Did he tell you anything about that?'

Livia sounded angry, which seemed about right.

'He was worried about phone traces. He knows mine isn't traceable – pre-paid. He said he's sorry about everything.'

'That narrows it down.'

'He wouldn't be more specific – believe me, Liv, I quizzed him – he was very upset.'

Livia raised her eyebrows.

'He sounded genuine.' As genuine as Greer could tell over a crackling line with limited time from someone who sounded as paranoid as he did.

'Where did he go when he left the hospital?'

'He didn't say, Liv, but he said he'd be in touch again.'

'Did he leave a number for me to call him on?'

'You know the answer to that one.'

Livia stood up and went to the kitchen. The space at the top of the gallery was entirely open plan, a loft of sorts, with exposed beams and wooden floors. Except for the *en suite*, you could see any so-called room from any other room.

'If I don't keep moving, I'll fall asleep,' Livia said. 'I think I've been set up as a mule. Why are they killing people? Minnie. Tibor. Even if Minnie's death was unintended, so are most murders. Are they going after Yani now, too? God, I don't know.'

'But you do know. You're not naïve. You know what collectors can be like, if that's what this is about.'

'It's about the gun case, something in the gun case, or the case itself. And they've got Karl scared witless.'

'He had wits to begin with? Sorry, old habits.' Greer couldn't resist one more opportunity to take Karl down, even in his absence.

'I'm sure he knew where the dogs were,' Livia said. 'He's terrified, he's unstable, and he's downing what he calls 'calmatives' by the handful.'

'If he has something to do with whatever's gone missing, and Gordon's too doddery to follow through, logic says Karl might be next in line.' Greer couldn't have cared less about her cousin, but she cared a great deal about her uncle Con. She cared that he should recover fully from his latest health scare and if he got wind of this debacle, it could cause a relapse. And she cared about Gordon, too; his well-being affected Sibyl, whose well-being, in turn, used to affect Minnie. There were dominoes everywhere, waiting to rock and fall.

'These people who saw Doug next door with Minnie – if they find out his name and where to locate him, he could end up like poor Tibor. I don't want that to happen.'

'Why don't I take him down to Avalon with me?' Greer suggested. 'He'll still be inside state borders, only his whereabouts will be on a need-to-know basis.' And going to Avalon, as she'd planned to do, anyway, would allow her to think through a few things. There was no point in springing the story of the murderous Miguel Rodriguez and his gang on her sister right now.

'You know,' Livia said, 'this business is beginning to remind me of how it felt on some of those operations we did with cousin Levi in France. The last ones. We were all sucked in, even Levi, because of one corrupt link in the chain, and it started to spread.'

Greer nodded. 'Only we knew more than this; even if it wasn't much, it was more than this, wasn't it?'

'We knew nothing, Greer. We were played like glove puppets.' Livia gazed at her sister across the room. 'I still dream about Jacques sometimes,' she said. 'Don't tell anyone.'

Greer didn't like to contemplate the darkness that had begun to envelope them on the sunny French Riviera when they'd realised that what had begun as a series of missions to preserve and promote human rights, freedom of speech and association, in short, democracy, had itself become the plaything of a kind of malicious star chamber. But back then, they'd finally learned enough to save themselves and their colleagues. And here in River City, the solar vibration was surely too strong and antiseptic to allow such twisted power to take over.

'Who would I tell?' Greer saw Jacques Foucault in her mind's eye, splashing around in the shallows with them on a deserted little beach south of Perpignan. They'd befriended him in Marseilles, two students from Lyons, Marie-Claire Claudel and Simone Blanc. They wined and dined and invited the son of one of Europe's richest arms dealers on a road trip around the Gulf of Lions, as they'd been instructed. He'd wanted to go the other way, to Cannes, and Nice, and Monte Carlo. But they'd insisted, begged him, and, twenty-something gentleman that he was, he'd agreed with good humour. Despite his father's predilection for selling landmines and all manner of missiles and offensive weaponry to rogue states and dictators hostile to the notion of allowing their citizens peaceful, quiet lives, Jacques was actually a decent young man. He had no desire to follow his father into the business, and Livia and Greer had followed their instructions to the letter, certain that their superiors knew this, too, and wanted the boy out of the way while they took care of the man.

'Can you, you know, speed it up a little bit,' Livia said, 'I need to know Doug's away and safe.'

'Sure, Liv.'

Livia was beginning to sound brittle. Greer knew she hated to be reminded of the old days, before Paul, before Dan, when they led different lives, but how was it possible to forget them?

She went to the bathroom and closed the door. She stared at herself in the mirror. Would she do the same today? She'd killed someone less than a week ago, a repugnant disgrace to his species, certainly, but she'd known exactly what she was doing. Two decades ago and more, she'd been clueless. There they were, a trio of happy children, frolicking on the sand, the sea almost motionless. A cabin cruiser motored along the shoreline, turning seawards and dropping anchor a couple of hundred metres out, directly in front of their beach. Eventually, the women shook out their towels and sat down beneath umbrellas, waiting for Jacques to join them for their picnic lunch. He walked up from the hard sand and then scuffed soft sand ahead of him, smiling at them all the while, his white skin turning pink under the Meditteranean sun. He was no beach bunny, this boy, and he looked to Greer as though he couldn't believe his luck. He'd reached their spot and picked up his towel when suddenly, he moaned and fell to his knees, and then forward onto his chest and face. A cluster of four red circles had appeared on his upper back, and his blonde hair wasn't only wet with sea water. It turned red and redder as Greer and Livia stared at it, and then at each other. Cousin Levi appeared from nowhere, white-faced, and told them to follow him down the beach where they boarded a skiff and almost levitated out to the cruiser. Levi seemed to know only one speed: as fast as the outboard would take them. Greer would still swear that he held his breath the entire way. When they boarded the cruiser, he lurched to the side and vomited. The cruiser captain took them across the gulf to Marseilles, where they immediately boarded the train for Paris. From Paris, they flew to London, and then to Glasgow, where they spent the remainder of their summer break working as bar attendants in jobs arranged for them by the star chamber. They never saw the shooter, and Greer still wondered if it was possible that Levi, without forewarning, had been initiated that day. She wondered whether, had he refused, they would still be alive today to do just that: wonder.

None of them spoke about Jacques Foucault for months, and months more went by, until Livia declared her intention to return to the great southern land. But Greer, Greer knew she'd stay, at least for a while. It was the first major separation of their lives together. After Livia flew out, she and Levi made contact with certain people that Levi knew in Tel Aviv, and they contacted others, until, finally, they found the one person who could find them a more satisfactory line of work, and she was still with him today. So, which, she asked her mirror image, had been worse: the sweet and fatal ignorance of youth, or the angry and fatal knowledge of maturity? She turned from the mirror, undressed, and stepped into the shower. Some days, she found it difficult to maintain eye contact with herself.

3

Trina volunteered to drive them to Avalon, the therapeutic resort Livia and Greer had established in the south coast hinterland with their Grandfather Wolfie's trust funds. Doug agreed readily to the plan once Greer assured him that he could camp in the surrounding rainforest if he chose. There were tents available, or private huts for special guests such as himself, where his privacy would be respected. The only intruders he could expect would be the likes of possums, koalas and snakes, wallabies and scrub turkeys. Even more appealing.

'I was going to be travelling north anyway,' he said, by way of explanation. 'Some of my old mates live in the bush year round.'

Livia saw them off and returned to the gallery office. She was about to tap in the security code for the building when the phone rang.

'We didn't know who else to call,' said Delia Clarke, the charge nurse at the Holy Mother and St Jude. 'Cosmo Dacey suggested you.'

'How can I help you?' Livia was anxious to return to Minnie's house and check on Ishmael and the dogs. The reminders of lives past, and lives destroyed, had made her even jumpier. She needed the calming knowledge that the rest of her loved ones were okay.

'As I say, we didn't know who else to call. Mrs Babitsky's gone, and Mr Trembath – you know Mr Gordon Trembath?'

'Yes, of course. What is it, is Sibyl all right?'

'Mrs Trembath's fine. It's Mr Trembath – I'm afraid he's passed away, Ms Galvin.'

'What? When?'

'We've had the body removed by Skelloe Funerals, as per the home's contract. But we need to tell them who to contact to make the arrangements. Are you the right person, Ms Galvin?'

'Wait. Gordon Trembath's dead.' Livia's hands had begun to shake. She sat down behind her desk. 'You're sure it's him?' As she spoke, she knew the question was ridiculous. Who else would it be?

'He died in his wife's room, Ms Galvin. It looks like a heart attack, or a stroke. Can you help us with the arrangements?'

She had to get a grip. 'You need to call Con Galvin at the Terrace Hospital. They'll put you through to his room. You'll probably get his personal assistant, Elias. He and Con will know what to do about the arrangements. Mr Trembath is a close personal friend.'

'Thank you, Ms Galvin. My condolences on your loss. There's something else that we'd really appreciate if you could spare the time. I wonder if you could come out and see Mrs Trembath, Sibyl. It would be good for her to see a familiar face, and I remember meeting you when you visited her yesterday.'

Livia waited. She looked around the office, Minnie's office, really; Livia hadn't changed much since she took over. Sibyl could be in a lot of pain, depending on just how much awareness remained to her.

'I'll be there shortly.' She went to the security panel on the wall behind the desk and tapped in the code. She wondered, as she walked to the car park, whether or not Karl had managed to speak to Gordon, and decided that she didn't like the answer that came to her.

CHAPTER TWENTY-THREE

River City
Friday 5 September 2008
Holy Mother and St Jude Retreat
Sibyl Trembath's Room

Some members of the CLEAR committee were busy on several floors when Livia arrived at the Holy Mother. She saw Cosmo Dacey strolling around the indoor terrarium with a watering can and a frown on his face. He didn't notice Livia walk by to the elevator. When she stepped out on Sibyl's floor, she came face to face with Verity Price, who was removing crucifixes and paintings from the hallway walls. A two-tiered chrome trolley, which looked like a double-layered shopping trolley, was almost full of wall furniture and parked behind her.

'Verity,' Livia said, 'this is a surprise.'

'Livia.' Verity was equally surprised.

'Was that Cosmo Dacey I saw downstairs in the terrarium?'

'Cosmo? Yes, that would be right,' she said, calculating something in her mind. 'Ruth should be on the second floor by now. Have you heard from Tibor?'

'Tibor.' The image of his gashed head and bruised face reprised its role in Livia's mind and turned her stomach again.

'Tibor Restik,' Verity said patiently, 'our friend. It's so out of character for him to be away for so long.'

'Yes, I'm sorry, Verity.' Livia tried to cough the nausea and Tibor's image away. 'Yes, I know who you mean.' She was tempted to say something to Verity – but what could she say? She had a right to know her friend was dead, didn't she? 'Did Tibor have any relatives?'

'Tibor was an only child, to my knowledge, a child of the circus, or rather, many circuses. He was always a bit of a loner, actually. Minnie and the three of us here today were probably his closest friends. His only friends.'

'I'm sorry about Tibor,' Livia said, which was about as much as she could say by way of expressing her grief.

'Well, we're sorry about Mr Trembath. He was a close family friend of the Galvins.'

'Yes. Were you here when it happened?'

'No, but I wish we had been. Who knows, maybe we could have helped.'

'I think it was very quick. Do you need any help here?' Livia asked. She rationalised her reluctance to proceed down the hall to Sibyl's room by deciding that she needed to ensure a certain level of calmness in herself before she visited. Noone could tell exactly how aware Sibyl was from day to day, and Livia had no desire to send yet another family friend to glory.

'No, Livia, but thank you for offering. We're taking things down so the professional cleaners can do all the walls. Cleanliness is next to you know what, not that they need any extra help here with their godliness. We clean up the pictures, and crucifixes, a couple of times a year, or whenever they're looking tired.'

Livia looked at the pictures Verity had already stashed in the trolley. Many of them were prints of the saints (especially St Jude) together with the Holy Mother and Jesus. There was one of the Pope, and there were what she assumed were original artworks along spiritual themes. These, Verity explained in answer to her query, had been done by current and former residents, and donated to the home as mementoes of their time here. So it wasn't entirely a God's waiting room: some of the residents returned to the world, recovered and rearing to go, or at least pushing their Zimmerframes and wheelchairs as fast as their reinvigorated arms and legs would take them. Not that it wasn't a good place to be, if it was the kind of place you needed to be: whatever floor you were on you could smell biscuits cooking. The terrarium was a central feature of the building, funnelling plant, grass and cooking smells up to every floor. Everything had a lightness about it, from the springy walks of the nursing staff to the bright colours in the art.

'See,' Verity said, holding one of the paintings, 'when we do our cleaning and restoration work, we note it here.'

On the bottom right-hand corner of the frame was a small square of something like pine or balsa wood. Etched into it were the words, 'Restored by Cosmo Dacey,' and beneath that in very tiny print, a date.

'What are those lines?' Livia asked, pointing at a series of horizontal and 45-degree angled lines etched along a vertical axis. Some of them went right through the vertical and others jutted out from one side or the other.

'That's a bar code,' Verity said, hesitating. 'It's a special bar code, I don't know much about it. It has something to do with where the painting or print came from, who donated it, or the original painter.'

There were more original paintings than prints on Sibyl's floor. The printed and original Sacred Heart of Jesus spilled blood from every corridor, it seemed, if Livia's memory of previous visits was accurate. And how long the Holy Mother could hold her welcoming arms out like that in so many repetitions beggared belief. Here she was in a grotto setting similar to the grotto near the car park outside; there she was at Fatima, or Lourdes. Here she stood on the world, snakes trodden underfoot; there she was with the baby Jesus; and over there mourning the crucified Jesus dead in her arms.

'It would be impolite to refuse a donor,' Verity said, reading Livia's mind.

Since she could no longer usefully stall, Livia wished Verity well and went to Sibyl's room, where she found the old lady asleep. She stood at the window and admired the view of the bay until she heard whispering from the bed. She moved quickly around to the visitors' chair and said a quiet hello as Sibyl woke, hoping that she wouldn't be upset at seeing someone in her room unannounced.

Ruth Gold stopped by with a pot of tea. After she'd said hello and goodbye, offering her condolences for Gordon in between, and after Sibyl had silently sipped at her tea, Livia wondered what to say. She couldn't be certain if Sibyl had registered Gordon's name when Ruth said it; she seemed not to react. Did she realise that he was dead?

'I'm so sorry, my dear Sibyl. How are you?' Livia spoke softly, not wanting to inflict even the slightest further harshness upon the poor woman. Her right hand was bandaged, and bruising from the heavy weight of Gordon's upper body falling and resting upon it had already become apparent. She had to be in pain. Had they given her something for it?

She stared at Livia, absently rubbing her bandaged hand. Finally, she whispered something, but it was inaudible. Would Livia understand it anyway, given Sibyl's reliance on the Bavarian dialect Cosmo had mentioned to cope with her aphasia?

'I'm sorry, I didn't hear you.' Livia leaned forward.

'Eine Frau? Die Frau. Du, Liebling.'

Livia understood that much of ordinary German: 'A woman. The Woman. You, Darling.'

Sibyl looked puzzled, her face animated with interest. Had she decided to practise her grammar on visitors? Was this how she coped with being unable to literally speak her mind, to say precisely what she was thinking?

'Ja,' Livia replied in her minimalist German. 'Je suis – I mean – ja, eine frau.' She couldn't remember the German for 'I am a woman.' 'Eine Frau,' she said again. 'And? Und?' She cursed her youthful immersion in French rather than the language of her ancestors.

'Eine Frau, und Mercator,' she said. 'Und Menschen.'

Sibyl smiled, uttering the words again as though they were an answer in themselves. Mercator featured again, and this time with a woman, presumably Livia herself, and men. Which men?

'Aber.' Sibyl stopped and took a breath. 'Die schönen Kunste. Überall.'

'I only know some numbers, Sibyl, a few words. Hund, Katze, Zimmer. Sprechen Sie Englisch?'

Sibyl had a laugh to herself, patted Livia's hand, and appeared to drift off. Livia waited. Half an hour passed.

'Gordon,' Sibyl said, seeming to wake from a fugue state. Her eyes moistened, and she raised her bandaged hand and stared at it. 'Unvermeidlich.' She let her hand drop back to the sheet, and stared ahead of her at something Livia couldn't see.

'I'm sorry, Sibyl, I don't understand,' Livia said. 'I'm so sorry about Gordon. Je suis désolé.' If Sibyl had once understood, and perhaps still did understand five languages, luck might be with them, and French could be one of them, if English had deserted her. But Livia was getting sick of that phrase.

Eventually, Sibyl slept. Livia kissed her forehead before leaving, and took the stairs down to the car park. The exercise would either freshen her thoughts, or make her appreciate the elevator more next time.

Sitting in the car, she called the Terrace Hospital. Elias answered the call put through to Con's room, and confirmed that things were underway for Gordon's funeral.

'Is he well enough to talk to me, Elias?' Livia asked.

'Livia, how are you? How is Sibyl?' Con's voice sounded strong and deep; he was almost back to his old self.

'I'm so glad you sound better,' she said. 'I'm not sure how much Sibyl understands. She was speaking in German. Do you understand any of it, Uncle C?'

'Not so you'd notice, my dear.'

'Do you feel up to a – well, a bit of mystery?'

'Of course. Always.'

'Do you recall anything about a project Gordon was working on?'

'The Beijing project. I'm looking into it, and I'm hoping against hope that Minnie's death, and Tibor's, are unrelated to it.'

'You know about Tibor?'

'Unfortunately, yes. I used to use the same cleaning outfit as Gordon. Elias is trying to arrange a meeting with Karl, but we're having trouble tracking him down. Have you seen him? He's not answering his mobile.'

'I'm afraid not.' She hesitated to mention Karl's frazzled, early morning visit, and then the moment was gone.

'I need to remind him that the death watch is over,' Con said, his voice hardening, 'and I'm still in charge.'

She had to choose her words carefully. Whatever trouble Karl was in, he didn't need to be spooked too far away from the family because of Con's rising wrath.

'There was another man at the funeral, from China. He was with the detective investigating Minnie's murder, Detective Petersen. An Inspector Bao – Petersen said he works with a group called Asiapol. When I saw him after the shootings, he was with the Beijing and Olympic security police. He's Yani Lee's boss.'

'Bing Lee's son? The Yani you and Greer travelled around China with. Gordon was a close friend of Lee senior. They collaborated on a number of projects before Gordon chose semi-retirement.'

'Perhaps they've collaborated more recently, Uncle C.'

'I'll follow it up. Livia?'

'Yes, Uncle C?'

'I know you're more than capable, but I can provide security for you – just say the word.'

'Thank you. I'll know it when I need to say the word. Rest up and get better.'

She put the phone on the seat beside her and drove out of the grounds. Karl couldn't wait to take over from Con, and Con knew it. In the meantime, Karl wanted to build his empire as quickly as possible and no matter how dirty things might get. But this time, he may have taken too many steps in the wrong direction, and he no longer had Gordon to lean on or to clean things up for him. Karl saw himself as a player, and he was, up to a point, but sometimes the old saying applied perfectly to him: he was a man among boys, and a boy among men.

CHAPTER TWENTY-FOUR

River City
Friday 5 September 2008
St Jude's Road Cemetery

1

Livia couldn't say exactly what encouraged her to turn left into the cemetery where Minnie's mausoleum, her so-called 'bed' of rest was located. Perhaps she simply needed a quiet, safe place to think. It was a growing town of the dead with narrow, macadam streets and lanes, and a socio-economically diverse mix of ordinary six-feet-under graves, above-ground vaults, and mausoleums. Some of the latter incorporated chapels, and were elaborately embellished inside and out, the names of the dead calligraphically etched into imported Italian marble facades and highlighted in gold or silver leaf.

Minnie had decided on a mausoleum, with chapel, when Livia and Greer were children – though she'd purchased it much later – not for reasons of religion or ego, she'd said, but because she liked the story of King Mausolus of Caria in the Persian empire, and his wife, Artemisia, who was also his sister. Some of the ancients, she explained to those children present whose faces had registered horror, liked to keep the wealth and power literally in the family. After Mausolus' death, Artemisia fulfilled his dream of building him a great resting place, and Greek architects and sculptors set to work, creating what later became known as the Mausoleum at Halicarnassus, so beautiful and impressive a structure that Antipater of Sidon declared it one of the Seven Wonders of the Ancient World. Minnie never missed an opportunity to give extra tutorials in ancient history, or any other subject that took her fancy whenever there were children around to be educated about the apparent craziness, or creativity of other eras. No less crazy or creative, Minnie had emphasised, than our own time.

Mausoleum Row, as Livia instantly dubbed it, was quiet, as quiet, she thought – feeling slightly hysterical after her interlanguage encounter with poor Sibyl – as a few thousand graves could get on a Friday afternoon, when the thoughts of the living were more focussed on weekends of fun and laughter. Most of the pruning and polishing probably happened on Sundays after Mass. Minnie's home was down the back in one of the relatively newer sections, but it wasn't in view from the top of the hill. She took the scenic route down through the older part of town, a narrow street with family and community mausoleums on either side. It was like driving through a suburban development, only the houses were smaller and there wasn't a millimetre of wasted space. No room here to display the acquisitions of a lifetime. The money was in the quality of the masons' work. The ostentation, or refined sophistication in some cases, was accompanied in many instances by photographs of the deceased in their primes. If one were to judge by these pictures alone, there had been an awful lot of unaccountably premature deaths of very healthy-looking, robust people.

Although the family mausoleums with narrow walk-in chapels surrounded by individual beds of rest, were more imposing, aloof even, Livia preferred the community mausoleums. They accommodated unrelated people, single interments rather than a whole family's members in one, rather like a block of apartments. Everyone got on, but they kept to themselves and chose their own methods of decorating their front doors. The body corporate was the body deceased.

She neared the turn at the bottom of the hill that would take her to Minnie, and pulled off to the side of the road, parking in the shade of the Boccabenna family's tidy structure. She could stay out of the sun by following the shady side of the lane to her left. It seemed more appropriate to approach on foot, more respectful, perhaps, and in keeping with the general absence of noise. Besides, this must be one of the few town-like places in the world where there was no need to fear that the neighbour's kid would steal your vehicle for a joyride. She left the keys in the ignition and the windows wound down – luxury.

She was reading the names and inspecting the photos on the mausoleums she passed when, from the corner of her eye, she caught a movement up ahead. When she focussed on the spot, it looked as though someone was slumped on the ground. One of the gardeners? Even on mild days along the 27th parallel, the sun could take its toll. She realised she had no water in the car, and continued along the path at a trot. When she reached the prone figure, she saw that they were near Minnie's chapel. She knelt down beside him and tried to understand his groaning and mumbling. He tried to push himself up onto his hands and knees.

'Wait,' she said, 'wait and I'll help you.'

Then she felt a terrible pain in the back of her head. The world disappeared into bright lights followed by blackness.

2

It was so nice to be resting at last, although Ishmael could have chosen less gritty sheets, and a much softer pillow. There was a smell: kind of earthy, a bit moist and cool, like a basement, and coppery, too. The smells of the night in the inner city – she'd have to get used to them now that she was chatelaine of Minnie's house. Somehow, she thought, she'd wrapped herself in the gritty sheet. She struggled to free her arms and pull it away from her face. It was hard to see in the darkness, and then she opened her eyes at last. It was still dark. She turned to check the clock on the bedside table and felt a sharp pain cut through her head as she simultaneously realised there was no clock. She felt the spot on the back of her head from where the pain was shooting at regular intervals, and detected a lump and wet, matted hair: blood? She tried to sit up and was instantly dizzy. She lay down very slowly and waited until the dizziness, and the resulting nausea, subsided. She thought she might be concussed; it wasn't a happy thought.

When she stretched out her arms on either side of her, she encountered walls. Keeping her head as still as she could, she placed her hands flat against the walls and felt along the rough surfaces. It was a narrow room all right, and none too comfortable. It was when she reached up and hit the ceiling that the panic set in. She remembered driving into the cemetery, and down the street towards Minnie's chapel. And then – then, it was fuzzy. But if she was in the cemetery still, she could only be in one place: a bed of rest, a rectangular concrete box just big enough to house a coffin.

Listen for the sounds around you, she told herself as she began to shake. Concentrate.

'Count your breaths.' Her voice sounded close, far too close bouncing back from the low ceiling. She began to hyperventilate. She was buried.

'Count, count. Eins, zwei, trois, quatre, cinq, sechs, sieben, acht, neuf, zehn, elf, douze, thirteen.' Where were those numbers when she was talking to Sibyl?

Wait. She lifted her head again, more slowly this time, propped herself up on her elbows, and swivelled slowly, slowly, to look behind her. Darkness. She turned carefully and looked down between her feet. Think. Would they have wasted time mixing cement to brick her in? Who were 'they?' Something must be blocking the way out and it was at the foot of the bed. Eventually, she saw that there were tiny pinpricks of light at the edges of the rectangular opening. She shimmied down to the point where her feet could touch the end of the bed and gave whatever covered the entrance a tentative push. It was rock solid. And then it happened. Something ran over her face. She yelled and smacked herself in the nose with her shaking hand, wanting and not wanting to touch whatever it was, fearing she would vomit at any second. Her nose throbbed in time with the back of her head, and her eyes watered. Her fear of the spiders, the beetles, the goannas here in bed with her, on top of the panic, sent a huge power surge through her body; she began to kick with the fury of not an Olympic shooter but a 50-metre swimming champion. Something gave, and something more. Light began to fill the cavity, and eventually the entire opening was clear. She wriggled out into the open air and fell a metre or so to the ground.

Momentarily winded, she lay on her back staring up at the impossibly blue sky. This resting place had certain advantages over the previous one, and she had a momentary insight into Doug Courtney's need to live and sleep in the outdoors. Thinking of Doug, she found enough strength to stagger to her feet, looking back at the concrete bed from which she'd escaped, and then ahead of her where a child about seven or eight years old stood, mouth agape, eyes goggling. She knew she must look dishevelled, that she was coated in a layer of what was probably grey concrete dust mixed with streaks of blood, but did she look as bad as the child's expression seemed to indicate? Yes, she probably did.

The boy continued staring, dressed in his Friday best, and Livia suddenly realised what he must have witnessed in the last couple of minutes. She took one, two, three tentative, reassuring steps towards him, more to test her ability to walk than anything else. He took a few more steps back. Okay, she thought, the residual hysteria of being buried alive kicking in. There was nothing like a Sunday School lesson a couple of days early.

'You better believe Jesus rose from the dead, mate,' she said, smiling at him.

He stared, horrified, mute, for a second longer, then turned and ran off along Minnie's lane. Livia followed him at a more sedate pace, wiping her mouth, thinking she was going towards the car when she was moving in the opposite direction. She reached an intersection, glanced to the left, and was surprised to see the gardener sitting in the doorway of a chapel, his head in his hands, elbows on his knees.

'Hello,' Livia said, not wanting to surprise him.

'Zise Gottenye,' he said, looking up. 'Sweet God. You're alive.'

Despite the assault, his light brown eyes were sharp with intelligence and presence of mind. They made a good pair, Livia decided, with the complementary streaks of blood on their faces and the dust and abrasions of struggle and burial all over them.

She joined the man on the Gandolfinis' porch and they sat together in the shade. A cool breeze blew down the lane.

'This is the life, eh,' Livia suggested by way of conversation.

There was something familiar about him. He was in his sixties and tallish, with a solid build, salt and pepper grey curly hair, an olive complexion, like a million other grandfathers, but maybe fitter than most, if he survived being viciously assaulted.

He said, 'I got one of them with these.'

He picked up a pair of red-handled secaturs and handed them to Livia. 'The other one hit me again – that was it. But something scared them off.'

There was blood on the blades of the secaturs. Livia placed them carefully on the concrete apron. He picked them up and slid them into a pocket on the pants leg of his overalls. There was nothing like carrying forensic evidence around with you to promote a conviction, although something told Livia this particular crime would never see the light of a court-room.

'A funeral procession, I think,' she said. That was where the well-dressed boy must have come from. They wouldn't have wanted anyone to see their handiwork in action, whoever they were, attacking a woman and an elderly man. They'd interred her with a bin full of bricks, gone to work on the handyman again, and then heard, or seen glimpses of the cars arriving and proceeding down the back to the newer areas.

'I'll call an ambulance,' Livia said, then remembered she'd left the phone in the unlocked car in this nice neighborhood. 'I'll get my phone.' She stood up and swayed a little.

'No,' he said, looking up at her. 'We'll go to the Holy Mother. I know the staff there.'

He must have been a gardener at both places, and maybe he'd surprised whoever attacked him, but what were they doing here in the cemetery? Livia realised then that her slowness could have been the knock on the head, the terror of reprising Ray Milland in *Premature Burial,* or plain old naivete, but it finally came to her as the man spoke.

'Before we leave,' he said, 'we have to collect her things.'

Livia looked over towards Minnie's chapel about six or seven metres away. From where she stood it was hard to tell if anyone had tried to break in. She couldn't imagine why they'd want to, but why else were they here?

'Who are you?' she asked, rapidly revising the gardener role.

'Help me over to the chapel, would you, Liebling,' he said, a slight accent to his speech. 'It doesn't matter who I am.'

'I think it does,' she said. They walked together, very slowly, to Minnie's chapel. Livia wasn't certain who was supporting whom, but she knew that together they'd make it.

'You'll have the key,' he said quietly. He turned to face her as they reached the door to the narrow walk-in altar.

'Look,' she said, distracted by the damage. Scuff marks on the steel-framed door indicated that their attackers had unsuccessfully attempted to kick it in. This structure was a miniature Fort Knox.

'Someone gave you a key recently, Liebling,' he persisted, his voice gentle but insistent, and Livia's hand went automatically to the belt loop where her keys were usually hooked.

The key that didn't fit anywhere, or unlock anything, until now. When the time was right, Minnie had told Ishmael. She nodded, restraining herself from asking further questions. She walked as rapidly as she could to the car, driving it down the lane and parking directly in front of Minnie's place. She removed the key from the ignition, selected the mystery key from the bunch, inserted it into the lock on the chapel door and turned it. She wasn't surprised to see that here was where it belonged.

'We should be quick about it,' said the stranger who became more familiar by the minute. 'In case they get bold enough to return. You just don't know these days – thugs aren't what they used to be.'

'You're telling me,' Livia said, and they both laughed, very briefly, until the explosive throbbing restarted in their matching bashed heads.

Her familiar stranger stepped into the chapel and then appeared to lose momentum, staring ahead of him at the items on the altar. There was a small dagger with a curved blade in its sheath, a ball of string, a sheela-na-gig that could have been a sister to the one Rosanna had; a number of small stones, a set of three pyramids, and a set of three trilobite fossils. Lying flat on the altar was an iPOD, its ear buds waiting for a heavenly body to listen in.

When her new old friend continued to stare, it was Livia's turn to be the prompt. 'Which things do we take?'

'Everything, Liebling,' he said, turning to her. His eyes glistened with tears, and his voice cracked when he spoke. 'We take everything, including that lovely picture on the wall.'

He indicated a painting that depicted scenes from mythology. The bottom half showed Charon the Ferryman on the River Styx, standing in his boat with several passengers, a three-headed Cerberus waiting on the shore at the entrance to Hades. The top half was a scene of lightness: sunshine lit up open fields in which indistinct figures sat and stood in ones and groups: the Elysian Fields, or was it the so-called happy world of the living? Was that Persephone on the far left, straddling both halves of the picture, a sad-looking, wraith-like figure in white, her long, braided hair floating out behind her? Yet again, Livia wished she'd listened to Minnie more carefully when she'd read stories from *Bulfinch's Mythology* to her and Greer.

'Do you have a bag at all, my dear?'

She went to the car's boot and plucked out a calico grocery bag, into which they carefully placed the painting and all the altar decorations including the iPOD. They eased themselves gently into the car and Livia drove them, slowly – her head throbbed and threw spins every so often – the short distance to the Holy Mother. She parked as close to the entrance as possible in the visiting doctor's bay – let him or her discover the joys of a more humble, mortal existence for a day. They sat in their seats, listening to the engine ticking down. Livia turned and looked at her passenger.

'I'm really glad to see you, Uncle Ari.' She leaned over and kissed his blood-streaked cheek, and he kissed hers.

'My dearest Livia.' He took her hand and held it in both of his.

CHAPTER TWENTY-FIVE

River City

Friday 5 September 2008
Holy Mother and St Jude Retreat

Inside the building, it was cool and the fluorescent lighting was positively soft compared with the daylight outside. In the kitchen, as usual, biscuits were cooking, sending the sweet scent of baking throughout the building.

Livia wasn't surprised to see Cosmo Dacey sitting in the small reception office to the right of the entrance. He left his station and hurried out, shaking Ari's hand warmly before embracing him.

'Together again,' Cosmo said, touching Livia's cheek affectionately and gazing at Ari like a long-lost brother. Then he stood back from both of them and made a few quick, unspoken decisions. He took them past the terrarium and down a hallway to a small room, where they sat drinking paper cups of water and explaining what had transpired at the cemetery.

Finally, Cosmo excused himself assuring them he'd return soon.

Livia noticed that Ari hadn't let go of the calico bag containing Minnie's *objets d'affection*. He clung firmly to its handles, obviously reluctant to let it go or set it down anywhere. It was his last link with Minnie and her final wishes. There were so many questions Livia wanted to ask him, but the effects of the events at the cemetery weighed heavily on both of them. It wasn't the right moment. Instead, they sat companionably enjoying each other's silent, exhausted company until Cosmo returned with Ruth Gold and Verity Price.

Verity set a medical kit down on the coffee table and took out the antibacterial wipes, which helped to remove the most obvious blood and dust. Livia hadn't realised or noticed until that moment how badly she'd grazed her hands and her arms when she thought she'd become a female Ray Milland and literally terrorised herself into escaping. If she hadn't been wearing her heavy-duty Doc Martens, she knew she'd have broken bones in her feet to add to the list.

As she listened to the flow of conversation, it emerged that Ari knew the three CLEAR committee members well from the old circus days, but they didn't seem especially surprised to see him in the flesh after 30-something years. Maybe that was one of the perks of older age, the shockproofing that came with decades of having seen it all.

'Do you think you could be concussed?' Ruth asked. She checked the wound and lump on the back of Livia's head, dabbing at the wound with something soft and soothing.

'I don't know, Ruth, I've never been concussed before.'

'Well, you remember our names and you managed to drive here,' she said, 'you don't have double vision, or a desire to sleep, but we should err on the safe side. You both need proper medical attention, you know, and you both need to get away to somewhere safer than here.' She glanced at Verity and Cosmo to confirm they agreed.

Safer? The Holy Mother was no longer safe? That was news to her. What about Sibyl and everyone else? She realised that what Ruth had meant to say was that this particular place wasn't safe for two particular people.

'It's lucky Livia came along when she did,' Cosmo said to Ari, who nodded and smiled a weak smile. He was fading fast.

'The funeral saved us,' Livia said. 'The little boy was a godsend.' Who knew how traumatised he'd be from watching her resurrection? Maybe she could trace the funeral notices and find him one day, and explain, somehow.

'How is the cleaning coming along?' Ari asked the group. He handed Cosmo the secaturs he'd used to prune the cemetery thug.

Cleaning? Was cleaning something people became obsessed with as they grew older? Goodness knew Rosanna kept a shipshape hotel, but that was her nature. Livia could take or leave housework, and usually the latter shaped as the preferred option. As Minnie always insisted, what were a few dust motes among friends?

Cosmo gazed at the secaturs in admiration, tore open a bacterial wipe and rubbed at the blades. 'A nice addition to the terrarium equipment.'

'The cleaning is going well,' Verity replied. 'Only, we can't find Tibor. He's been gone for a couple of days, but if we work longer shifts each day, we'll make up most of the difference.'

She moved around to inspect Ruth's work and placed a warm and comforting hand on Livia's shoulder. It was all she could do not to blurt out the truth about Tibor. She concentrated on the stinging in her hands. Someone needed to know about Tibor besides the thugs and Gordon Trembath's cleaning crew. The man deserved far more than a wheelie bin and a mystery gravesite. He deserved, no less than Minnie did, to have someone find out why he died, and now that she had even more skin in the game, a victim of assault herself, and even less desire to go to the police now that Ari had arrived, she could feel a sense of – she could only find the word duty to describe what she felt welling inside her.

'Where are you staying, Uncle Ari?' She stood to test her balance, insisting to her physical self that she was not concussed.

'The Metro Central in the CBD,' he replied. 'The city has exploded since I was here last.'

'You're right, it has. And I know where we can go, but we'll need a driver, and we need to make a stop on the way.'

CHAPTER TWENTY-SIX

River City

Friday 5 September 2008
Metro Central Hotel, CBD Mall

1

He'd been reluctant, but Livia had insisted that Ari accompany her into the biggest shoppingtown in the country on their way into the city centre from the Holy Mother. There were a few stares; you couldn't go through what they'd been through and still look like your everyday self. They'd shopped for half an hour with Ruth by their side, in case concussion became an issue, she said. Then they'd gone to the food court where they ate kebabs and drank strong coffee. They'd bought new sets of clothing and stayed a little longer than necessary, idle shoppers in search of nothing other than a moment or two of peace, a short delay before their journey continued.

A change of look, Livia knew, was as good as a change of identity, if it was radical enough. And now, after they'd washed the cemetery dust away with refreshing showers, Ari had joined her in her suite. She'd taken one on the same floor as his, down the hall and on the opposite side, at the Metro Central, coincidentally one of Karl's growing list of property development success stories. When too much money just wasn't enough. She and Ari looked like visitors from the country in their new moleskins and double-pocket shirts, Livia the gothic cowgirl all in black. They'd even bought riding boots, but Ari baulked at the hats, preferring instead a Driz-a-Bone jacket. It was far too warm to wear in spring but it was the finishing touch that made them look the part: the grazier and his daughter, in the city for special appointments and meetings, the sale of thousands of hectares, or its purchase.

The shopping trip had been the only light moment in what seemed like years to Livia. If time truly was elastic, this week had stretched it as never before. She picked up the remote and turned on the large plasma screen television on the wall opposite their sofa. She resisted the urge to quiz her godfather straight away, hoping he might decide to volunteer something himself. The calico bag sat against a leg of the coffee table in front of them; he'd relaxed enough to release his grip on it.

As the news broadcast got under way, she picked up the tube of antiseptic cream they'd bought when shopping and rubbed some on the laceration on the back of her head, and more into the palms of her scratched hands. She'd swallowed several painkillers and they'd taken the edge off the headache and other pains.

The news went through the usual motions of infotainment disguised as news, stories beaten up to seem important, excessive sports coverage, and inaccurate weather forecasts. At the end was a 'breaking' story about a body found at the bottom of a cliff face on a beach at Deception Bay, north of River City. The body, as far as police could tell, or as much as they would tell the media, was of a man in his 60s or 70s, but as he was headless and handless, identification would be difficult. Livia sat up and put the tube of cream on the coffee table.

'Investigations are continuing,' the newsreader told viewers, 'and there is speculation that the man may be the victim of an underworld hit, given the missing body parts. Police spokesperson Detective Greg Petersen, refused to comment on the possibility of a mob connection, but indicated that identifying the man was a priority.'

Plausible deniability. Livia slumped back in her seat. She could readily deny knowing exactly whose head belonged on the shoulders of that body because she'd had no notion of the cleaning crew's plans, thanks to Jerry's reticence. Self-deception is an art.

'That's Tibor Restik,' she said to Ari, nodding at the TV screen.

'Tibor?' Ari put his plate down and turned to face Livia, his own face impassive but alert.

'You didn't know?' Livia had thought that somehow he might discover – even as he flew home – all that had been going on in River City over recent days, given the motivation of Minnie's death.

'No, no, I didn't. Tibor, too.'

'Greer hasn't had a chance to contact you today?' She played the hunch.

'No, I haven't heard –' He leaned back a little. 'Was it the call the other day?'

'You phoned and then Greer rang. And now, here we are, finally.' Livia felt a tear sliding down her face. 'Where have you been, Uncle A?' The day had been so long, and she'd all but given up on sleeping ever again. Even the bugs in the concrete bed of rest wouldn't give her a chance beyond a cat-nap.

Ari leaned over and cupped her cheek in his hand, wiping away the tear. He may have been as distressed as Livia, but his face gave nothing away.

'I'll tell you, my darling, once and never again, where I've been.'

He picked up the remote and turned off the television.

'Are you sure you want to know?'

Livia nodded. 'I'm in the dark about a lot of things, Ari, this doesn't need to be one of them, not anymore.'

'In 1972, Minerva and I were building the business, art restoration and so on, and working more and more closely with Con, and Gordon. I'd been travelling extensively, especially in Europe, arranging deals, organising acquisitions – it was much easier in those days to fill orders and to send them anywhere, really. You understand what I'm telling you?'

'Yes, I understand.' It was a side of the family business Livia had deliberately distanced herself from, especially since she'd taken over Minnie's gallery. She'd always hoped that the legitimate acquisitions and sales, and the family's involvement in the restoration, through their extensive connections, of stolen works to Jewish Holocaust survivors and the looted Iraqi museums, outweighed, or at least balanced the ledger's darker columns.

'The art world is an interesting place, I'm sure you'll agree. There's your own involvement, Livia. You've seen documentaries, news reports. Collectors – of art and artefacts, antiquities, and the like – are single-minded people, rich or poor, but the rich especially. Some of them have virtually unlimited resources, and for some of them, the provenance of works – where they've come from, their pedigree papers, if you will – doesn't matter as much as possessing them. Call it ego, call it a mental health disorder – they want to possess because then they control. It's an addiction, and it's also a lucrative business if you have certain skills, which I do. We all benefited from those skills, the entire family.' He paused. 'You remember I'm Jewish?'

'Of course.'

Livia knew the story of how Ari's parents, Moishe and Sarah, had been murdered by the Nazis in Poland, sometime in 1944. Before their arrest, they managed to arrange for the infant Ari – Ariel Moishe Babitsky – to be smuggled out of Poland to relative safety in France. He never found out where they died, only that they disappeared and were never heard from again. His life in Europe after the war as a young boy was one of extreme hardship with his adoptive family. Minnie had told Livia and Greer stories of how he'd been homeless, travelling with his adoptive parents and other adults and children through the towns and countryside, begging, stealing, doing what they had to do to survive. Although the family eventually managed to migrate to Australia where life became so much better for them, Livia had always felt that Minnie held back on the worst aspects of his young life in Europe, to spare them the nightmares. But Ari became, in short, a very tough cookie, though with a heart of pure compassion and love for those he trusted and cared for. The flipside, of course, was the ability to hate with a vengeance.

'In 1972,' Ari continued, 'Minerva and I were very happy. Although we couldn't have children, we had a full life together, and I felt invulnerable, I truly did. Business was booming, I travelled everywhere for the boys – Con and Gordon. Minerva accompanied me sometimes. I, both of us, made all sorts of connections, networks all over Europe and into North America. Dealers, galleries, private collectors. I loved my work. I loved my Minerva Helena.' He stopped and gazed around the room. 'But then Munich happened.'

'The Israeli athletes murdered by the Black September PLO terrorists in the Olympic Village.'

'A shocking crime.' The memory seemed to wind Ari.

It had been one of the most horrific acts of terrorism the world had witnessed, and it was played out on the television news. Although Livia and Greer were only eight at the time and sitting safely in the TV room at the Bender, Livia remembered their collective fear watching the grainy black and white film of the masked gunmen on the balcony of the Village accommodation block. Even as children, the girls felt the terrible sadness, knowing, like so many others, that there was almost certainly no way out for those athletes, some of whom were horribly tortured before they were shot. And afterwards, there was the debacle when the German government tried to save the remaining hostages and capture the terrorists.

The hostages died, and the murderers escaped. Over the years, analysts had raised suspicions of a deal with the terrorists. But in the end, everything that could go wrong, did.

'For months I tried to put it out of my mind,' Ari said, 'but I couldn't. I lived in Israel for several years in the early '60s, and I made a lot of friends there; some of them were related to the athletes who died. That's where I learned my trade restoring artworks, curating antiquities. The short of it is, Minerva and I discussed how I felt, I flew to Tel-Aviv and contacted a man who knew a man who knew a woman, and so on. I became, eventually, a contractor.' He waited.

'An assassin.' Livia recalled the documentaries and films about the so-called Golda's List, a decision by the then Prime Minister of Israel, Golda Meir, to draw up a list of, and systematically eliminate the terrorists involved in the Munich massacre. Ari had helped them – Mossad, the Israeli secret police – but had he become one of them? How did he feel about the cases of mistaken identity when the 'contractors' had killed the wrong people? That was a question for another time.

'Why didn't you come home after you'd – finished your contract?'

'Something like that – it changes you – the idea of life and how one lives, it changes. In any case, I don't exist, Livia. The plaque in Minnie's park is accurate. Ariel Moishe Babitsky has returned to where he came from: the ashes of Nazi Europe. I would be glad to join my Minerva now. I, too, have a part in her murder.'

'How could you possibly – ?'

'Who do you think procured the art work for Gordon, without realising he was unwell, that he would make mistakes, that Con had no idea what Gordon was doing?'

'But it wasn't Gordon who made the mistake, if there was a mistake. It was me. I sent the gun case back because I had no idea it was supposed to take a different route home. I still don't know what's significant about it.'

'A map, my dear. A very valuable map, a Mercator. For a collector of cartographic rarities.'

Livia thought back to the conversations with Sibyl.

'A Mercator map. That's what Sibyl's been saying. Gordon must have told her. His fantastic stories.'

'I beg your pardon?'

'Never mind. How was it to be handed over?'

'That I don't know. It relates to your gun case, certainly, but everything was done according to NTK principles. My only contact was with Gordon, and I organised it all from Europe. I was just as happy to do that; I had other plans to execute and Gordon's payment for the map helped me to do that.'

'NTK – need to know. Each participant in the project knows only as much as he or she needs to know to carry out their segment of the plan. Obviously, it was thought I needed to know nothing at all, as the mule.'

'That was their first mistake,' Ari said.

'No, their first mistake was picking me, and my trip to Beijing.' Karl really wasn't suited to this type of intrigue.

'But we test drove it, in a manner of speaking,' Ari said, 'before it was presented to you. Gordon requested the map from me. He knew I'd procured just such a map a few years ago, from a chalet in France. The owners didn't even know it was there, sitting among the other decaying texts in their ancient library. I was curating their collection – I'm still on the lookout for Nazi plundered art and artefacts – you can't imagine what we've found in respectable castles and stately homes over the years. I found the map quite by chance. I was so elated at the time that I mentioned it to Gordon when he was holidaying in Bonn.'

'But how did it get here?'

'I'd speculate that the map was somehow placed in the case in Europe, when Michael Morris was doing the design work in Amsterdam. Your leg of the journey should have been the easiest. The case had already passed through European and Australian customs checks with no trouble at all. The Olympics would have been the final security test. I know that there are plans to use it as a prototype to make others to transport items in the future. If this case proved successful, travelling across several continents, and through the maze of Olympic security as it did, then it would come highly recommended to the people who use such things to avoid nosy authorities and their awkward questions.'

'You can't think I would have agreed to carry such an item if I'd been told about it.'

Livia felt the old anger rising again, and she didn't like it. It was the silent rage that had stayed with her for so long after Jacques Foucault was murdered with her help, and Greer's.

'Better it's with new owners than those ignorant descendents of Nazi collaborators whose wealth is tainted with innocent blood.'

She took a breath and tried to push the comment, and her anger far away. It wasn't about who might be the original owners, it was what its presence in her gun case had caused to happen, here, now. But Ari was grief-stricken for Minnie, and bringing the past forward might be how he was coping with his unintended part in her death. It was time to take a different path.

'So how long has Greer known about you – that you weren't dead?' How long had her sister kept the secret from her? A twinge of jealousy sparked and fizzled.

'She found me, quite accidentally, through mutual friends in Tel Aviv, after you returned to Australia. You remember how the two of you helped those people out on a few operations, with your cousin Levi?'

'It's a bit hard to forget, Uncle A.' Those need to know principles were at work in the kibbutz days, too, of course. And Livia would never know who she may have helped to imprison, or liberate, or even who else may have been killed as a result of her slight involvement during the time she and Greer worked in Israel and when they were studying in Europe during the '80s. To them, the liaisons and the exchanges of documents during their tourist trips around certain Meditteranean countries, were adventures, organised by friends they'd met on the kibbutz. Friends she'd left in the past, once she'd decided on a career path that didn't involve brushing sleeves with mystery people who asked her to initiate an acquaintanceship with this Frenchman, or attend a seminar with that Egyptian student. She got sick of not knowing more than her apparently simple scripts, that was the truth of it; need to know became need to leave, and she did.

'Levi and Greer left that group and got in touch with a re-lated contracting organisation, one that was less inclined towards fatalities, and more interested in art and artefacts. In the course of conversations, she mentioned my name. They let me know, and eventually, I called her. I wanted to look out for her – like you, she was Minerva's goddaughter, after all, and mine, until I 'died.' The best way to do that was through direct contact.'

'And now? What do you two get up to these days?' Livia had thought Greer spent most of her time researching PTSD and counselling trauma victims. Avalon was devoted to trauma rehabilitation for soldiers and civilians. It was the only way Livia had been able to assuage her conscience about her grandfather's trust fund.

'I'll leave that for the two of you to discuss, Livia.' He stood up and went to the kitchen, pouring himself a glass of water.

'All right, Uncle A.' She couldn't understand the sudden abruptness in his tone. Jetlag, the ever-present grief? 'Why did we take these things from Minnie's chapel?' She nodded at the calico bag on the floor.

'Knowledge is power, Livia. You learned that the hard way. We took them so noone else would take them, or see them, and come to a misunderstanding about what they mean. Especially Karl, but also these people at the cemetery today. I doubt they saw enough to read anything into the collection.'

'And what do they mean, Ari?'

'Even I have to figure that out, liebschen. They may not mean anything.' He returned to the lounge, leaned down and pecked her cheek. 'Good night, my dear. I am not the man I used to be.' He glanced at his watch.

'Good night? Don't you think we need to figure a few things out?'

'I'm sure you can put the puzzle together for all of us, Livia.'

He closed the door gently and was gone. She looked at the calico bag. Even he had to figure it out? She didn't think so. Minnie's husband should know exactly what every single item signified, shouldn't he?

She turned the television back on and pressed the mute button; there could be more news of Tibor on the next update. She went to the kitchen and filled the electric kettle. In the cupboard was a white teapot and English breakfast tea. On the dining-room table was the hotel's gift basket to its favoured guests: anyone with the funds to afford a suite on this floor. She opened it and removed the small cakes and chocolates. If she was to engage in a test of some kind, courtesy of Ariel and Minerva Babitsky, she'd better equip herself for the trip with caffeine and sugar. As Minnie had always told her and Greer, justifying the liberal quantities of Viennese delicacies she fed them, 'No child can think on an empty stomach.'

2

Livia propped the painting against the sofa's arm, and placed the other items on the coffee table. She had to think like Minnie. Minnie, who had more than a passing interest in mythology, and an enduring affection for the strange artefacts and antiquities valued by different cultures. She had a collection of small objects, sprinkled throughout Fortescue Street, brought home to her by friends returning from holidays and business trips overseas.

The sheela-na-gig was a replica of the one Rosanna had, a small stone figure about seven centimetres tall baring her teeth and exposing her genitals. She was supposed to frighten away evil spirits, or draw the sun's fertility, or she was a mystery icon from pre-Christian, happily pagan Ireland. Noone really knew for sure. Livia put her aside as an object of affection rather than information; she knew that Tanya Skelloe had bought her a few years before for Minnie, an emergency substitute for an Aran rock, which she'd forgotten to acquire on the islands.

The dagger could have been from Ireland too, or Egypt or Greenland or Mongolia, for all Livia knew. It had a curved blade and a carved wooden handle, and looked like the real thing rather than a touristy replica. She pulled it out of its sheath and saw that the blade had similar markings carved into it as those on the handle. She put it aside with the set of three small brass pyramids, the collection of stones, and what looked like trilobite fossils: the prehistoric shells of ocean-floor animals. Minnie's collection was more eclectic than Rosanna's, but they had similar tastes in many ways.

She could make no sense of the ball of string other than as a reminder of the myth of Theseus – one of the Argonauts – and the Minotaur. The Minotaur, she remembered, was a monstrous hybrid – half bull and half man – and lived in a Labyrinth on Crete where he happily feasted on the youth of Athens, offered as tributes to King Minos of Crete, after he'd defeated the Greeks in a war. The Minotaur itself existed because of some previous malarky relating to Poseidon and sacrifices not made when they should have been. The old mythological soap opera standby, an adulterous and unnatural union, featured somewhere, too. Theseus used thread provided by Minos's daughter, Ariadne, to find his way into and out of the Labyrinth, slaying the beast with a sword, also provided by Ariadne. She was a resourceful princess.

Livia realised, as the knowledge fought its way out of her childhood, that she must have listened more than she'd thought when Minnie told her stories. But she couldn't imagine the significance of this particular ball of thread, except as a reminder that if she entered any kind of maze, she'd better be able to find her way out again.

She leaned back and gazed at the painting. Maybe it was the sort of artwork that bore a closer inspection. She picked it up and held it out in front of her. If the top half wasn't the Elysian Fields, perhaps it was a representation of ancient Avalon. Greer named their resort and therapeutic centre after one of her favourite songs, Brian Ferry's *Avalon*. Not long after they'd registered the company name and made everything legal, they'd remembered Minnie's tale of the Celtic Avalon where King Arthur was taken after he was mortally wounded. Greer had had second thoughts for a while, but it was, in its own perverse way, a fitting kind of name for a place that was a paradise of sorts, one you went to when you were broken or broken-down, and hoping, often against hope, to recover yourself.

'What can't I see, Minnie? You should never have trusted me with your Will, and your house, and poor Sibyl. I should never have sent you the gun case.'

But even as she spoke, Livia knew, surrounded by Minnie's things, old and new, that whatever this was about, this collection of so-called mysteries, it had started long before the gun case, long before she and Greer could tie their shoelaces.

Old and new. The iPOD was very new. She cursed herself for not checking it sooner. She propped the painting on her lap so she could continue to peruse it, and plugged in the iPOD's ear buds. She turned it on and her inner world was flooded with Glenn Miller, swinging and rhythmic, majestic fluid notes, the joyful bliss of perfect melody. She clutched the painting to her chest, and remembered Minnie as she used to be: bustling, laughing, dancing around the kitchen as she cooked up a roast, or baked scones, or made fudge and coconut ice for any passing child. The tears she'd restrained for so long began to flow, and she clung to the painting for comfort, knowing how much Minnie must have loved it.

Through blurred vision, she saw again on the television news update the beach where Tibor's body had been found. She removed the earbuds and reached for the remote control to turn on the sound. As she reached, she held the painting more firmly with the other hand, worried about dropping or somehow damaging its frame or glass, one of Minnie's last conversational gestures. She switched the sound on and heard the reporter say there had been no further developments in 'the headless man' case. At the same time she felt something beneath her fingers on the back of the painting. She turned it over and looked, then looked again. There was nothing, until she felt again with her fingers – ridges – then saw lines notched into the back of the frame.

She slid to the end of the sofa and held the painting beneath the light from the table lamp, rubbing her thumb along the spread of the lines. They appeared in clusters with breaks between them, although there was no apparent logic to where the breaks occurred. She'd seen the lines before: they were the 'bar codes,' as Verity described them, on the artworks at the nursing home. Perhaps Sibyl had given Minnie this painting as a memento of something or other, a nursing home resident they'd both known?

There was something else, too. She picked up the dagger and removed it from its sheath. There along the top of the blade were similar markings. They weren't bar codes, that was certain. But why bother with something so elaborate to name a painter or a work and designate its last cleaning? Why not simply use initials, and Roman numerals if fancy work was desired? Perhaps the bar codes were words, or a combination of numbers and letters forming words, like mobile phone text messages. That would be one explanation for the apparent lack of logic in the number of lines before a break occurred. And if they were words, were they hiding something? Everyone seemed intent on concealing something at the moment.

She turned off the television, replaced everything in the grocery bag, put it on the floor next to the coffee table, and wondered what to do next. What would Minnie do? She went to the bureau and sat down. The desk was positioned near a wide floor-to-ceiling window and offered a panoramic view of the cityscape. The CBD had acquired a succession of tall and taller buildings over the last decade: a phallic cluster, for those who saw the panorama from a certain angle. Others saw success, profit for the taking, reasons for envy and greed, the literally concrete (and glass) proof of corporate achievement. That would be Karl's take, and Con's, Livia had to admit.

She went to the balcony door and stepped out. It was cool, but not bitingly so; the last of winter was behind them. Down below, the city's backing band played incessantly: thousands of motor cars, bikes and trucks, revving, slowing, idling, rumbles and screeches, purposeful, directionless. Restrictions on building heights in certain areas had eased considerably and, every so often, an announcement appeared in the media to the effect that the tallest building in the Southern Hemisphere was about to rise from muddy or stony foundations (along with – and Livia had never heard this mentioned in the rosy reports – the perfect ratio of illusory solidity to built-in obsolescence). She supposed such monoliths were designed to strike River City's residents mute with respect and pride for their hometown, given its drab and scrubby beginnings. It wasn't the sort of place you could mythologise, like Los Angeles, for instance, another summery, dry town, but then, L.A. had Hollywood, a myth factory. River City would never be the capital of the world, as New York claimed to be, and it had no history to speak of, by comparison with London, say, or Paris. On the other hand, it was home, it made its history every day, for better or worse. The myths would take care of themselves.

She went inside and found her mobile phone, punched in the numbers, and waited. Minnie would take care of business, of course, but first, she'd take care of something far more important: family and friends, a couple of them, for now. The rest would have to wait.

'Hello?'

His voice, so timid on the other end, never knowing exactly what to expect, but willing himself to take a chance.

'Ishmael, it's Livia. How's everything?'

'The dogs are good, Livia. They're good. They're eating and drinking.'

'And you? Are you okay there with them? You don't mind dog-sitting for a while longer on your own?'

'I love the dogs, Livia. I'm their carer. It's no problem. And I've been fixing the house – after the burglars.'

Livia saw the house, every room turned upside down. It wasn't so much pillage and break as turn it out and mess it up. She didn't know what was worse, throwing out the broken and irretrievable once and for all, or picking every last item up and returning it to its assigned place, closing doors and draw-ers, righting chairs, squaring rugs and pictures. She'd bet that Ishmael, with his obsessive leanings, would know where eve-rything belonged.

'Ishmael, you don't have to do that – we can do it together when I get back. They left such a mess.'

'It was as easy as a-b-c, Livia,' he said. 'Room by room. I'm going out to feed the possums now. The dogs can take a little walk around the park. They're still tired.'

'Be careful,' Livia said, going to the sofa. 'I don't think the burglars will be back, but be careful anyway.' She picked the painting out of the calico bag.

'I will, don't worry. Be careful, Livia, be careful anyway.'

As easy as A-B-C, Ishmael said. As easy as the alphabet. She turned the painting over. If the clusters of straight and crooked, and half-sized lines were letters, or words, they would be derived from some sort of alphabet, but was it a pri-vately constructed one for Minnie and Sibyl and their compa-ny of colleagues and friends to enjoy? Or could it be a system they'd borrowed from somewhere else, another culture, perhaps another era? Minnie's love of myths and legends pointed towards the latter option, and it would add a dash of interest to their mundane cleaning tasks.

She sat on the sofa again and retrieved the dagger from the grocery bag, placing it beside the painting on the coffee table. It wasn't as though they shared anything obviously in common other than the markings: horizontal and 45-degree angled lines struck through a vertical axis. She noticed that all of the angled lines went through the axis, but some of the horizontals were halved and stopped at the axis, jutting out from one side or the other, all of them forming strange little ladders. The only thing she knew was that they weren't Egyptian hieroglyphs: there was nothing pictorial about them at all. They were basic and simple to the people who understood them well, but Livia wasn't one of those people.

She had a choice: she could lie in bed for hours and speculate, in between falling dreams and nightmare images of Tibor's wrecked body, on what the lines could mean, or she could move, now. She pocketed her mobile and the room's card key, pulled her new riding boots on, and went to the elevator. Perhaps Minnie's ball of string was there to remind her that there was always a way out of the maze. But she had no sword, at the moment. The sword she needed was a sword of knowledge, if such a thing could be found.

3

Downstairs, the night had just begun for many of the hotel's guests and visitors. Groups of happy people in costumes ranging from five-star designer-silk splendour to Livia's own cowgirl gothic came and went through the foyer on their way to the gaming tables in the casino bar, or the seafood smorgasbord in the open-plan, multi-level atrium dining-room, or private functions in one of several chandelier-sparkled ballrooms.

Livia made her way across the foyer in front of the registration desk to the modest internet café tucked in a corner beyond the reach of the atrium's busyness. The atrium was the central feature of the building, running its entire height. It was only natural that the space should be reserved for eating, and greeting: near the dining area were clusters of armchairs and low tables, where guests and visitors could rendezvous and decide which indulgence to test first. There were no clocks to be seen. A person could stay in here all day and all night and never know what time it was, or if the world outside had gone on holiday or disappeared forever through a portal.

She slid her room keycard, as instructed on the screen, into a slimline box beside the monitor. She started with Google, typed in 'alphabets,' and checked the first site listed. Hundreds, or maybe thousands of alphabets were available, in alphabetical order. She'd never really gotten the knack of interrogating the internet, and comforted herself by remembering a librarian's comment that 98% of its content was irrelevant rubbish, probably the 98% most visited. Everyone was entitled to her or his opinion. Narrowing down, she thought, that was the key to the internet. There were mountain ranges of facts, oceanic depths of information. Her mystery lines might be an old alphabet, and mightn't be referred to as an alphabet at all. She strung a few words together and eventually came up with 'ancient writing systems.' The first site had fewer listings, but there were still too many to check in a limited time. She needed an expert, the stern librarian with a heart of gold who could direct her to the two per cent of worthwhile data. She pulled her phone out of her pocket, flipped it open and dialled.

'Who is it?' A sleep addled voice.

'Jill? It's Livia. Your cousin.'

'I know who you are, Livia. Do you know what time it is?'

'No, I um, I'm sorry, Jilly. Is it late?'

'Never mind. I assume you have a query?'

Jill was used to the family regarding her as an oracle. The cousins referred to her as Jilly of Delphi.

'As a matter of fact, yes. You're a librarian.'

'Cut to the chase, Livia. There's still time for me to get back to sleep before I remember I'm awake.'

'I'm trying to track down a writing system that consists of a vertical axis criss-crossed by horizontal and 45-degree angled lines. Some of the horizontals are half-size – they stop at the axis, others go straight through. There are gaps between them suggesting they might represent letters, or words. Any thoughts?'

'Any wiggly bits, or crosses? Other shapes drawn across the axis?'

'Not so far,' Livia said, 'but I've only seen a couple of examples.'

'It could be runic.'

Livia waited while Jill trawled her brain for connections. When they were children, Livia thought her cousin was consumed with daydreaming, just as the rest of the cousins were distracted, like their cats, by dust motes and shiny ribbons and their place in various fantasies. But she came to realise that Jill was busy processing into easily retrievable parts of her cognitive system the information and knowledge she'd most recently gathered from her extensive reading activities. No wonder she became a librarian.

'Write this word down,' Jill said. 'O-g-h-a-m.'

Livia grabbed the convenient post-it pad and pen from beside the monitor and wrote down the letters. 'Ogham?'

'That's one way of pronouncing it. There are others. I'm not saying that's the exact thing you're after, but it's a start. Ogham, or oo-um is supposedly connected with Celtic runes. Researching the family tree, are you?

'Something like that. Say hi to Trina. And thanks for this. I'll be in touch.'

'No trouble,' Jill replied. 'Wake me anytime, Livia. My night is yours.'

She hung up before Livia could apologise again, knowing her cousin wouldn't hold a grudge. She loved her status as the family's oracle, and the family demonstrated their love for her by phoning and texting and emailing her at odd moments with even odder queries.

Once Livia returned to the web site she'd found for ancient writing systems, it was a simple matter of checking the A to Z index and calling up Ogham. It appeared to be the one, all right. She selected the relevant pages depicting the Ogham alphabet with its equivalent English letters, and read its potted history while she waited for the printer to warm up and give her a copy. Ogham was an early Celtic alphabet, used to etch inscriptions on stone slabs. Its origins were mysterious; some researchers connected it with runes, as Jill had mentioned; others with the Roman alphabet. Still others credited it as being a unique invention of the Celts.

Livia picked up the pages from the printer and noticed, as Jill had also suggested, that there were other characters besides the lines she'd already identified. They seemed to represent combined letters that produced a single sound, such as 'ch,' which was an 'X' shape through the vertical axis. A cross-hatch image of three vertical and three horizontal lines sitting to the right of the axis represented 'ae,' 'x,' and 'xi.' It looked like a noughts and crosses game panel with extra lines each way.

Livia folded the pages and slipped them into the pocket of her moleskins, retrieved her room keycard, and made her way through the atrium space to the elevators. It was the only time she felt vulnerable, wondering if, somewhere in the groups of people coming and going, the same eyes that had regarded Minnie with such malevolence, the same thugs who'd left Tibor on her verandah, were watching her. There was no point in trying to pick anyone out of the crowd, the killers could be from anywhere, and, she realised at that moment, they didn't have to be male, not necessarily. Doug Courtney had seen men, non-descript men, bland men in bland clothing, who could as easily be women in disguise, she supposed, or a man and a woman, as readily as two men. How reliable, after all, was Doug's testimony?

She kept her hand protectively on her pocket as she travelled up in the elevator. With the translation cipher, she knew she could decode the lines on the dagger and the painting. And what good would it do her, she wondered, sliding the card into its slot and turning the doorknob, to know how 'dagger' was spelt in Ogham, or to have it revealed to her that Minnie's chapel painting was probably called 'Persephone between Worlds?' She would know something for sure that she hadn't been certain of previously. Wasn't that a plus? Elimination could be as important as accumulation. And when she visited Sibyl again, she could try out her new-found knowledge on the artworks at the Holy Mother. Debunking the bar code theory, she could find out who cleaned them, and when. Big deal. Was it?

4

Livia settled herself on the sofa and wondered, momentarily, if she should wake Ari, then determined to do the work herself, for what it might be worth. She pulled the dagger out of the grocery bag, and the pages of the Ogham alphabet from her pocket, unfolding them on the coffee table. She went to the bureau and found a notepad and pen. In Ogham, according to her web source, the letters and words could be written along a vertical or a horizontal axis. The dagger sported a horizontal axis, but the first letter wasn't 'd,' as she'd anticipated, but 'b,' represented by one vertical line drawn down from the horizontal, a 'T' shape. The next letter was 'o,' two vertical lines drawn all the way through the axis, then came 's,' four vertical lines below the horizontal; 't,' three vertical lines above the horizontal, another 'o,' and an 'n,' five vertical lines below the horizontal.

'Boston,' was the word. She double-checked her translation, and confirmed it was correct. Had the dagger come from

Boston in the United States, or another Boston? Boston in South Yemen. Was it made by someone named Boston, or could that be the brand of the knife: a Boston Dagger? It could have been from the era of Paul Revere, or even the Civil War. It sounded cool enough: the Boston Dagger. There were Boston buns, and the Boston Red Sox, or White Sox, players of baseball or basketball, or both. They'd even had a tea party in Boston, though what a dagger would be doing at a tea party Livia couldn't imagine.

She replaced the dagger in its sheath, trying to remember where she may have heard Boston mentioned and in what context, and pulled out the painting. It was a direct enough translation exercise, once you knew how, and as long as you were a suspicious type and, in addition, had a cousin like Jill to guide you in the right direction. This time the word was 'Gardner.' She confirmed its accuracy with a re-check – Gardner, not gardener as in tidy Elysian Fields – then turned the painting over to examine the picture again. The word sounded recently familiar, but she couldn't remember when she'd heard it or where. She was tired, but it would come. Let the mind settle, Rosanna counselled her girls when they couldn't think properly. Imagine a stirred-up pond and all the sediment settling again, leaving crystal clear water above. Yes, it would come, but when?

Persephone continued to hover, undecided, between worlds. There in the bottom right-hand corner, amid the swirling blue-grey waters of the Styx, was a small signature, smaller than a 10-point font: Gardner, with what must have been the year it was painted: '90. Was Gardner a nursing home resident? Was Mr or Mrs, Ms or Miss Gardner, a friend of Minnie's, an early CLEAR member? Who would know? Livia assumed it was 1990, not 1890, unless it was a production of the famous Mother Magda Mesmer, nun extraordinaire, olive grower, and artist. But surely such treasures would be kept at the home for all to appreciate, not banged up in a chapel devoted to the dead at the far end of a seldom-visited necropolis.

She placed the painting on the coffee table next to the dagger and wondered what possible connection there could be between the two items. She leaned back into the sofa and made herself comfortable for some heavy thinking. Boston. Gardner. How did the two go together? Did they go together? There were no similar marks on the other things from Minnie's chapel. She found the iPod in the grocery bag and turned it on. The ear buds were like guardians against the outside world, and inside all was Mr Armstrong and Ella as 'Let's Call the Whole Thing Off' flowed over the Styx and lured her into oblivion.

CHAPTER TWENTY-SEVEN

River City

Saturday 6 September 2008
Metro Central Hotel, CBD Mall

L ivia had curled up on the sofa during the night. It was as
comfortable as most of the beds she'd ever slept in on her
travels. She stretched her arms and legs, and twisted her body
as far each way as she dared after the previous day's adventures. She acknowledged the dull ache that had set itself up
with the lump on the back of her head; her hands throbbed,
and she felt more exhausted as the minutes ticked by. She
reached over and picked up her phone, meaning to call Greer
before she could think too much about it. She had to know
why her sister hadn't told her about Ari. No, that wasn't right
– she knew why, it was a simple matter of safety and protection, especially for Ari. But she had to hear it from Greer's
lips. What she had to know was that it would still work, their
relationship, the way it always had. Apart from this particular
secret, there should be no others. Was that reasonable, she

wondered? She had no idea, and, no, she couldn't think straight, so she put the phone down and waited to feel the urge to rise.

CHAPTER TWENTY-EIGHT

Gold Coast Hinterland, south of River City

[27.55S 153.9E]
Saturday 6 September 2008
Avalon Resort and Therapy Centre

1

'I could stay here, liebling, right here in this chair, forever.' Ari leaned over and plucked a steaming mug from the table.

They sat together on the balcony of Greer's bungalow on the banks of Avalon's creek. It was running hard and fast after a series of spring thunderstorms. Within its boundaries, the resort boasted volcanic hot springs, bore springs, rainforest, waterfalls, an embarrassment of floral and faunal riches. It offered everything for nothing more than one's presence; that was its magic.

'Perhaps you're right, my dear, a very sunny place to tempt a shady person.' He raised his mug in a salute, and Greer responded with hers.

'You're welcome anytime, you know, Ari, now that Livia's in the loop, more or less.'

'You're not still thinking of telling her, surely?' Sometimes, it was impossible to predict which way she'd jump. He hadn't thought she would see Rodriguez through to his end, for example. He'd always been the finisher, had seen out the rest.

'Well, when does it end, Ari?' she asked.

'When I say. Someone worked Rodriguez like a marionette, someone with primary connections in government and policing, and with the guerillas. Therefore, someone extremely dangerous. The fewer people who know about our South American project over the last few years, the better.'

'But Livia has a right to know. I hate keeping secrets from her. You, for instance, your life after death.'

'Listen to me. Eamon was my friend, he was your partner, Greer. Dan, little Dan, was family. Perhaps you're right, perhaps it's over. In either case, over or not, leave it to me – I want to follow a few threads just a bit further. All right?'

He paused and waited, staring out at the expanse of green dappled in sunlight. A red-backed possum sat sleepily in the fork of a leopard gum, her baby perfectly balanced on her back, its black eyes staring hard at him. Had Greer taken it in, the importance of silence on the matter?

'Shouldn't you be helping Livia to find Minnie's killers – and the gun case? The police can't be brought into it.'

The sidelong response. So be it. He'd hope for the best from her, then, hope that she could resist the temptation to tell all to the one person in the universe who could tempt her beyond the edge.

'I'm here to see Doug Courtney – he'll help me find the killers – if not now, then very soon. And Livia is fine for the moment. She's on a quest of her own, and she must be allowed to complete it alone.'

'Then you'd better cross the creek, my friend. Mr Courtney prefers sleeping under the stars in an Avalon tent. Four walls are far too overwhelming.' She glanced back into the bungalow, its order, the artificial lights and sounds, and back out to the rainforest. 'He's a lucky man.'

2

He called out once he saw a sliver of tent, a good 20 metres away. He'd just stepped off the walking track, passing all manner of green things, listening carefully to the miscellaneous squawkings and shriekings, the chirpings and rustlings of birds and small marsupials and reptiles. He stopped and stood beneath a giant tree fern, prehistoric-looking, the tall, brown, fibrous trunk reaching up to the canopy, the curled and uncurling fronds bowed towards the ground, its fragile lacy green leaves. Ahead of him was a glade where a cluster of large boulders rested alongside a stream, and there were more towering tree ferns here and there, smaller ones too, ready to rise. Had a child suggested the nearby presence of Jurassic era animals, he wouldn't have been surprised to see a family of raptors amble in to sip at the clean, clear water and chat amiably before deciding who got to snack on him.

He ducked under a succession of fern fronds heavily laden with raindrops. The fronds stretched out from a dark gully running down to the creek, and he'd bumped them hard enough to feel trickles of cool water across the back of his neck. It was refreshing rather than unpleasant.

'I wouldn't go that way, if I were you.'

The voice was low and firm, not a metre behind him. He spun around and came face to face with a dark-haired man sporting a two-day growth of salt and pepper beard. He'd heard neither footstep, nor breath.

'They're killers.' He nodded at a sleek black and red snake on the flat top of a rock, basking in narrow fingers of sunlight that had found their way through the canopy.

'Thanks.' Ari put out his hand. 'Doug Courtney?'

'Ari Babitsky – Greer described you, so I'd know, and not kill the wrong man.'

'Thank the gods then, that my Greer got it right.' Ari lowered his hand; the man wasn't interested in contact, yet.

'I would've asked first,' he said. 'Maybe.'

Ari noticed that Courtney's hands trembled but the rest of him appeared as solid as the boulders surrounding them.

'You know what I'm after, Mr Courtney? What you didn't tell the police.'

'I know. You come recommended, in a roundabout sort of way.'

'Oh, yes?' said Ari.

'Greer via Livia via Trina – she's the one who sprung me. You should've seen the look on that bastard detective's face when she wrote the bail cheque, told him a Senior Counsel was in my corner from now on – her brother, apparently – pro bono. Hah.' Courtney smiled at his luck.

'Via Minerva,' Ari suggested.

Courtney stared at Ari. 'I'm sorry for your loss, Mr Babitsky.' He offered his hand, and Ari took it. Neither man tried to win the hand wrestle, a refreshing change in Ari's experience.

'You and I can make it up to Minerva – a little anyway. I've brought a thermos, and sandwiches. No room service this far out.' Ari indicated his backpack.

'Time's the enemy, Mr Babitsky. You never know who's likely to show up out here.' Doug Courtney strode off through the glade in the direction of the tent.

Ari followed him, eyeing off the black and red snake on its big grey boulder, half covered in velvety green moss. Was paranoia contagious, he wondered? He looked for creatures more out of place than himself on the way to the tent.

CHAPTER TWENTY-NINE

River City

Saturday 6 September 2008
Metro Central Hotel, CBD Mall

'**M**r Cordoba checked out, Ms Galvin.'

'That's suite P4? And it's under Cordoba?'

'Yes, ma'am. A Mr Cordoba was in suite P4.'

Livia stood at the kitchen bench, a glass of fizzing painkillers in one hand, the phone in the other. Cordoba? A sense of familiarity, not unpleasant, hovered briefly and then fled from her thoughts.

'Did he leave any messages for me?'

There was a silence at the other end of the phone, then Livia heard typing on a keyboard.

'One message. It's a name.'

Another name.

'Eleanor Roosevelt.'

'That's it?'

'Yes, I'm afraid so. Will there be anything else?'

'No. Thank you.'

Livia hung up. She tapped her fingers on the bench and swirled the glass before drinking the sweet tasting liquid. Cordoba. Eleanor Roosevelt. One name was enough to worry about for the moment. She tapped another number into the phone.

'Hello?'

'Mum, it's me.'

'Livia, where are you? What's going on?'

'I don't know. Do you know what's going on? Have any arrangements been made for Gordon yet?'

'This one won't be as fast as Minnie's was, Livia. Gordon only died yesterday.'

Her mother sounded tired, as tired as Livia still felt, even after a night's sleep on the world's most comfortable sofa. She couldn't do what she now realised was unavoidable until she either slapped herself into some kind of wakeful, alert state, or took the more sensible approach. It was only yesterday that Gordon died? It seemed so far away, so stretched beyond her understanding.

'Have you heard from Karl lately, Mum?' There was no harm in asking, however unlikely it was that Karl would contact Rosanna.

'As a matter of fact, he phoned late last night, asking me if I was certain I didn't have your gun case. I told him nothing had changed since the last time he asked me, and if I planned to rewrite history, I'd buy a time machine and make a few other changes he mightn't like very much. He sounded drunk, Livia.'

'Mum, don't worry about Karl. I'll look after him now. And don't worry about the gun case. That's a work in progress. Look, do you remember Eleanor Roosevelt?'

'Franklin D. Roosevelt's wife, a great feminist, a wonderful, brave woman. Knew her own mind, Eleanor Roosevelt, a hard worker. I could use someone like her around here. Which reminds me, Livia, when are you coming home? I mean, to the Bender, darling? I miss you.'

'I miss you, too, Mum. I'll be coming home as soon as I can. I just have a few things to do. There isn't anything else about Eleanor Roosevelt you can remember?'

'That isn't enough?'

Livia had to suppose that it was. Ari must have thought invoking Eleanor's name would inspire her.

'Okay, Mum. Jerry's in residence, is he?'

'He's here. You must do the thing you think you cannot do.'

'Yes, I know, Mum. And I'll be there for the spring stock-take, don't worry.'

'No, silly. That's the quotation: 'You must do the thing you think you cannot do.' Eleanor Roosevelt said that. I haven't heard it in a very long time. Your godfather used to tell you and Greer that when you were little – when you learned to walk, when you learned to swim, what with your father away so much even then. You were too young, you've forgotten. And by the way, that fellow rang for you.'

'Which fellow?' Rosanna sometimes referred to Paul Clifford as off-handedly, but Paul knew how to contact Livia on her mobile.

'That boy you went to school with. Grady what's-his-name?'

'Crabtree. What did he want?'

'He wants to talk to you. He's a strange one. He said he'd lose his head, those were his exact words, lose his head if he couldn't talk to you soon. He said he'd rather have both his hands cut off than miss a chance to speak to you. Now what could he mean by that, Livia? I've told you for thirty years that boy is crazy, an hysteric.'

'That boy is in his forties, Mum. He's a respected journalist.'

'There you go – another oxymoron – 'respected journalist.' There's no such thing and you know it.'

Rosanna hated the fourth estate. She resented their intrusions into the family's life over the years with their features on organised crime families – 'a thing of the past,' she always insisted – and their allegations about the Galvins' involvement in complex international money laundering and art theft franchises. More recently, Livia had heard from the fourth estate – that crazy boy in his forties – that Karl was rumoured to be aiming for the big-time with Armenian or Russian drug manufacturers: the kinds of drugs sold in massive volumes and cheaply through the internet or to third-world countries, the kinds of drugs that turned out to have either no active ingredients, or dangerous ones that maimed and killed rather than cured. She couldn't believe he'd even consider it, but there was belief and then there was reality. If Grady's research had thrown up the possibility, were the police on the money, too?

'You're right, Mum. Can we meet for lunch, next week maybe? Thursday sounds good, or a day ending in 'y."

'Call me when you're more settled, darling.' She was gone.

You must do the thing you think you cannot do. Livia re-dialled.

'River City News – Eyeline and Sunday Blinker desk. Blink and you'll miss it, but we won't. Do you have a story to tell?'

'With that patter, you could get a job selling mobile phone plans from Mumbai.'

'I'm filling in for my cadet, last seen heading for Dreamy Donuts three days ago.'

'Paying them a living wage would help, Grady.'

'Says you.'

'So you've got my attention. Do you have a story to tell me?'

'The body washed up, or was dumped, or dropped at De-ception Bay. I'm assuming you've seen or heard the news. A man in his mid- to late sixties, no identifying marks, exact cause of death to be determined. I remembered our conversa-tion at Mrs Babitsky's funeral, how uninterested you were in Tibor Restik being a potential murderer.'

'Because I know he couldn't have done anything like that.'

'He was such a quiet man, so kind to his elderly neigh-bours, helpful in every respect. I can't believe he could have done such a thing. Now, for $20, no, make that 20 pesos – I'm saving for a new cadet – 20 pesos and a chance to win an all-expenses paid trip to Australia Zoo, was I referring to a) Ted Bundy; b) Dr Crippin; or c) Jeffrey Dahmer? Come on, Livia. And if he murdered Mrs Babitksy, I'm left to wonder who took their revenge on him? And then I ask myself, what could CLEAR be a front for? Ex-circus types, some well-heeled, with international connections. Karl Galvin lurking nearby,

fake pharmaceuticals, a local sub-plot filled with illicit am-
phetamines – all these dodgy pills are connected somehow, in
the long run. You can see the possibilities.'

'Forget it,' Livia said, suddenly feeling nauseous. It must
have been the painkillers; she hadn't eaten enough before she
took them. She breathed deeply. 'Tibor Restik was a gentleman, a close friend of Mrs Babitsky. Take it from me, Grady,
CLEAR isn't a front for anything, and Mr Restik had nothing
to do with Minnie's death.' And to the extent that he may
have complicated matters by removing the gun case, he'd paid
with his life.

She walked to the sofa and sat down. She'd begun to
sweat, but the room was underheated if anything.

'Try this update anyway, from beneath the police desk.
Scenario one: the Deception Bay corpse is connected with the
booming amphetamine trade – River City is one of the country's biggest sources, and our headless poor bastard is a mid-
dle-man or a messenger for a big wheel who also dabbles in
those internet pharmaceuticals. Something went wrong
somewhere along the track: betrayal, greed, who knows?
Some other big wheel has sent a message of ill-will via the
decapitation and handectomies, hallmarks of organised you-
know-what. When Headless is identified, the trail should lead
to someone's front and back doors, whereupon Petersen's size
11s will kick down said doors and boot at least one wheel's
arse into maximum security, until their brief finds a techni-
cality. Petersen, of course, would like both wheels to be super
big-time operators whose downfall can help him into a better
cut of suit and a more heavily braided dress uniform.' He
paused. 'Response, Dr Galvin?'

'Why did you bring up Tibor Restik? I didn't think they'd identified the body yet.' Dehydration. She got up and went to the kitchen, turned on the tap and filled a glass. River City water tasted shocking – the drought, they said, all those years of treating sediment and pond scum, forcing it through the pipes – but it was safe, so far. Wasn't it?

'But they will identify him, by a process of elimination if nothing else – and when they do, Petersen will have his second scenario, a connection with Mrs Babitsky's death, and another excuse to knock down more doors, the CLEAR office, again; the victim's home in Fortescue Street. He'll put both scenarios together, formulate a plausible story, and try it out. It can't hurt, and the public will feel slightly safer in their beds with the thin blue line bringing up the rear after the ball is over, so to speak.'

'By which you mean that none of this speculation is leading to Minnie's murderer, nor is it about to.'

'That's the one certainty at present, I'm sorry to say – they don't have a clue, they're brainstorming, doing differential diagnoses on their mystery man. And since their prime suspect and possibly prime eyewitness was sprung by a generous bail-poster, they have even less. It was all circumstantial with Mr Courtney, and it'll probably be circumstantial with anyone else they'd care to arrest, too. In reality, no witnesses, or none willing to talk, no DNA as far as I can gather, and no clear motive apart from some outraged pro-development psychopath.'

'I have to lie down now, Grady. Thanks for the update.' She opened the fridge and saw bottled spring water.

'Don't forget Beijing.' Livia heard his voice fade as she took the phone away from her ear and pressed its red button.

She returned to the sofa with a bottle of water and lay down, sipping at the tasteless liquid, staring at the white ceiling, soothingly cool and, from a few metres away, apparently blemish free.

She dozed for a while, waiting for the water to do its job, for the nausea to pass – perhaps she had a slight concussion, after all? – then picked up the room phone and organised a wake-up call and dinner in her room. She forced herself to her feet and went into the bedroom, drawing the heavy drapes so that the room was as dark as it could be in the middle of another perfect day. She undressed and lay on the fresh, cool sheets, and was asleep long before the first clouds crossed Spring Hill.

CHAPTER THIRTY

River City

Sunday 7 September 2008
Holy Mother and St Jude Retreat

1

Livia had never thought of her hometown as anything but unremarkable. Flat suburbs and hilly ones sprawled all over the 27th parallel, interrupted by the muddy river: satellite shots revealed a narrow, black progression of turns and bends that resembled nothing so much as a demented snake. Some claimed River City as the biggest municipality by area in the world. Others said, no, it was second, but then couldn't remember number one because what was the point, they didn't live there, did they?

To outsiders, River City's quirkiest feature were the so-called houses on stilts, purpose-built for the summer months, the design probably stolen from Asia – a hallway running straight through the house from front door to back, verandahs at the front, or some combination of front, sides and back, depending on the size of the house and the wealth of its owners. Breeze-catchers, dream-callers, that was how Minnie described her verandahs. Livia was looking forward to enjoying some breezes and dreams, rather than the nightmares that had descended once she'd fallen asleep in the hotel room. It wasn't the room that caused the heart surges of anxiety, the sense of dread as she hovered between sleep and wakefulness. The entire suite managed to be disturbingly bereft of atmosphere and personality and at the same time comforting, an icon of the transitory. And it wasn't the head knock, she'd realised, once she'd showered and eaten dinner, checked the news for further police developments: there were none, or none reported. She was glad to be awake, even with the headache and other leftover cemetery injuries; some bruises were only imposing themselves now. There was something else, nagging away at the edge of her memory, but she knew it so well. It was like seeing a famous film star or politician and not being able to place a name with the face, noun deprivation. It was something someone had said, something familiar, someone familiar, like the Gardner memory – there it was, and there it wasn't, millimetres from her grasp, in shadow.

It became a waiting game. She'd forced herself to the sofa after dinner, conscious of conserving her energy, wary of the headache regaining its momentum, although it seemed spent at last. She'd taken the precaution of setting the alarm on her mobile phone, in case the excitement of late night television soccer replays didn't do the job. At 3am – heart-attack hour, the hour Scott Fitzgerald chose as the soul's darkest – the theme from *Lost in Space* startled her awake, and within 30 minutes she was driving down St Jude's Road, flipping a wave to Minnie in the cemetery, and slowing to a crawl at the T-intersection, wipers flicking the last of an early spring shower from the windscreen.

She took a right and headed for the Holy Mother's entry gate, killing the headlights before turning in. She stopped briefly while her eyes adjusted to the darkness, then inched the car forward, parking near the first roundabout where St Jude stood watch on his pedestal, hoping, no doubt, for an easy night shift.

She had her hand on the door-handle when she remembered to reach up and turn the cabin light from automatic to off. Torch in hand, Ogham alphabet page, notebook and pen in her pants pocket, Livia stepped out onto the driveway and noiselessly pushed the door closed. She shoved the car keys as deeply into her other jeans pocket as they'd go to muffle jingling.

Although the rain had let up – most of it had fallen as she slept – the air was heavy and the cloud cover was still thick, blacking out the available moonlight. It was so dark that she'd walked to within a couple of metres of the hearse before she could see it properly, parked near the entry to the high-care building. There were security lights at each corner of this building, the largest in the complex, but at its entrance, low wattage fluorescent tubes cast barely enough light to identify visitors. Beyond this feeble glow, it was almost pitch black. The single-storey independent living duplexes dotting the grounds had porch lights at their front and back doors, and there were small, twinkling lights around other outer buildings, but it was no stalag. There was no reason for the elderly and the frail to be out in the middle of the night, and therefore no reason for football stadium floodlighting. Any residents suddenly filled with an irresistible desire to nighttime strolling would have to rely on St Jude for support.

Livia moved along the side of the hearse, whose open rear door was about three metres from the sliding-glass entry door. The management must have decided it would be less distressing to the surviving residents for the undertaker to perform under cover of dark. The prayers and Mass would come later when everyone felt more secure, and healthy, in the light of day. For a few moments, she wondered if it could be Sibyl, and hoped Rosanna would have had the presence of mind to phone her. She pushed the thought away – there had been enough death already – and glanced around before moving to the entrance.

She hadn't thought of how to gain access, and couldn't have been more underprepared when she noticed that the sliding-glass door wasn't fully closed. Wedged at ground level between the door and the door-frame was a toad, struggling to pull itself free. She felt her toes contract inside her boots as she scanned the immediate vicinity for its other family members. The rain must have lured it out of its usual hiding place. Not only did she have to break and enter a property she partly owned, she had to get past an object of fear in order to do so. But if the toad hadn't entrapped itself, her plan might have come to a dead-end.

Gratitude was in order. Keeping her eyes focussed on the toad, which didn't appear to have the same level of interest in Livia, she leaned across, placed her hand around the glass edge of the door and pulled. It resisted, pushing against her pull, the automatic closing mechanism cranking itself up. Imagining the worst outcome for the toad shot a dose of adrenalin into her extremities. She applied herself with renewed vigour, and both hands. She had no desire to read anything into the exploded entrails of one of the earth's less-loved creatures. Even so, the door wouldn't budge. She moved closer and spread her hands as widely as she could towards its top and bottom, distributing her pulling weight more evenly. Her right foot was less than half a metre from the toad's nose. The toad began to make strange grunting sounds. When Livia heard the faintest of noises coming from inside, she pulled as hard as she could. Finally, the door moved with, rather than against her. She pulled again, quickly, and it moved a few more millimetres, just enough to free the toad, which lurched and hopped towards the gladioli garden beside the doorway. She pulled again and again. The door racheted back by centimetres until it finally gave up and shuddered open.

Livia stepped through into the foyer and heard the elevator doors opening at the end of the hallway to her right. The undertakers. To her left, she heard a muffled conversation, the family of the deceased. The ridiculous thought occurred to her that she was trapped between life and death, her choices diminishing rapidly. She took two long steps across the hall, plunging into the greenhouse on the third. Her foot made contact with something slippery and she lost her balance, sliding along the aisle between tree ferns, between kentia and golden cane palms. A large clay pot full of basil stopped her. She remained still, listening for voices and footsteps, which came, in due course, past the greenhouse doorway and disappeared outside. While the night staff saw off the bereaved and deceased, Livia pulled herself up, felt the renewed throbbing and stinging in her grazed hands, and returned to the hallway.

She took the stairwell up to the highest-care level, level four, where Sibyl lived and where the residents were more likely to be sleeping, with the aid of sedation. Still in the stairwell, she checked the torch before entering the floor, which was quiet and dark. Pilot lights along the hallway skirting guided staff and ambulatory residents into and out of rooms. Most of the paintings were still missing, but the volunteers – Verity, Cosmo and Ruth – had either left some behind, or had returned some spick and span ones already. Livia moved along the hallway and decided to try the painting nearest to Sibyl's room. If disturbed, she could visit with Sibyl, very quietly.

When she tried to lift the painting off its hook, it wouldn't budge. The Sacred Heart of Jesus was immovable. She turned the torchlight onto it and saw why. The frame itself was attached to the wall by screwed-in corner mounts. A cordless drill, or at the very least, a screwdriver, would be necessary. When the stairwell door opened, she slipped into Sibyl's room and stood behind her door in the gap between it and the wall behind her. There was just enough space.

Footsteps proceeded and then stopped every so often: a bed check? Livia leaned out from behind the door and tried to focus on Sibyl in her bed. She was a little bundle of sheets covered with a blanket, and appeared to be sound asleep. Livia took several deep breaths to calm herself, and eventually, the nurse's shape briefly darkened the narrow crack where the door was hinged to the doorframe. She walked in and stood at the foot of Sibyl's bed, her back to the door. She stood there for hours, or, more accurately, about 30 seconds, to confirm that Sibyl was still attached to this world, and then left.

Livia let her breath go, dropped her shoulders and bent her knees. She slipped out of Sibyl's room, and stood in the doorway. Attempting to pry the Sacred Heart or any of the other well-secured works off the wall no longer made sense. Even if she'd been aware of when the nurses' rounds took place, even if they had a strict schedule and usually kept to it, tonight it had been disrupted by a resident's death. There was no telling who else might come or go, or stay. She'd naively hoped that a nursing home at this hour would be a quiet place. The only venue that was quieter, more out of the way, may not offer what she sought, but she'd have to try it. In shooting, when you weren't hitting the targets, you had only Hemingway's choice: to go on regardless and see your way through to the end of the damn round, somehow.

2

The chapel, with a separate bell-tower at the rear, was sandwiched between the old convent and the high-care centre. It was a wooden structure, seventy or eighty years old, sitting on stumps about a metre and a half high. Next to the multistorey brick building, it looked small, but the body of the chapel, incorporating a choir loft over the front entrance, could hold a congregation of probably 300 or more celebrators of the Word, or more frequently these days, mourners. Narrow verandahs ran along both sides and were accessible from strategically placed sets of steps. A series of doors led off the verandahs into the chapel. It was built in the days when churches overflowed and the traffic in and out for every Mass and other service was high-volume. The doors also provided much-needed cross-ventilation in summer. The sacristy, a room of its own behind the altar at the eastern end, had its own separate entrances and stairs on either side for the priest and his assistants.

Livia, surveying the chapel from the shadows of the Holy Mother grotto, decided on the most direct route and chose the front door. There didn't appear to be any security lights on the front porch, which sported a single, lonely bulb. She crouched and ran from the cover of the grotto across an open space and up the front steps. She turned the left doorknob. Nothing moved. She glanced out at the darkness and gripped the other knob, listening for voices, footsteps. It turned easily, as though recently oiled and serviced. She sidled in and closed the door, silently thanking whoever had forgotten to lock up.

Inside, it was darker still, but Jesus was at home. The red light burning on the wall to the right of the altar, which signified his presence, cast part of its low glow towards the tabernacle. In between the doors and windows, on the wall space on either side of the chapel were the Stations of the Cross. In the corner to the left of the front doors, the shape of a small side altar faced out from the north wall beneath the choir loft. Two straight-backed chairs with attached padded kneelers were set before the altar. Livia turned on the torch and walked towards the corner, picking out devotional candles, boxes of matches, a small wooden donation box for the candle-lighters and, on the wall above the altar, a framed painting of Our Lady of Perpetual Succour. Unlike the screwed-in frames in the big house, this one was attached the old-fashioned way, hanging by a length of wire from a nail. She leaned across the altar and unhooked it, then sat on one of the altar seats and turned the painting face-down on her lap.

She inspected the frame using the torch, found its 'bar code' running up a vertical axis from the bottom left corner, and unfolded the Ogham alphabet page. She took the pen and notebook from her pocket, copied down the marks and checked them against the printout. Five backslash strokes through the axis, a space, four horizontal strokes through, another space, and a single backslash stroke through the axis. According to Ogham, they spelled R E M. There was a bigger space after these three 'letters' and then four horizontal strokes to the right of the axis, a small space, and what seemed to be an X with a shadow X beside or behind it: double vision. S P. Another wider space indicated another set of letters, which may or may not be a word. The next set of strokes spelled out the letters S C A P. A code within a code. It meant something to someone, somewhere. It occurred to Livia that she and Jill may be entirely mistaken with Ogham, that these letters, REM SP SCAP, were utterly wrong. But what about Boston, and Gardner? What about them?

She pulled her keys out of her pocket. They jingled and echoed noisily in the big open room. She found the penknife, flicked it open, and stared down at the frame. Would anyone regard it as sacrilegious to slash open a painting of Our Lady, in a church? It was a very old frame with cardboard backing taped around the wood. She tried to slice carefully, holding the torch in one hand and the knife in the other, so that the painting itself wouldn't be damaged.

Eventually, holding the torch between her teeth and using both hands, she levered the backing up and away from the frame. The painting was intact, although foxing marked its reverse side. The original creamy colour of the thick paper had turned shades of brown around the edges and there were light and darker brown spots across the paper. The chapel could hardly be regarded as an atmospherically- controlled environment for great or worthless art, being so close to the salty bay air and without the benefit of air-conditioning. She leaned back in the chair. There was nothing else but a Byzantine Mary here, hopefully not an original sent across the waves with Mother Magda from her family's Viennese palazzo and then forgotten.

Risking discovery should any night stroller happen by and see the light inside the chapel, she played the torch along the wall above the altar, where another wall hanging was displayed. It was neither painting nor print, and it wasn't a Station, but it was framed. It was much smaller than the others and there was a plaque fastened to the bottom edge of the frame. It read, 'Scapular hand-made by Reverend Mother Magda Mesmer, circa 1918. Blessed by His Holiness Pope John XXIII, 1960.'

Livia remembered attending a scapular ceremony as a child with her classmates, honouring St Iphigenia – her primary school's saint of record – and Our Lady of Mount Carmel. Once the priest blessed it, the scapular was hung loosely around the neck, a square dangling front and back to either warn off evil spirits, or bring good ones closer, something like that. Some children wore theirs constantly beneath their pinafores. Livia, uninterested in religion, lost hers immediately after the ceremony. It would turn up some day when Rosanna decided it was time to spring clean the Bender of childhood things.

Mother Magda's scapular consisted of two small squares of cotton fabric about 50mm x 50mm joined by lengths of string, with images of Our Lady of Perpetual Succour sewn onto one square and St Jude of Thaddeus, the patron saint of lost causes and the hopeless, sewn onto the other.

'You could earn your stripes now,' Livia whispered to the little images smiling out at her.

She turned the frame over and found more Ogham script. On this frame, the letters REM and SP reappeared, but there was no SCAP. It took a few seconds for her 4 a.m. synapses to fire, for her to recognise that SCAP could be an abbreviation for scapular. The Catholic cognoscenti had nothing on her.

The penknife slid through the backing tape easily. After removing the backboard, there was a thick sheet of backing paper inside as well. Livia pushed up an edge with the penknife and lifted it out. The scapular came with it, stitched to it at strategic points so that it wouldn't collapse to the bottom of the frame and lose its impressiveness as an object of reverence.

She turned the scapular this way and that, training the torch on each image, edging the fabric squares away from the backing paper. There was nothing behind either square. There was, however, a fold of fabric sewn over the top of the St Jude, turning it into a miniature envelope. Inside was a small piece of paper: Mother Magda's scapular pattern? There was enough space around it to slide it out without too much effort. It was difficult to see much detail in the torchlight, but the image on the paper was a drawing of a bearded man with long hair wearing a cap tilted at an almost rakish angle. He looked near to smug, his lips closer to forming a smile than a frown, and his eyes seemed to say, here I am, ladies, aren't I a catch? Even in this light, it was easy to see that it was the work of an accomplished artist.

'REM SP,' Livia said aloud. A tiny portrait that may once have resided with Our Lady of Perpetual Succour, before the damp threatened to impose itself. Perhaps the scapular was a marginally better insulator. Was REM SP related to Boston or Gardner, by any chance? If her suspicions were correct – but she'd have to check.

Livia turned off the torch and stared ahead of her. She had to repair the frames, return the pictures to the wall. Whoever else might know about this, she couldn't risk them becoming aware of tampering, not right away. How much danger had she stepped into here? Was there really a Mercator map in the gun case, after all, or was something much bigger going on under her nose, something Ari knew nothing about? She stared at the portrait, not much bigger than a postage stamp.

'How did you end up here? And who were you waiting for – Minnie? Did she put you here?' She looked to the altar for inspiration. That's what altars were for, but they seldom seemed to deliver, in her experience.

Candles and matches. There were dozens of candles in tealight holders, in varying states of melt, on the altar. Livia took a box of matches and lit four or five of them, more as a comfort than anything else. There was no tape here, though there might be a gaffer roll in her car, but the risk of coming and going again was too high. She picked up one of the candles and turned it so that the liquified wax dripped onto the palm of her hand, an activity she and Greer enjoyed as children. It was hot, then comfortingly warm and soft. They would make shapes and write words in wax until Rosanna or Minnie discovered their folly and asked them if they wanted to spend the next cyclone in the dark. This wax quickly began to cool on her palm and reset itself, like an old-time seal. She picked the white circle off her palm and returned it to the holder for a second life.

'Thanks, Jude,' she said aloud looking at the solution.

3

'Father? It is Father, isn't it?'

'Yes, Sister. Father Chen. The new priest.'

'You're so early, Father. I'm Sister Immaculata.'

Voices outside the chapel, and close enough. Too close.

Wax dripped into, onto and across the cuts in the backing tape on the larger of the two frames as they lay face-down on the altar. There was no way of telling how long it would hold; just long enough. Livia started on the second frame, pouring as much wax as she dared along and beside the cuts, willing it to drip faster and harden quickly. She strained to hear the voice again as she tidied the altar.

'The early priest, Sister, catches the congregation, although I was not expecting to see anyone here just yet.'

The early priest, at least two people outside. Maybe it was a simple morning walk past the chapel for the ascetics among the Holy Mother's residents and staff.

'Our residents tend to take life a little easier than this, Father, at their stage of life. Didn't Father Shand explain – no early Masses, except by request. Like the top forty.' The woman laughed at her own joke.

Mass. Livia returned Our Lady's portrait to the wall and waited. Shuffling feet beyond the wall. Where could she go?

'I'm afraid Father Shand forgot to give me his keys. Do you have a chapel key, Sister? I would like to get started.'

You don't need a key, Livia thought, it's open to all-comers.

'Well, he was certainly hasty, all right. He didn't give us any warning about you, Father. But you're very welcome, of course.'

'Father Shand's brother was taken ill very suddenly, so he told me.'

More walking, and some of their conversation blown away on the wind. But Father Chen, at least, was coming in. Livia blew out the candles and hooked Magda's reframed scapular up, slipped the REM SP into her shirt pocket and trotted down the aisle to the main altar: not the old-fashioned kind, heavy oak with spaces underneath where an intruder could seek respite. It was modern, Ikea modern, all steel legs and minimalist benchtop, out of place. A donation they couldn't refuse from an influential parishioner or resident? Usually, they preferred the in-your-face majesty of a stained-glass window.

'You're very lucky we ran into each other, Father.'

The voices were only a few metres from where Livia stood. They'd followed her down the chapel. She swerved over to the sacristy door and found it unlocked. He'd come in here, once he'd paid his respects to Jesus out in the body of the church, to arrange things for Mass. She stood in the doorway and saw that there was nowhere to hide. The place was simple and old but it held more than a touch of class: polished boxwood floorboards, a silky oak wardrobe – with brass door handles – for the vestments, a matching chest of drawers for related paraphernalia, a white porcelain wash basin with a gilt-framed mirror on the wall above it and a small cupboard beneath, also silky oak. There was a table in the middle of the room – silky oak if Livia wasn't mistaken – for the priest to spread out his gear as he dressed for Mass. What was it about River City Catholics and silky oak?

And why, she suddenly wondered, standing in the priest's sacred space, did he come without a key? Hasty Father Shand forgot, but Father Chen knew that before he got up this morning, didn't he? And he didn't know the place was unlocked. Livia knew Father Shand, from a distance. He'd been the priest at the Holy Mother and the local parish for 30 years. He was a man of deliberate habits and routines, he preferred the Latin Mass because he believed it sounded sweeter, and he'd never forget to give a new boy the keys, would he? Father Chen. Did Father Chen sound foreign? Chinese? His accent was global-English neutral. Livia never would have credited a church with encouraging such paranoia, and suspicion. But this was no ordinary church, not anymore, not after what she'd found. Adrenalin had begun to pump into her extremities; it was making her jumpy; she wanted to run.

'If you're going to celebrate Mass, you'll need flowers, Father. Come.' Sister Immaculata, bless her, was a woman who knew when she held an ace. She'd make him work for the redundant keys.

'Sister, I really must get on with my office.' The walking stopped near the sacristy's southern door.

Livia had to leave, but she knew she had to find a suitable container for the miniature portrait. If the postage stamp print was valuable, a real piece of work, she'd need something other than her shirt pocket to protect it.

'Very well, sister, let us pick flowers.' A sensible card player knows when to fold them. The feet started up again and moved off.

The wardrobe revealed a line of finely embroidered white, green, purple, black and red chasubles, along with albs, cinctures and maniples, several stoles, a dalmatic. In the first and deepest drawer of the chest of drawers were two chalices with accompanying patens and palls, a ciborium and, folded beside them, half a dozen linen purificators and two chalice veils, leftovers from the glory days. A rummage through the other drawers and a quick check of the cupboard under the basin produced nothing in the way of an appropriate container.

Livia returned to the chest of drawers and at the same time she heard voices entering the church. They were walking down the aisle. She opened the chalice drawer again and lifted the palls and then the purificators. Nothing. What she assumed were corporals – long linen cloths spread over the altar before Mass begins – were folded at the back of the drawer behind the purificators. She lifted them and there it was: a portable host carrier. It was round and silver and looked like a large fob watch. She took the print from her pocket, flipped open the portable and dropped it in: a more or less square print in a round hole. It would have to do.

Livia tiptoed to the sacristy's southern door and turned the doorknob; it didn't budge.

'Will you be needing an altar server later this morning, Father?'

'I won't be needing anyone else this morning, Sister. I would like to familiarise myself alone. Thank you.'

Father Chen sounded anxious to be rid of his helper.

Livia crossed to the other door. Immovable.

'But, Father, Father Shand always –'

'Father Shand isn't here, Sister. If you'll leave the keys with me, I'll make sure the chapel is locked this time.'

'Well, I, I'll just arrange the flowers for you, shall I?' The sister's resolve was beginning to crumble.

Silence.

Livia darted to the cupboard beneath the wash-basin.

'These peonies are Father Shand's favourite.'

More silence.

Inside the cupboard was an array of wine bottles whose contents stood at different levels. Father Shand liked a drop, and he liked variety. Who could blame him? On an impulse, Livia grabbed a bottle and removed the cork, swallowing a good snort. The warmth of it hit her like a hammer and she sat down on the floor.

'Sister Joan, how lovely of you to join us.' The sisterhood would save the day. Another annoyance for Father Chen, who remained silent, and fuming? Why was he in such a rush?

'I saw lights, earlier, Sister Immaculata, Father. I couldn't sleep. You two are early birds, all right.' An elderly voice. There were night strollers, after all, at the Holy Mother, all of them used to the terrain, unfazed by darkness. Their Lord was with them twenty-four-seven.

'We've been out in the garden, Sister. We just came in. This is Father Chen. He's saying Mass.'

'Not today, Sister. Tomorrow.'

'Oh, but Father Shand –'

There must be a sacristy key, a spare one, there had to be, one seldom used and probably forgotten about. There'd been no keys in the drawers. She lifted up each wine bottle, terrified of clinking one against the other. There were round red stains, hardened or still sticky, a line of ants through one section, a couple of dead cockroaches and, on the top shelf, third row, left, a piece of string. Livia pulled on it and drew out a key, rusted and dusty. She got to her feet, took the few steps to the door, inserted the key, turned it.

Outside, the sky was lightening, and soon the sun would rise over the bay and steam away the dew and the morning shower. Livia bent low and moved towards the Holy Mother's garden and shrine. The air was cool and fresh after the chapel and sacristy. She stood shielded by the Holy Mother's statue, and inhaled deeply; the host carrier pressed against her left breast.

She waited for more early birds to appear, but there were none for the moment. When would Father Chen realise that he hadn't been shining the lights that Sister Joan had seen inside the chapel? Livia took her chance and walked out of the garden at normal speed, her head erect, a dawn stroller. Her training kicked in automatically: body language is a prime indicator of guilt, so when you're out of place, and unauthorised, behave as though you fit like a hand in a glove. As she walked, she considered her ties with Sibyl and with the home, through Minnie's Will. She'd come out early to inspect the premises, she could tell an inquiring nun or nurse; she had no idea how early it was because her watch was running fast. She looked at her wrist. She didn't have a watch, even better.

She kept walking, getting faster, until she reached her car. She drove around St Jude's roundabout like any other soul lost on Border Rd and looking for a place to turn and redeem herself.

CHAPTER THIRTY-ONE

River City

Sunday 7 September 2008
West Bend Heritage Hotel

1

At the Bender, Livia showered and changed out of her gothic cowgirl disguise into her usual uniform: black trousers, white shirt and leather jacket. She risked being mistaken for one of the bar staff and buttonholed to take a drinks order, but she'd never minded that; it meant she blended in and was taken for granted as part of the furniture. She'd slipped into the living quarters with a nod to Jerry and without disturbing Rosanna, and now she sat on the bed in her room, the mystery portrait in front of her on the bedspread.

Could this small drawing have something to do with Minnie's death, or an association with what was presumably still in the gun case? She had to know what she was dealing with, and whether or not there were more REMs hidden away.

Sibyl's safety could be at stake, too, and Rosanna's, Uncle Con's, the CLEAR committee.

. 'Hello again, handsome,' she said. 'Rembrandt Harmensz Van Rijn. How are you? None the worse for wear, I hope.'

There was nothing like talking to an inanimate object, albeit a valuable one, if it was the real thing, to reinforce one's sense of occasion. She felt liberated from one small burden of ignorance. If Minnie and the others had been storing art works behind other paintings and prints at the nursing home, the place could be full of Rembrandts and others, even fakes, waiting to be re-homed, taken out of the art cooler at last. Could this be what Rosanna had meant about Minnie doing special things for the family when she spoke at the funeral: she managed an art cooler at the Holy Mother and St Jude?

She looked into Rembrandt's benign eyes, which seemed to be a little out of focus or slightly crossed. It was probably her imagination, although she remembered reading about some artists whose view of the world, altered by visual problems, affected the art they produced. She couldn't remember if Rembrandt was one of them.

'Where are your mates?' she asked him. Eventually, she'd have to return to the Holy Mother and St Jude and find out for herself. The alternative was to simply confront Verity, or Cosmo or Ruth and ask them for the truth. Which assumed they knew what they were removing from the walls and taking it to who-knew-where? They could simply be couriers without knowledge of the real prizes within the frames. Need-to-know could be in action here, too. And if Karl knew the whereabouts of the cooler, the temptation to plunder it would be far greater than he was designed to resist. He'd sell or barter away every last painting, drawing and etching to secure entrée into particular international operations whose CEOs had more money than they could handle, but too few artistic rarities in their greedy possession.

She closed her eyes and pressed her fingers to her temples, wishing she was at the beach with the dogs. Life could be so simple, if it would just leave her alone for long enough.

2

'Someone tried to break in last night.' Rosanna stood at the kitchen bench, cup in hand.

'Where? When?' Livia stood with her plate in one hand, a fork in the other. She no longer felt hungry. The gun case, were they chasing it here in their ignorance?

'The private quarters, after midnight. The security people arrived in good time, but by then they were gone.'

'Are you okay?' Livia had a sudden vision of Rosanna on the kitchen floor, unconscious, bleeding. 'Did you call the police?'

'Jerry's changed the codes, and he's looking into upgrading the system, today. You know what he's like. The place is already Fort Knox. I don't know what's happening in this world anymore.'

'Me neither. As long as you're all right.'

'Yes, darling, I'm all right.' Rosanna smiled at Livia. 'The eggs?'

'The eggs?'

'Good manners are the hallmark of a civilised society, Livia.'

Livia followed her mother's gaze to the plate she still held, the scrambled eggs forgotten. Another of Rosanna's coping skills: micro-manage, focus on the routine events of life. Not a bad plan when you thought about it.

'These eggs are delicious, Mum.' Livia stood at the kitchen bench. 'Silken, soft, on the cusp of floating away. And the toast. I don't know where to begin.'

'There's no need to gild the lily, dear, and you don't have to eat any more of it.' Rosanna poured herself another cup of tea. 'You know this is your home, as much as that little loft at the gallery. The fact that you sneak in at the crack of dawn is neither here nor there. You're lucky Jerry was on duty, or one of the other security boys could have arrested you by mistake after last night. You're lucky he's so switched on, and he wasn't at early Mass.'

Rosanna had never taken to the idea of Livia moving into the loft, which wasn't so small. She'd returned to the Bender when she and Paul broke up and Rosanna seemed to relax with the idea that her move was permanent.

'Early Mass? Jerry?' That was something to think about. 'By the way, Mum, do you know what happened to Father Shand out at the Holy Mother? He's taken off, or something.'

'Who told you that?'

'There's a Father Chen there now. Sister Immaculata mentioned it.'

'Sister Immaculata drifts in and out, Livia. She has dementia, sort of – she's on her way, but occasionally, she comes back to us for a visit. Father Chen, I haven't heard of him, but sometimes they have to bring them in from other places.'

'But Father Shand? I heard his brother was taken ill.' If Chen was on the money.

'His brother? I don't know, but Father Liam Shand's mother, Betty, died recently, prompting her son to announce his departure from the priesthood.'

'Oh.'

'Betty left Liam a fortune and a country house in a remote part of County Clare. Liam has taken off, as you say, with his housekeeper, Denice. There are marriage plans afoot.'

'Why wouldn't they stay here?'

'Well, it's a better outcome than being sentenced for kiddy fiddling, but it's still not a good look for the Church. Denice has been his housekeeper for 30 years, Livia. Better to go missing in the wilds of the Irish Republic.'

'Mum, do you remember when Uncle Ari disappeared?'

'What a question. It was terrible, terrible for Minnie, everyone.'

'How did they make sure he was dead?'

'Make sure?'

'I mean, confirmation that he'd died, somewhere. A proper death certificate.'

'They didn't have any way of making sure. They couldn't confirm anything. He was in touch with Minnie, and then he wasn't. We didn't even know exactly where he was – Europe or Israel. Or somewhere else entirely. Why?'

Why? If Rosanna knew anything more, she was both a good actress, and she had no intention making revelations to Livia, not right now anyway.

'I've just been thinking about him lately, wondering what might have been, you know, with Minnie that night.'

'There's no light down that road, Livia, you know that.'

Rosanna studied the leaves in the bottom of her cup; she moved back to the teapot, a plus-sized version to cater for all-comers on cool mornings. It was shiny and gold coloured on the outside and white inside, and Rosanna's hands had worn the paint on its golden handle to white over the years of pouring and pouring.

'You mean Dan, don't you?' Livia said.

'Minnie and this business in Beijing, it's stirred you up, darling. It's PTSD, you know that better than anyone. Triggers, setting off alarms in your mind. Reminding you of Colombia.'

Rosanna sagged momentarily, lost her usual straight-backed poise, revealed for a second in her eyes the eternal grief for her little boy lost, long enough for Livia to notice, and tack away.

'Mum, is it all right if I use your PC for a while? A bit of research, some gallery stuff.'

She brought her plate and fork to the sink and stood beside her mother, put her arm around her shoulders. They stood together gazing at the teapot. Dan had been too young to lift it when it was hot and full, but he was determined to play when it was empty. Rosanna would half fill the sink with water, drag a chair over for him to stand on, roll up his sleeves, and let him pour the dregs in, black leaves of tea swirling around making patterns, gliding effortlessly around his hands, fingers trying to catch the leaves as they sped by.

'You don't have to ask, Livia.'

'Thanks, Mum.' She squeezed a one-armed hug and left her mother in the kitchen. More than once, she'd wondered if

Dan's death had been some kind of cosmic ledger-balancing act after Jacques Foucault. The innocent sons taken for the sins of their parents. But where did that logic leave Minnie, and Tibor, Gordon and Ari? What sort of ledgers were they trying to balance?

CHAPTER THIRTY-TWO

Gold Coast Hinterland
Sunday 7 September 2008
Avalon Resort and Therapy Centre

'I don't think this was a good idea.'

'But you must agree the result was great.' Yani kissed her neck.

'Hmm.' Greer smoothed his black hair back from his forehead. 'You've still got some war wounds from Beijing.' She lightly touched the laceration near his right temple. The tissue around it was still bruised, the darkness standing out against his olive skin. 'Livia said you'd been injured, poor man. And this.' She leaned over and kissed his right shoulder where the bullet had grazed his collarbone.

'Thank God Livia was there to save me.' He shifted position and placed his hand on her flat, bare stomach. 'Anyway, I don't recall this particular scar the last time we met.' He walked his fingers up to a rough circle of skin, whiter than the rest, just beneath Greer's left breast.

'The less said about that the better. I've done some re-search into trauma in a few places a little more dangerous than I expected them to be.' She rolled onto her back and stared at the white ceiling. 'You still haven't told me what you're doing here.'

His arrival had been quite a surprise. He'd crept into her room earlier in the morning and was sitting in the chair oppo-site her bed when she woke up. Apparently, he'd bypassed security, used his lockpicks – cat burglar Lee – and found his way into the owners' bungalow. He'd smiled at her, she'd smiled back, and somehow, he'd ended up in bed with her. She supposed she could blame it on exhaustion rather than misjudgement, or the discombobulation of having killed a man without hesitation. And there was their history, a scat-tergram of meetings in distant places as they moved around the world doing whatever it was they did to feel fulfilled.

'You still haven't told me what Livia's doing, or what you're doing here, for that matter.'

'Me? I'm taking a break from my research. And Livia, she's trying to understand who could have attacked Minnie and killed her. Our godmother.' When she said it, she felt a throbbing pain in her chest. She wanted to cry, but the tears wouldn't come, not yet. Instead, she felt the heat in her eyes and on her cheeks, and knew he'd notice.

'I'm sorry,' Yani said. 'I didn't mean to upset you. But I'm worried about Livia, too.'

'It's all right. She thinks she's getting closer. There's a chance she might even find what they were looking for, who-ever they are. And they've killed Tibor as well.'

She stopped. There was something convincing about Yani, she thought, convincing enough to get her into bed with him almost every time they met. He encouraged self-disclosure, and worse, the disclosure of other people's secrets.

'Tibor? Who's Tibor?'

'A dear friend of Minnie's.' She decided not to tell him everything. 'He's gone missing, and Livia's convinced he's been murdered, too.'

'By the same people?'

'She isn't sure of that.'

'You know, I was only supposed to collect the case and re-move the contents, Greer. I have no stomach for murder. And I'm not returning to China.'

He was so close to her, she could feel his breath on her face.

'Why not? You love China. China's your life.' There was far more to Yani's simple courier story than he'd let on, she was convinced.

'I'm going to Greece to start again. I'm going to be an art dealer. My mother has family connections, in Athens and London. After what's happened, I'm a liability in some peo-ple's eyes.'

'Whose eyes? Surely you have support, your father's a bigwig, isn't he?'

'Dad's playing his own games at the moment. I don't really know what he's doing, and he's obsessed with the Sister Cities program and the Museum exhibitions – he's in River City now.'

'Bing Lee is here?' Greer was surprised; Mr Lee rarely ventured outside his comfort zone in Beijing from what Yani had told her over the years.

'I'm keeping a low profile with everyone for the time being. There's one person in particular who I'm almost certain decided to take the gun case for himself rather than deliver it. But I didn't know enough about the rest of the plan to make it right.'

'NTK,' she said, staring into his eyes.

'How did you – ?'

She looked down at the scar near her breast. 'That happened because of Need To Know and its major shortcoming: the essential trustworthiness of everyone else in the chain, especially if you don't have backup.' Which was why, after that particular accident, Ari had shadowed her every move, and she'd done the same for him. She still wondered why it had taken her so long to learn the lesson, especially after Perpignan and Jacques.

'I think someone's tried to double-cross Gordon on this deal,' he said, 'and they're still trying to score. Mrs Babitsky was caught in the middle.'

His eyes glittered with unshed tears as he leaned over and took her in his arms. Who was he talking about? Himself? And how could he have known that it would lead to this?

'Watch that shoulder, boyo,' she said. Boyo. She never used the word, not after Eamon. She tried not to think of him, and now she felt that old sense of trying to swim through higher and higher waves, swallowing water, unable to see the life she could have lived. She'd become Dan's and Eamon's avenging angel, with Ari, and now it was over, and here she was with another man on the edge of mortality. She wouldn't get involved, couldn't jump in, not again. Yani had been an occasional indulgence, and she knew that he saw her in the same way. It had to end. The vendetta against Dan's and Eamon's murderers had followed its natural course and it had ended, she hoped. She wanted another life, even if its details were hazy at present. She could allow herself to savour this last encounter with a man she barely knew and worry about any guilt later. There was always plenty of time for that.

'Greer?'

His voice was a long way off.

'Greer?'

'Mmm.'

'Can you tell Livia for me? Please? Mrs Babitsky was in the wrong place.'

He'd been talking, but she hadn't been listening.

'She has to know the truth. She has to know who it is, if she hasn't already guessed.'

'Of course,' she replied, 'all right.' She leaned into him and his arms tightened around her.

CHAPTER THIRTY-THREE

River City

Sunday 7 September 2008
Fortescue Street, Spring Hill

1

In Rosanna's study at the Bender, Livia had Googled Sibyl's contribution, Mercator, confirming its history and the location and value of some of Gerardus Mercator's creations. She could make no connection between it and Boston or Gardner, but the Mercator story itself had checked out. There was, unsurprisingly, no mention of stolen Mercators, or Mercators turning up unannounced in French castles. Ari had seen to that. And as Ari had speculated, the map's presence in her gun case, if it was still there, wherever there was, explained everyone's inexcusable actions, from the top, whoever was pulling the strings up there, down to Yani's taxicab and the street assassins.

Boston and Gardner, though, were different kettles of art. They could explain something of Karl's interest beyond the Mercator, part of his intense desire to take over and acquire all that there was to know about the family's more clandestine business arms. There was enough motivation behind Boston and Gardner for more than a few murders. And Livia had a piece of the puzzle in her pocket: the tiny Rembrandt self-portrait. It came down to three words: follow the money, because what money, and things worth a great deal of money did, was to open doors and bestow power.

She'd taken the Rembrandt out of her pocket and out of the host holder and compared it with the picture on the screen in front of her. There was no doubt, although without authentication, and sometimes even with it, 100 per cent certainty was never a given. Despite her close associations with the art world and its products, Livia felt an even heavier burden of responsibility with this particular work. She returned it to her pocket and left the Bender, anxious to be out in the world where clear air and exercise awaited.

Ishmael was sitting on Ari Babitsky's park bench when she arrived, the dogs nosing around the perimeter, looking ready to enter the Melbourne Cup.

'They could use a walk, a long walk,' she called from the footpath.

The dogs looked up at the sound of her voice, and Ishmael rose with a smile, as though he'd been waiting and wishing for her to show up and say just that.

'Livia,' he said. 'You're back.'

Caddie and Tilly ran to her and she dropped to her knees and held them both, breathing in their clean, canine scent.

She hadn't realised just how much she'd missed them until that moment. Ishmael attached their leads, handed Tilly's to Livia, and they set off down Fortescue and into Boundary.

'Are you all right, Livia?' Ishmael, reticent as usual, had waited for a block and a half before he spoke. Caddie pulled at the lead and the words jerked out of him.

'I'm fine now,' she replied, and she realised that she was fine at that moment. She knew what she had to do, but would the others fall into line and help her out? 'I really appreciate you taking care of the dogs, Ishmael. Minnie would be proud of you.'

'I'll be able to take care of them a lot more soon.'

'Really? That sounds good, for them, and me, with the gallery to look after. Patrons may not appreciate a couple of Baskerville hounds galloping around the exhibits.' What was he trying to tell her? Should she ask him?

'I'm taking long service leave.'

'You are? You don't seem old enough for long service leave.'

'I've worked for Dad's firm since I was 18, full-time since I was 20.'

'That's quite an achievement.' What else could she say? She couldn't begin to imagine working in one place for so long that someone would pay her something called long service leave. It sounded, somehow, like a reward that combined persistence and doggedness with a recognition of defeat. You made it, now go away, and while you're away, contemplate wasting ten years of your life in the singular pursuit of this very moment. Perhaps she was being too negative.

'Not really, Livia. I'm leaving after the leave. I'm looking for a new job.'

'Why are you leaving?'

At that moment, Livia's phone rang. She looked at the screen.

'Where are you?' she asked, mouthing 'sorry' to Ishmael, who took Tilly's lead. He continued ahead towards a vacant lot where the dogs could poke about and amuse themselves.

'Avalon. Yani's been in touch.'

'And?'

'He thinks Minnie's death –'

'Murder, Greer, use the right term, it's murder.'

'He thinks it was a terrible accident, a misunderstanding. She was in the wrong place.'

'She was in her own office, her own place, minding her own business.' What was Yani thinking?

'I know. He also said he had nothing to do with Tibor's murder.'

'How does he know about Tibor's murder? Did you tell him?'

'I might have. He's very upset about the whole thing. It all went wrong.'

'The fewer people who know about Tibor, the better. It's bad enough that the poor man's body got treated so horribly.'

'Are you any closer to finding out who killed Minnie? And Tibor?'

'Only if Doug happens to see the bastard again, somewhere, sometime. I'm not holding my breath. I'm waiting on Karl to surface again. He knows more than his prayers.'

The thought flickered through her mind like one of those moths that, when they stop and turn at a certain angle, seem to disappear completely. Then they flap their wings, and they're back for another try. Could Karl be the murderer? Livia had no idea where he'd been that night. She had to assume that Detective Petersen had investigated all of Minnie's loved ones as potential perpetrators, but without an eyewitness – Doug – able and prepared to testify, there was no hope of anyone being charged. And if Karl was the murderer, improbable though it sounded, would Livia hand him over to Petersen, and destroy the family? Or would vengeance be wrought by Karl's own blood? His father? She pushed the moth away.

'Do you know anything about the Mercator map, Greer?'

'Only what you've told me – buggerall.'

'Gerardus Mercator was a sixteenth-century map-maker. He designed something called the Mercator projection – it was to do with creating more accurate navigational maps and the way they represent longitude. I'm not sure about all the technical details, I –'

'The *Reader's Digest* version will do.'

'Mercator maps are prized items among the cartographic crowd. An avid collector would be very interested in something rare – something, for example, that's so rare it hasn't been on the market before. The underground market, I mean, or any market.'

'Hasn't been on the market before because?'

'Because it was stolen – by our godfather. If it came to light, a museum, or an alleged owner, or the country of origin might claim it – like the Egyptians do with their artefacts.'

'Unless the damage is already done, like all the mummies the stupid English explorers sent back to the mother country for fertiliser and fireplace kindling. Good old nineteenth-century values.' Greer laughed to herself but Livia could tell her heart wasn't in it.

'There's something else, but I'm not sure how it's connected with the map, or with Minnie's murder, or Tibor's.'

'What?'

'In 1990, 13 items were stolen from the Isabella Stewart Gardner Museum in Boston. They've never been recovered, and their combined value ranges from $180 million to over $500 million, depending on which article you read. There are Rembrandts, a Vermeer, a Manet, some Degas, a couple of strange artefacts. It's the biggest art theft in history, and importantly, the statute of limitations has run out on prosecuting anyone for it, if they could ever catch them, which they haven't.'

'Go on.'

'Every year the museum issues a press release pretty much begging anyone in the know to contact them so they can arrange returning the stuff. There's a five million dollar reward. But I think they know it's hopeless, because the press release also includes information about how the paintings and drawings should be stored – the temperature and humidity, as if they accept the kidnapper isn't bringing the baby back, so here's how to make up the formula.'

'So?'

'So – I think we have one of them,' Livia said. 'Maybe more, but almost certainly one. A Rembrandt.'

'Some of the – I can't imagine that the family would have anything like that.'

'Not the family as such. Minnie. And Ari.'

'Even so.' Greer sounded sceptical, but Livia couldn't let it go, not now.

'What if they had no choice? What if they had to help someone because they owed them a favour, or there's some kind of outstanding debt. Ari was still stealing stuff up until recently. How do you think the Mercator ended up in my gun case?'

'He was still doing a lot of things up until recently,' Greer said.

'Pardon?'

'Never mind. That's a lot of speculating, and a lot of art for River City to cope with.'

'Nowhere is a backwater these days, Greer. Everywhere's accessible and useful – one cooler's as good as the next. River City may be even better because it's unlikely.'

'It would explain Karl's loopy behaviour, I suppose,' Greer said, 'if he's suspicious that Minnie was looking after some pieces, even one. Unless he's injecting, or inhaling or swallowing too many fast pills. What would it be worth, this Rembrandt?'

'I don't know – up to fifty million.'

'What?'

'You heard me. Get over it.' But even as she said it, Livia began to sweat. The host carrier was nestling uncomfortably in her trouser pocket, probably at the wrong temperature. She wished she'd bought an extra pair of soft moleskins, and an esky.

'I don't know what you can do with information like that.'

'I'll take Yani's advice, and say nothing to noone. By the way, are you able to stay in touch with him?' If Livia could talk to him when she knew more, knew what to ask, something might come of it, he might remember something else.

'In a manner of speaking, yes.'

'Is Ari okay?'

'He's in a different part of the resort. He's gone bush with Doug, across the creek.'

'That'll do them both good.' But what would they bring out of the bush with them, she wondered, watching Caddie dig frantically at the base of what was left of the demolished home's brick fireplace. 'Stay in touch with me, too, Greer, okay?'

'Okay. Mind how you go, Liv.'

Livia closed the phone, and yelled for the dogs. 'Caddy. Tilly. Come on.' Tilly had joined her sister at the fireplace.

'What is it, Livia?'

Ishmael trotted over to join her on the footpath. He'd been inspecting the interior of a new sports car parked a few bays along from the vacant lot.

'Probably nothing,' she replied. 'But there could be rats – we don't want to disturb that nest.'

Ishmael took off towards the dogs and Livia turned towards home. She didn't want to be late for any two-legged rat who might come calling with his tail between his legs.

2

The dogs were sleepy after their longer walk, but they still had energy enough to alert Livia to an arrival on the back verandah. They growled their deep and low Baskerville notes as Karl made his way up the steps, then hesitated before actually taking the last step onto the verandah. Livia, sitting in the lounge with a direct line of sight to the back door, watched him smiling at them and cooing some nonsense in what he must have thought was his dog whisperer voice.

'Easy, girls,' she said, walking out to greet Karl. She reached down to pat their heads. 'They won't hurt you.'

Karl stared at her from red-rimmed eyes. He looked as though he hadn't slept in a while, or had slept far too much for his own good, and he looked more despondent and desperate than menacing.

'After you.' Livia stepped back, and followed him through the kitchen and into the lounge-room. The dogs followed both of them.

'What's going on, Livia?'

She watched his face change as he spoke. He seemed to realise he'd have to shape up to confront her successfully.

'Why don't you take your coat off, Karl. You look hot.' His face was sweaty and reddening, even though the afternoon was mild. 'Care for a glass of water?'

'Cut the crap.' He removed his coat and flung it on the sofa, then leaned over and rummaged in its inside pocket for a handkerchief. As he wiped his forehead, he spat the words at her. 'I want that gun case. I've told you before and you still haven't fronted with it. Where is it, Livia? I know you know where it's stashed, just like you knew exactly what you were doing when you shot those two scumbags to death in Beijing. If you hadn't done that, we might have had a chance to finish the job properly.'

She had to give him credit for showing up, even though he was talking ten parts rubbish to one part sense. At least this time he hadn't decided to turn and run the way he did with Lakshmi. Livia knew she had an advantage at last. He'd come to her. She gazed at him, into his eyes, the pupils far too dilated, this time, for the level of light in the room.

'Well?'

His belligerence was too much for the dogs. When he took a couple of steps towards Livia, the rage building in his face, Caddie and Tilly began to bark, standing on either side of her, ferocious, deep barks, the sort she remembered from the night she landed on her elbow in Minnie's kitchen.

'I don't think they like you, Karl.' Livia stood her ground as he stopped and tried to work out what to do next.

'Where's the Boston stuff, Livia?' He hissed at her, his voice a loud whisper, with a dash of fear thrown in. He held his hands out in front of him, trying to placate the dogs. 'All I want is the gun case and the Boston stuff. It's nothing to do with you.'

He didn't really know what the 'Boston stuff' was, of that she was almost certain.

'Where have you been, anyway?'

'Gardening leave, what's it matter, Livia, I'm here now.'

Gardening leave. Gardner. That was where she'd heard it, when she went to visit Con at the hospital, and surprised Karl trying not to browbeat his father. She'd thought he'd said the 'gardener project,' and Con had told him there was no such thing. If it was good enough for the family's CEO, it should be good enough for her.

'Karl, I'm about to make you an offer you can't refuse. Come out to the kitchen, and we'll sort this out like cousins, not enemies.' Livia left the lounge-room, not waiting for an answer. The dogs followed her but kept a watchful eye on the visitor as he brought up the rear.

Livia found a bottle of mineral water in the fridge and poured two glasses. Karl gulped down his glass and poured himself another, drinking that one just as quickly. He made it half way through the third before he stopped. Livia waited through the first and second, mustering her most convincing, authoritative persona, something Greer called the language of expectation. When he slowed down on the third, she began.

'Here's how it's going to go, Karl,' she said. She sat opposite him at the kitchen table. The dogs settled themselves on the floor beside her.

'Who are you to be telling me anything?'

The mineral water was restorative, it seemed. Malevolent energy was powerful.

'I'm the one to be telling you, Karl, because I'm the one who's going to save your rancid bacon.' Did she sound confident enough? As though she knew exactly what was going on? She tried to think of him as a target, concentric circles of twirled suit, spaghetti limbs, and startled face. It was only partly successful and he ended up mangled.

'And I'm telling you, Livia, cousin, that I need to do something quickly about the Beijing project. I'm being threatened. Even if the gun case turns up, we'll have to give them Yani –

you surely know where he is? You two must have been fucking each other senseless all these years.'

'I'm glad you've decided to be more open about the Beijing project, Karl.' Even calling it a project gave it legitimacy as a family endeavour. 'And what I do with Yani is none of your business.'

'That prick deserves to end up in a wheelie bin like that other fucking idiot. You know Con would agree. We might even have to give Bao some of the Boston stuff.'

'The thing is, Karl, for Con to agree would mean he'd have to know everything. And once he knew everything about this debacle, you'd be taking a back seat in the business for the next hundred and fifty years while Elias and his colleagues run things. You don't want Con to know about any of this.'

'How do you know he doesn't know everything?'

'He'd allow me to be set up as a mule? He'd allow Gordon to make all the contacts in Beijing, given his failing health, mental and physical? Come on, Karl. There's a reason why Con's the boss. Think about it.'

'Gordon was fine at the time – it was months ago – he organised it all – I don't even know where he got the bloody map.'

That much Livia could believe. Need to Know: Gordon would have simply put in the order and told Karl it was underway.

'After this was done, Gordon was going to tell me everything – all his contacts, not just for this job, the whole network. But I do know that Yani Lee was the connection in Beijing, and he brought that creep Bao in to give him Olympic security access – triple A rating, access all areas, so he could keep an eye on you when you arrived, when you competed, when it was over. The fuckwit couldn't manage to get the map off you, even with all that help.'

'I'd be careful who I was calling a fuckwit if I were you, Karl. There's a lot of thin ice around here at the moment.' Livia felt as though she'd been standing on the thinnest spot for days.

'Gordon paid Yani very well for his services, and he extended the payment when he brought Bao in.'

'I thought you didn't know what was going on?'

'Bits and pieces, that's all.'

Livia remembered the old joke about politicians that Rosanna was fond of: how can you tell when a politician's lying? His lips are moving. She realised she would never know exactly how much Karl was aware of, how much of the project he'd controlled.

'There's something you and Gordon missed though. The one thing even adequately paid people have to offer in return – loyalty.'

Karl didn't look at her, but stared into his glass as though its emptiness was a magic trick. Bao's magic trick had been simply to act as himself, a police officer investigating an apparent car-jacking gone horribly wrong. And when he spoke with her at the hospital in Yani's room, Livia had revealed to him that she'd sent the gun case home. Later, when he interviewed her, she'd actually told him Minnie's name and location. He couldn't have made it to River City in time himself, but he must have despatched an associate, or two, or even three, given Doug's account, one of whom, the last to visit Minnie, had killed her. No wonder Yani had fled the hospital;

otherwise, Bao would have ensured that the injuries he sustained in the car-jacking were unavoidably fatal.

'I think I know the answer to this question, Karl, but I need to hear it from you. Why, why do it at all?'

'Why? Jesus, I don't know how you keep the doors to that gallery open, Livia, you wouldn't make a businessman's –' He hesitated, leaned back in his chair. 'Look, it was a joining fee, a way to get an entrée into one of the richest corporate groups in the world. The shopper doesn't need money, he wants something noone else has, something unique, which makes it priceless. And Gordon supplied it, or tried to.'

'And Minnie paid the price, Tibor paid, and now Gordon's gone. Who's the shopper, Karl?'

'Wouldn't have a clue.'

He'd hold out if he could, but like the soda water left in the bottle, the last bubble was about to burst.

'Aren't you in danger of being whacked, Karl? Bao's here in River City, a respected police officer from Asiapol doing the rounds with the detective investigating Minnie's murder. You're the direct descendent of one of the country's most notorious crime lords. Who are they going to believe? Who will Detective Petersen want to believe?'

'Bao's a fucking liar, a crim, he screwed us over, screwed Yani, he's probably killed more people than we've had hot dinners, Livia.'

'Probably. And I don't want to have to worry about anybody else adding to his score, Karl. People like Sibyl, for instance, or the CLEAR committee, or Con, or my mother. Relatively innocent people, Karl. Bao and his mates don't have a clue who knows what's going on. And Con doesn't have to know you've been involved in this. As long as you trust me to make the appropriate corrections. But I need to know who ordered the map.'

Karl sat and stared out the back door. Livia followed his gaze. The dry grass in the yard was too long and due for a mow. It looked as though it was reaching up to the sky, begging for more rain, a good, full-bodied storm. She didn't want to spend much more time in the same room as her cousin.

'Karl?'

He put both hands on the table and pushed himself to his feet. The effort seemed to wind him, and he took a few deep, wheezing breaths as he went back to the lounge-room and retrieved his coat. He pulled a business card from its inside pocket and returned to the kitchen, threw the card onto the table in front of Livia. She looked at it for a long time.

'Well,' she said, finally, 'I didn't know he was in town now.'

She looked up at Karl, impatient but silent, standing on the other side of the table.

'How ironic? As they say in the classics, I'm surprised but not shocked.' There could only be a few people as interested in cartographic rarities at this level of sophistication and value. Livia had always thought such items should be in public galleries and museums for everyone to enjoy, not hidden away in private collections.

'You do know where the gun case is, Livia, don't you?'

'Leave it to me, Karl,' she said, injecting what she hoped was a brisk tone into her voice. 'What you need to do is this: make yourself scarce, go on gardening leave until tomorrow. Be at the Bender by noon. And Karl, two ears, one mouth. Don't talk if you can help yourself.'

Karl's face reddened and he looked ready to begin again with a new diatribe about Livia's inferior place in his grand scheme of life, the universe, and so on.

'Put your coat on, Karl,' Livia said, 'wipe your face, and walk out of here calmly, as though you've been visiting to arrange a dinner party, which, in effect, you have. Okay? You never know who could be watching.'

She stood up and the dogs stood with her. Karl put his coat on, drew a handkerchief from his pocket and wiped his face. He walked to the back door, looked out as though the devil might be waiting out there somewhere for him, but managed to affect a strolling pose down the steps and around the path.

Livia went to the phone and dialled the number on the business card Karl had given her.

3

'Mum, a quick question? When's Uncle Con getting out of hospital?'

'He's out, and I've convinced him to stay here for a few days, before he goes home to Faith Island. He has revised dietary guidelines for his heart, and new medication. I'm going to have to reorganise the menu and go shopping.'

Rosanna secretly enjoyed fussing over family members who needed the metaphorical equivalent of chicken soup and a hot water bottle. She liked to let Livia know that, on any day you'd care to mention, complications would surely arise, and, after a short but refined period of complaint, there was no point in doing anything other than dealing with them.

'So what's he doing now?'

'He's upstairs with Elias, working, against medical advice.'

'He's all right. You couldn't kill him with a tank, Mum. Can you tell him I'll be over to see him later on, for dinner. And I need to book a couple of rooms there for tomorrow at lunchtime, the meeting room next to the dining-room, and the billiards room upstairs.'

'What's going on, Livia? You can't be upsetting your uncle.'

'He won't be upset, Mum. This'll be mother's milk to him. All right about the rooms? I'll explain later when I come over. I'll give you the catering numbers.'

She hung up before Rosanna could ask more questions, and phoned Grady Crabtree at *The River City News*.

'How are things at the *Guano Gazette*, my friend?'

'When am I getting my feature, Livia? Your kind of fame has a shorter shelf life than yoghurt, you know.'

'Do me a favour, Grady, and I'll meet you at the Bender tomorrow at 3.30 for an early sundowner.'

'You Olympians are hard to resist. What is it?'

'You do the police beat, don't you? Know the detectives?'

'Yes. So? There's nothing more on Mrs Babitsky, I'm afraid.'

'That's what I thought. But my favour is to do with the Chinese police inspector visiting from Asiapol – I think his name's Bao. I want to thank him properly for his kindnesses when I was in Beijing. Actually, my mother wants to thank him, plus he left his briefcase behind at Minnie's funeral reception, so I was hoping to get it back to him.'

'You've taken this long to figure out it's his briefcase? Wouldn't the Chinese characters have made you suspicious?'

'I've been a bit busy, and Mum didn't know what to do with it. Can you get the message to him? Give him my mobile number, and tell him to bring his offsiders with him, would you? Mum wants to treat them all to a Wagyu lunch at the Bender. Noon tomorrow. His briefcase will be waiting for him.'

'This exclusive had better be good, Livia.'

'You have no idea, Grady.'

Livia had no idea herself what she would tell him about Beijing. At this point, she was a trapeze act without the aid of a net. How had Minnie ever done it? Before she could lose momentum, she made the last call.

'I don't have much time, Greer. Can you round up Ari and Doug and bring them to the Bender tomorrow at 11, no later?'

'You're not going to explain, are you?'

'Trust me, I'm your twin.'

'Good enough.'

'And Greer?'

'Yes?'

'Bring them through the private quarters. Elias will be there to meet you – he'll take you to the right place.'

'All right. Are you sure I can't help you with something else? Today?'

'Do you have a contact number for Yani?'

'Possibly.' There was a pause. 'Yes.'

'I need to call him so we can sort out the Beijing mess once and for all.'

'You know who it is, don't you?' Greer asked. 'Who killed Minnie, and Tibor.'

'I don't make assumptions,' Livia said. 'Let's wait and see. There's one more thing. Don't mention any of this to Yani, if you should happen to have any close encounters with him between now and then. I don't want to worry him. All right?'

'How did you know?'

'I've always known.'

Karl hadn't been too far from the mark when he alluded to Livia's relationship with Yani. He'd simply chosen the wrong twin.

CHAPTER THIRTY-FOUR

River City

Sunday 7 September 2008
Holy Mother and St Jude Retreat

1

Sibyl and Gordon. Gordon telling his stories to his wife. Wonderful stories, the nurse had said, about art works, Chinese names, and a man named Karl. Sibyl had aphasia, which meant she found it difficult to express herself, but unlike Sister Immaculata, she seemed to be free of dementia, so far. She didn't drift and visit, visit and drift.

Livia checked each floor on her way to Sibyl's room, noting that more of the paintings the CLEAR group had removed had been returned and fixed to the walls once again. She could only imagine the beauty they concealed behind their less attractive façades. She also knew that these disguises weren't hiding a gun case. But if the Mercator had already been removed from the case, it could be in any building on any floor, in the chapel inside a Station of the Cross, under the tabernacle, screwed to the underside of a pew.

Sibyl was awake and sitting up when Livia arrived. She smiled at Livia and beckoned her over. Livia kissed her cheek, took a seat and held her hand.

'Hello, Sibyl, how are you today? Is there anything you'd like to tell me? About Gordon? And Karl? The gun case?'

Sibyl kept smiling, but had nothing to say, unlike her ancient Greek namesake. The moment for Sibylline fortune-telling was now, Livia thought, willing herself to sit back and pass the time of day in the old lady's quiet company, letting her get used to the visitor's presence, calming the way for clear thought, should it arise.

When Sibyl dozed off, Livia slipped her hand away and turned to the built-in wardrobe behind her chair. There was hanging space, drawers and a shelf across the top for extra blankets and sheets. She opened one of the doors, pushed the chair closer and climbed up to rifle under the manchester, just in case. What did people do with their possessions, their furniture, their households full of everything when they moved into places like this? Did they pay for storage elsewhere; did their children – those who had children – take it off their hands. Was it dumped?

She pushed open the other door, and as she did, noticed the flag draped over the towel bar half a metre beneath her. She stepped down and inspected the flag, confirming that it was the Olympian-autographed flag she'd sent to Sibyl from Beijing with the bronze horse. The last time she saw it, it was inside the gun case.

'Good afternoon.'

Livia turned to the door.

'May I help you?' The nurse, a thin woman in her fifties with swept-back blonde hair, looked suspiciously at Livia standing at the open wardrobe.

'I'm Livia Galvin, a friend of Sibyl's – Mrs Trembath. And you are?'

'Sister Klewes. Have you lost something, Ms Galvin?' She tried to force a smile to her lips, and failed.

'I just found something, actually.' Livia pulled the flag from the rack and held it up. 'This flag. Has it been here long, do you know?'

'God, that flag. We didn't realise what it was until it went through the laundry – it got caught up with Mrs Trembath's washing. Then we saw all the names. Mr Restik brought it in last week.'

'Mr Restik brought it in? Was it in something? A case of some kind?'

'Did you say your name's Galvin?'

'Yes. Was it in a case? The flag?'

'Your Olympic flag.'

'That's right.'

'I'd really appreciate your autograph, for my daughter.' Now that she knew who Livia was, she'd begun to beam.

'Anytime, but I really need to know if the flag came in a case or something similar.'

'Mr Restik dropped by and he had a few things. I was on shift that day. Let me see.'

Sister Klewes stared out the window at the multi-million dollar view of the bay.

'There was a leather suitcase with buckles and zips – an old-fashioned thing. It had some books and clothes in it. And there was another case inside of it as well. The flag was in that case. Very nice looking – beautiful etchings on the outside.'

'Do you know where it is now?'

Sister Klewes moved to the wardrobe.

'It should be in here where Mr Restik left it.'

She stood at the open door, looked down and then up. Down again, left and right.

'Someone's moved it. There isn't a lot of room in these wardrobes.'

Sister Klewes walked to the end of Sibyl's bed and picked up her chart.

'Is there somewhere that they put suitcases, excess luggage?' Livia asked.

'Hmm. Some of the rooms in the old convent, they're full of suitcases, furniture, but I don't think they use it anymore. They ask people to sort that out before they come here. Most of the stuff over there belongs to the old nuns.'

The nurse closed the wardrobe and left Livia with Sibyl. The flag, Livia thought, should at least be visible. Sibyl loved flags, or used to. She went to the door, which seemed always to be open, and threw the flag up to the top so that part of it hung over the other side as a temporary anchor.

'I'll get some hooks, Sib, don't worry.'

'Magda.'

Livia turned and gazed down at Sibyl in her bed. Had she spoken?

'Magda.'

Her voice was frail, barely audible. She stared up at Livia, who came and sat beside the bed, smiling reassuringly at her. She took Sibyl's hand.

'It's okay, Sibyl, I'm looking for something, and I thought it might be here.'

'Magda,' she said again. And then, 'Mercator.'

She seemed to have Magda confused with Mercator.

'What do you mean?' Livia asked.

Sibyl turned her head carefully from side to side.

'Mercator, ist in Magda Zimmer.'

She'd managed an entire sentence, although each word took a second or two for her to organise.

'You mean the Mercator map, don't you?'

She nodded. 'Magda Zimmer.'

'Mother Magda?' Mother Magda was surely around long before the Zimmerframe was invented.

'Ja. Magda Zimmer.' She raised her bandaged arm and pointed out the door.

Zimmer. Not Zimmerframe. Magda Zimmer. Magda room. Zimmer meant room in German.

'Mother Magda's memorial room?' Minnie's Mother Magda Mesmer Memorial project had only just begun. She'd mentioned it to Livia a while before the Olympics. Livia had commented on the presence of so many Ms, and Minnie had been a little miffed to say the least.

Sibyl nodded and smiled. It had been a huge effort of concentration for her to get the words out. She lowered her arm, relaxed into her pillows and closed her eyes.

'Thank you, Sibyl.' Livia leaned over and kissed her pale, warm cheek. 'Danke.'

She left the room and hurried down the corridor to the far end of the building, turning left into an alcove which led to a smaller room behind the linen cupboards. She opened the door and entered, feeling for a light switch. Two fluorescent lights flickered on to reveal a room about four metres by five. It was mostly empty except for some cardboard boxes and a couple of tea chests. One wall featured built-in cupboards with sliding doors. There was a balcony which ran around the north-eastern corner of the building and offered views to the northern mountains in the far distance, and the sparkling blue bay in the east.

Livia went to the double doors and unbolted them. She pulled the heavy, navy blue curtains aside and pushed the doors out, opening the room to the sea breeze and natural light. She went out to the balcony and hooked the doors back. Down below, she could see the densely overgrown area that ran along the front of the old convent and the high-care centre. There were plans to clear the thick lantana and assorted ragged trees and create a contemplative garden for the residents and staff, but nothing had happened yet. They'd have to fill in the gully immediately in front of the fence protecting residents and visitors from slips and falls. Livia took a few deep breaths of the late afternoon air, catching a whiff of possible rain to come. There were some promising clouds making their way across the bay.

Returning to the room, she quickly checked the contents of the boxes and tea chests: dozens of books, sets of rosary beads, evaporating Lourdes water in poorly-sealed plastic containers, holy pictures, crucifixes in many sizes, colours and materials;

manchester, old-fashioned nuns' habits, and any number of small and medium sized statues of saints.

She went to the built-in cupboard and slid a door along. Most of the shelves were empty except for one, which contained a brown leather suitcase with buckles and zips. She pulled it out and placed it on the floor, unbuckled and unzipped it, flicking back the lid. Inside, as Sister Klewes had said, were books and clothes. Livia would bet that they were actually Mother Magda's very own missal, bible, and a leather-tooled folder that was probably part of her writing set. Nestled on top of her faded brown habit was Livia's gun case, looking totally out of place with its high-tech graphics and its lightweight polymer plastic shell, harder than steel but far more versatile and flexible. The corners were curved not sharp, and the handle was positioned exactly for the best balance once it was loaded up with the weapons it was designed to carry. It had a combination lock, which Livia had set to Dan's birthday, 310194, and it still worked. There didn't appear to be any indication of tampering.

Livia opened it up and turned it this way and that, looking for something she'd never seen in all the time she'd owned it. Either the map was gone, or it was concealed somehow within the shell. An expert would have to look at it. She closed the lid and spun the lock's numbers and heard, as she rose with the case, the slightest noise near the entry door.

'Hello? Sister Klewes?' she said.

'Father Chen.'

A man about Livia's height but a little heavier entered the room. He wore black trousers, and there were tiny gold crosses on the collar of his white, short-sleeved shirt. He was smiling, but the smile didn't reach his eyes. There didn't appear to be any place for him to hide a gun, except if he had an ankle holster.

'You've replaced Father Shand,' Livia said.

'Not really,' he said. 'I'll take the case, Ms Galvin.'

He moved towards her.

'Did you kill Minnie Babitsky? Tibor Restik?'

She took a few steps back towards the balcony as he advanced on her. She could see the pulses in her eyes as her heart began to hammer and the adrenalin surged.

'Restik died before we could get the rest of the information out of him.'

'You killed him.'

'He was weak, old, stupid. The case.' He lunged at her, but she stepped away to the left, and this time the smile reached his eyes.

'What about Minnie?'

'This is 20 questions? The case, Ms Galvin.' His voice was hard, even for a priest.

'This is my case. You can't have it.' Livia backed out to the balcony and he followed her.

'I don't want to hurt you,' he said.

'Like you didn't hurt Tibor? And Minnie.'

She dropped the case to the floor and kicked it to the opposite corner of the balcony. Chen looked at her and then at the case, and back at her. His eyes went dead as he came towards her. She dipped and moved sideways and he followed her, grabbing her by the arm and pulling her in to him. He was very strong, could probably snap bones or dislocate joints if she zigged when he zagged. She went with him, putting her other arm around his torso, creating a bear hug, clutching at clothing and skin, knowing she had a better chance close in, but so did he. For 20 pesos, would you want to be in this position? The strange things people think of in extremis, and suddenly she remembered Grady's comment when she was at the hotel, and she remembered why she felt sick then. Dan. Dan, who'd asked her in Bogota for the five countries, for 20 pesos. Dan. She slammed Chen as hard as she could against the balcony rail, knocking the breath out of him, but he slammed back, pivoting, grunting, puffing. They were a couple of drunks wrestling for the last slug of whiskey. If the momentum slowed or stopped, she was done for. He'd be too strong in a fair fight, and her hands, though powerful, were too sore to last for much longer. She had to act, now. She'd only have one chance.

She pushed her upper body back from him and saw that his eyes had lit up again: excitement, the thrill of the imminent kill? It wasn't going to be her. She was here for Minnie and Tibor, all of them. Dan. She released her free arm, focussing all her energy into one movement, breathing in as deeply as she could, and then out as the power came from her core, through her shoulder, down her arm, into her closed fist, all of her self driven into his throat, crushing his larynx.

She broke away from his grip and he stared at her, shock and pain in his eyes, his legs wobbling. He had enough in him for one last lunge, but when he came at her, she ducked and fell to the ground, gasping for breath. He was gone, over the side. The balcony was silent. Livia pulled herself up to the railing and looked over in time to see his body rolling down the gully and into the lantana. He hadn't uttered a sound on

the way down. She could see a speck of white shirt, unmov-
ing.

2

'Ms Galvin?'

Sister Klewes entered the Mother Magda room as Livia
walked in from the balcony wondering if she looked as bad as
she felt. She was still getting her breath back.

'Are you all right, Ms Galvin?'

'Fine, I'm fine. I get vertigo sometimes, from the height.'
Livia nodded back at the balcony. 'Some fresh air into the
room.' She placed the gun case on the floor next to her.

'You found it, then?'

'Yes, safe and sound.' Her hands were shaking, her legs felt
like melting putty, her head was light and she wanted to run
three miles, and another three.

'I wonder if you'd be so kind.' The nurse held up a polaroid
camera. Livia knew they took polaroids of all the residents in
case anyone wandered off – the police would have a recent
shot. 'For my daughter.'

'Sure, why not?' Livia ran her hands through her hair and
straightened her jacket. Now she was laughing.

Sister Klewes took a shot of Livia on her own, then came
over and stood next to her, turned the camera on the two of
them, holding it up and away at arm's length, *Thelma and
Louise* style. The flash so close blinded Livia temporarily. She
needed to know if there was anyone else around who might be
with Chen, and she couldn't afford to be blind for long.

'Many visitors today?' she asked, blinking away the dots.

'Surprisingly few, for a Sunday,' the nurse replied. 'Must be the lovely weather – they're all out yachting or something.' She handed Livia the polaroids and a marking pen. 'Your autograph? Can you make it to Aleshyah?'

'Oh, yes.' She looked down at the pictures in her hand, looked at herself staring back, eyes unfocussed, capable only of a frowning, questioning kind of smile. The camera didn't lie, it just didn't know she'd seen a man off the balcony not five minutes before. 'Anyone new around, Sister Klewes?'

'I couldn't really say, Ms Galvin. I'm new myself, still getting used to the faces. That's A-l-e-s-h-y-a-h.'

Livia dutifully wrote the name and scrawled something that may have been her name at the bottom of each photograph. She pressed hard to minimise the shaking.

'Thank you so much, Ms Galvin,' said the nurse, accepting the pictures and pen. 'Is there anything I can help you with today?'

'No, ah, I don't think – wait, yes, there is. Do you know a resident named Michael Morris?'

'Mr Morris, yes, he's our youngest. He's in unit 4, one of the self-contained, semi-detached apartments across the roundabout from here. You can't miss it once you cross the road.'

'Thank you.'

Sister Klewes left Mother Magda's future shrine a happy woman. Two autographs, a brush with Olympic glory, and her life still her own. If she'd arrived a few minutes earlier, her daughter could have been an orphan by now. Livia went out to the balcony and stared down at the lantana. It took a while for her eyes to adjust to the light and the shrubbery below before she could again identify the white speck that was Chen's shirt. Noone else was out there. Had noone seen him fall, or land, or roll into the thick undergrowth beyond the fenceline? Had anyone even taken notice of him, the invisible priest gliding around the floors, apparently visiting residents on Sunday? Had he entered Sibyl's room in his quest for the gun case? Why hadn't Livia thought to demand who he worked for? Not the shopper, surely? That would be far too disappointing.

There was a white plastic chair at the other end of the balcony where the view drew the eye out to the ocean and beyond. The shower clouds seemed to have stopped to dawdle over the bay. Livia sat and pulled out her mobile.

'West Bend Heritage Hotel, Jerry speaking.'

'Jerry, it's Livia Galvin.'

'Yes, Ms Galvin, would you like to speak with your mother? I can put you through.'

'No, no. I want to talk to you, Jerry. I, um, I have a cleaning job that I hope you can help me with.' Was this the right approach, she wondered?

'No problem.'

Just like that. Livia gave Jerry the details, described the scene and where Chen could be found.

'Will you be there, Ms Galvin. Do you want to meet with me beforehand?'

'No, not today, Jerry. But I'm going to need a photograph of the – subject, a close up of the face, if it's not too, you know, damaged. Look, even if it is, I'll need one, and can you hang onto it until tomorrow. I'll meet you at the Bender before noon. Is that okay?'

'Perfectly fine, Ms Galvin.'

Livia waited. 'Jerry?'

'Yes, Ms Galvin?'

'Don't you want to know what happened?'

'No. We'll come out after dark. You can forget about it now, Ms Galvin.'

'Right. Okay. Thank you, Jerry.'

'No problem.'

'Oh, Jerry. How do I pay you?'

'I work for your family, Ms Galvin. The payroll works itself out.'

'Okay, then. Well, thanks again.'

'Good afternoon, Ms Galvin.'

Livia could almost imagine Jerry doffing his hat to her, if he wore a hat. In some ways, he was as old world as Grandad Wolfie used to be in his three-piece suits, with his furled umbrella and the ubiquitous cigars. In her childhood memories, Wolfie had always reminded Livia of Sigmund Freud, with the beard and the intensely focussed eyes. What would he make of his granddaughter now when his final desire had been to garner the respect of the so-called legitimate business world? She had no time to worry about it as she took the stairs two and three at a time down to the ground floor, the gun case slapping at her leg.

She peered out at the car park and the grounds, not sure exactly what to look for, and draped her leather jacket over the gun case before she left the building. Was there another priestly figure, waiting to do her in? She crossed the roundabout and found unit four, semi-detached from unit three, part of a cluster of small, cream-brick buildings with no character to speak of, but they represented a huge step for any residents who moved from the high-care centre into their snug environs. Instead of going up, floor by floor, jumping the queue in God's waiting room, they returned to earth, literally, surrounded by Mother Magda's olive trees with shades of green native ferns and shrubs to contrast the brick.

Livia stood at the screened security door and pressed the buzzer. Michael was in. She heard his motorised wheelchair purring towards her before she saw him in the shadows behind the door.

'Michael?' She felt tentative all of a sudden. Maybe he'd been sworn to secrecy and couldn't tell her anything. 'Michael Morris?'

'That's me.'

The words were precise but firm. He followed them up with a smile that lit up his face. He must have moved beyond the wired jaw stage.

'Michael, my name's Livia Galvin. We haven't met, but you designed this gun case for me when you were in Europe last year.' She pulled the jacket away, revealing the case. 'For the Olympics in Beijing.'

'Come in,' he said, reaching up to flick the lock on the door. He reversed his chair and Livia opened the door, walking ahead of him into the living-room. It had been converted into a gym full of weight-training equipment. Dumbells of varying colours and weights littered the floor like chicanes on a grand prix racetrack. A Nautilus style home gym sat to one side of the sliding doors leading out to a shady patio area.

'Can I get you a drink? Something to eat?' He came to a halt beside her. 'Have a seat.'

'Thanks.' She sat on the sofa, and placed the case beside her. 'I'm okay for drinks and food.'

It was obvious that all the equipment was in use. Michael was developing the body of a gym junkie.

'How are you going?'

'Better. Since I've come down here, I can work on my own. The rooms over there,' he nodded towards the high-care centre, 'are nice, but small. And some of my older friends don't like the sound of grunting, or weights hitting the floor.'

'I'm sorry to bother you, and rush you, but I was wondering if you could help me with something.' There was no point in drawing the wrong kind of attention to Michael Morris's unit, should any other friends of Chen be nearby. Michael was obviously fit, but still wheelchair-bound.

'Your gun case?'

'My gun case. I sent it home early from Beijing and some issues arose as a result. Have you heard anything about what happened in Beijing, and here afterwards?'

'No, I tend not to watch the news. I have other priorities. But please accept my sympathy on the loss of your Mrs Babitsky. I'm sorry I didn't make the funeral. Some weeks I have bad days and worse days. Don't worry – this has been a good day, so far. Please go on.'

'The short of it is, I need to open the case, the special part that you designed into it, the bit that counts.'

'Well, I guess since you're the owner,' he said, 'and your uncle has paid for the best care anywhere, as they used to say on *MASH*. But you'll have to do the tricky stuff.' He held up his hands, which had a constant tremor. 'Looks like yours have had a bit of a beating, too.'

Livia looked down at her hands; some blood had seeped from beneath what was left of the band-aids after Chen. 'Never mind,' she said. She set the case on the coffee table between them, spun the combination, and opened it.

The lid could be removed from the base with simple snaps of the interior and exterior hinges. Suddenly, they had two pieces of luggage. There was a narrow lip around the base, part of which turned out to be strongly magnetised.

'Feel around under the lip and you'll find a piece of metal about six centimetres long.'

Livia felt along the lip and, sure enough, there was a piece of metal. She had to use some force to pull it away from the magnetic strip. It was an unremarkable triangular prism, shaped like a tiny piece of black cheese sliced from the corner of a block.

'The key,' Michael said, answering her unspoken question, 'to the base and the lid.'

He directed her to each corner of the base, where she inserted the key and turned it 180 degrees. She did the same with the lid, and felt a mounting tension. The contents were what two strangers had been willing to kill her and Yani for in Beijing. The contents were responsible for Minnie's and Tibor's murders. They were responsible for the dognappings and for her premature burial at the cemetery. The contents drove Father Chen to his high dive.

'If I did my job properly,' Michael said, 'and I did, you should be able to lift them out very easily. Hook your thumbs under the lip.'

Livia placed one hand on either side of the base and her thumbs under the lip and pulled gently. The interior shell lining the base – she'd thought it was fixed and permanent – came up and out without a scrape. It was much lighter than it looked, but black has the effect of appearing heavy. She set the shell on the parquet floor before looking at what lay beneath.

'Looks old,' Michael said.

'You didn't know what's in here?'

'I'm just the designer.'

There were several layers of paper, parchment, and it looked old, all right. Someone had sensibly placed sheets of what appeared to be tissue paper – acid-free, she hoped – between the leaves of parchment. She wouldn't dare to touch any of it with her bare hands.

She said, 'We'll leave it where it is.' At least until she could get it to the gallery, put her gloves on and remove it to something equally as protective as the gun case.

Michael nodded. 'Cartography,' he said. 'There's no accounting for taste.'

'There isn't,' Livia replied. Some of them went for millions, and that would be the case here, assuming it was a Gerardus Mercator original, and she had no real doubts that Ari knew what he'd stolen. The Library of Congress in the United States had one, for which they'd paid about ten million dollars. According to her internet search, it was the only extant example that featured the North American continent with the word 'America,' written on it, but what about this one?

Livia returned the shell to the case and turned the key in its four hidden keyholes to lock it in place. Then they turned their attention to the lid. She followed the same routine and discovered rectangular pieces of what must have been leather

– it was showing its age, cracked and discoloured – with words embossed on the top piece in a language other than English. It could have been Latin. The pieces were around the same size as the parchments in the other half; she assumed they were covers.

'It's an atlas, all right,' she said, locking the shell back into place and rehinging both pieces. She replaced the key on its magnetised strip and closed the lid.

'You found what you wanted?'

'There's more to come. Thank you for your help with this.'

'Would you like to stay to dinner?' he asked. 'You look like you could use some home cooking.'

'I'd love to, but I have to see a man about a lunch. Can I take a raincheck?'

'Looks like the rain's going to beat you to it,' he said, gazing out at his courtyard, where the shower from the bay had begun to fall.

CHAPTER THIRTY-FIVE

River City

Monday 8 September 2008
West Bend Heritage Hotel
Ground Floor Meeting Room

'Uncle C.' Livia stood with her uncle and Greer in the kitchen. They watched Rosanna discussing lunch menus with her staff. 'How are you feeling?'

'I'm fine, Livia. A little tired. A little older.'

He looked like a slightly younger version of his father, although Livia knew the beard was temporary, a convenience while he was laid up in hospital. He'd lost weight, and his suit appeared ever-so-slightly too large, but only a trained eye would detect any loss of strength.

Greer said, 'You might have to channel Grandad Wolfie to keep this rabble in the meeting room in line.'

'I've always had enough of Wolfie in here,' Con pointed to his chest, 'to keep me going when necessary. Don't worry, my dears, it'll work. I'm still the alpha male in this pack of dogs. Come along.'

Livia had explained almost everything to Con the night before at dinner, judiciously leaving out Karl's part and emphasising – feeling guilty for defaming a dead man – Gordon's role. Karl could wait.

As they entered the meeting room, Livia noted that the guests she'd invited were present and sitting silently around the long mahogany table. Karl, on his own, fiddling, as usual, with his wedding ring, sat at one end on the long side. Two-thirds of the way down on the same side, were Inspector Bao and the assistant who'd accompanied him at Minnie's Wake. Diagonally opposite Karl, at the other long end was Yani, staring at Bao with undisguised anger. Greer made her way over to sit next to Yani, whispered something in his ear that caused him to soften his stare, and Livia sat with Karl. Con strode to the head of the table nearest to Karl and sat on a chair that seemed to elevate him above the rest.

'I'll keep this brief, ladies and gentlemen,' he began. 'It isn't a discussion or a debate, and there will be no room for consensus. I'm aware that, while I've been indisposed, a few problems have arisen in relation to a project involving the delivery of an item to a Beijing investor.

'The project manager was my close friend, Gordon Trembath, who died only a couple of days ago. His death, though sudden, was due to natural causes, unlike the two deaths that have occurred this past week. My beloved friend, Minerva Babitsky, and her beloved friend, Tibor Restik, both murdered.

'There is an eye-witness to Mrs Babitsky's murder, some-one who has been able to describe in detail those who visited her that night, and who killed her. When he sees them again he will be able to confirm their identities.'

Con paused and poured himself a glass of water. He took a sip, and another.

Livia watched the small group for movements that would give away their guilt. Karl twitched uneasily beside her, either going up or coming down from his latest handful of drugs. Yani, sitting beside Greer, was focussed on his glass of water, turning it slowly on the table. Inspector Bao might as well have been a statue, but his offsider shifted around in his seat and occasionally rubbed his right thigh, as though he'd injured himself.

'This is very painful for me – I loved Mrs Babitsky dearly, as did all of the members of my family, some of whom are here with me today. More importantly, Mr Trembath also had a wide network of connections in many spheres, all of whom regarded him with great respect. They would be keen to know who murdered his beloved sister-in-law, and who could have tampered with his project. He has left his dear wife, Sibyl, a grieving widow, and even frailer.

'To be blunt, ladies and gentlemen, there are no options available. I was Mr Trembath's employer, and I therefore carry responsibility for his project. As much as it grieves me, I must also protect my family and our interests. And I am certain that Mrs Babitsky would agree. I suggest to you, therefore, that if you know who visited her on the night of her death, you advise them to leave this country immediately. That is the most generous offer I can make. The pursuit is over, and the family will assume the responsibility for Mr Trembath's contract as part of Galvin Corp's business plan.

'I believe the hotel's owner, Mrs Rosanna Galvin, has invited you all to a meal. You'll forgive me if I don't attend. Please remain seated, lunch will be served here.'

Con stood and nodded at Livia and Greer, then at Karl, who nodded back, stood and followed his father out of the room. Livia knew the performance had taken a great deal out of her uncle. She sat and waited, remembering a Chinese saying that Yani had taught her: how goes the enemy? The enemy is time. How long would he take, she wondered, glancing up at the security camera in the corner of the room.

West Bend Heritage Hotel

Security and Surveillance Room

'He doesn't look too well.' He stared at a polaroid photograph of a man whose face was bruised and bloody, the worst of the blood hastily wiped away, his eyes swollen shut, scratches on his cheeks.

'No, he had a fall.'

'It's him, though, one of the first two. I remember that scar above his eye now. He was with that bloke.' He pointed at the monitor.

'And the other fellow, the third man?'

'That one. There.' Doug continued to stare at the monitor.

'Him? Are you sure.' Ari stared, too. 'It's very important.'

'You don't have to tell me that, Ari.' Doug leaned forward and touched the screen in front of them again, clearly pointing to the man he'd seen. 'He's the one who hit Minnie. He killed her.' Doug slumped back in his seat, clearly distressed. 'I should have saved her. I shouldn't have left her alone.'

'You did the best you could, Doug. Because of you, Minnie will get the justice she deserves.'

Doug began to cry, and Ari put an arm around his shoulders. He continued to stare at the screen and watched as Con and Karl left the room, the others, as ordered, meekly waiting for the next course with Livia and Greer.

Jerry, taking his cue, moved to the door and slipped out.

West Bend Heritage Hotel – Ground Floor Meeting Room and First Floor Billiards Room

1

'Before lunch begins, Inspector Bao, I wonder if we could clear something up.' Livia rose and went to the inspector, who stood and faced her.

'Of course, Dr Galvin.' He nodded, and followed her to the side of the room.

What next, he thought, wishing he hadn't surrendered his weapon to that doorman, what was his name, Jerry? And where was Chen? His mobile had rung out several times and he hadn't returned to his hotel room.

'This is Elias, Mr Galvin's colleague,' Livia said, looking at the man who'd entered the room.

'Inspector,' Elias said.

'How do you do?' Bao managed, staring all the while at the briefcase Elias carried in his right hand.

'Thanks, Elias.' Livia took the briefcase as Jerry entered the room followed by Rosanna with an assistant who placed plates in front of Yani and Greer and Bao's man, who rose from his seat. Jerry moved to stand behind him.

Bao whispered to his colleague in Chinese, instructing him to sit and stay, to follow any directions that were given, and to stop drawing attention to himself and the stab wound in his leg with his restless movements.

'This way, Inspector,' Livia said, leaving the room with the briefcase.

He followed her along the hallway, up the staircase and into a room containing a billiards table. At the far end of the room was a man he knew only by reputation. They had never met.

'Inspector Bao Jinmin, I would like to introduce you to Professor Wu Xiaoping.'

Professor Wu moved forward, smiling, and greeted the inspector with a bow and a firm handshake.

'As I explained to you earlier, Professor, Inspector Bao is in town for Asiapol. Part of the Sister Cities program, and I thought it would be nice for someone from home to be present, someone from the police service, no less, when your briefcase was restored to you.' She turned to Bao. 'It was lost in transit for a while.'

'So kind of you to make the time,' the Professor said as Livia placed the case on the billiards table.

Bao stood, silently, staring at the unopened case, his case. How had she found it? Where? But this wasn't the same case. There was nothing on the outside. It must be a bluff. Chen, he'd found the right one, he had it now. He could be on his way to anywhere with it.

'Won't you join us for a drink, Inspector?' Livia asked. 'The Professor is leaving very soon. We were lucky enough to catch up with him after his Sydney and River City conferences.'

Bao couldn't stay, he could do nothing but think of Chen and his whereabouts. And the other one downstairs, gorging himself on that beef, was he in on it, too? He'd hired them as partners.

'Sadly, I must decline, Dr Galvin,' Bao said, nodding his gratitude at the Professor. 'My schedule, like yours, Professor, is very tight. It does not allow for – changes.' So many changes, he couldn't keep track. 'A pleasure to meet you, Professor.'

'The pleasure is all mine,' Wu replied, absently patting the briefcase.

Livia walked to the door, and Bao followed her.

'I don't think my mother catered for dessert, Inspector,' she said.

'Be careful, Dr Galvin, you are walking near thin ice.'

Livia opened the door. Elias stood outside in the hallway.

'Sometimes,' she said, 'none of us are aware of just how thin it can be, Inspector. Elias will escort you back to lunch.'

2

'Dr Galvin, you are full of surprises. I had no idea.' Professor Wu gazed in at the contents of the briefcase.

'Neither did I.'

'Normally,' he said, 'there would be third parties. I don't usually have such direct involvement in this kind of acquisition.'

'I understand. I'm tying up loose ends for one of the family's closest associates, the late Mr Trembath. His death caused some confusion.'

'I am very much looking forward to poring over this beautiful atlas when I return home.' He closed the case, placing a proprietorial hand on the lid. 'Is there anything I can offer you in return for your obvious generosity.'

Livia paused. 'As a matter of fact, I'm establishing a foundation in honour of my godmother, Minerva Babitksy. She was Mr Trembath's sister-in-law. Perhaps you'd consider an endowment.'

'Of course.'

'Would you care to join me for lunch at the Mesmer Babitsky Gallery? I have a classic Mayan funerary urn and a sacrificial knife that might interest your wife for the Sister Cities galleries exchange program.'

'It would be my pleasure, Dr Galvin. And I wonder if you would kindly convey for me a message to Mr Karl Galvin. Please tell him that I extend my hospitality to him to contact me after I return to Beijing. There is a project that may interest him, and his father, of course.'

'Certainly. I'll let my uncle know without delay. Time is the enemy, as we're all aware.'

CHAPTER THIRTY-SIX

River City

Tuesday 9 September 2008
Fortescue Street, Spring Hill

Minnie's clock said 12:08am. Caddie and Tilly had draped themselves across the bed but Livia had managed to retain a few centimetres for herself. She'd fallen asleep playing solitaire Scrabble and there were letters scattered on the sheets and the dogs. She couldn't tell if they'd woken her with their sudden rise to sitting positions, or if she'd heard the sounds downstairs, too. The moment she made the move to get up, they were off the bed and out the door, flicking vowels and consonants around the floor, and growling those low growls that Livia hoped would terrify the hardiest of thieves into rethinking his decision.

She followed them down, barefoot, hesitating at the bottom step. Whoever it was had gone into the study – the light was on – and left the door ajar. The dogs waited for her to join them in the lounge-room. Could it be Bao, unphased by Con's threat, or his offsider, determined to get what he could?

'Come out now, and keep your hands where I can see them.' Against the silence of midnight, her voice sounded hard and distant. The threat wasn't entirely hollow, there were guns in the kitchen wall, only metres away.

'Livia. Darling. Come in.'

She walked into the study. He was rolling up the carpet. Somehow, she wasn't surprised. She glanced back, told the dogs to stay, and closed the study door.

'If you're looking for a smoke to help your arthritis, you only had to ask. Do you know what time it is?'

'Darkness becomes me.' He smiled.

'Since you're here.' She went back out to the lounge-room, opened the third drawer of the sideboard, and removed the host-holder. She gave the dogs a pat and returned to the study, where Ari had grabbed the paperweight and opened the trapdoor to the basement.

'What do you make of this?' She flipped open the holder and handed it to him. He looked inside.

'I haven't seen you for an age,' he told the Rembrandt. 'Have you told anyone else about it?'

Livia shook her head. 'Don't you want to know where I got it?'

'Provenance can be a thorny issue in art and antiquities cir-cles, Livia, as you know. This little fellow needs the right temperature.'

'There's only a few marijuana plants in the basement.'

'Come, my dear. It's time you saw for yourself.'

He gestured for Livia to lead the way down, flicking a switch on the underside of the floor as they went. The ante-room which preceded the curtained hydroponics was bathed in a dull yellow glow.

'I haven't been here for so long. The last time was with Minerva.' He looked around, slowly turning a full circle. 'It hasn't changed. Look over there.'

On the wall was a framed copy of the print that had been in Minnie's chapel at the cemetery, the one with Ogham let-ters inscribed on it spelling 'Gardner.' There was Persephone, still caught between worlds: Charon, Cerberus and the Styx below, the light and sun above. Livia hadn't noticed it at all the last time she'd been down here with Ishmael. He hadn't turned on the yellow light, and then the phone had rung like a fire alarm.

'Do you have the key to Minnie's chapel, my dear?'

It was still on her key ring. 'Yes, it's here.' She unhooked the key ring from the belt loop on her jeans and handed it to Ari.

'You do it, Livia. It's your home now.'

He went to the wall on which the picture hung and moved the empty bookcase sitting beneath it. Behind the spot where the bookcase had been was a door lock. Once she saw it, Livia could also see the outline of a door in the planked wall. She leaned down and keyed the lock.

The area beyond the door she opened was large and, when Ari flicked the light switch, appeared to be virtually empty of furniture. Along one wall was something that resembling an office compactus unit. There was a distinct hum coming from somewhere, but she didn't guess what it was until Ari closed the door and they walked into the middle of the room. The space was a different temperature from the rest of the house; was it drier, too?

'Over there, liebschen.'

Ari put his hand on Livia's shoulder and pointed towards the far corner, where a single armchair faced the wall.

She walked over and stood in front of the armchair, staring at the wall two metres ahead of her. Ari had turned the spotlights on as she approached.

'Wheel the chair back,' he said.

She wheeled it back another metre or two and sat.

'You recognise it? It was Minerva's favourite.'

'*The Storm on the Sea of Galilee*,' Livia replied. For some reason, tears pricked at her eyes.

Ari said, 'Oil on canvas, 1633. Rembrandt. Probably one of the last things of beauty Minerva saw. She told me she came down here almost every day, to watch, and breathe it in.'

Ari stood beside Livia and they gazed at the painting in silence. There was no need to hurry as they observed Jesus in the open boat with his twelve apostles, about to be swamped. Was that the moment before he decided he'd had enough? He was the only one who didn't look worried. Livia couldn't believe she was so close to something so beloved, whose loss was so desperately mourned.

'We have two works from the Gardner Museum, then,' she said, turning to Ari.

'Liebschen.' Ari squatted beside her and took her hand in his. 'Yes, we have two of the works. And we have the rest.'

'We have them all?'

He nodded. She recalled the information she'd found on the theft.

'We have them here?'

'Die schönen Kunste. Überall. The fine arts, the beautiful arts. Everywhere.' He nodded again and glanced towards the compactus wall.

The words Sibyl used that Livia couldn't translate. Sibyl knew about the fine art works at the Holy Mother. Did she know about these?

'Which is why Minnie's Will stresses that I should live here and undertake no renovations or redevelopment of the site. I thought it had something to do with her CLEAR activities.'

'Yes. She knew you would observe the letter of her wishes. You and Greer. Keep the cooler safe.' He waved his arm around to indicate the room. 'A place where art –'

'Stolen art. Worth hundreds of millions.' Livia couldn't seem to take in the enormity of what was in the room with them, directly beneath Minnie's modest park. 'In a cooler.'

'Where it can rest, and cool down. The Holy Mother and St Jude is a cooler, somewhat lesser, but a cooler nonetheless. Once the heat is off – and these pieces are the hottest of all – they can be circulated for sale to collectors who aren't fussy about provenance. They simply want what they want. You know that.'

'Like Wu.'

'Some collect because they are obsessed, some because they are business people, first and foremost. Wu is both, I think.'

'Minnie's looked after these coolers for a long time, hasn't she?'

'A very long time. Since before I had to leave. Of course, these works weren't here then. There were others before them.' He stood up and flexed his knees, all the while gazing at the painting.

'What are we going to do with all this now? We'll have to return it to the Museum. The statute of limitations is up on prosecutions.'

'Which is just as well for me. May I borrow the key?'

Livia handed it to him and he went to the compactus, unlocking it and rolling it open. He pulled out the first of the works, Vermeer's *The Concert*. Like all the others, it was suspended inside a loose cellophane envelope hanging from a steel frame that rolled silently out of the compactus on nylon runners.

'You were one of the thieves.'

They stared at the light and contrasting darkness in the painting, the two women's faces visible, but the man's back was turned.

'It's better that you know as little as possible about that. It was a long time ago. 1990. A lifetime away.'

'We have to send it all back, Ari. It's important art.'

'So were Gerardus Mercator's maps. Do you think Minnie left this legacy to you, and Greer, so you could return it?'

He pushed the Vermeer back into the compactus and moved along, pulling out each work in turn and staring at it.

They were all there: the Rembrandts, five by Degas, the Vermeer, a Manet, a Flinck, and in plexiglass boxes on a shelf at the end were the eagle finial, about 25 centimetres high, and the Chinese Ku, a goblet-shaped vase, 30 centimetres tall, made of bronze.

'Was this a shopping list, Ari?' There had been rumours that the thieves, who'd bypassed far more valuable works, were working from a list, stealing to order. Otherwise, some of their choices, such as the eagle finial, made no sense. Unless.

'I've always loved eagles,' Ari said, touching the plexiglass and tracing the line of the eagle's wing. 'So did Minerva.' He placed the open host holder on the shelf next to the Ku, Rembrandt's small face looking up at them.

'I see.' But she didn't really see at all. 'So it is a shopping list. Yours.'

'Not at all. Those items – a coincidence. The thing is, I and some others, we worked for someone else. That's the way of things – and he alone knew who the pieces were for – need to know, as the planning goes – and he died, leaving no trace of where the groceries should be delivered. We've been waiting to be contacted ever since. One day, perhaps, someone will be bold enough.'

'You don't really believe that. If they don't know who to contact, then how?' Livia began to wonder if retaining the works was Ari's way of keeping Minnie's memory alive. All this beauty to remind him of her, wherever he might be in the world.

'You'll be moving in permanently here,' he said, ignoring her question. It was a statement, not a suggestion. 'Minnie would want nothing less.' Then it became a law.

Livia watched as he closed the compactus carefully and locked it up. He pressed the key into her hand.

'Thank you,' he said.

She could dump it all somewhere, she thought, have Jerry do the lifting, and then make an anonymous call to the authorities. But the art would be damaged, no matter how careful they were; who knew what had already happened to the tiny Rembrandt? It all needed to be kept in specific climatic conditions: 70° Fahrenheit and 50% humidity, according to the Museum's press release. The same release said the Museum was confident of having the works returned some day, that such art had the power to 'inspire thinking and creativity.' The only thinking they inspired where they were now was the fearful kind. Their beauty was literally buried.

'Livia? You're far away.'

'Sorry.'

'You will be fine, my dearest. You decoded the Ogham – Minerva's idea of initiation. You couldn't come to harm researching this alone, my dear. The Mercator was an unfortunate complication, but they weren't after all this.' He gestured at the compactus. 'Now that Minerva's gone, apart from you and me, not another living soul knows where these precious things are. Come.'

Ari led the way this time. They returned everything to their former positions. The dogs were waiting in the lounge-room, faithful as ever. They growled at first, but then seemed to sense that Ari belonged, temporarily. Ari bent to cuddle them and when he stood he said, 'Never tell Karl about this. Any of it.'

'Of course not.' Who could she tell without causing chaos in so many lives? Her sense of shock was the least of it, and Karl's suspicions would remain just that.

'Thank you liebschen,' Ari said, 'for all that you have done. And all that you will do for Minerva. My darling goddaughter.'

He took her in his arms and held her tight, and she reciprocated, wondering if she'd ever see him again.

'I'll call you,' he said. 'I used to ring Minnie whenever I could. It's hard to break an old habit. And now that you know I'm alive.'

He trailed off and she wondered if he felt very much guilt over the deception of decades, or if it was just another unavoidable decision, like Greer's and Minnie's choices not to tell her about his existence.

'Where are you going to go now?'

'I have another project, in Europe, a lot of research to do. But no more Mercator maps. That was the last. I'll say goodbye to Minerva in the park.'

He kissed Livia's cheek and walked out to the front verandah, checking the street for movement before he continued. He sat, silhouetted, on the bench that featured his plaque. Was he right above the *Sea of Galilee*, Livia wondered? She returned to the study to straighten up the rug and stare at the floor and contemplate her future. In this house?

When she looked out the window a few minutes later, Ari had gone.

CHAPTER THIRTY-SEVEN

Boston, Massachusetts
[42.20N 71.05W]
Thursday 2 April 2009
Tremain Inn, Rowes Wharf

Minnie had been right, of course. Livia kept the gun case. It had become an invaluable mode of transportation for her laptop and her gold medal, and other items, when required. Apart from her gallery commitments, she was frequently invited to speak at sports psychology conferences on the nature of motivation, of what made a winner a winner, of how to persevere when doubt is ever-present and defeat a near certainty, of how to solve moral and ethical conundrums. What does one sacrifice in order to reach the pinnacle? How selfish does an individual need to be – selfish, at all? – to succeed? What, in any case, defines success?

She removed the laptop now, and the gold medal in its red lacquer box – kindly replaced for her by Professor Wu – found the triangular key, turned it in the appropriate places, and lifted out the shell, placing it on the bed beside the case. She went to the bureau, pulled on her new leather gloves, collected a DVD mailing box and a padded envelope and returned to the bed. She picked up the cellophane packet and gazed into his slightly off-putting, out-of-focus eyes.

'You're a looker, there's no doubt at all,' she told him, placing the packet carefully inside the DVD box, and the box inside the padded envelope to which she affixed two labels, one each on the front and back.

The label on the front read: Director of Security, Isabella Stewart Gardner Museum, 280 The Fenway, Boston, MA 02115.

On the reverse, the label quoted: 'for the education and enjoyment of the public forever,' Isabella Gardner's intention and wishes for her collection.

On her way to the airport, Livia directed her cab to a Post Office, purchased several dollars worth of stamps, and took the package to the nearest U.S. Mail box. Before she slid it through the slot, she took out her pen, and on the reverse, beneath the quotation, she wrote: 'Love from Dan, XOX.'

At the airport, she took off the leather gloves and placed them in the nearest rubbish bin. She checked her gun case through the usual security points and at one, the inspection official picked it up and idly remarked: 'You'd think it'd be heavy, wouldn't you ma'am, by the sturdy look of it? But it's actually very light.'

'Yes,' Livia said, 'and beautiful. A work of art.'

The official smiled and checked her through.

CHAPTER THIRTY-EIGHT

River City

Wednesday 22 April 2009
Oyster Point, Moreton Bay

Livia fished the water bowls out of the gym bag, took them to the tap, filled them up and set them on the grass next to the picnic table. They had the shadiest spot, beneath a gigantic Moreton Bay fig at the far end of the park. Caddie and Tilly fussed around the bowls, lapping water as Livia took out two more bowls for their dry food.

'This is the first real chance we've had to get together since everything with Minnie and Tibor. I was thinking of all that the other day after I moved the last box from the gallery loft to Minnie's. It's good to live in a house full-time again.' And it had been more than good to arrange for brass plaques in the park to farewell Minnie – hers was on the rotunda – and Tibor – he had his own new bench, although the police still hadn't identified the Deception Bay body. That hadn't stopped

429

them from holding Minnie's memorial party for both her and Tibor.

'Happy birthday,' Greer said, 'by the way.' She took a tablecloth, plates, cutlery and serviettes out of a calico bag, and proceeded to set the table.

'Happy birthday to you,' Livia replied. 'And anyway, I was up in Minnie's bedroom and I remembered when you rang in the middle of the night and Tibor was out on the verandah; you said you had something really important to tell me.' She looked over at her sister as they sat down at the picnic table. 'Anything I can help you with, now that we're free and clear, for a while at least?'

'Ah,' said Greer. 'Yes.' She leaned down and patted Caddie. 'Well, I'm thinking time has sorted that out, for the moment. So, don't worry about it. Okay?'

'The fewer worries the better, as far as I'm concerned.'

'I couldn't agree more.'

They watched as Rosanna and Ishmael emerged from the fish shop at the other end of the park. They each carried a rectangular package wrapped in butcher paper. Ishamel was swinging a plastic bag at his side.

When the dogs saw them, they took off to meet and greet. It was as though they hadn't seen Rosanna and Ishamel for ten years rather than ten minutes. Livia could hear them laughing and talking from halfway down the park.

'A new project for Mum, do you think?' Greer asked.

Livia watched them getting closer.

'The son she never had.' Or the grandson, instantly grown up. 'What are you planning to do now that you're all Avaloned out?'

Greer had spent several months at Avalon, resting, researching, writing journal articles on PTSD in soldiers tortured in wartime. Doug had given her several interviews on the promise of anonymity. It seemed to have done them both good.

'I heard from Ari the other day – he made an enticing offer, he's finishing a project that was interrupted when Minnie died. It could further my PTSD research – case histories and so on – but I'm not sure. I'll have to think about it. How about you?'

'The gallery, of course. And Minnie's Will. You'd be amazed at the cultural and community activities she was involved in. I seem to have been appointed to every board and committee she ever sat on. But mostly, Ishmael and I are sorting out the Holy Mother. He's the new Accountant.'

'Mrs Bradbury's retired?'

'You sound shocked. She's only a hundred and forty not out, a slip of a thing. But I've convinced her to go part-time, handover to Ishmael, and keep a watching brief on all things figurative over there.' Livia waved her arm in a northerly direction. They weren't that far from the Holy Mother, as the seagull flew. 'Have you heard from Yani?'

'Not recently, no. You know, it's a shame about Beijing. After all, you won a gold medal, and then the assassins, Minnie, Tibor.'

'I prefer to remember our first visit there. When you could buy sweet buns from hole-in-the-wall bakeries, and not get sick.'

'When you could buy toffee apples from a man with a wheelbarrow full of them, and live through the night.'

'When that young man – what was his name? – Yani – Yani –'

'Yani Lee, as I recall – would take us to cafés and restaurants that you'd swear would kill you on the spot.'

'But didn't. They had the best food in the city.'

'All the locals ate there.'

'And there were more bicycles than cars on the streets.'

'And the cars that were there actually got out of second gear.'

'They positively flew past the Forbidden City.'

'What are you two talking about?' Rosanna asked, arriving with a flurry of dogs and packages and barking, and a laughing Ishmael.

'Old times,' Greer said.

'Before the war,' Livia added.

'We bought dessert,' Ishmael said, 'but we might have to eat it first.'

He pulled cans of Coke from the bag and put them in the esky, and then handed around Drumsticks.

'Listen,' he said. 'Listen.'

Ishmael turned to the creek and everyone, including the dogs, turned their heads and followed his gaze.

A small blue and white cabin cruiser slowly made its way along the sliver of a creek that ran beside the park. It was off to the bay for fresh fish and prawns, and Gene Krupa's drums throbbed from its sound system. They helped the boat's engine gain extra energy, its speed increasing as Gene and the saxophones and trumpets wound themselves up playing Benny Goodman's 'Sing, Sing, Sing,' sending the fishermen out with the promise of – who knew, exactly? One of Minnie's credos swam to the front of Livia's mind as she watched the little boat clear the creek and motor out beyond the breakwater: 'Do what you like, my dears,' she'd tell Greer and Livia as they'd butter up a third pancake, or put off their homework for another half an hour, 'and live with the consequences.' Then she'd smile, stifle half a laugh, and hum something jazzy.

'Happy birthday, my girls,' Rosanna said, leaning down to kiss each daughter. 'Happy birthday from Minnie.'

'All right, everyone.' Ishmael had arranged the plastic plates in perfect parallel with each other, and the plastic cutlery was aligned at perfect right angles. The salt and pepper sachets were piled up in the middle of the table like sandbags.

'All right, Ishmael,' said Rosanna, as he tore open the hot fish and chips. 'Did you remember the extra tomato sauce, boyo?'

CHAPTER THIRTY-NINE

London, England

[51.30N 0.10W]
Wednesday 22 April 2009
Tamarind Bar, Soho

1

Peter Crane and Yani Kefala, formerly Yani Lee, dined together, and Crane invited Kefala to a night on the town. It would kill two birds with one stone, Crane had said, since he had to meet up with another trader in the course of the evening, and these younger fellows seemed to operate twenty-four-seven. He preferred to take meetings in public places, he said, so each person stood on even ground. Yani had no objections; he was at a loose end until Crane confirmed his interest in sourcing some art works for one of his shoppers. It would be a lucrative contract, if he could pull it off, and he needed it badly, so he saw the evening as a business expense, billable hours, to himself. If it worried him that Crane was

435

trying for a younger man's look with dyed, dirty-blonde hair and unnaturally blue eyes – contact lenses, no doubt – he wouldn't show it. The man gave his age away in any case, rugged up against the cold, wearing gloves and a heavy over-coat, even though the weather wasn't severe at all. As long as Crane delivered, it didn't matter what age he chose to be.

Eventually they arrived at the Tamarind Bar in Soho, and Crane indicated a booth at the far end of the dark, crowded space. Yani made his way through the crush of drinkers and sniffers – the place was on the edge of slipping into seedy – while Crane muscled into the bar to order a round of drinks.

Yani slid across the leather seat, feeling a little tired now that they were in this warm environment and he could relax with a drink. He was surprised to see a familiar face before him as he settled into the booth and prepared to say hello to Crane's associate. He hesitated for only a moment, a mere blink, and saw that the other fellow had no interest, either, in acknowledging their previous meeting in River City. He simply nodded. The less said about that, and Bao, the better; a sensible approach. As far as Yani was concerned, they'd all moved on, and life was very different now, certainly for Yani, perhaps for this fellow too, although his appearance – the close shave, the short hair, the dark suit, looking for all the world like an old-time CIA agent, or a London banker with-out the furled umbrella and bowler hat – hadn't altered much from that day at the Bender. The only jarring notes were the six empty shot glasses in front of him. He'd either been wait-ing for quite a while, or he had a problem.

When Crane arrived with the drinks, Yani looked up ex-pectantly, waiting for Crane to make introductions, but he set

the glasses down in silence, and then sat down himself opposite the two of them.

'Last year you spent some time in River City, Mr Brown.'

Crane wasn't a man to waste time on small talk, Yani
thought, and he'd gone straight for the jugular with this fellow. But the man seemed unimpressed.

'That's right. Do you need some work done there? I can
re-familiarise myself.'

Yani was surprised to hear that the man wasn't slurring his
speech, but something was off, something more than alcohol
was at work, he'd bet.

'No work there. You attended a lunch – Wagyu beef, as I
recall.'

'So?' Brown appeared uneasy. He took a gulp of his whiskey. 'You have good sources.'

'I happened to be there myself.'

'At the hotel? I didn't see you.'

'I saw you, a couple of times, one of them at the hotel. A
friend of mine saw you as well, and he mentioned to me that
you visited an office in New Farm where you spoke with a
lady called Minerva Babitsky about some lost property.'

'That job was a cockup from the start and I was only following orders. We had instructions. It was a last minute
thing. You shouldn't judge our professionalism by one job.'

'Ah, yes, ' said Crane. 'Instructions from whom?'

'I suppose it doesn't matter now that it's done and dusted.
Bao. An Olympic security guy, a seconded policeman. I think
he got in way over his head, if you want my opinion. He shut-
tled us from Beijing to River City on a government flight –
seemed to be in a real hurry. I ended up getting stabbed, got

an infection out of it. I've got permanent pain as a reminder.' He rubbed at his thigh.

'You aren't a policeman, too?' Crane asked.

'I freelance, Mr Crane, like your friend here.' He looked at Yani. 'But I have a new partner – you get two for the price of – two.' He gave a quick laugh. 'My partner from River City vanished. It's all in the past now. My new partner, White, and I are excellent procurers of rare art and artefacts. We do other jobs to order.'

'I don't quite understand, Mr Brown.' Crane leaned forward. 'About Mr Kefala here also being a freelancer. I thought he was a legitimate art dealer from Athens.' He stared at Yani, but Yani wouldn't give him the satisfaction of looking away. He knew his psychology.

'I don't know what he is now, but he was there in River City, chasing that case.'

'What are you talking about,' Yani said. This couldn't be right. 'I've never seen you before that day at the hotel. I was there with a friend for lunch, a member of the Galvin family.'

'But like the man said,' Brown flicked a glance at Crane, 'Chen and I visited the old lady, except we were there earlier than you, but some street tramp was there, too. We left and drove around the block, parked down the street and waited. It would have been easier if you'd let the old lady go home, you know, pal. But you had to muscle in there and knock her down. We knew that old guy Galvin wasn't bluffing about the eyewitness – seems you didn't.'

'It was an accident,' Yani said, 'I never meant to harm her. She hit me with something. And I reacted – I –'

'You knocked her down and ran away. Pathetic.' The fellow smiled a nasty smile at him. 'That street guy called the ambulance, and then we left. Bao told us to go to ground so he could figure out what to do next. Never work with policemen, or animals. Or old men who think they know everything.' It took him a couple of beats. 'Present company excepted, of course. I meant Restik – dropped dead of heart failure before we could get anything out of him. Very inconvenient.'

'Of course.' Crane raised his glass and took a sip, then slammed it down on the table. At the same moment, Brown sat back in his seat. He looked surprised, and then, quite slowly, slumped sideways against the large seat cushion next to him.

'What? What are you doing? What have you done?' Yani stared in disbelief at Brown's lifeless face. He'd been shot, by this stranger whom Yani had thought trustworthy. Greer had connected them, after all.

'It's a question of balance, Mr Lee. Don't move, I have a pistol here under the table. You can die now, or hear why, and then die, although I think you know the story fairly well.'

Time, that was what he needed. Somehow, he managed to sit perfectly still. 'If it's the Chinese shopper angry about not getting his map, I can fix that.'

'It's not that, Mr Lee. The shopper is completely satisfied. He has his map.'

'Then what? Whatever it is, I can fix it. I have the resources.' And if he didn't, what did it matter, as long as he walked out of this bar.

'The first rule in this business is: when opportunity knocks, open the door. You had your chances to get the map before Livia, poor darling, sent it home and you followed it and killed my Minerva. The only reason you didn't take it earlier was because you planned to steal it yourself and leave the country. But you and Inspector Bao missed the boat, and my Minerva paid the price. That's unacceptable.'

'I was just the courier, you don't get it. Bao wanted to steal it, not me. He sent those car-jackers; they were assassins, for God's sake. Gordon Trembath set the whole thing up. He's responsible for the old lady.'

'Gordon is dead. There is no satisfaction in killing a man twice, and his suffering was great enough. He knew what he'd done. He loved Minerva, too. But don't worry, Mr Lee, I took care of Inspector Bao during his recent visit to Paris from Asiapol. Already, he is enjoying a new life in Morocco, as a pallet of creamed eels, I believe.'

'I don't understand. What's your connection? Who are you?' If he could just talk the crazy bastard down.

'My name is Ariel Moishe Babitsky. My wife was Minerva Helena Babitsky, God rest her sweet soul.'

Yani felt the warmth of his own blood in his lap as the man in the booth with him slammed his shot glass down again. He must have muzzled the pistol; clever fellow. The slam was extra insurance but he didn't need it; the second and third shots were disguised by the roaring voices and loud, driving music.

'Goodnight, Mr Lee.'

Yani watched as Ari rose from his seat and walked slowly to the bar's rear exit. He tried to speak, but no sound emerged from his mouth. The man who'd shot him was so sure of his work, so experienced, he didn't even bother turning back for a last look. Yani thought of his mother, Antigone, but the face that came to him as his eyes closed was of the old lady in the office in River City, and she was smiling a loving, motherly smile. She didn't blame him, after all.

2

Several blocks down the street from the Tamarind Bar, Peter Crane stopped and entered a café. He ordered a Turkish coffee, removed his gloves, and made a call from his cellphone.

'Liebling, happy birthday.'

'Uncle Ari, how are you? What a surprise,' Livia said.

'That gift from Dan to the Gardner. It made all the papers.'

'Yes?'

'Unvermeidlich.'

'Pardon?'

'Inevitable, I suppose, knowing you. But, no more, Livia. All right?'

'Sure. I'll put Greer on.'

'Ari, how is it?'

'Happy birthday, my dear. I miss our work together.'

'When are you coming home? Rosanna wants to talk to you. She says she has thirty years worth of questions, and you left too soon in September.'

'I have some business in Bogota, but it shouldn't take too long. As I've said, you're welcome to join me. There is a man called Arroyo, Minister for the Arts. I believe he is a puppeteer of note.'

'Be careful,' Greer said.

'Always. And by the way, I caught up with the referral you gave me.'

'Yani?'

'Everything is in balance. Have a lovely day, my darlings. Give my regards to your mother. Tell her I'll be home in springtime.'

ABOUT THE AUTHOR

Jay Verney is an Australian author who has published novels, essays, short stories, poetry, memoir, magazine and newspaper columns, book and film reviews, and comics.

Jay's first novel, *A Mortality Tale*, was shortlisted for the Australian/*Vogel* and Miles Franklin Literary Awards. Jay has a PhD (in genre and crime fiction), and a Master's degree (memoir) in Creative Writing from Queensland University. In 2009, she received a Dean's Award for Outstanding Research Higher Degree Thesis for her PhD, of which *Summon Up The Blood* is the direct result. Unsurprisingly, her cats, both ectoplasmic and here, remain unimpressed.

Jay's second novel, **Percussion**, is now available in both ebook and paperback, as is her third novel, **Spawned Secrets**.

Visit virtual Jay at her websites for **free** entertainment:

Transient Total Focus – www.jayverney.net

One blink at a time

Minty fresh stuff and nonsense and even some useful things.

Veranda Life – www.verandalife.com

Breathe ~ Relax ~Drink Black Tea Often

999 lovely haikus with lovely images.

Zen Kettle – www.zenkettle.wordpress.com

It makes tea

Zenkus, teeny tiny haikus about life, the universe, and everything. Also lovely.

Last Cat On Mars – www.lastcatonmars.wordpress.com

Would you want to be the first?

Dr On Mars welcomes you to a comical world of fun and laughs. It's laughly, and lovely, yes.

You can give Jay all your money by visiting Amazon to purchase even more of her lovely works. Ask Prof. Google for **Jay Verney Amazon**. You know you want to, grasshopper.

If you enjoyed this novel, please don't hesitate to ***make haste to Amazon and post a review***. The author will be eternally, or at least for a while, grateful and bless you and all of your children with a cheesecake-shaped blessing device.

ACKNOWLEDGEMENTS

This novel is the result of several years of research and a lot of trips to the refectory at Queensland University (who knew their egg and lettuce sandwiches were so more-ish?). Also, the university library, which smells the same today as it did when I first entered its forbidding portal as a wee country mouse way back in dim and dark 1980, otherwise known as the Paleolithic era. Actually, it wasn't dark at all – it's sunny, sunny Queensland and the library has fluorescent lighting, but I'm sure you take my point. Oh, the smell – a very good smell, but indescribable unless you've been there. Don't worry about it, grasshopper. Books and air-con and the thoughts and theses (you heard me, I said theses) of countless students over countable decades learning and laughing and lifting their sights and spirits higher and higher. That kind of smell.

I'm thankful to the faceless, nameless committee (one day they'll find those faces and names and celebrate) who awarded me a scholarship (an Australian Postgraduate Award) to research my doctorate (and buy egg and lettuce sandwiches). And I'm especially grateful to writers Jan McKemmish (writing in the ethers these days) and Amanda Lohrey who convinced me to actually apply for said scholarship over morning tea in the Great Court one late-winter day. It's funny what you remember, isn't it? I think I had a blueberry muffin.

Of course, I'm very, no, eternally grateful for the University of Queensland Dean's Award for my finally done and dusted creative writing thesis, half of which is this novel when it was but a manuscript.

Thanks also to Nicholas Jose and Sue Turnbull for their generous and insightful comments and suggestions. And thanks to the staff at the School of English, Media Studies and Art History and at the Graduate School, who contributed their time and effort to assisting me.

I could go on, but this is the last page, so let me sum up by saying that a certain confluence of circumstances and cats, of Bette Midler show tunes and Makybe Diva winning three, read it and laugh, three Melbourne Cups, of friends new and old, both here and recently gone to glory (see you in a while – quite a while, one hopes – Jan, Dorothy, Mottle, Rosie, Jo, Michael, Lawrence, Dotty, Pat), have brought me to this point in life. And it's at this point where I'm very lucky indeed to sit on the veranda with the love of my life (and our cats, here and ectoplasmic) and quietly sip my tea and scarf my delicious scone and say thank you for reading. I hope you enjoyed the ride very much, or at least to the value of the recommended retail price. See you next time, grasshoppers.